THE CASE OF THE ASPHYXIATED ALEXANDRIAN

THE MASKED MAN OF CAIRO

BOOK FIVE

By Sean McLachlan

Copyright 2021 Sean McLachlan, all rights reserved

Cover design courtesy Andrés Alonso-Herrero

This Book is sold subject to the condition that it shall not, by way of trade or otherwise, be lent, re-sold, duplicated, hired out, or otherwise circulated without the publisher's prior written consent in any form of binding or cover other than that in which it is published and without similar condition including this condition being imposed on the subsequent purchaser.

For Almudena, my wife
And Julián, my son

THE CASE OF THE ASPHYXIATED ALEXANDRIAN

THE MASKED MAN OF CAIRO

CHAPTER ONE

Cairo, Spring 1920

Murder can make even the most irritating company bearable.

Sir Augustus Wall did not want to have an early dinner at Shepheard's Hotel with Cairo's chief of police. He was already in the habit of having breakfast with him on the hotel veranda most mornings in order to hear the latest inside information on Cairo's endlessly fascinating parade of crime. Adding a dinner meant spending more time with Sir Thomas Russell Pasha than he could stand, but he had already said no to three previous dinner invitations. Even Augustus could not snub the chief of police forever.

So he sat in the dining room of Shepheard's Hotel, its ostentatious décor of gold-painted columns shaped to look like papyrus stems, its ceiling covered with random and illegible hieroglyphs, and its plaster statues of pharaohs nauseating him almost as much as the company. Sir Thomas was holding forth on the empire's colonial policy. Egypt was technically a protectorate, not a colony, but that mattered little. All of the empire's policies were unraveling before their eyes, no matter how much Sir Thomas fulminated at the head of the table like a dissenting minister from his pulpit. Augustus dug into his beef Wellington and wished he was elsewhere.

To make matters worse, Sir Thomas had brought his wife along.

Not that Augustus judged Lady Dorothea Russell any more harshly than any other member of the human race. A healthy, tanned woman of middle age, she had more intelligence than the average run of colonial wives. Actually, that was a poor and unfair measure, akin to saying a number was large because it was higher than zero. In fact, Lady Dorothea showed a great deal of intelligence. Well-traveled, disinclined to gossip, and well-versed in Egyptology, she was actually the antithesis of a colonial wife. She even enjoyed sharing in her husband's hunting trips.

And yet she had one unforgivable trait that put her permanently beyond the pale—she invited him to things.

Tea dances, bridge parties, dinner parties, military parades, wildfowl shootings, there was no end to the number and variety of social occasions she tried to get him to join. A steady and unwavering series of answers in the negative had failed to dissuade her. Long after all the other Englishwomen had given up Augustus as a lost cause, Lady Dorothea still hammered away at his reclusiveness with the stamina of an ancient tomb robber burrowing into a pyramid.

She used the opportunity of the dinner to burrow further.

Right when Sir Thomas started an interesting tale about catching some Bedouin smuggling hashish across the Sinai, his wife dove in, interrupting him.

She did that often.

"I was wondering, Sir Augustus, if you would be interested in coming to a charity dinner at the Turf Club next week."

"I am afraid I'll be engaged."

Lady Dorothea gave him a look that, had she been a man, would have earned her a job as an interrogator at the Citadel. "All week?"

"Yes. Terribly busy." He glanced at his watch. "And as I mentioned, I regret that I will have to leave you early."

He'd been stared at enough for one evening. The mask that covered his war wound always attracted attention. Many people were polite enough to pretend they weren't staring. Others, like the Americans at the next table, did so openly. Loud husband, louder wife, and two squalling children talked to each other in that horrible excuse for English but had eyes only for him. It amazed Augustus that the family had managed to eat anything.

"Oh yes, that man of yours and his bookshop," Sir Thomas said. "Giving a talk, isn't he?"

"It's the first of a series of lectures he is hosting. I shouldn't miss it," Augustus said. Even though Moustafa no longer worked for him, he was a good chap and proved useful at times.

Sir Thomas cleared his throat. "Indeed. Now as I was saying, this particular band of Bedouin belong to the Al-Tirabin tribe and—"

"It's a pity you can't make it, Sir Augustus," his wife interrupted again. "I think this charity would be near and dear to your heart."

"Financial support for recluses? A whipping society for slow waiters? Pressure on the government to enact a National Day of Silence?"

Where most Englishwomen would sneer or look appalled, Lady Dorothea merely laughed. The woman was unstoppable.

"No, it is a support charity for mules."

"Mules?"

Augustus had to admit he wasn't expecting that.

"Oh yes. Donkeys and horses too. As I'm sure you know, the Egyptian Expeditionary Force used a huge number of animals for transportation. The government deemed it a waste of money to ship them back to England, so they were sold to the Egyptians. Well, who could have foreseen the terrible conditions these poor beasts have been put into! Beaten. Starved. Worked to death. These animals did not volunteer for His Majesty's service, and yet proved as brave and as loyal as any Tommy. Don't they deserve a better fate than this?"

Augustus could not think of any answer that would be both honest and courteous, so he held his tongue. Perhaps the question was rhetorical.

Sir Thomas cleared his throat. "Dear, as I said before. The Egyptians look upon animals not as God's creatures, but as tools. The natives live in too poor and uncivilized a state to do anything else."

"Exactly why we need this charity! As we help the mules, we help the

Egyptians, by giving to them the same noble feelings we have for animals. This will cultivate a kindness and charity in the Egyptians that is sadly lacking. The animals have served the empire and deserve better."

"Indeed," Augustus said. "I knew many an ass in the officer corps."

"Steady," Sir Thomas said, taking a sip of wine.

Lady Dorothea turned to Augustus. "Now, this charity dinner will take place next Wednesday and—"

Augustus drew out his wallet faster than the cowboys drew their guns in those Western films Faisal liked so much. He pulled out a pound note.

"For our four-legged veterans."

"Oh! That's most kind."

An act of self-mercy, I assure you.

Lady Dorothea was stopped from further gushing by the arrival of a rather worried-looking waiter. The Nubian was dressed in the hotel's version of traditional Egyptian attire—fez, red vest and matching slippers, and billowing white pantaloons—a mixture of Ottoman Empire and Arabian Nights. After the briefest of apologies for the interruption, he leaned close to Sir Thomas and whispered something in his ear.

The chief of police frowned, took a sip of his wine, wiped his mouth with his napkin, and turned to his wife.

"If you will excuse us, dear, Sir Augustus and I need to deal with a little business upstairs."

Intrigued by this unexpected and mysterious salvation, Augustus followed him out of the dining room.

"There's been a spot of trouble," the chief of police told him.

"What sort of trouble?"

Sir Thomas waited until they passed a group of guests chatting in the front hall, and then in a low voice said, "A man appears to have been murdered."

The waiter took them to the second floor, where in front of one of the rooms stood a shivering Egyptian bellboy, the manager, and a florid-faced Scot who Augustus recognized as the hotel detective.

"What have we here?" Sir Thomas asked.

The manager, a stoop-shouldered man with a receding hairline, mopped his brow and glanced nervously at Augustus.

"This gentleman is a friend of mine," Sir Thomas told him. "I trust him implicitly."

"O-oh. I see," the manager stuttered. He gestured at the bellboy. "Mohammed here was told by the guest of this room, a Mr. Saunders of London, to come at this time and pick up a letter to be posted in the evening mail. Mohammed knocked and found the door slightly ajar. He peeked inside and found the man dead."

"Strangled," the hotel detective said.

"We don't know that," the manager hastened to add.

"Yes, we do," the Scot affirmed.

The manager let out a groan.

The hotel detective opened the door and flicked on the electric light switch to reveal the sitting room of one of the hotel's mid-priced suites. A few plush chairs, a coffee table, and a loveseat comprised the main furnishings. Doors led to the bedroom and bath. In one of the armchairs sat a bearded man of young middle age wearing a dinner jacket. His eyes and mouth were open. The way he sat slumped and motionless told them he was dead.

It was only as they approached that the signs of violence became apparent.

"Note the bugged and bloodshot eyes and bruising around the nose and mouth," the hotel detective said. "He was suffocated."

"Perhaps he choked?" the manager suggested hopefully.

"That would explain the eyes but not the bruising," the hotel detective said.

"You know your business," Sir Thomas said. "There's also swelling around the neck, as if he struggled against his opponent and wrenched it."

Augustus leaned over the body. There was something unusual about this fellow's appearance.

The hotel detective went on. "There don't seem to be any other signs of a struggle or theft. I made a quick investigation before calling for you. No overturned furniture. No bloodstains. His wallet and gold watch are on the bedside table."

"No scuffs on the knuckles, either," Sir Thomas noted. "He didn't get a chance to punch his murderer. I wonder why? Looks fit enough."

Augustus was barely listening. He studied the victim's beard. He either had the world's worst barber or …

"Perhaps there were two murderers," the hotel detective suggested. "One held his arms and the other pressed a pillow or some other object over his face."

"He's wearing a disguise!" Augustus cried, grabbing the dead man's beard and yanking it off.

Augustus staggered back, shocked to the core.

Lieutenant Gregory Marshall crawled by his side through a series of shell craters in No Man's Land, the shattered terrain dimly visible through the early morning mist. German artillery had hammered this area the previous week in preparation for an offensive. The Oxfordshire and Buckinghamshire Light Infantry and neighboring regiments had held the line at the cost of two hundred lives. The Germans had lost many more.

Now No Man's Land was even more chewed up than before. He and Marshall, pistols in hand, crawled along the edges of water-filled craters, occasionally pausing to disentangle themselves from stray strands of clutching barbed wire or lifting themselves over a shattered hunk of flesh that had once been a man.

Marshall tapped him on the shoulder and pointed into the murk to their left. He gave the lieutenant a questioning look and Marshall nodded, then shrugged. It was hard to find one's way even in broad daylight, and Marshall was trying to retrace his steps from the night before, when he had led a scouting party and lost a man to a sudden burst of sniper fire.

A man they hoped to find alive.

After crawling for another hundred yards, Marshall pointed to two heaps of rubble that might have once been farmhouses.

He nodded. Marshall had told him the private had been hit somewhere around there.

The poor chap couldn't have been shot in a worse area. The mounds of broken brick and splintered beams were prime spots for observation posts. One objective of the scouting mission had been to check out these two ruins for just such a thing. There had been no observation post—the firing had come from the German forward trench a couple of hundred yards further on, but that didn't mean the Germans didn't have an observation post there now.

Only one way to find out. They crawled forward.

The rubble formed two low eminences in the undulating terrain of No Man's Land. Between them, in a little swale of mud, they found him.

The private lay on his back, a bullet through his chest, face turned up to the sky, mouth agape. A field dressing lay unraveled in one hand. The man had just managed to pull it out before his wound overcame him. He had died alone in the darkness as his comrades retreated.

Marshall closed his eyes and mouth and slumped for a second, his usually chipper face going grim.

Then he snapped off half of the man's identification tag and they started crawling back to their own lines.

They didn't make it five feet.

Several rifles opened up from the further rubble pile. They scrambled into a shell crater.

"Let's give them the grenades and run for it!" Marshall shouted over the gunshots.

They each pulled out a grenade, yanked out the pins, and tossed them at the rubble heap.

There was a pair of loud thuds and fragments of bricks and clods of mud flew into the air.

They bolted, running several yards before throwing themselves on the ground.

Machine gun fire tore through the mist, seeking them out. They crawled further, got into a crater that overlapped with another, giving them cover for several yards. From there they crawled, smearing their bodies through the mud.

Just as they made it back to their own wire, a German field gun opened up.

The first shell hit fifty yards to their right, close enough for shrapnel to fly over their heads. They scrambled through a gap in the wire and leapt into the British forward trench, not stopping until they got into a dugout, their comrades *cursing them for bringing on artillery fire.*

More field guns opened up. The shells came one right after another, shaking the dugout. That didn't bother him much. This was simply the Germans' daily hate, thrown over a little early because he and Marshall had been spotted. He sat on a supply crate in the back of the dugout, the regular booms of the explosions shaking him.

And yet it didn't feel like shelling. The dugout began to fade. Earthen walls and floor were replaced with wallpaper and carpeting. The sound of explosions faded, replaced with a concerned, familiar voice.

Someone was shaking him. An insistent voice forced itself on his memories. The hotel suite came into focus.

"Good God, man! Whatever is the matter?"

Sir Thomas stood over him, shaking him by the shoulders. Augustus realized he had fallen onto the loveseat. If it hadn't been there, he would have ended up on the floor.

He looked from the chief of police to the victim and back again.

"I … I know this man."

CHAPTER TWO

Moustafa Ghani El Souwaim glanced at the clock above his bookshop door, growing increasingly worried. Mr. Wall was never late unless he had gotten into trouble, and trouble followed that man like flies on a camel.

And those flies always ended up buzzing around Moustafa.

He tore his gaze away from the clock and turned to address the score of gentlemen and one lady who had assembled for the lecture.

Before he spoke, he could not help but cast a proud eye over what he had built.

The Egyptian Reader was a tidy bookshop fronted by windows prominently displaying the latest releases. Floor-to-ceiling bookshelves lined the walls, and a waist-high bookshelf ran down the center of the room. The shelves carried books on every subject in Arabic, English, and French. In the back was an open space for lectures, and a small crowd had assembled for the very first one since the shop's opening.

Moustafa felt proud he had arranged a speech by no less a figure than Heinrich Schäfer, the preeminent Egyptologist. The men in the audience, filling the small space to capacity, were mostly foreigners, with only a few Egyptians among them.

While his countrymen's lack of interest troubled Moustafa, he also took it as a challenge. For too long Africa had been sunk in ignorance. One of the reasons he had opened this bookshop was to play a small part in changing that.

He spotted a few familiar faces in the audience. In front sat the expert antiquities forger Suleiman Hanzade, his eyes red and hooded from hashish, and his stunning Turkish wife Zehra, who was receiving more attention from the men in the room than poor Herr Schäfer, who sat next to them smoking a pipe. The Hanzades' two adult sons had also come. Joseph, a young Coptic researcher who had briefly been a workmate and later became a friend, also sat in the audience. Other than that, everyone was a foreigner and a stranger to him.

It didn't matter. Many of them had purchased books already, and they had all come to hear the great scholar speak.

"Thank you for coming and welcome to my humble bookshop," Moustafa began. It nettled him a little that he had to speak in English. Wouldn't it be better if everyone in the room spoke Arabic? "This is the first of a series of lectures we will have here at The Egyptian Reader. Tonight, we are proud to have the noted scholar Heinrich Schäfer speak on the Greco-Roman antiquities of our great country."

A flicker of annoyance passed over the faces of some of the foreigners at the term "country." Joseph the Copt sat a little straighter.

Moustafa sat down by Joseph as Herr Schäfer rose to stand at the podium. Moustafa could not help but give the audience a nervous glance. The last time he had seen a distinguished Egyptologist speak at a podium, the fellow got killed with a poison dart. Moustafa hoped he had put that part of his life behind him.

"Thank you, Mr. Ghani. I am very happy to be here and even happier to have found a good edition of Nerval's *Voyage en Orient* at your excellent bookshop. Our purpose here today is to examine a little-known phase of Egypt's past, namely the Greek and Roman periods. Mr. Ghani himself has done some research in this field, sketching the temple of Alexander at Bahariya Oasis. His sketches have been transferred to lantern slides that we will see shortly."

Joseph elbowed him and shot him a smile. Moustafa felt like he might burst with pride. One of the great Egyptologists mentioning his work!

That was the other part of Moustafa's plan. He had already published one scholarly paper, and he had nearly finished another. For too long, the history of Egypt and the Soudan had been written by foreigners. Now it was time for Africans to study Africa's past.

But why did so few Africans care?

He relaxed as Herr Schäfer started his lecture. Of course, he knew most things the scholar spoke about, but to hear it from such an important researcher in his very own bookshop made it a real treat. When the Egyptologist asked him to turn off the lights so they could see the lantern slides, Moustafa as thrilled to find the first slide was a photographic reproduction of one of his very own sketches.

"Here we have one of Mr. Ghani's drawings of the temple of Alexander the Great at Bahariya Oasis in the Western Desert. As you can see, the bas-relief on the back wall shows the Macedonian king making offerings to the various Egyptian gods. It is a standard scene that we are familiar with from countless Pharaonic monuments. The scene is significant by its lack of uniqueness. Alexander wanted to be seen as a pharaoh, not as an invader."

The front door bell tinkled as someone opened it. Had Mr. Wall come at last? Moustafa slipped away as quietly as he could and went to the front.

Although he had switched off the lights, enough illumination filtered through the windows from the streetlights outside for him to see a white man in a slouch hat and overcoat that looked too warm for this late spring evening.

"The talk has just started," Moustafa whispered. "There are a couple of spare seats."

The man nodded and moved to the back of the store, where Herr Schäfer was showing a lantern slide of an inscription in both ancient Greek and hieroglyphics. Moustafa smiled as he glanced at the picture, able to read both languages as readily as his own.

The man did not sit, but rather stood near the edge of the audience and looked at their faces bathed in the light of the screen, as if searching for someone.

Moustafa gestured to an empty chair, but the man ignored him and checked his watch, a military one with hands painted in luminescent radium. Looking around again, as if at a loss, he moved back to the front of the store. Curious, Moustafa followed at a discreet distance.

The man quietly left the shop. While Moustafa watched from inside, standing well away from the window so he could not be seen from the better-lit street outside, the man glanced both ways before crossing to the other side. He moved into the obscuring shadow of a building.

And there he stood, as if waiting.

Moustafa's heart began to beat faster. He had been in too much danger in his life not to know when a new threat approached. What was this man up to?

He glanced back at the talk in progress, tempted to return to it and ignore the strange man in the street, but he knew that he could not, that he should not. Something was going on, and it might threaten his shop.

So he waited, listening to the talk while watching the man across the street, who did not move from his spot in the shadows.

And then it struck him. What if this fellow had come to find Mr. Wall? He was the only person of note that Moustafa knew intended on being there and who had not shown up.

Moustafa felt a wash of fear like a bucket of cold winter water pass over him.

That lunatic is getting me in trouble again, I just know it.

Now he really felt tempted to return to the lecture.

Except he couldn't. Ignoring trouble only made trouble worse.

Taking a deep breath, Moustafa moved to the desk by the front door and pulled out a short, stout club. Egyptians and Soudanese were forbidden proper weapons, and while Moustafa knew he could mete out a good deal of damage with this, he would have preferred a sampling of Mr. Wall's vast collection of armaments.

Hiding the club in the sleeve of his djellaba, he opened the door to his shop.

The man noticed him immediately, and visibly stiffened.

Might as well be direct.

He walked boldly across the street and right up to him.

"Is there something I can help you with, sir?"

"No thank you. I came to the wrong place," the man replied in an Australian accent.

Moustafa didn't believe that for a second. "Are you looking for someone?"

"None of your business, darky. Get back in your master's shop," the Australian snapped.

Moustafa's hand, hidden in the sleeve of his djellaba, gripped the club tighter.

"It's my shop, and my country. You will not speak to me in this fashion," he growled.

Moustafa expected one of two reactions. The most common was a surly response, an arrogance implying that despite Moustafa's large stature and burly frame, his black skin negated any real threat. The other response would be a turning away, ignoring him. Too proud to give an apology and too intimidated to continue with the abuse, the person giving the insult would simply pretend Moustafa no longer existed and would assume Moustafa would not want to risk his liberty by escalating the situation any further.

But the Australian did neither of these things. Instead he looked Moustafa up and down briefly from under the brim of his slouch hat, glanced either way down the street, and said, "Sorry, friend. I spoke out of turn. Go on in and enjoy the lecture."

Moustafa said nothing, momentarily at a loss. Then he nodded, said, "I'll forget all about it," and turned and left.

He cast several glances over his shoulder as he returned to the shop. The man did not move.

All through Herr Schäfer's lecture, the strange man troubled him. Twice Moustafa slipped away to peer through the window to see if he was still there, but he had vanished.

CHAPTER THREE

"You little thief, if I catch you I'll kill you!"

The fruit seller ran after Faisal, who scampered away, an armful of oranges tucked into his torn and filthy djellaba. He darted between the adults in the evening crowd of shoppers, his growling stomach giving him speed. He hadn't eaten all day, and with the stalls closing for the night, this was his last chance for dinner.

"Stop him!" the fruit seller shouted.

A man reached out to grab Faisal, but he ducked to the left, avoiding the outstretched hand by inches, then had to shift back to the right as another man tried to stop him.

What was going on these days? A boy couldn't do a simple grab-and-run without getting harassed. People used to mind their own business.

Faisal glanced over his shoulder and grinned. The portly fruit seller was losing ground. Faisal could outrun anyone in the market, even on an empty stomach.

A strong arm struck his chest. Faisal came to a stop, the oranges rolling in all directions.

Another of the market sellers, a grain merchant who Faisal had robbed twice in the past month, grabbed him by the front of his djellaba.

"I got you!" he announced. "You've been nothing but trouble since you were born. I—"

Faisal kicked him in the shin. The grain merchant howled and let go.

Faisal ran, but the grain merchant managed to stumble after him for a few steps and smack him on the back of the head. Faisal staggered but kept on going. He ran and ran until he left them all far behind.

Panting, he passed through some side streets and then made his way to the little alley where he shared a makeshift shelter with some of the other street boys. Faisal wrinkled his nose at the smell of rotting trash and cat piss, and took care to keep his bare feet from tripping on the heaps of bricks, splintered boards, and other refuse.

He rubbed the back of his head. It still hurt from where the grain merchant had smacked him. His stomach felt worse, though. No food today.

The shed was made up of warped boards and musty blankets scavenged from some of the collapsed old buildings and waste heaps of the neighborhood.

He parted the blanket that acted as a door and entered. Half a dozen boys sat glumly inside, their faces looking sickly in the light of a single flickering candle. Faisal sat down in his corner amid the piles of castoff clothing and rags that counted for his bed.

"Any luck?" Hamza asked.

Faisal shook his head.

"I didn't get anything either," Mehmed whined.

"I haven't eaten all day," Faisal said. "Does anyone have anything to share?"

They all said no or shook their heads. Faisal looked at each boy in turn. He knew some of them must be lying, and he also knew they wouldn't give him anything. It wasn't fair. He shared his food when he could, especially with the smaller boys like Mehmed who weren't so good at stealing and begging, but nobody ever gave him anything. With a resigned sigh, he stretched himself out on the heap of rags and tried to make himself comfortable.

A man's voice echoed down the alley, followed by another. Someone quickly blew out the candle.

"Who's that?" Hamza whispered.

"Shhh," Faisal said.

Everyone sat silent in the darkness. The voices continued, drawing closer. It sounded like several men, talking in the loud, angry tones of drunks. The clatter of a board as one of them tripped over it made Faisal jerk. The man cursed. They continued talking, but trying to make out words from their slurred speech while hiding inside the shed was impossible.

Then one word came loud and clear.

"Look!"

The men whispered. One barked out a laugh.

Mehmed's quavering voice came out of the darkness. "They've found us."

Faisal woke with a start. He lay under his blankets for a second, staring into the darkness, ears perked to the sound of approaching danger.

He heard nothing. It was very late, too late even for most of the human jackals who prowled the alleys.

I'm not in an alley. I'm in my little house on the Englishman's roof, he told himself.

Was he? It didn't smell like an alley. He ran his hand over his blankets. New and good quality, and there were two of them. He lay on a bed too. He wriggled deeper under the covers so they protected his head.

Keeping well tucked under the covers so nothing could get him, he reached out to the shelf nearby for a box of matches and the ancient oil lamp Moustafa had given him. Its familiar shape reassured him that he had woken up in the right place.

That didn't mean everything was all right, though. He needed to check.

Faisal hated checking, but he knew he wouldn't get any more sleep unless he did.

Striking a match and jumping a little at the sudden sound and flare of light, he lit the wick in the lamp. Its steady, warm light illuminated the interior of his little house, a rooftop shed the Englishman had fixed up for him. He set the lamp on the shelf next to his row of ripped tickets from the moving pictures and dressed quickly. It was cold this late at night, and dampness rose from the Nile to clutch the city in a clammy hand.

He parted the curtain in the doorway to the shed and came out onto the roof, pausing to look for a moment out over the quiet city. Moonlight shone off the whitewashed rectangles of buildings. Here and there a slim minaret rose above the skyline. No lights shone in any window. All was silent. No drunken laughter. No approaching footsteps. He moved to the door that led downstairs.

This part always made him nervous. The big rooms on the third floor of the Englishman's house were mostly empty. Djinn loved empty spaces. Of course Faisal had set charms to keep them away, but you could never be sure. Faisal moved quietly, afraid even the slightest sound would bring something leaping out of the wavering shadows.

At the bottom of the stairs he came to the sitting room, set under some rooftop windows that caught the breeze. The only furnishings were a comfy chair and a low table that had originally had books. The Englishman used to read up here sometimes but he had plenty of places to read, so now the table had a few of Faisal's things and a covered dish of dates.

Faisal crept out of the room to the walkway that went around the inner courtyard. He could hear the splash of the fountain below. That fountain was tricky because it hid other noises, bad noises.

He dreaded this part the most, because he had to lean over the balustrade and check nothing lurked in the courtyard.

Faisal's skin prickled as he saw four white figures standing around the fountain. He had to count them. One. Two. Three. Four. There were four old statues in the courtyard. Not three. Not five. So if he saw four white shapes he was safe.

Unless something had taken away one of the statues and stood in its place. Djinn could be tricky like that.

Faisal stared at the shapes, wishing his little lamp shone strongly enough to throw more light down there.

Once he had mostly convinced himself they were only statues, he crept to the next set of stairs and down to where the Englishman slept.

At least he hoped he was sleeping there. The Englishman had been late coming home last night. Faisal had tried to stay up but had fallen asleep.

Faisal hated it when the Englishman came back late. Faisal got stuck all alone in a dark house and he always worried the Englishman might not come back at all.

What had Moustafa said? "They always go back to their own country eventually." Moustafa had worked for a bunch of Europeans and they had all gone back, leaving the Nubian to fend for himself.

Who's to say the Englishman wouldn't leave the house one afternoon, board a train, and take it all the way to England? Then Faisal would be alone with all those statues and mummies and other things. The house would get bought by someone else and he'd get kicked out. What would he do then?

Faisal came to the next floor and felt a little better. There were more furnishings here. In the hall stood the bureau where the Englishman kept some of his things, right next to the door to his study where he had his desk and papers and lots of books. And over there was the door to the Englishman's bedroom. He crept over to it but didn't try to open it. It was always locked.

Instead, Faisal pressed his ear against the wood while keeping an eye out for sneaking djinn.

From inside the room he could hear a faint, regular snoring.

Faisal let out a long, slow breath of relief. He stood there for a moment, head against the door, listening to the reassuring sound.

**

The next morning at breakfast, the Englishman seemed distracted. He didn't tell Faisal to sit up straight or not make so much noise while eating or be careful not to get crumbs on the tablecloth. He sat picking at his food and not saying much of anything.

Faisal watched him over his eggs and bread. The Englishman kept touching his mask, which was a sign that he was busy thinking about something.

Faisal knew better than to ask.

Once they finished breakfast, the Englishman stood and said quickly, "I won't be opening the store today. I have some things to do."

"Um, all right. I'll clean the dishes and then I need to go too. I'm seeing Cordelia."

The Englishman didn't even seem to get annoyed by that. He really was distracted!

"Very well. Make sure you lock the door," was all he said.

Within a minute the Englishman had grabbed his cane that had a sword hidden inside and had gone, leaving Faisal alone again.

Faisal worried over this problem the entire time he cleaned and dried and put away the dishes, dressed in his nice new djellaba, and washed his hands and face. The doorman at Cordelia's building hated him, so he had to look his best to avoid trouble.

He couldn't do anything about his hair, though. Standing in front of the mirror, he tried to comb it, but no matter what he did it went every which way. When he had first come to the orphanage, they had cut off all his hair, leaving him bald. That got rid of the lice that had plagued him all his life, but he didn't like how it made him look like a brown egg. But soon enough his hair had grown back just as thick and curly and unruly as ever. At least the lice hadn't come back.

Once he finished, he went down to the pantry and took some bread and dates and vegetables. Not too much. Just a little so the Englishman wouldn't notice. He'd need them as soon as he got outside.

Sure enough, he had barely shut and locked the door behind him before every street boy on Ibn al-Nafis Street and all the adjoining streets crowded around him.

"Hey Faisal, you got something to eat?"

"Do you have half a piastre? Just a half. I need to get my sandals fixed."

"Do you have a spare blanket?"

Faisal began to hand out the food he had taken, first to his old friends from the shed in the alley—Hamza and Mohammed and Abdul and the little Turk Mehmed—and portioned out the rest to the other boys, boys he knew a little or did not know at all but who knew him.

Faisal had become famous among the street boys because he had been taken in by the Englishman. Every street boy dreamed of being taken in by someone who had a real home. No one but Faisal ever had.

The food quickly ran out. It always ran out, so Faisal began to hand out small coins. He tried to keep as many small coins in his pocket as he could so he could give something to everybody. The Englishman gave him money for his meals when he was out of the house but most of it ended up in another boy's hands. Faisal sometimes had to steal to eat. At least today he'd eat at Cordelia's.

Assuming he could get through this crowd and make it there. There were more than yesterday. It seemed every day the crowd of street boys got bigger.

Pretty soon the coins ran out just like the food. Two boys he didn't know, one about his age and the other bigger, didn't get anything.

"Come on," the small one whined. "Just a little something."

"I don't have anything left," Faisal said.

"Liar," the big one said. "What's that in your pocket?"

"My house keys." It always gave Faisal a sense of pride to say that. He had never had house keys before.

"Nonsense! You got something else in there." The big boy tried to reach into his pocket.

"Hey!"

Faisal pushed him away. The bigger boy pushed him back, making him stumble. The smaller boy darted in, trying to get into Faisal's pockets.

"Leave him alone!" Hamza shouted. Hamza was fourteen or so, and the biggest of Faisal's friends. He slugged the bigger boy while Faisal slugged the smaller boy.

Soon all four of them were fighting and a few other boys dove in too. Nobody liked to pass up a good fight.

"Get out of here, you scamps!"

Karim the old neighborhood watchman came running in with his stick, smacking everyone within reach as the men lounging in the café across the street cheered. Faisal got behind the boy he was fighting and let him take the watchman's blow. Karim wasn't fooled, though, and went for him. Karim had always had it out for Faisal.

Faisal laughed and ran for it. He could run way faster than that old grump.

"You stop causing trouble, you little louse!" Karim bellowed after him. "One day the Englishman will realize his mistake and you'll be back on the streets!"

Once Faisal got safely out of reach, he turned back to Karim and gave him a crude gesture, then ran off into the crowd.

It was a long walk to Cordelia's, and Karim's words followed him all the way there. He tried to put them out of his mind, but they echoed in his head like Moustafa's words.

He had a nice house and plenty of food for the first time ever. It was hard to believe it, and even harder to believe it would last.

Cordelia had taken an apartment in a nice area of town filled mostly by foreigners. It wasn't just English people there, but also Italians and Greeks and some others too. Faisal still had trouble remembering all the different countries in Europe. Cordelia had given him a map to study but since he hadn't learned to read yet, it didn't help much.

The doorman, a fat Egyptian man with bad teeth and an even worse temper, frowned at him. Faisal gave him an innocent look. The doorman grunted and let him pass into the small foyer with its stone floor and big mirror so people could check they looked good before going in or out.

Faisal inspected himself. A bit of a scuff on his chin where he had been punched, but nothing too bad. Cordelia and the Englishman both got cross if they thought he had been fighting, and never believed him when he said it wasn't his fault.

Whistling, Faisal went up three flights of stairs and knocked on the door. Cordelia answered. She was a young woman with blue eyes and that bright yellow hair Europeans often had. Her white dress made it look even brighter. She smiled at him.

"Good morning, Faisal," she said in English.

"Hello. Nice to see you. How are you I am fine," Faisal replied in English. He was getting better.

"Shall we practice some Arabic today?" Cordelia asked in Arabic. It was one of the only things she could say in Arabic but she said it very well.

Faisal switched to Arabic. "Sure, I'll teach you some words."

Cordelia got that lost look she always got when Faisal spoke his own language.

"Come in," she said in English. Then remembered to say the same in Arabic. "*Tfaddel.*"

Cordelia had a nice apartment. It wasn't big like the Englishman's with lots of empty rooms and the others all full of weapons and dead things. There was a sitting room full of comfy furniture and a big rug on the floor to keep it cozy. There were vases with flowers and boxes of sweets. In the corner was a phonograph they liked to listen to and some pictures of England on the walls. There was a bathroom and a bedroom too, a kitchen with nice smells, and a balcony where you could look out onto the street.

"Are you hungry?" Cordelia asked in English.

"Yes, please," Faisal replied.

Even though he had just had a big breakfast, he didn't have any money left so this would have to be an early lunch. He hoped the Englishman wouldn't be so distracted that he forgot to come back for dinner.

He sat at the table while Cordelia went to the kitchen and returned with a plate covered in a cloth. When she removed the cloth Faisal saw some English things called *grum bets*. You put butter on the grum bets and ate them with tea. Faisal didn't like English tea much, it was too weak, but the grum bets were nice. Faisal's eyes widened as she put three on his plate, each with a generous dollop of butter.

Faisal fidgeted as she poured the tea, stifled a groan as she only put one spoonful of sugar in his cup, and waited until she served herself. The Englishmen, he had learned, wouldn't eat until the Englishwomen started eating. This was the opposite of Egyptians. The men ate first and the women ate what was left later in a separate room. The English did everything backwards.

Cordelia served herself and then moved over beside Faisal, pointing to his chest and saying something in English. The only word he caught was "wound."

Faisal blushed. Cordelia wanted to check how his wound was healing. She was a nurse and had saved him when he was shot, but it still made him shy when she checked the circular scar on his chest.

Faisal opened up the neck of his djellaba and pulled it down a bit to expose the scar. It was on his upper chest, just above the heart. The doctor at the hospital in Luxor said it had missed his heart by less than an inch and he was a very lucky boy. Faisal could have told him that if he was a very lucky boy he wouldn't have gotten shot in the first place, but he didn't think the doctor would listen.

"Does it hurt?" Cordelia asked in English, examining it. He knew this question.

"A small."

"A *little*," Cordelia corrected. Faisal shook his head. Why have two words for the same thing with one of them being wrong half the time?

Cordelia probed it with her fingers. Faisal winced. It didn't hurt. Actually it tickled a little, but if he pretended it hurt, Cordelia got all concerned and usually gave him an extra grum bet.

Cordelia tut-tutted and sat down. Faisal did up the top of his djellaba. Faisal looked at Cordelia. Cordelia looked at Faisal. When was this woman going to start eating?

Faisal looked at the grum bets and back at Cordelia. Maybe she would take the hint.

Nope. She just sat there staring at Faisal.

Faisal wished his stomach would grumble. That would tell her what to do, but he had just eaten breakfast.

He looked at the food again. Still Cordelia wouldn't eat. What was the matter with her?

A smile slowly spread across her lips. Faisal smiled back. Cordelia covered her mouth and laughed. Faisal giggled. Cordelia reached for a grum bet, then pulled her hand away. Faisal laughed.

Cordelia finally stopped fooling around and started eating, which let Faisal eat too. After a minute he remembered his job and picked up a spoon.

"*Gafsha*," he said.

Cordelia tried to pronounce the Arabic word. Faisal made her try several times until she got to something that might possibly sound close. Then it was her turn.

"Spoon."

"Spun."

"*Spoon.*"

"Spoooon."

Next Faisal put the spoon in the sugar bowl, pulled out a heap, and pointed.

"*Sukker.*"

"Sukker."

That was an easy one. So close to the English word. He moved to put the sugar in his tea but Cordelia took his hand and gently but firmly made him put the sugar back in the bowl. Faisal rolled his eyes and Cordelia said something in English he didn't catch. He didn't need to. The tone said, "I know all your tricks."

Well no, she didn't, but she knew a lot of them.

They ate their grum bets and traded words. Even though Faisal was already learning a lot of words from the Englishman he liked these mornings before Cordelia had to go to work in the hospital, because Cordelia was nice despite what the Englishman said and she was a better cook too.

Finishing off his grum bet, Faisal hoped it would be like this forever, that he would have a nice snug bed on the Englishman's roof, breakfasts and moving pictures with him sometimes, and mornings trading words and eating with Cordelia.

He didn't want anything to change. Never. Not ever. He didn't want any more dead bodies or severed heads or running around after bad people. He certainly didn't want to get shot again. The doctor had been right in a way. While it hadn't been lucky to get shot, he sure had been lucky to survive. He didn't think he'd be so lucky next time, if there was a next time.

He had to make sure there wasn't a next time.

CHAPTER FOUR

"Are you quite sure this is Lieutenant Gregory Marshall, formerly of the Oxfordshire and Buckinghamshire Light Infantry?" Sir Thomas asked. "Sorry to make you go through it again, but it has to go into the coroner's official record."

"Yes," Augustus said in a quiet voice. "I served with him throughout the war."

Augustus and Sir Thomas stood with the city coroner in the chilly cellar of the morgue. The body, now missing its false beard, lay on a gurney before them, covered by a sheet with only the face exposed.

Sir Thomas put a hand on his shoulder. "Sorry, old boy. It's always hard to lose an army chum."

Augustus wouldn't have exactly called Gregory a chum. While a nice enough fellow, Gregory was utterly uninterested in any intellectual pursuits and his reading about the past was limited to last week's cricket scores. A gambler and womanizer, always ready with a crude joke, he was the opposite of the young, retiring intellectual Augustus had been even when he still had his face and his original name.

But Gregory had been a good man to have with you on the line. Steady as a rock and always ready to share the last of his rations when the German shelling kept food from coming up the communication lines. On trench raids, wire cutting expeditions, and scouts, Gregory always did his share and more.

That made the brash, uncouth fellow far, far more than a chum.

"So what have you discovered?" Augustus asked the coroner. The thin, pale fellow had said his name but it had passed in a blur.

"Cause of death was suffocation, mostly likely with one of the pillows on the loveseat. A few red threads of red velvet were found in the false beard matching the threads on the pillow. Swelling of the neck due to the struggle, but no other injuries except some bruises on the upper portion of both arms, probably from someone holding him in place while a second man suffocated him."

"They must have been titans," Sir Augustus said. "Gregory was quite fit, and they kept him immobile enough that his false beard didn't slip."

"Indeed. The body shows that he was in the prime of health. No diseases and no injuries other than a fully healed bullet wound through the side."

"Bloody Bosche! I'm bleeding like a stuck pig."

"I got you, Gregory. Only a few more yards now."

Augustus shook himself, forcing his mind to focus on the here and now. The coroner continued as the faint sound of artillery fire echoed through the cellar.

"I found no poison or drugs in his system. His stomach contained only his last meal. I'm afraid that's all I have for you."

Sir Thomas shook his hand. "Thank you, Dr. Klepper. It is a great help. We will leave you to your work now."

They left the gloomy cellar, taking the stairs up to the ground floor of Cairo's central hospital. Augustus barely saw the clean white corridors and uniformed nurses and doctors passing by.

Augustus lit a cigarette and asked, "So what did that hotel detective discover, McHaggis or whatever his name is?"

"MacHugh. He says your friend registered at the hotel earlier that day, having been picked up by a hotel cabman at the station. He came on the morning train from Alexandria. I'm making enquiries with my colleagues there. He registered under the name Peter Saunders."

Augustus stopped in his tracks.

"Does that name mean something to you?" the chief of police asked.

"He served in the Oxs and Bucks. Killed in action at the First Battle of the Aisne."

Sir Thomas scratched his chin. "Curious. Do you think he came down here to see you?"

"Impossible. No one knows my true name here, except you."

"And I only found out after a rather extensive investigation. But you must admit it's too much of a coincidence. Perhaps he heard of an antiquities dealer of your, erm, description."

"You mean my mask."

"Sorry, I—"

"It's quite all right. I see your point." They walked out of the hospital and into the blazing noonday sun. "Even when I served with Marshall, I had a great interest in the past and spoke frequently of wanting to visit Egypt. I didn't think Gregory paid much attention. He wasn't at all interested in intellectual pursuits. So yes, coming to Cairo would be an unusual step. Coming under the name of a fallen comrade and in disguise is even more unusual. What did that Scot say, McGinger or whatever his name is?"

"MacHugh. Really, Augustus, do you have something against the Scots?"

"Not at all. They took the worst part of the British Isles for themselves, saving us from having to live there. Do go on."

"Your friend tried not to be noticed. He did not speak with any other guests or go to the bar."

"That's not typical of him. Gregory was gregarious and liked a drink in the afternoon. He was a past master at scrounging bottles of wine from the cellars of ruined buildings. Sniffed them out like a pig sniffs out truffles."

In the street in front of the hospital, Sir Thomas's car waited. A uniformed officer sat at the wheel. They both got in the back.

"Shall we drive you to your house?" Sir Thomas asked.

"Thank you."

The chief of police leaned forward. "Ibn al-Nafis street, sergeant."

"Yes, sir."

Sir Thomas turned to Augustus as the car pulled away. "Your friend didn't eat in the dining room, either. Instead, he had a meal sent up to his room. The concierge said he purchased a detailed map of the city and asked how long it would take for a letter to reach an address in Cairo. The concierge said it was too late for it to reach the recipient that day, but that if he gave him the letter at any time in the evening it would go out with the morning post and get delivered with the afternoon post."

"At what time was this?"

"The concierge couldn't recall exactly. Sometime around dinner."

"And the bellboy who delivered his dinner was told to come back to get the letter."

"To be precise, he came back to clear the plates and was told to come back in half an hour to get the letter. The bellboy returned to the room at 6:30 PM, which was when he found the body."

"So the killers must have come into his room some time in that half hour," Augustus mused. "It sounds like they were watching."

"Indeed."

"So he didn't leave the hotel at all?"

"It appears not. We can't be entirely certain, of course."

"What was found in his room?"

"Nothing unusual. No papers of interest. And no letter or blank sheets of letterhead. The concierge gave him some hotel letterhead, and the bellboy never picked it up, so the killers must have gotten it. If he was trying to contact you, they know where you live. Would you like me to post a policeman outside?"

"No, I'll be quite all right."

Sir Thomas frowned. "I was afraid you would say that. Look, old boy, I know you're cut up about this and I don't blame you, but don't go off on one of your wild goose chases. It will only muddy the waters. I'll put my best men on this."

I'm sure you will, but I'm a better man than all of them.

Augustus kept quiet as they drove into the native quarter of Old Cairo.

As they approached his street, Augustus told the driver, "Drop me off here, if you please. It's best if I don't drive up to the house with a police officer. The neighbors speak of me enough already."

Augustus walked the rest of the way, lost in thought. Sir Thomas was right, it was too much of a coincidence that Gregory came to Cairo, a place he had no business being, and wanted to send a letter to someone here. And the chief of police was correct that a masked man running an antiquities shop was a fine description of the man Gregory knew him to be.

But how would he have known Augustus had moved to Egypt at all? No one back home knew.

Augustus unlocked the door and entered his house, locking and bolting it securely behind him. As he passed through the showroom of his shop with its statues and glass cases full of shabtis and scarabs and bits of papyrus, Faisal came hurrying up, looking out of sorts.

"There's been another murder, hasn't there?"

Augustus blinked. "Why do you say that?"

"Because you were distracted at breakfast. You didn't shout at me. Not once. And then you were on the phone with Sir Thomas Russell Pasha. And you didn't come back for lunch. But this is a bad one, because you're not excited like usual."

"Since when did you become a detective?"

"Since I met you. What happened?"

Augustus sighed and passed through to the back sitting room. He reached for the whiskey decanter, then stopped himself. He needed to keep his head clear. Augustus sat on the sofa. Faisal sat beside him.

"I thought you were supposed to be at Cordelia's."

"I was. She's at work now, you silly Englishman."

"Remembering her schedule is a very low priority."

Faisal looked glum. "You're going to investigate this murder, aren't you? You usually have a drink from that stinky glass thing when you come home but right now you want to think."

"In English it's called a decanter."

"I don't need that word. You usually drink from it when you come home, but not if you're thinking of something important."

Augustus slumped. "Indeed I am. The murdered man was a friend."

Faisal's jaw dropped.

"Not Moustafa!"

"No, I would have told you from the start."

"Herr Schäfer?"

"No. No one you know."

Faisal looked relieved, then put his arm around him. "I'm sorry about your friend."

Augustus extricated himself. "Thank you. Now kindly leave me alone. I need to think."

Faisal did not leave, but Augustus barely noticed. He was too busy trying to unravel the mystery of why a lieutenant would take on a dead private's name in order to come to a city that he had no interest in.

Or did he have an interest? Since being wounded, Augustus had lost track of the men of the Oxs and Bucks. Everyone in the regiment, at least those who had made it through, had sent him letters. He answered none of them. Those who visited him in hospital got turned away by the nurses at his request. Augustus didn't want them to see him in his present state.

He tried to remember what he knew of Gregory Marshall's civilian life. Some second-rate public school. Oxford for university. He had graduated, certainly not with a first, in some subject Augustus couldn't remember and Marshall may never have mentioned. Then he had gone into his father's business, a large construction firm that had done very well with war contracts.

Marshall had been the second son. Augustus remembered him laughing how his older brother had gotten a deferment because he had been running the day-to-day affairs of the family business, his sickly father in charge in name only.

"My brother always was better at games," Marshall had said once. *"Used to thump me good and proper if I gave him any backtalk. Now there he is, getting fat in an office while I'm out here saving civilization. I stick his nose in it with every letter I write!"*

He had said this, however, without heat. Marshall was a boor, but not a brute. He extended a hand to everybody.

Going out into No Man's Land by day to retrieve a man who was almost certainly dead had been typical of him. It had been only one of countless acts of selflessness.

Marshall held up a bottle in the candlelight of their dugout. "Look what I found, my boy, an old bottle of wine."

He looked at the label, faded and dusty. "A 1892 Beaune Grèves. A good vintage."

Marshall chuckled. "I knew you'd know more about it than I do. For me it's just wine. I found half a dozen of them in the ruins of that chateau we passed today. Had some of the men help me dig around."

"Where are the rest?"

"Don't get greedy," Marshall said, punching him on the arm. "I gave them to the men."

"You gave vintage French wine to a pack of squaddies?"

"The finest pack of squaddies you or I will ever see. I'll give every one of them a job after the war, and if my brother kicks up a fuss, I'll give him a left hook that will change his attitude. I love these men. I'd do anything for them."

"I know, Marshall. You're the best officer in the regiment."

"After you, you old swot. Come on, help me drink this and tell me what I'm drinking. Quite a find, eh? And to think you're the one who wants to be an archaeologist!"

Marshall poked him in the side.

The scene faded and Augustus's sitting room in Cairo came into view. Faisal was poking him in the side.

"Stop that!" Augustus snapped.

"It was someone from the army, wasn't it?" Faisal asked.

"Why do you say that?"

"Because you went away in your head."

"Yes," Augustus sighed. "It was someone from the army."

"Sorry."

Faisal put his arm around him. This time, Augustus didn't push him away.

CHAPTER FIVE

Moustafa almost didn't recognize Faisal when he came through the door of his bookshop. He hadn't seen the boy in a couple of months and the transformation was remarkable.

Most notably, he was clean. Not just clean clothes, but his hands and face were freshly scrubbed and he even looked like he had tried to comb his hair.

He had grown a bit too, not just up but out. While still thin, he no longer looked scrawny and underfed. Mr. Wall's regular meals were having an effect.

The boy didn't look happy about his improved condition, though. Moustafa could see something troubled him.

Moustafa rose from his desk by the entrance. "What are you doing here, Little Infidel? Why the long face?"

"There's been another murder."

Moustafa groaned. He knew it. That strange visitor at his bookshop a couple of nights before, Mr. Wall's unexplained absence from the lecture … trouble followed that man like a desert wind.

"Who is it this time?"

"Some old Army friend. He keeps slipping away in his head."

This was bad. Mr. Wall had a strange affliction that made him return to the war anytime there was danger. If he was having these spells even without a gunfight, then he had grown even more mad than usual.

"What has he said?" Moustafa asked.

"Not much, that's what worries me. He usually gets all excited when someone gets killed. Now he just shuffles around mumbling to himself. He hasn't opened the shop and he keeps going out without telling me where."

"Didn't he hire an assistant?"

"He did, but he let him go. Then he hired another man and let him go too. He said neither were as good as you. I wish you still worked there."

Moustafa shook his head. "I couldn't continue working for that man."

Faisal looked around. "He said your shop is doing well."

"It is, praise be to God."

"He tells all his customers about it."

Moustafa smiled. "Does he? And what about you? How's the wound?"

Faisal shrugged. "Oh, that's fine." He plucked a book off the shelf.

"Don't touch that!"

"Why not?" Faisal said, flipping through the pages.

"Because I don't want your dirty fingers leaving stains on the paper."

"My fingers aren't dirty. Besides, I like to look at the pictures. Hey, this is a pharaoh, isn't it?"

"Yes, that's Ramesses X. Instead of looking at the pictures, you should learn how to read."

"The Englishman says he doesn't have time to teach me. He's been teaching me lots of words, though. And about ancient things too. Did you know those little statues called shabtis came to life and helped the dead Egyptians do their work?"

"Yes. They're common finds in tombs from all eras."

"Why don't they come to life anymore?"

"They didn't really come to life, you idiot. That was just a belief the ancients had."

"Oh," Faisal said, not sounding convinced. He continued to flip through the pages, looking at the pictures. Moustafa wanted to snatch the book from him but with the boy actually appearing interested, he decided against it.

"Perhaps he should put you into a school."

Faisal made a face. "No."

"You need to learn how to read. Make something of yourself."

"I'll help in the shop when I'm older. He said I could."

"You need to be able to read for that."

"Maybe Cordelia will teach me."

"She's still in Cairo?"

"She got a job as a nurse. Aunt Pearl left, though. Went to someplace called India. I'm teaching Cordelia Arabic and she's teaching me English. I'm better than her, though. She sounds like a strangled cat!"

"Don't speak of a respectable woman like that! You're lucky she's taken an interest in your education."

Moustafa smacked him upside the head, making Faisal drop the book.

"I knew you'd do something like that," Moustafa growled, retrieving it.

"That was your fault. I wouldn't have dropped it if you hadn't hit me."

"I wouldn't have hit you if you weren't such an ungrateful little street parasite."

"I don't live on the streets anymore. So what are we going to do about the murder?"

Moustafa felt tempted to say that he would do nothing and kick the Little Infidel out of his shop before he did any more damage, but the memory of the mysterious visitor tugged at him. Mr. Wall needed to know about that.

Cursing to himself, he closed up his shop and followed Faisal to the familiar old house on Ibn al-Nafis street.

They found the shop closed, but Mr. Wall came to the front door as the boy opened it. As Faisal had said, he looked distracted, although he brightened a little at seeing his former employee.

"Moustafa! How good to see you."

"I told him about the murder," Faisal said. "He's here to help."

Mr. Wall merely nodded, as if that was the most natural thing in the world.

How irritating. He simply assumes I'll put myself in danger for him.

And yet he's right.

Why is he right?

They entered the front hall, a large space with an arched ceiling that used to give access for carriages to the courtyard. Now it was lined with Egyptian statues, an introduction to the main room beyond.

As they stepped into that room, Moustafa felt a tug of nostalgia. It looked much the same. The giant statue of the crocodile-headed Nile god Sobek still stood sentinel in one corner. In the center of the room, he recognized the massive Old Kingdom sarcophagus that had been delivered one night with the body of a French police chief inside. Here was a shelf of shabtis and figurines, arranged in a subtle pattern that signaled which were genuine and which were Suleiman Hanzade's clever fakes. Another shelf held a stack of animal mummies—cats and ibis, hawks and crocodiles.

"The shop looks well, Mr. Wall."

"It's doing well, although finding an assistant as good as you were is proving an impossible task." Mr. Wall turned to him. "Look, my good man, I'm very grateful that you came to help, but if you don't want to get involved, I won't hold it against you. You have your family and your business and—"

"I am already involved, Mr. Wall. I think the murderer, or someone associated with this case, hoped to find you at the lecture last night."

A spark of excitement flashed in his old boss's eyes. "Really? Come, let us sit in my downstairs study and discuss it."

They passed through the shop and to a back hall. On the left was a small, cozy study with armchairs and bookshelves. Mr. Wall told him to sit.

"I'll put the kettle on," Mr. Wall said. "Faisal, why don't you go outside and play?"

"Don't you need me to help find the murderer?"

"No."

The boy made a move for the door, then stopped.

"You sure?"

"Quite sure."

Faisal thought for a moment, then seemed to come to a decision.

"I need to stay here and help you solve the murder." He sounded reluctant.

"You're doing nothing of the sort," Mr. Wall snapped. "You got shot last time, if you recall. I'm not going to risk such a thing happening to you again."

"But you need me," he said uncertainly.

"Go."

"I promise I won't get shot," Faisal said, in a tone that made it sound like he was trying to convince himself as much as Mr. Wall.

"GO!"

"I'll go to the courtyard," Faisal moped. "Come get me if there's something you can't figure out on your own."

Faisal left. Mr. Wall waited a moment, poked his head out the door and shouted, "Wherever you're hiding, go out in the courtyard. And I want to hear you out there."

"All right," Faisal grumbled.

A few minutes later, after he had made tea and evicted Faisal a second time, Mr. Wall returned with a tray of tea and biscuits. "He's gone, but let's speak in English just in case. I don't want him involved."

"Good idea," Moustafa replied.

Mr. Wall then told him of what had occurred at Shepheard's Hotel a couple of nights before. Moustafa listened with increasing interest, and despair.

He could feel it happening. He could feel his pulse quickening and his mind racing. Once again, he felt the lure of the chase.

He is going to pull me away from my family to hunt down this killer, I just know it. Why did God saddle me with this man?

Moustafa did not express his feelings out loud. Instead he asked, "What do the police say?"

As if a police investigation will stop him from taking up the case. It will only encourage him!

"Sir Thomas Russell Pasha has received some interesting information from his colleague in Alexandria. Gregory Marshall had been living in Alexandria for several months under an assumed name. He became a member of the local Egyptological and Geographical societies, as well as the Classical Society. This is most unlike him. When I knew him, he showed not the slightest interest in any of those subjects."

"People change," Moustafa said.

"So much? Also, the police questioned some of the members of these societies who said Marshall had very little knowledge of the subject matter, although he had a keen interest in Alexander the Great's conquest of Egypt. He asked all sorts of questions about it, and little about any other subject. He also made friends with many educated members of the Greek community and asked similar questions."

"Curious. The reason I came was because something happened at the lecture the other night, a lecture, as you know, about the Greco-Roman period."

Moustafa told him everything he could remember about the man who had appeared.

"Interesting. You say he had an Australian accent?"

"Yes, but not a refined one like some of the officers. They sound almost English. His was more of a working man's accent. Like what I heard from many of the lower ranks during the war."

"And you had the impression this man was looking for someone who hadn't come, and then waited outside in case that person did?"

"Yes. He moved out of sight after a few minutes. Whether he left the street entirely I am not sure. As you know, my street is long and straight at that section, and he could have hidden quite a distance away and still seen if anyone arrived or left my shop."

"I'm surprised he posted himself directly opposite your shop, then."

"He probably didn't think I would come out and challenge him."

Mr. Wall smiled. "Many people have underestimated you and ended up regretting it."

A regular thumping in the courtyard cut off what Moustafa planned to say next. Mr. Wall grumbled and got up from his chair, moving to the doorway.

"Faisal, I told you not to play football in the courtyard!"

"You told me to play out here," the boy's voice whined from outside.

"I told you to play, not send footballs around the courtyard! The way you kick that thing, you're liable to decapitate a statue."

"You bought him a football?" Moustafa asked.

"Don't you remember that boy teaching him football in Bahariya? He loves the game. He's started a neighborhood league."

"Full of lice-ridden street imps, no doubt. Careful he doesn't bring any contagion home."

"It started with only street boys, but the boys with homes also became interested. Now boys whose parents never allowed them to speak with Faisal are beginning to do kickabouts with him. It's helping him be accepted into what passes for respectable society around here."

"I wouldn't be too optimistic about that," Moustafa said, knowing full well how long the Egyptian memory could be when it came to social differences. The children might like his football, but their parents would never forget where Faisal came from.

There was a thump and a crash outside.

"What was that?" Mr. Wall called out.

"Nothing!"

They could hear Faisal muttering to himself and the sounds of broken pottery being gathered up.

"I hope that wasn't something ancient," Moustafa said.

"No, a flowerpot. He's decimated them."

"That boy needs a good thrashing."

"That boy needs a lot of things." Mr. Wall leaned forward. "But I need something a little more urgently. I need your help. Gregory Marshall was a comrade-in-arms. I don't know why someone murdered him or who that man at your shop was, but I intend to find out. I need a strong, intelligent man at my side."

And there it was. Mr. Wall had asked him.

"Mr. Wall … I have my shop. My family."

"I know, I know. Of course I'll pay you your usual danger pay as well as compensation for lost time at your shop."

"It's not about the money, Mr. Wall. It's my wife. She doesn't want me going off."

Mr. Wall rubbed his temples and didn't say anything for a moment. His fingers trembled slightly. Moustafa stared at him. He had never seen the man so out of sorts. His former employer went on with some difficulty.

"It's just that I'm … known in Alexandria. I lived there for some time, as you know, and a few people came close to discovering my identity and I was forced to leave. I cannot move about the city very freely, and I cannot move about the native quarter freely at all. Plus there appears to be some sort of Greek connection. You speak modern Greek and I don't. Even without these complicating factors it would be difficult for me to conduct this particular investigation alone."

"He keeps going off in his head." Wasn't that what Faisal said?

"Alone?" Moustafa asked.

"I can't bring Faisal. Not after what happened last time."

"I agree, Mr. Wall."

The memory of Faisal lying in the darkness in a pool of his own blood made him shudder.

"I've sent a telegram to Jocelyn in Jerusalem to inform her of the situation. I'm hoping she can take a train or a boat down to Alexandria. She would be of great help, but I haven't heard back and I don't know if she will make it in time."

Jocelyn Montjoy? That fallen woman with the trousers? She was almost as mad as the man in front of him. Still, Moustafa had to admit, she was a good shot. She could, indeed, be of great help, not the least in keeping Mr. Wall on an even keel.

Assuming she made it on time. That was a big assumption. There was a railway between Jerusalem and Cairo, built during the last war, and fast steamers, but it was still a long journey. If she didn't make it, Mr. Wall would be up in Alexandria alone.

Alone with his madness.

Moustafa felt a mixture of dread and exhilaration.

Perhaps this is what drunks feel, knowing their favorite vice could ruin them but rushing to the bar all the same.

"I will come, Mr. Wall."

His former boss looked inexpressibly relieved. "Thank you, Moustafa. This will be of great assistance. We won't be going for another day or two yet. First we have to check on a few more things here, namely the identity of the man who visited your shop. If he was trying to find me there, that means he either doesn't know about my shop, which seems unlikely considering the stolen letter, or didn't want to come here for some reason."

"But how will we find him?"

Mr. Wall scratched his chin. "Good question."

"I know! I can put a sign in my window announcing that you will give a lecture tomorrow night. I'm sure he's keeping a watch on my shop. He'll see the notice and come."

"Guns blazing into your place of business?"

Moustafa grinned. "We'll set a trap for him."

Mr. Wall smiled and clapped him on the shoulder. "That's the man I know. Let's get to work."

"So what do I get to do?" Faisal asked, bounding into the room.

Moustafa turned to him with surprise. "Did you understand our conversation?" he asked in Arabic.

Faisal shrugged. "Enough of it. Something about trapping somebody. Is that the murderer?"

"I'm not sure," Mr. Wall said. "But I'll wager he's involved."

"All right. What can I do to help?"

"Nothing," Mr. Wall said.

Faisal looked equally surprised and disappointed. "Nothing?"

"Nothing. You'll stay away and stay safe."

"But—"

"But nothing. I don't want you getting shot again."

"I promise I won't get shot."

"The answer is no. Now go outside and play with your friends."

Faisal left, an unreadable expression on his face.

CHAPTER SIX

It was absolutely, totally, completely unfair.

The Englishman and Moustafa were off solving a murder and he was stuck eating cabbage and bratwurst.

Herr Schäfer and his wife Inge had never invited him to dinner before. Faisal had come over with the Englishman once or twice, but that was it.

It was obvious the Englishman was trying to get rid of him for the evening.

"Don't worry," the Englishman had said. "Inge Schäfer is an excellent cook, and promised that she'd use beef instead of the usual pork for the bratwurst. It's a type of sausage. You'll like it. Germans always serve big portions."

No pork? Like that was supposed to make everything better! He didn't expect these Germans to poison him anyway. What he resented was being left out of the investigation.

Well, he wasn't going to be left out for long.

Herr Schäfer had picked him up at the Englishman's house right on time (Europeans wanted everything to happen on time, rather than the time things should naturally happen) and drove him in his motorcar to his own house. At the front door they were greeted warmly by his wife Inge, a plump woman with a round face who pinched Faisal's cheeks like he was a baby, and then disappeared into the kitchen. Herr Schäfer took him into the living room.

It looked cozy enough, and Faisal plopped into an armchair and looked around. There were books everywhere! Even more books than the Englishman had.

Herr Schäfer smiled, lit his pipe, and tried to have a conversation with him.

This was the first problem. Herr Schäfer didn't speak Arabic, and Faisal's English wasn't good enough for a long conversation yet. Pretty soon Faisal got bored and his head hurt. He looked around, hoping for some of that German chocolate. The Germans made the best.

To his delight, Herr Schäfer got up.

The delight was short-lived, because the German came back with an armful of books. Europeans were really bad at taking hints.

Still, the books were interesting, full of pictures of the ancient things the Europeans liked so much—giant pharaohs and djinn with animal heads, and big temples with tall pillars. Herr Schäfer talked and talked about these things, Faisal only getting one word in ten. It was funny, because this should be really boring, and it was, kind of, but it was nice too because Herr Schäfer was paying attention to him and being kind. Hardly anyone had been like that to him before, and now he had lots of Europeans who were nice to him.

That made him feel bad that he had to sneak away and help Moustafa and the Englishman.

Faisal wouldn't be rude, however. He wouldn't sneak away until after dinner. Inge had obviously been working hard in the kitchen, so it was only right that he eat what she had cooked. He'd need a full stomach to catch that murderer anyway.

At last dinner came. They sat at a table with a frilly white cover and a vase with flowers in the center. The walls had colored prints of castles and forests in what he assumed was Germany, and some photos of people who must be relatives. One photo showed two young men in military uniform and funny helmets with spikes on top. A black ribbon was draped around this photo.

Inge brought out a huge plate piled high with sausages, and another plate piled high with potatoes, and a third plate piled high with vegetables. Faisal hoped he would be able to move after all this.

It was all Faisal could do to keep himself from grabbing some food and stuffing it in his mouth. The Englishman had told him a bunch of times that it was rude. Gobbling was also rude, and so was belching, farting, and picking your teeth. Europeans thought everything was rude. Most of all grabbing food. In English it was called "being greedy."

"You don't need to do it in any case," the Englishman always said. "Your food grabbing days are over."

Faisal liked the sound of that, but he kept some bread and nuts and dates hidden under his bed. Just in case.

Besides no grabbing, gobbling, belching, farting, and picking your teeth, you also couldn't put your feet on the table, put your head on the table, or even put your elbows on the table. You couldn't even leave the table without saying sorry, as if leaving the table was bad somehow. You also couldn't scratch your armpit, swirl your food around your plate, drop peas into your juice to watch them float, or crush insects with your spoon.

How did Europeans remember all this? He certainly couldn't, and the Englishman always got mad if he forgot something. He wouldn't be happy about all the things Faisal did remember, just mad about the things he didn't. So if Faisal managed to get through the whole meal without belching, farting, scratching, or putting his elbows on the table, the Englishman would shout at him for gobbling his dessert. Or if he managed not to gobble, but rested his elbows on the table for just one moment, or tried to scratch between his toes with his fork when he thought the Englishman wasn't looking, he'd get in trouble for that instead of getting praised for all the stuff he did remember.

Then there was the time he did everything right, got through absolutely the whole meal remembering everything. When he finished, he leapt up, very proud of himself, and raced to get his football. The Englishman angrily called him back and berated him for "not asking to be excused."

Excused for what? Doing everything right?

And now he was a guest in somebody else's home, two very proper-looking Germans. He had to be careful. Maybe the Germans were more relaxed than the English. He hoped so.

After laying out all the dishes, Inge sat and she and her husband put their hands together and bowed their heads.

Uh-oh. They were praying. He didn't understand the words but it was pretty obvious what they were doing. A lot of Europeans did it before eating. The Englishman never did, and Cordelia only did it when she was with other Europeans, so he had never been sitting at the table when Europeans prayed before eating.

What was he supposed to do? He couldn't join in a Christian prayer, could he? Wouldn't that be a sin? He had enough of those already. That's what Moustafa said. But wouldn't it be rude if he didn't join them? He wasn't sure. The Englishman should have told him what to do!

The Schäfers both had their heads bowed and their eyes closed, so maybe they wouldn't notice him just sitting there.

The prayer only took a moment anyway, and pretty soon Inge started heaping a bunch of those wonderful sausages onto his plate. She tried to speak with him, but she spoke English funny and he understood her even less than her husband.

Everyone started to eat, and he discovered that bratwurst tasted really good. He tried to remember to sit up straight, not gobble, use his knife and fork properly, and not belch.

Well, he let out one or two. Just little ones, and only when Herr Schäfer or his wife were talking. That way they didn't notice.

And he didn't gobble at all. He didn't get the chance. Inge started pointing out things on the table and said the word for them, encouraging Faisal to repeat. This was annoying because it slowed down his eating. Talking with your mouth full was one of the many things Europeans thought were rude.

The words were hard too, and Inge and her husband had a good chuckle at Faisal's expense. At first Faisal thought it was because Inge spoke English funny and Faisal tried imitating her too much, but then she pointed out things that he already knew the words for.

She wasn't teaching him English at all. She was teaching him German. Like he didn't have enough to think about!

Still, the bratwurst was good.

As he finished his plate, she heaped more on it. Perhaps he should learn some German after all.

Once Faisal polished off his plate a second time, he realized he needed to go if he wanted to get to the bookshop before the murderer. He had a plan for that. All he had to do was ask to use the bathroom.

"May I be excused?" he said. The Englishman had made him learn that question and repeat it every time he wanted to leave the table, so he was good with that. At least when he remembered.

He didn't expect the answer he got.

Herr Schäfer said something he didn't catch, except for the word, "home." He looked concerned, and so did his wife.

Of course the Englishman had told them to keep an eye on him. Faisal couldn't let them figure out the truth.

"No ... um ..." What was the word for bathroom? He knew it, and now he had forgotten.

He pointed to the front hall, where he thought one of the side doors might lead to a bathroom. The Germans gave him a blank stare.

"Um ... water?" Faisal said.

Inge poured him a glass of water. Faisal rolled his eyes.

"No ... um ... *my* water."

Inge nodded and set the glass closer to him.

Faisal stood up and made a gesture. The Germans must have understood because Inge turned the color of a beet and Herr Schäfer put his hand to his mouth and tried to hide the fact that he was chuckling. The scholar got up, led Faisal down the front hall, and opened one of the doors to a bathroom. He showed him how to pull on the little chain to make the water go through the toilet.

Like he didn't know how to do that! It was one of the first things the Englishman had taught him. Then Herr Schäfer left. Faisal closed the door.

Faisal waited enough time for Herr Schäfer to make it back to the dining room table. Easing the door open without a sound, he found he was alone.

Good. Now he just had to sneak out the front door and get across town as quickly as he could. It was far, so far that Herr Schäfer had even picked him up in his motorcar, but Faisal had saved enough money for the tram. He loved the tram, and since he had cleaned up extra well for tonight, the conductors wouldn't kick him off like they sometimes did.

Faisal tiptoed to the front door, feeling good about himself for being so clever and bad about fooling Herr Schäfer and his wife. They were nice. He'd apologize to them later. Hopefully they wouldn't be too mad.

At the front door he paused, suddenly afraid. He hadn't been in any real danger since that horrible night in Luxor. What if there was shooting and fighting? That happened a lot with the Englishman around. He'd been sent to dinner here to keep out of it.

But he couldn't leave the Englishman and Moustafa to do this alone. They never got anything done without him.

Still, if the Englishman wanted him here, he must be expecting a fight.

No, Faisal had to help. He wouldn't be a real friend if he didn't.

He got the door opened and closed without a sound and hurried off into the night, his heart hammering in his chest.

The first problem was finding the tram stop. There were only houses on this street and the tram only stopped on bigger streets with shops. He saw some Europeans but of course they wouldn't speak Arabic so he wandered for a bit until he saw a Nubian man dressed as a servant.

"Where's the nearest tram line to the Old City?"

"Just two blocks down there and to the left. That will take you to Ismailia Square and from there you'll have to transfer."

"Thanks!"

The Nubian stepped in front of him. "Hey, I don't recognize you. Are you a servant in this neighborhood?"

"I'm not a servant. I was a dinner guest."

The Nubian laughed. "That's the worst lie I've ever heard. What are you doing here?"

"It's true!"

"Then which family invited you?" the servant asked in a tone that showed he didn't believe a thing Faisal said.

Faisal hesitated. If he told the man he was at the Schäfer home the servant might tell them where he was going. Then Herr Schäfer would chase him in his motorcar.

"None of your business." Faisal said, going around him.

"I won't take backtalk from you. Tell me what you're doing here!"

The Nubian lunged for Faisal, but Faisal was too quick for him, darted around, and ran for the tram stop.

"Thief! Thief!"

Faisal got half a block down the street, turned and stuck out his tongue at him. Several Europeans on the street stopped and stared. The Nubian started shouting a word in English. It must have been the word for thief because the nearest European man ran for him.

But if Faisal could outrun a Nubian, he could easily outrun a European. The only European he couldn't outrun was the Englishman.

Faisal darted down a side street, clambered over a wall into a garden, ran across it just as a dog came out of the shadows all barks and teeth, vaulted over the opposite wall, and ended up on the street he needed to be on. The tram stop was just ahead, with the tram just pulling in. What luck!

Faisal hurried over just as the last European was boarding.

The Egyptian conductor looked at him suspiciously.

"And where do you think you're going?"

"I'm going home." Faisal produced the 24 millièmes needed to get a ticket. That was more than two piastres and pretty expensive. No wonder so many Egyptians walked.

The conductor looked at him closely. "Are you a servant in this neighborhood?"

"Yes."

"Then why are you out of breath?"

"I was late for the tram."

"You were probably late at your master's house too. Here you go." The conductor gave him a ticket.

Faisal sat near the back where none of the Europeans would bother him. They always made you give up the better seats.

But that didn't bother him as much as what the Egyptian conductor said. Him, a servant? Not for anyone! The customers at the Englishman's shop thought the same. Just the other day one clapped at him and demanded tea. Faisal had picked his pocket to teach him a lesson.

He understood why Moustafa had quit. He said he quit because his wife nagged him and worried he'd get killed on one of these murder cases. That wasn't the truth. Moustafa loved the cases as much as he did. He just didn't want to work for someone else. Especially not a European.

Moustafa supported the people who wanted independence. Faisal didn't know what he thought about that. It would be nice to get rid of the English police. They killed people. But the Egyptian and Soudanese police were even worse. And if the Europeans all left, they might take all their trams and trains and moving pictures.

And the Englishman would leave too.

They all leave in the end, Faisal. That's what Moustafa always said. He had told him how all the archaeologists he had worked for had left. The Englishman was different, though. He hated Europe and said he never wanted to go back.

He wouldn't change his mind, would he?

The tram moved through the European neighborhood, past all the fine houses with their walled gardens and phonographs and good food. It would be a shame if all that disappeared.

The tram let him off at Ismailia Square. The big museum stood to one side, its pale red walls all lit up even though it was closed for the night. Ismailia Square was an exciting place with lots of people and motorcars and trams going every which way. He felt relieved to be back somewhere familiar. He waited for the tram that would take him past Moustafa's shop, itching with excitement. He'd arrive right on time to help, he knew it.

The tram came and he waited until the Europeans got on before he climbed aboard.

"That will be 24 millièmes," the conductor said.

"I already bought a ticket," Faisal said, holding it up.

"Tickets are nontransferable."

"What?"

"You can't use the ticket from one tram for the other. Didn't your parents ever tell you that?"

Faisal bit his lip. He had never used two trams on the same day before. "But I paid!"

"You paid for one ticket. Now you have to buy another," the conductor said. He sounded like he was losing patience, sort of like the Englishman when Faisal forgot not to belch at the table.

"I don't have enough money."

The conductor shrugged like it wasn't any of his concern. Deflated, Faisal stepped off the tram.

The bell rang and the tram pulled away. Faisal ducked behind it just as it sped up and grabbed the big brass back light. He pulled himself up and sat on the fender.

He grinned as the tram sped up. This was a much better way to ride. Free!

It was uncomfortable, though. Noisy too. Some European in a motorcar behind him kept honking and shouting in English. Faisal figured out what he was shouting pretty quick when the tram pulled to a halt between stops and the conductor got out and chased him. That was all right. He was faster than the conductor and he was almost at Moustafa's shop anyway.

Once the conductor gave up and went back to his tram, Faisal hurried until he got to the right street. Then he approached Moustafa's shop with more care, looking around him for suspicious people. This city was full of people who broke the law and thought they could do anything they wanted. It was really terrible.

The street outside Moustafa's bookshop was still busy at this time of night. It was wide with a tramline cutting through the middle, plus streetlights and plenty of people about.

That didn't make it any safer, though. Once the Englishman saw a murder happen on stage in front of a big hall full of Europeans. The Englishman could get in trouble anywhere, so Faisal always had to be on duty to get him out of it. Even if it meant getting in danger himself.

Faisal walked slowly, keeping close to groups of people so he would be less visible. He tried to choose Egyptian groups, so anyone who noticed him might assume he was with them. He had discovered he was more visible now that he wasn't unwashed and dressed in a ragged djellaba. As a beggar boy nobody noticed him. Europeans still didn't notice him much even though he dressed better, but Egyptians saw him.

He had to be careful.

He approached Moustafa's bookshop from the opposite side of the street. The lights were on inside and he saw a big new sign in the window saying something. He could see people inside and as he got closer a pair of older European gentlemen entered.

Directly opposite the shop he saw an Egyptian man, dressed in a white djellaba and skullcap, standing in a doorway smoking. His eyes scanned the crowd, glancing every few seconds at the entrance to the bookshop.

That man was spying for sure. Faisal stifled a chuckle. If the murderers were this obvious, this would be an easy case.

He strolled by, acting casual. It was a big enough street with enough people that he wouldn't look out of place. The spying Egyptian didn't even look at him.

Faisal decided to walk down the block and then come back along the other side of the street, the side where the Egyptian spy stood. He pretended to look in some of the shop windows to give him a chance to sneak a peek at the spy. Sure enough, the man still stood hidden in the doorway, only the faint trail of his cigarette smoke catching the light of a streetlamp to show he remained in place.

Faisal chuckled out loud this time. He didn't even need to act casual. The dummy couldn't see him at all!

He decided to linger where he was, but first he glanced around to make sure no police were about. They'd shout at him for loitering and that would alert the spy.

No police in sight. What luck!

After a while no more foreigners entered Moustafa's shop, and all Faisal saw was the usual foot traffic passing back and forth. The cigarette smoke still curled out of the doorway where the spy hid, waiting.

A foreigner passed by him, stopping just a few feet away and looking across the street at the bookshop. After a moment, he put his hand in his pocket and crossed the street, angling to the left so that he could come to the bookshop.

He must be late. I didn't think Europeans were ever late.

The spy in the doorway threw his cigarette on the pavement and moved out of the doorway, reaching in his pocket. He pulled out a pistol just enough that Faisal could see the butt end of it. It looked like the spy was checking to see if it was loaded. A moment later he tucked it back in his pocket and started to cross the street.

Faisal tensed. The spy was going to go in right after the latecomer and shoot the Englishman!

Faisal looked around him for some way to stop the spy. Not far off, a man in a gray djellaba and white turban was pulling a cart piled high with watermelons in the direction of the spy. That gave Faisal and idea. He ran behind the cart.

"Here, let me give you a hand," he said, pushing at the cart with all his might.

"Hey! Stop that!" the watermelon seller said from up front.

Faisal only pushed harder.

"You're going to run me over!" the man cried.

"Then get out of the way."

He did, because he had to. As the watermelon seller ducked to the right. Faisal gritted his teeth and shoved the cart as hard as he could toward the spy, who turned around to look curiously at the rattling cart. The European heading for Moustafa's shop seemed unaware. Europeans usually didn't pay attention to what Egyptians did.

"What the—" the spy started to say. He didn't have time to say anything more because the watermelon cart was almost upon him. He braced his legs, reached out his hands, and stopped the cart with a jolt that sent the watermelons pouring down on him.

Faisal jumped in the air and spun. That was exactly what he wanted to happen!

Now the European did stop. Everyone stopped.

Everyone except the watermelon man.

"You little brat!"

He rushed at Faisal, who ducked around the cart.

That turned out to be a bad move, because Faisal ended up tripping on the pile of crushed watermelons and falling flat on his face.

Just as he did, the spy rose up from the red and green pulp, a gun in his hand.

The watermelon seller let out a cry and backed off.

"Stop! Police!" the spy shouted in English, pointing his pistol at the European, who still stood a few steps away from the door to Moustafa's shop.

The European whipped out a pistol and fired. The bullet hit a watermelon right next to Faisal, which burst and covered him in red juice.

The spy tried to fire, but his pistol, dripping with pulp, didn't work. The European grinned and aimed his gun.

CHAPTER SEVEN

At the sound of the shot outside, Augustus and Moustafa sprang into action. Leaving the startled audience, they dashed through the bookshop as Augustus drew his compact automatic. Augustus had taken the precaution of providing Moustafa with a heavy Webley revolver from his personal arsenal. The Nubian had hidden it behind a multivolume set of *Description de l'Egypte* and grabbed it on his way out the door.

They burst outside, startling a European who fled down the street. In the center of the street they saw a strange sight—a cursing Egyptian with a pistol in one hand and Faisal in the other, both covered in watermelon pulp and surrounded by a sea of broken watermelons.

"Stop right there!" Augustus shouted, leveling his gun. "Let go of the boy or I'll make your head look like one of those watermelons."

The Egyptian dropped his gun and let go of Faisal, raising his hands.

"I'm Egyptian police," he said in Arabic.

"Don't move a muscle," Moustafa said, drawing closer to him.

Augustus rushed up to Faisal and grabbed him by the shoulder. "Are you all right?"

Faisal looked pale, and only nodded.

Enraged, Augustus whirled on the Egyptian. "If you hurt him by God I'll—"

"He is what he says, Mr. Wall." Moustafa pulled a police identity badge from the pocket of the man's djellaba.

"I was sent by Sir Thomas Russell Pasha. When he heard that you were giving a talk here, he suspected you wanted to trap the murderer of the man at Shepheard's Hotel. I was sent to protect you." He turned and snarled at Faisal. "I was about to apprehend a suspicious person when this little imp stopped me."

"I knew you'd cause trouble!" Moustafa shouted, giving Faisal a hard enough clout upside the head that the boy slipped on the crushed watermelons and landed in the pulp with a splash.

"No time for that," Augustus said, then turned to the police officer. "Where is this man?"

"He ran off that way. He just went around the corner."

"Blast! We'll never catch him now. Give us a description of the man you saw."

"European. Tanned, not sunburned, so not a recent arrival. Wiry frame, about five ten, looked about thirty but hard to tell because his features were obscured under a slouch hat."

"That's the same man I saw," Moustafa said. "I would have recognized him immediately if I hadn't been looking at this mess!"

"And I didn't see him either," Augustus grumbled. He turned to Faisal, who had picked himself up from the mound of broken watermelons, even more covered in pulp than before. "So you ran off from the Schäfers? That's hardly polite after all the trouble they went through to host you."

"I wasn't rude. I ate dinner and thanked them."

"Oh, so you got your chocolate cake and then ran off."

Faisal's jaw dropped. "There was chocolate cake?"

"Yes, and you were so eager to get yourself shot that you missed it. Let that be a lesson to you."

"Sorry." Faisal slumped, then brightened. "But since I helped you, maybe Herr Schäfer will save me some."

"I certainly hope he doesn't. You need to learn to listen to me."

"And you didn't help at all," Moustafa said. "You let the murderer get away."

"We don't know he's the murderer," Augustus mused. "Although he is certainly the lead suspect, indeed the only suspect at the moment."

"It must be him," Moustafa said.

"Not necessarily. If he did kill Gregory Marshall, then he got his letter to me. He would know my address. Why not ambush me as I come out the door, or simply walk into my shop as a customer and shoot me there? Indeed, we don't even know if he wants to shoot me at all. He might just want information."

"He pulled out a gun quickly enough when I tried to stop him," the policeman said, wiping bits of watermelon off his djellaba. "I—"

Whatever the officer planned to say next got cut off by the watermelon seller, who, having recovered his courage now that there seemed to be no threat of further gunplay, stormed up to them, shaking his fist.

"Who's going to pay for my watermelons!"

"Quiet," the policeman snapped. "This is a police matter."

"So is this!" the watermelon seller bellowed. "Arrest that boy."

The officer turned to Faisal, who stepped back. Augustus intervened.

"You'll do nothing of the sort. I'll fix this." He pulled out his wallet and handed over fifty piastres, probably more than the man earned in a week.

"I apologize for the reckless behavior of my, um, assistant."

The man took the money, managed to mumble a thank you, glared at Faisal, and pushed his now empty cart down the road.

"Well at least that's taken care of," Augustus said, frowning at Faisal. "And at a high cost too."

"Sorry," Faisal said.

"Um, Mr. Wall?" Moustafa said, pointing to his shop. "We have another problem."

The entire audience for the lecture stood at the doorway and windows to his shop, staring at the scene.

"Oh dear. And I here I came to Cairo to be anonymous. Erm, tell them that there was an attempted armed robbery outside and I intervened. Nothing to do with us, of course. Give them my apologies and tell them I'm too shaken up to proceed with the lecture. I'll take our little watermelon destroyer home and we'll discuss it in the morning."

"All right, Mr. Wall. Give him a good beating."

"I think you'd be better at it. Why don't you take him home?"

"God preserve me! That boy will never set foot inside my house."

Moustafa went to speak with his customers. Augustus and Faisal started walking away from the scene, the policeman following.

"I should escort you home," he said.

"That's quite all right, thank you."

"Actually, sir, my orders are to see to your safety."

"Oh, very well," Augustus grumbled. He didn't like Sir Thomas meddling in his affairs. Couldn't the man leave him alone and let him solve this mystery in peace?

Augustus hailed a motor cab and got in the back with Faisal. The policeman got in front.

Faisal, usually so happy about riding in a motorcar, sat slumped in his seat, leaving watermelon stains on the upholstery.

"You all right?" Augustus asked as the motorcar merged with the traffic and headed for their side of the city.

Faisal didn't reply.

"He didn't hit you. Might the bullet have grazed you, or sent up a ricochet from the pavement that hurt you?"

Faisal shook his head.

The boy's hands started to tremble. The trembling increased and spread to his arms. Within moments his entire body was shaking like a leaf.

"It's normal, mate."

Marshall sat with a new recruit in the trenches. The youth, who claimed to be eighteen but who had almost certainly lied about his age, had just had a near miss from a German sniper on his very first day. The bullet had dinged off the edge of his metal helmet, leaving a dent.

The young man was unhurt, but couldn't stop trembling, and couldn't stop apologizing for doing so.

Marshall put an arm around him.

"We all get the spooks the first time one comes close."

Augustus reached over, hesitated, then put an arm around Faisal. The boy shuddered and leaned on him. Augustus noticed watermelon juice staining his suit but didn't complain. Instead he gripped him closer.

***

The next morning, feeling groggy from the extra dose of opium he had taken the night before to keep the dreams at bay, Augustus did a thorough search of the house and saw no signs of attempted entry. Next he went to every window to peek through the mashrabiya, looking for any suspicious characters on the street outside. He saw no one.

After looking out the windows a second time, he turned and saw Faisal standing behind him, watching.

"Feeling better?" Augustus asked. The boy had gone straight up to his shed after they got in.

Faisal looked at his feet. "I acted like a baby last night."

Augustus walked over to him, put a hand under his chin, and made the boy look at him.

"No you did not. You nearly got shot. That's enough to spook anyone."

"I was never like that before," Faisal said, his eyes growing damp. "I've turned into a coward."

"You weren't scared before because you're a child and it didn't seem real to you. Now that you've been shot, you know what it's like."

"You're not afraid."

Because I don't care what happens. "I've grown accustomed to it."

"Oh." Faisal seemed uncertain. "So what are we going to do today?"

"I'm going to check on a few things. I have to find our friend in the slouch hat."

Faisal looked away, glanced back at Augustus, then looked away again.

"I'll come and help," he mumbled.

"You can help by watching the house. Peek out the windows every now and then and look for suspicious characters. And don't let anybody in except me or Moustafa. This place is built like a fortress. You'll be safe unless they have your climbing ability, and I've never met anyone who can match you in that."

"All right." Faisal sounded relieved. "Is that … are you sure that counts as helping?"

"It does."

"All right," Faisal said quietly. "Is Moustafa going with you?"

"Yes."

"Good."

Augustus prepared to go, taking his sword cane and placing his compact automatic in the pocket of his jacket. Faisal followed him around the house. It was one of his more irritating habits, but Augustus forgave him since he was still obviously shaken from the events of the night before.

"Where are you going?" the boy asked.

"First to the Citadel," Augustus said, trying to suppress a shudder. "Don't be tempted to follow because you won't be allowed in." Augustus managed a smile. "Besides, I need you to guard the house. That's important."

Faisal nodded. "All right, Englishman."

Augustus left, taking a motor cab across town to the Citadel, the great fortress built by Saladin atop the Moqattem Hills on the eastern edge of town and used by every ruler of Egypt since. There he went to speak with Sir Thomas in his office. He found the man in the center of a frantic scene, talking on two telephones at once and surrounded by assistants awaiting orders. Augustus had to cool his heels in the hall for half an hour before he got a minute with the chief of police. When Sir Thomas finally managed to wave away the last of his assistants with a curt order, he called Augustus in.

"Sorry for the wait, old boy. Things are kicking off again. Have you read the morning papers?"

"No. I came straight over."

"The government has released Sa'ad Zaghloul. He's returning to Egypt."

"Good Lord! You're in for a long week."

Sa'ad Zaghloul was one of the main leaders of the independence movement. A prominent merchant, he lived in a fine home in Abdeen, from which he had formed a political party and an independence movement that had united reformers and conservatives, Copts and Muslims, and all strata of society. The British tried in turns to ignore, threaten, and cajole him, and when Zaghloul didn't budge, they sent police into his mansion one night, bursting into his bedroom where he and his wife were asleep in an act that seemed fine tuned to offend the sensibilities of everyone in the protectorate, many liberal foreigners included. Zaghloul had been sent into exile in Malta.

"When does he return?" Augustus asked.

"Unclear." One of the telephones on the desk started ringing. Sir Thomas ignored it. "The independence movement is planning a big rally for later today. I'd go home and stay home if I were you."

"I'm afraid I have a friend's murder to solve."

"Yes, about that. Sorry my man loused it up. He had some ridiculous excuse about a boy attacking him with watermelons."

"Don't be too hard on him. That's actually true."

"Oh dear. I shouldn't have shouted at him then. Was it that street beggar you employ?"

"Former street beggar."

"Well whatever he is, he should thank his lucky stars he's a minor. I could have him brought up on charges of assaulting a police officer and interfering with an investigation."

Augustus felt like reminding him that Sir Thomas's men had arrested many minors before, but decided to hold his tongue. The chief of police went on.

"I'm afraid I've had to pull every available officer for this circus show. I won't be able give many man-hours to the Gregory Marshall investigation for the next few days." Sir Thomas got a strained look on his face. "I'm afraid we've had a spot of bother regarding that. We have a good description of the man who tried to enter the bookshop, and have instructed our agents in the train station and the docks to be on the lookout."

"Good."

Sir Thomas grimaced. "I'm afraid that description didn't make it to everyone. Since I'm pulling in all available officers, some of the men I posted at the train station had been on leave and hadn't read all the reports. One of them, once he did, remembered a man of that description boarding the morning train for Alexandria. He telephoned Alexandria but the train had already arrived and the passengers all gone."

Augustus's hand gripped the arm of his chair so hard it squealed in protest.

"I see," he growled.

"Terribly sorry, old boy."

Augustus tried to control his rage and think.

"I'm surprised he left Cairo. He still hasn't got whatever it is he's after," Augustus said.

"Any idea what that could be?"

"None whatsoever. It seems strange that he hasn't tried to reach me at my home. It's not difficult to find. And if Gregory managed to finish that letter before he got attacked, our murderer would have had the address right away."

"I'm sure you've gotten a good description of the man from my officer and that Nubian who owns the bookshop. Does he sound familiar?"

"No. I don't think I know him."

But he knows me. He knows who I really am, as did Gregory. I'm sure of it. How did they find out? No one else has. I thought I covered my tracks.

"You all right?" Sir Thomas asked.

Augustus blinked. "I beg your pardon?"

"I was saying that because there was no sign of forced entry, we are working on the assumption that your friend knew the murderer or murderers. He trusted them enough to let them in. I was hoping they might be known to you as well."

"I haven't seen Gregory in three years, and I never went on leave with him. I don't know his civilian friends."

"Hm, that's too bad." Sir Thomas stood. "Well, I must be away to see to the positioning of our troops. I'm sorry I can't put more men on it at the moment."

"I understand."

Actually I approve. I want to handle this myself. All your men will do is interfere.

"May I use a private telephone?" Augustus asked.

"Certainly. My adjutant is out. He's just next door. You can use his." Sir Thomas paused a moment. "I hope you're not thinking of chasing that fellow up to Alexandria. You'll only land yourself in trouble."

"I have to guard my shop from the riots."

"Good. We'll make your friend's case the highest priority once the independence crowd has let off some steam."

I have no doubt that you will, but by then I'll have solved the case and killed the guilty parties.

Once he made his call, Augustus took a motor cab down to Moustafa's bookshop. The motor cab passed through streets that had grown eerily silent, with most shops closed. Few people were out. Even the street vendors had disappeared. Augustus checked his gun.

Moustafa's shop was closed too, the lights off, but the big Nubian opened the door when Augustus rang the bell.

"Sorry to keep you out of business for the day," he said as Moustafa came out and locked the door behind him.

"I wouldn't have opened in any case, Mr. Wall. I am sure you've heard the news about Sa'ad Zaghloul. There is a general strike and a big independence march today."

Moustafa brought the metal shutters down with a crash.

"And you don't want your books burned and windows smashed, eh? Smart man."

"Something like that. So where are we going?"

"Alexandria," Augustus said. "On the morning train. It's already too late to get the one this afternoon. I just called the station and it's fully booked. Many Europeans have decided a breath of sea air would be preferable to the stench of burning buildings."

Moustafa turned away from his shop and faced him. He did not look happy.

"I don't suppose we have any solid leads or any clear idea how long we'll be up there."

Augustus shook his head. "No. I do apologize. It seems to be the pattern of our little adventures."

"Indeed it does, Mr. Wall," Moustafa said with a sigh. "Indeed it does."

CHAPTER EIGHT

Moustafa waited until the children were asleep before he told Nur he had to go away again.

They sat in the back garden, the moon floating high in the night sky, illuminating the garden in its soft light. He sat on a cushion smoking a waterpipe as Nur sat next to him knitting.

He had waited for the children to be asleep because he didn't want a scene like last time. Still, he dreaded speaking the words.

Finally, after he had refilled his pipe for the second time, he took a deep breath and said, "I must go to Alexandria for a few days."

Nur looked up at him sharply, then hunched over her knitting again.

Silence stretched out for a moment. Moustafa went on.

"Mr. Wall needs help again. He will pay well. He has also promised train tickets and a hotel for us to go to the seaside again. You know how much we enjoyed that."

"You go to Alexandria without us," Nur said softly, not looking up from her work, "and our reward will be to go to Alexandria without you."

"I'll be fine."

"That boy you always complain about nearly got killed last time. I dreamed it would happen."

"Have you had any bad dreams this time?" Moustafa couldn't help but feel nervous asking the question, although it was unworthy of an educated man like himself.

"Just because I didn't have a bad dream doesn't mean something bad won't happen."

"I'll be fine," Moustafa repeated.

Nur put down her knitting and turned to face him. "What are you after, Moustafa? It's not the money. We have enough now. You have your own shop and money in the bank. Why do you keep going with him?"

"Loyalty is important among men. He needs me."

"He is not your friend."

Moustafa shook his head. "No, he is not."

"So why feel loyal to him? He wouldn't help you if you were in trouble."

"Yes, he would. For all his many flaws, he would go through fire for me."

"A European?"

"Yes, a European."

Nur smiled the way she did when she thought he was doing something foolish. "And of all the Europeans you've worked for he's the only one who would do that. You admire these foreigners and you want them to admire you."

Moustafa shifted on his cushion. "I'm a Nubian Muslim and I don't want to be anything else. But there's a lot to admire in European culture. We need to take the best from their world and make it our own, otherwise—"

"—Egypt and Africa will remain in ignorance for centuries to come," Nur said, mocking his tone. "Yes, Moustafa, you've told me this many times before."

"Because it's true."

"We need you here. That's the real truth."

"It will only be for a few days, and then we can have another trip to Alexandria."

Once all the murderers have been cleared out, Moustafa added silently.

Nur poked him in the side with the knitting needle. "You better bring me back something nice."

Moustafa put an arm around her. "So you're not angry?"

"Of course I'm angry," she said, poking him in the side again. "But being angry won't change anything. Besides, I said yes to marrying you because I could see you would go on to do great things. Leaving your village when you were still half a boy. Making it all the way up here. Learning all those things. You have a fire in you. Just don't let that fire burn us, Moustafa."

***

The next morning, Moustafa and Mr. Wall took the early morning train to Alexandria. They had a private compartment with the blinds to the door lowered as a precaution. Mr. Wall had brightened up considerably. It had become, once again, a game to him. He looked out the window as eagerly as Moustafa's children had when he had taken them north on a special trip to the sea. The only difference was that his children hadn't brought along a small arsenal in one of their bags.

Nur's words from the night before haunted him. He knew he was putting his needs before those of his family, and it hurt him to think he was such a man to do that. The fact that Nur understood did not make it any better. If he was a good husband and father, he would stay at home and work in his shop, building his family's future.

But that future had been secured through the reward money he had made on the last case. He owed this madman sitting across from him everything he currently had.

No, that wasn't quite right, because Mr. Wall wouldn't have solved that case without him. Of course, Moustafa would never have been dragged into the case if it hadn't been for this Englishman who so urgently needed to prove himself.

Or, as Nur had so often pointed out, Moustafa wouldn't let himself get dragged into these cases if he didn't want to prove himself too.

God help me, am I mad too?

Moustafa looked out the window at the broad fields of the Nile delta and found himself missing Nur even though he had said goodbye to her only a few hours before. Being a Nubian and a stranger in Cairo with no family or friends to vouch for him, it had been difficult for the matchmaker to find an Egyptian girl for him. Nur was a simple farmer's daughter with no education. Her family only had a single feddan of land and could barely scrape by. By society's standards he had married beneath himself.

He did not look at it that way. Moustafa had seen she was a religious woman, and noted how well she had taken care of her younger siblings, proving she would be a good mother. Nur had not disappointed him.

Still, it would have been nice to have someone who could appreciate his work.

He would make sure his sons grew up with a proper education. His eldest son, Muhammed, who was still just a child, would inherit the bookshop. He'd find Bachir a good job somewhere too. Who knew? Perhaps in a newly independent Egyptian government. That march yesterday had been a big one. The independence movement would not be stopped. And his three daughters he would marry to educated men.

The next generation would be so much better than this one. He was building on a small scale what Egypt and the Soudan needed to build on a grand scale.

And here he was risking his life chasing after a murderer.

"At least Faisal is safe," Moustafa said to himself, looking out the window at the broad green fields.

"Indeed," Mr. Wall said. "We've shaken him at last."

Moustafa roused himself from his reverie. He hadn't realized he had spoken out loud.

"You've worked wonders with him, Mr. Wall. He looks much healthier. He's even clean."

"The health comes from eating me out of house and home. How such a small body can pack in so much food I'll never know. It's like he's eating for every street boy in the neighborhood. As for the cleanliness, I cannot claim responsibility. We have to thank young Ahmed Fakhry for that."

"That officer's servant in Bahariya Oasis?"

"Yes. Quite a good influence. Not only got him to bathe in the hot springs, but actually taught him the worth of learning about his nation's past. Not that he's the best student, his mind is still full of ideas of giant pharaohs and animal-headed djinn, but at least now he has some glimmer of curiosity."

Moustafa shook his head. "It's hard to imagine that boy ever being educated. At least he's no longer infested with lice."

"He's done a complete about face. Now he wants to have a bath every night. Heats up water on the stove and lugs it up two flights of stairs to fill the tub, then splashes around in it for an hour. He's made a little fleet of feluccas and dahabiehs and races them. Water gets everywhere. Thank God the house is made of stone or he'd have soaked through the floor by now. I'm still trying to teach him how to mop up afterwards."

Moustafa laughed. "God has given you a great burden."

"Indeed," Mr. Wall said, lighting a cigarette. "But he won't be a burden on this case. He'll be safe back in Cairo the entire time. I foisted him on some friends."

"Some friends?"

"Well, I couldn't very well leave him alone at the house. Those chaps who were trying to track me down might not realize I've left and try to break in."

"So you sent him to the Schäfers again?"

"Good Lord, no. An academic and his hausfrau lack the resourcefulness and low cunning to control a former street boy intent on causing mischief. No, I gave him to someone whose wits are more than a match for him."

CHAPTER NINE

This was bribery.

Suleiman and Zehra Hanzade had "invited" him to stay at their mansion. The Englishman thought he'd be so distracted by the good food and nice rooms and bouncy cushions that he wouldn't mind getting left behind when he and Moustafa went off to Alexandria.

The Englishman was being extra silly if he thought he could leave Faisal behind.

He sure had been clever, though. The Hanzade mansion was amazing, like something out of a storyteller's tale. The front hall was twice as wide as the front hall in Cordelia's building and on each side stood ancient statues of men and women with no clothes on. That made Faisal feel embarrassed. Suleiman said these were Classical statues and works of art and nothing to be embarrassed about. Faisal wasn't so sure. There was also a nice lounge with lots of soft divans covered in silk and tins of sweets they let him eat and a big dining room in the Turkish style where everyone sat on cushions and ate wonderful food with their hands the way normal people do.

It was a relief to eat with his hands again and be surrounded by people who spoke his language. Faisal felt tempted to stay here forever and ever, but as great as everything was, he could tell it was a prison. There was a high wall around the grounds and servants who kept an eye on his every move.

Those servants even watched him while he sat with Suleiman and Zehra as they drank coffee in one of the lounges. They said he'd get too excited if he drank coffee and gave him sherbet instead. Fine by him.

Zehra wore a brilliant emerald caftan with gold embroidery down the front. Unlike every other Muslim woman he'd met, she wore her hair down like a girl, not tucked into a headscarf. Even Mina wore a headscarf. She was just twelve, and hadn't worn a headscarf until she had been promised in marriage to that old man. Faisal had gotten rid of that nasty old crook, but her parents still wanted her to wear a headscarf.

That was too bad. Faisal liked her hair, even though he hadn't really noticed it until he couldn't see it anymore.

Zehra wore a jeweled ring on nearly every finger, and gold earrings in some complicated design he couldn't figure out. Her husband Suleiman dressed more simply, in a white djellaba and red tarboosh, but of the finest quality. Suddenly Faisal felt embarrassed by his appearance. He'd been proud of his new djellaba, but it looked cheap next to what these two wore.

He tried to remember all the things the Englishman had told him not to do when eating. He wasn't sure they all counted, though, since he was lying on a divan next to two Turks.

Zehra studied him for a minute. "You look much better than when I first met you."

"Um, thank you."

"Augustus certainly has been feeding you well. Are you happy there?"

Faisal nodded.

"You have certainly helped on many of his cases," Suleiman said, taking a sip of his coffee. "He thinks you're a very clever boy."

If I'm so helpful and clever, why am I being left behind?

Zehra gave him a warm smile. "Very clever. You're a good friend to him, and any friend of Augustus is a friend of ours. If you don't mind me asking, how did you end up living on the street?"

"My father got killed in the Egyptian Expeditionary Force and my mother was a good woman who died giving birth to me."

Neither of these things were true. His father had been a slapping, stomping, shouting drunk who had disappeared one day, thank God. Faisal had never made up this lie about him before. It sounded good. He hoped they'd believe it.

He hoped they'd believe what he said about his mother too. Nobody in his neighborhood did. They seemed to know things he didn't. Some even said she was a window girl behind the fish market. It made Faisal ill to think about that.

No. She had been a good woman who died giving birth to him.

"That's very sad," Zehra said.

Faisal shrugged. It was just the way things were.

"Have you thought about your future?" Suleiman asked.

Faisal took another spoonful of delicious sherbet. "My future?"

"What you want to do for a trade?"

"Oh, the Englishman said I could work in his shop. I'm already studying the ancient things."

Suleiman looked surprised. "You've learned to read already?"

"No. But I look at the pictures. I know all about shabtis and giant pharaohs and the djinn with animal heads."

"I see," Suleiman said. "To truly understand the past, you'll need to learn to read."

Faisal suppressed a groan. Everyone kept telling him to read!

"Would you like some more sherbet?" Zehra asked.

"Oh, sure!"

She motioned to a servant, who took Faisal's empty bowl and went away.

Two servings of sherbet? This place was like paradise. He wondered if Mehmed had lived like this when he had a home. Mehmed was a Turk like the Hanzades. During the war the English had sent many of the Turks to prison and confiscated their homes. That's why Mehmed ended up on the street.

"My Turkish friend Mehmed lost his home in the war. How come that didn't happen to you?"

The Englishman had told him that while it was all right to ask questions, one shouldn't be nosy. He didn't feel this was nosy. They were asking so many questions about him, after all.

"Many of the leading families kept their property," Zehra explained. "You see, we've been in Egypt for many generations and we've shown our loyalty."

"So Mehmed's family were spies for the Sultan?"

"Probably not. The English didn't know who were spies and who weren't, so sadly they punished many innocent Turks."

"But not the rich ones."

Zehra smiled. "That is the way of the world. Surely you know that."

Faisal nodded. Yes, he knew that.

"We do help the Cairene Turks in need," Suleiman said. "There are several charities for them."

"Could Mehmed come to lunch?" Faisal asked.

"Maybe some other time," Zehra said.

That didn't sound convincing.

The servant came back with another bowl of sherbet.

You're trying to make me so comfortable I'll forget all about the Englishman and Moustafa going to Alexandria. Well, I'm not going to forget. I'm going to get out of here.

I better eat the sherbet, though. Just so they don't get suspicious.

The Hanzades sure were generous with the food. He felt like stuffing his pockets to share with the other boys, but the servant kept such a close eye on him he didn't dare. The Hanzades would notice too. The Englishman said they were clever, and he rarely said anything nice about anybody, so it must be true.

By the time he had finished his second helping of sherbet, he felt really sleepy. He hardly ever got to eat this good. They had given him an appetizer, a main course, a second course, some side dishes, and the sherbet. It hadn't been a meal, it had been a feast.

Suleiman got up. "I need to get back to work. Come on out to the shed today and you can see how I make the fake antiquities your English friend sells."

"All right," Faisal said, his eyelids feeling heavy.

The servants cleared away all the cups and dishes and left.

Zehra came up to him. "You look like you need a nap. Lie down on the divan. It's all right. Here, I'll put this blanket over you."

Faisal smiled as she tucked him in. He could get used to this. He'd just take a little nap and then he'd have the energy to escape and help the Englishman.

She smiled down at him, tousled his hair, and left. Faisal settled in and relaxed. He felt sleep tugging him down.

A minute later, the servant came back in, carrying a letter.

"This is for you."

"I can't read," Faisal said without getting up.

The servant glanced at it. "It's in Arabic. Shall I read it for you?"

"All right."

The servant opened the letter, held it at arm's length because he was old and read,

"Dear Faisal,

Moustafa and I are going to Alexandria. My friend being murdered has reminded me of my old life back in England. I was wrong to leave it. After I solve the murder I will get on a train and go back there. I've already sold the house and the new people will be coming in next week. That gives you some time to find a new place to live. I left some coins in your shed for your next few meals. I know you will be able to take care of yourself after that.

Good luck,

The Englishman"

Faisal sat bolt upright on the divan, breathing hard. The room was dim, the light coming in from the windows faint. He had slept almost until dusk.

He looked around and didn't see any servant. He didn't see any letter either. That had been a dream, like his other ones.

A dream that could come true. Alexandria was where all the foreigners came into Egypt, and where they all left it. The Englishman could leave and go back home if he wanted to. The case might even make him go back to England to investigate who killed his friend, and once he got back there he might decide he liked it better than Cairo.

Faisal threw the blanket aside. He needed to get up to Alexandria! But how?

First things first—he needed to get out of here.

That was going to be tricky with all the servants.

He heard footsteps in the hallway outside, real footsteps this time. He got back under the blanket and pretended to be asleep, leaving his eyes open just a crack so he could see a little.

A dim form stopped at the doorway for a moment. His eyes were closed too much to see who it was, but it was definitely a man. Probably one of the servants since Suleiman had gone to work in the shed.

The man moved out of sight. Faisal heard footsteps receding.

Faisal got up and tiptoed to the doorway. The hallway was empty. He sneaked in the direction of the front door and peeked around the corner and down the big front hallway of Classical statues. At the far end, one of the servants was mopping the marble floor near the front door. Another servant used a feather duster to clean the statues. Faisal held back a giggle as the servant dusted a Classical lady's rear end.

Those servants didn't look like they'd leave anytime soon. He'd have to try the back door. The Hanzades had already given him a tour of the ground floor, and Faisal never forgot the layout of a house. He used to be Cairo's best housebreaker before the Englishman took him in.

Making his way toward the rear of the house, he didn't see anybody except for once when he had to duck into a dark room to let a servant pass. He also passed a closed door where he heard Zehra's voice. He pressed his ear against the door. She spoke in Turkish, stopping to listen to someone he couldn't hear before speaking again.

She must be talking on the telephone, Faisal thought.

Faisal had gotten to use a telephone once, when he had been in Luxor. Just before he had gotten shot and the Englishman left him in an orphanage.

Faisal frowned. He was still mad at him about that.

Passing through a gloomy dark dining room that must have been able to hold a thousand people, he went down another hallway to the back door. Suleiman had already shown him this. It led to a large back lot with a big workshop at the end where Suleiman and his son made fake old things.

He opened the door a crack, peeked out, and got a surprise.

A cart stood in the yard, with a pair of donkeys hitched to it. Suleiman, his son, and another man were loading big crates onto the back of the cart.

What luck! In a minute the servants would open the back gate and that cart would roll right out of here.

But how to get inside?

"These will sell well," Suleiman said. "Let's get the last lot and then we can have a nice smoke before you go. After all this work I think we deserve a bit of relaxation, eh?"

"Thank you, sir," the cart driver said.

The three men headed back into the workshop. Faisal hesitated. He didn't know how long they would be inside before coming back with the last load. It might be better to wait until they went inside to smoke. Men took ages while smoking.

But then he saw a waterpipe and three chairs sitting in the shade of a bougainvillea in another part of the lot. If they smoked there, Faisal would never make it to the cart.

Now or never. The instant the three men went back inside, Faisal sprinted to the cart, leapt onto the back, and opened the nearest crate.

Yuck! A mummy lay inside.

But wait. These were Suleiman's fakes. The Englishman always laughed when he sold some fakes to foreigners. He liked cheating foreigners as much as the merchants in Khan el-Khalili.

That mummy sure looked real, though. It even had finger and toe bones sticking out of the wrappings.

Voices came from the workshop. Faisal hopped in beside the mummy and put the lid back on the crate.

It smelled funny inside. At least it wasn't a real mummy beside him. He tried to push against the wrappings and get the thing to move over. Why hadn't Suleiman made more room inside these crates?

He heard voices outside the crate, and felt a vibration and heard a thud as the men loaded more crates onto the cart. There was a bigger thud and his whole crate shook as they put a crate right on top of him.

The movements and the voices stopped. They must have gone for their smoke.

The air inside the crate began to grow stuffy. Uh-oh. He wasn't getting any air in here, and he'd almost used up what was already inside the crate.

Good thing he had a solution for that. He pulled a penknife out of his pocket. He stole it from the Englishman a month ago. Well, not really stole. He found it all dusty on a shelf. The Englishman obviously didn't use it, so it didn't really count as stealing, even though Faisal hadn't actually asked if he could have it. That was OK, though, because if he didn't use it and Faisal did, then it counted as helping the Englishman.

Especially right now, because he could carve some airholes through the side of the crate. He wouldn't be able to save the Englishman if he suffocated.

So by taking (not stealing) his penknife, Faisal had actually done the Englishman a favor.

Proud of his good deed, Faisal set to work, and pretty soon had bored a couple of holes into the side of the crate. Now he could breathe better, although it still smelled funny inside.

The men took forever with their smoking, but at last he heard the cry of the driver, the snap of a whip, and felt the cart jerk forward. The mummy jostled him as the cart rattled onto the cobblestone street, and Faisal elbowed the thing. Old wrappings came off on his arm and dust puffed into the air, making him sneeze. Luckily the cart rattled so much the driver didn't hear.

He elbowed the thing again, trying to get more room. He was sure glad it wasn't a real mummy. It might come alive and eat him.

After a long and uncomfortable ride, the cart stopped. Faisal wondered where they were. Had he gotten even luckier and ended up at the Englishman's shop?

Probably not. The Englishman always closed his shop when he had a mystery to solve. It seemed like he didn't really need his shop to make money, which made Faisal wonder why he had it at all.

Probably so people came to visit him. He always said he didn't like Europeans visiting him but Faisal didn't believe it. He missed his own kind.

He might miss them so much he'd go back to Europe.

That was only a bad dream, Faisal told himself. He didn't feel convinced so he told himself that again.

The cart shook and rattled as someone started removing the crates. He could hear the cart driver and another man talking. At last he heard the scrape of the crate above him being taken off.

Faisal popped the lid off his crate and jumped out.

"Boo!"

The two workmen screamed and ran off. Faisal looked around. He was in front of some shop in the nice part of town. Several people on the sidewalk stared at him. An Egyptian policeman came running up the street, probably attracted by the two men running past him while screaming their heads off.

"I'm a mummy!" Faisal shouted at the policeman, hooking his fingers like claws.

"You will be when I get you!" the policeman shouted.

Uh-oh. Police didn't scare so easily. Faisal hopped off the cart and ran through the crowd, the policeman huffing and puffing behind him. Within a minute Faisal lost him.

It took him ages to get across town to Cordelia's apartment. He tried his trick with the tram again, but the conductor was too smart for him and kicked him off. So he had to walk as quickly as he could clear across Cairo. Not that that tired him out. He used to walk around all day begging and stealing.

When he got there, it was dark and the snobby doorman told him Cordelia was at work.

Faisal groaned. Cordelia worked late. He'd have to wait half the night!

He couldn't wait here, though. The Hanzades would be sure to look for him here.

Cordelia took the tram to work, so all he needed to do was keep an eye on the nearest stop.

Waiting got really boring really quickly. Because he had to watch the tram stop, he couldn't wander and explore like he usually did most of the day. And he didn't have his football or the fleet of wooden boats he had made or any books with pictures in them.

Before he had a home and all those things he hardly ever got bored. Searching for food took up most of the day, and the rest of the time he spent watching things going on in the street, like fights or other boys stealing from the merchants. There was always something to watch.

But this street was dull, just a mix of foreigners and some rich Egyptians. He sat around for hours, hoping each tram would bring the one woman who could help him.

And then, after hours and hours, there she was! She wore her nurse's uniform of red and gray and looked tired after a long day at the hospital. Cordelia had to take care of lots of people.

"Cordelia!" Faisal hurried up to her. Cordelia turned to him with a look of surprise.

"Faisal?" This was followed by a question he didn't understand. Probably asking what he was doing here. Faisal had already thought of what to say, picking out the unfamiliar words and practicing while he waited.

"The Englishman and Moustafa big bad. Man …" He still didn't know the word for "murdered," which was silly considering how many people got murdered around the Englishman. He drew a finger across his neck. Cordelia understood because her eyes grew wider. "Go to Iskenderia."

"Where?"

"Iskenderia."

A European man stepped forward, said something to Cordelia, and tried to shoo Faisal away.

"No, no." Cordelia said something to him. The man frowned at Faisal. Cordelia said something more and he shrugged and walked away.

Cordelia turned back to him. "What happened?"

"Dead man."

Cordelia sighed. "Again?"

Faisal nodded. "Again."

Then Faisal saw something in the woman's eyes he did not expect—delight. Her eyes got all shiny and bright the way the Englishman's did when he investigated a murder. They didn't look as crazy as the Englishman's, but it still made him take a step back.

"Come with me," Cordelia said, taking his hand and leading him to her building.

On the way, Faisal tried to tell her the details of the case, but his words got all muddled and he could tell Cordelia only understood a tenth of it. She really needed to get better in Arabic. They passed the frowning doorman and went upstairs.

While Cordelia made them some coffee, Faisal tried to make her understand again.

"Englishman and Moustafa to Iskenderia. Train. Dead man Englishman friend."

"Where is Iskenderia?" Cordelia asked.

Faisal rolled his eyes. How couldn't she know Egypt's big port? She came through it on the way to Cairo!

"It is on al-Motawassit."

"What?"

Another eye roll. She sailed across the sea and didn't even know its name?

"Water. Big water." Faisal spread out his hands. "Big ships. Nile but more please."

Cordelia's brow furrowed, then her face lit up.

"You mean the Mediterranean?"

"Huh? No, al-Motawassit. Iskenderia."

"Alexandria?"

Faisal snapped his fingers. He'd heard the Englishman call it that. The English had different names for everything, even Egyptian places. Silly English. "Yes! They train today."

Cordelia smiled and put her hands on his shoulders. Her eyes had that glimmer again. "Faisal. Us train tomorrow."

CHAPTER TEN

Augustus sat at the window of his room in the Windsor Palace Hotel, smoking and looking out over the bay of Alexandria. The wide, oval harbor was calm, protected by a pair of long moles of massive stones to either side with only a narrow entrance between them. At the end of one mole stood the imposing old castle of Qait Bey, built atop the foundations of the famous ancient lighthouse and now modernized with naval guns.

The great sweep of the harbor shore was studded with ornate buildings in the European style, hotels and government buildings and a few palaces of the very rich. Along the Corniche, people of all nations strolled, and just below his window he could hear the hoofbeats of horses and donkeys, and the occasional roar of an engine. A fresh sea breeze blew in through the open window. The Royal Navy ships were moored at their places and there were clear skies over the Mediterranean. All looked well.

Except it wasn't. Yesterday there had been another massive demonstration in Cairo and smaller ones in several other cities. The morning papers said there hadn't been much of a disturbance here in Alexandria. Unlike the rest of Egypt, the Alexandrians looked outwards, not inwards, and felt more comfortable with foreigners.

That didn't mean he would be free of trouble while up here on the investigation. He'd have to take care. He had seen more than one sour look on the streets already.

And then there were the people who might know him …

Augustus lit another cigarette. He wished he could take some opium and sleep the day away.

A knock at the door. Augustus rose and, holding his compact automatic out of sight, opened the door with the chain still on.

Moustafa. Finally! The man had been gone for hours.

He unhooked the chain, let him in, and quickly locked the door behind him.

"What did you find out?" Augustus asked, indicating that the Nubian should sit.

"I searched all the fine hotels. It took some time to locate him because he did not go to any of them. A Peter Saunders registered at the Cheops Pension, however."

"Never heard of it."

"It's quite modest, sir. Barely respectable."

Augustus scratched his chin. "Gregory always liked to live well, although that didn't stop him from thriving in the trenches. I suppose he wanted to be unobtrusive."

"He only stayed there for a few nights before moving to an even more modest pension called the Soter. I pretended to be a servant with a letter for him like you suggested."

"Sorry for that. I know it nettles you."

"It does indeed, Mr. Wall," the Nubian said with a note of tension.

"So how does this Pension Soter look?"

"I did not go in, fearing the Australian or one of his friends might be lurking about and recognize me. I asked one of the staff about it. It's a simple place, with the distinction that it has modest cooking facilities in each apartment."

"Gregory wanted to limit his going out."

"That is my guess, Mr. Wall."

Another knock on the door. Augustus and Moustafa exchanged

glances.

As Moustafa grabbed his revolver from its hiding place in the bureau and positioned himself to cover the door, Augustus went to answer it with the same caution as before.

One of the hotel staff presented him with an envelope.

"A telegram for you sir."

"Oh, thank you." This was a surprise. Hiding his hand behind the still chained door, he put his pistol away and gave the man a tip.

Augustus closed the door and examined the telegram. Seeing it was from Zehra Hanzade, he could tell what it contained. A glance confirmed what he thought. And feared.

"Faisal has given them the slip," he told Moustafa.

"The little ingrate! You stick him in a palace and he runs off?"

"I suspect we shall be seeing him presently."

"How could he manage to make it up here ... oh yes, of course he could."

"Blast! The boy nearly got killed down in Luxor. I can't work on this case and worry about him at the same time."

The memory of Faisal flying back, blood spouting from a bullet wound in his chest overcame him. The boy had lain, still as a corpse, in the middle of the darkened temple of Karnak. Blood had flowed freely from his chest. Such a small, thin body and so much blood. If Cordelia hadn't been there ...

Augustus shuddered.

Moustafa said in a calming tone, "If he shows up, well, *when* he shows up, I'll guard him. I won't take my eyes off him for a second. I know all his tricks. He won't elude me."

"But I need you for the case." Augustus thought for a moment, then snapped his fingers. "I know! We'll fob him off with busywork. Have him watch buildings we know are safe. Follow men who aren't involved with the murder. We'll mislead him every step of the way and keep him out of danger."

Moustafa did not look convinced. "That might work."

"Or he might see through it," Augustus conceded. "He's a crafty little fellow. That's why he's been so useful. No more. I can't have him on my conscience. We'll mislead him somehow or other. But perhaps fortune will smile on us and we'll solve the case before he gets here. Let's check out that pension you found."

Within a minute they were out on the street, Augustus with his sword cane and automatic pistol, Moustafa with a Webley revolver tucked into a voluminous pocket of his djellaba. Once again Augustus felt the prickling of his skin that told of his excitement for the chase. His steps hastened along the sidewalk, putting the lie to his cane, as he and Moustafa hurried through the crowd of Egyptian vendors and idling Europeans. Augustus glanced over at Moustafa and saw a gleam in his eye that he knew matched his own.

The Nubian led him away from the Corniche, five city blocks inland. While still in the European part of the city, the buildings here grew less grand the further they went from the water. They saw no fluted columns or ornate balconies, no fancy brickwork or cast iron railings. Instead the narrowing streets were lined with solid, functional, rather dull buildings.

Moustafa made a small motion of his head. Augustus looked across the street and saw a building opposite with an open brass door and an aged, stooped Egyptian sweeping the steps. On either side of the door were metal plaques advertising various physicians and accountants and, amid all of these, a modest sign saying "Pension Soter."

Augustus smiled. Somebody had a sense of the historically ironic.

Neither of them broke step as they walked past.

"So how shall we do this?" Moustafa asked in a low voice.

Augustus thought for a moment. "Since we don't have our little housebreaker along for the moment, we can't wait until night and scale the building. I suppose we have no choice but the direct route."

"The owner of the pension will ask questions, Mr. Wall."

"To the Devil with his questions. I need to get into Gregory's room."

"Perhaps I can find a better way. I already talked with that doorman. Allow me to do so again."

"Very well. I'll take another walk around the block."

By the time he returned, Moustafa was openly waiting in front of the building. He feigned like he was seeing Augustus for the first time and waved as if to get his attention. The doorman looked up from his sweeping for a moment, then went back to work.

"This way, Mr. Smith," Moustafa called.

"Thank you, my good man," Augustus said, playing the part.

They strolled past the doorman and through a gloomy front hall to a small lift of wood and glass that rose up the middle of a winding staircase.

"You could have been more original with my *nom de guerre*," Augustus said.

"It was the first name I thought of," Moustafa replied, pressing the button for the fourth floor. "The doorman says there's only one person working at the pension at this time of day. The cleaning lady has already left."

"And he wasn't curious as to why you wanted to know this information?"

"A tip took care of that, plus an explanation that you wanted to know. You are a foreigner and are expected to ask strange questions."

"I don't suppose he knew which room our so-called Mr. Saunders was staying in."

"No. If you distract the man at the front counter by asking to see a room, I'll sneak a peek at the register."

"Crafty. I think Faisal is rubbing off on you."

"There is no need to be insulting, Mr. Wall."

Augustus chuckled. The lift stopped.

"I get out here," Moustafa said in a low voice. "Take the lift up one more floor to the pension. I will wait five minutes before coming up."

Augustus did as he asked, and found himself in the foyer of a modest pension. There was no carpet on the scratched tile, and nothing on the walls except for photographs of local scenes of the kind churned out by the ton for the tourist industry. Why someone would want to buy a photograph of the Serapeum or Pompey's Pillar when they could go see those things themselves was beyond his understanding. Behind a battered wooden counter sat an aged Greek in a cheap suit and a fringe of gray hair.

"How may I help you, sir?" the Greek asked in heavily accented French.

"I have need of a room. May I see one?"

The Greek gave him a quick look over and Augustus realized he hadn't dressed for the part. His suit was too fine, his shoes too new and unscuffed.

"For one night?" The Greek cast a significant glance at a sign by the front counter that read, in several different languages, "No female guests in rooms."

That must have been pure torture for poor Gregory.

"For the week," Augustus replied.

With a little shrug that expressed that the man had long since given up trying to figure out the eccentricities of his guests, the Greek removed a heavy brass key from a row hanging on the wall and shuffled out from behind the counter.

"Right this way, sir. You are English? I regret I do not speak your language. We have two other Englishmen staying here so you will feel right at home."

Two?

Augustus thought quickly. "How interesting. I would very much like to meet them."

"One of them is a gentleman. He is away at the moment."

Gregory. So who is this other man who apparently isn't a gentleman?

They passed through a modest lounge. Armchairs with frayed cushions, a few darkened prints, and a coffee table with a scattering of newspapers in various languages.

"Well, then I will have to satisfy myself with the company of only one Englishman," Augustus probed.

The Greek said nothing.

Augustus was shown a small set of rooms. The bedroom, sitting room, and bathroom were all clean but modestly and rather drearily furnished. The window, sans balcony, looked out over the narrow street at a similarly lackluster building.

Augustus took his time looking about the room.

"It's 300 piastres per week, sir. Breakfast and linen included. And you can use the kitchen if you wish to cook your own meals."

"Sounds satisfactory," Augustus replied, trying to remember a time when he had stayed at a pension that felt the need to state that linen was included.

Augustus kept the man there by asking a few questions about the neighborhood and local sights. After a few minutes of this, and feeling he could not delay any longer without arousing suspicion, Augustus walked slowly back to the foyer. Moustafa was nowhere to be seen. Augustus took the man's card and went back down to the ground floor.

Moustafa waited for him there.

"We are in luck, Mr. Wall. The pension takes up two floors and Mr. Saunders is on the sixth floor in room 607. We will not have to pass the front desk."

"Good. The manager won't know we've been."

"Unless he notices the key is gone," Moustafa said with a grin.

"Faisal really is rubbing off on you."

They took the lift back up to the sixth floor. Augustus started to feel his heart beating faster. Perhaps now he would find out what this was all about.

Whoever killed you, old comrade, I promise they will see justice.

My brand of justice.

They stepped out into a long hallway of identical doors. Other than a side table with a vase of rather wilted flowers, there were no furnishings. Moustafa pulled a key from his pocket and they moved to Room 607.

They listened at the door. Nothing. Moustafa unlocked it.

Mr. Wall paused. The faint sound of distant artillery fire drummed in his mind. He shook himself and pushed the door open.

A clatter of falling metal made them leap back. Both of them whipped out their guns.

No one came out of the room and they heard only silence within. Leading with his gun and keeping his body protected by the doorway, Augustus peered inside.

He found it similar to the one he had just seen, although obviously lived in. A few newspapers and personal items lay scattered about the sitting room. Just behind the door was a small pile of frying pans, pots, and, to Augustus's surprise, several tent pegs and an old Army entrenching tool.

A trap to alert anyone of intruders. But no one seems to be here.

Unless they're lurking further inside.

Motioning for Moustafa to follow, Augustus edged through the half-open door, eyes darting to the open door leading to the bedroom and the closed door to the bathroom.

Moustafa's huge frame couldn't pass through the door without opening it further. Augustus gritted his teeth as the Nubian carefully slid the door open another few inches, making the metal objects scrape against the tile.

Augustus pointed to his companion, then to the bathroom, while he pointed to himself and the bedroom.

They moved as one, leaping into the respective rooms with guns at the ready.

And found no one.

Augustus made another quick search, checking in the closet and under the bed. There indeed was no one at home.

"It seems we have another puzzle," Augustus said.

Moustafa joined him in the bedroom. "Indeed. I just glanced out into the hallway and no one has come to investigate the sound."

"Good. I'll search the room. You take another look out in the corridor and shut the door so we won't be disturbed."

Moustafa left. Augustus noted a sheaf of papers on the bedside table and moved to check them.

Just then he heard the sound of a blow outside the apartment. Moustafa cried out and there was a thud of a heavy body hitting the floor.

CHAPTER ELEVEN

Moustafa saw the attack coming just in time to dodge, but not in time enough to avoid getting hit.

A short, tough-looking European smacked him on the head with a sap. The leather sack, which felt like it was filled with ball bearings, landed only a glancing blow, but enough to make Moustafa fall to the floor, half in and half out of the room.

The man loomed above him, ready to let fall another strike.

Moustafa lashed out, his limbs barely obeying his commands. He managed to knock the man to the side, shoulder hitting hard against the doorframe, buying Moustafa a precious moment to scramble to his feet.

He only made it to his knees before his attacker recovered. He raised the sap again. Moustafa grasped his elbow. For a moment they struggled. For such a small man, this European had amazing strength.

Mr. Wall's shout made them both turn.

"Moustafa, stop! I know him. He's …"

He tried to finish, but he was already fading away.

"It's you!" the attacker said, eyes going wide as he spotted Mr. Wall. "Did you find who got Gregory?"

Mr. Wall crouched, clutching his pistol and looking all around.

"The bunker is empty for a moment, Tim," Mr. Wall whispered. "Let's see if the Bosche left any maps or orders."

"What?" the man called Tim said, staring dumbfounded. Moustafa still grasped his arm but he no longer struggled.

Moustafa took a chance on letting go and backing away.

"Quick, Tim! Before they get back," Mr. Wall whispered. "You've never been slow on a raid before."

"What's the matter with you?" Tim turned to Moustafa. "What's the matter with him?"

"He fades back into the war sometimes," Moustafa said, moving over to Mr. Wall, his steps unsteady. He took him by the shoulders. Mr. Wall looked up at him, eyes trying to focus. "We are in Egypt, Mr. Wall."

"Right. Egypt, old pal," Tim said, visibly shaken. He closed the door to stop anyone passing in the hallway from seeing the scene.

"Egypt?" Mr. Wall said, looking around.

Tim moved over and put a hand on his back. "Yeah. Bloody war's over and good riddance. Been over for two years."

"Over?" The question came out soft, strangled. Then his eyes lit up in recognition. "Oh, Lord!"

Mr. Wall turned away. Moustafa took a step back and turned to the man named Tim. "Leave him for a bit. He'll be all right in a minute."

Tim watched, jaw hanging as Mr. Wall staggered into the bedroom.

"You sure he'll be all right?"

"He has these spells sometimes. It will pass."

Moustafa's head throbbed. The shock of the moment having passed, the blow to his skull hurt twice as much as before. He moved to the bathroom, wet a towel in the sink, and dabbed the growing bump on his head. He winced. Couldn't he go anywhere with that madman without getting hurt? Nur was right. He was a danger to everyone around him.

"So who are you?" Tim asked from the door.

He was a short man, not even reaching Moustafa's shoulder, but solidly built and seeming to brim with energy. He had close-cropped blonde hair that revealed a jagged scar just above the hairline on the front. Another scar on the cheek looked like a graze from a bullet. Two other scars, apparently from knives or bayonets, cut across the side of his neck and the back of his right hand. Pale blue eyes studied him.

"My name is Moustafa Ghani El Souwaim."

"You his manservant?"

"No," Moustafa snapped. "I own a bookshop."

"A bookshop?" Tim chuckled. Moustafa didn't see why that would be funny.

"I help your friend when he has a murder to solve," Moustafa explained, dabbing more water on the bump.

"Has there been more than one?" Tim asked with surprise.

"There have been far too many," Moustafa grumbled.

"Sorry for the knock on your noggin. I thought you was one of them."

Moustafa turned to him. "And who are they?"

Before Tim could answer, Mr. Wall reappeared. He looked pale and shaken, but back in the present time.

"Timothy Crawford! My word, I can't believe it. Whatever are you doing here?"

Tim took his hand.

"Looking up old friends, what do you think? How have you been doing, H—"

Mr. Wall raised a hand, shuddering.

"My name is Sir Augustus Wall."

Tim grimaced and shook his head.

"Yeah, Gregory learned your new name and told me," Tim jabbed a finger into Mr. Wall's chest, a familiarity Moustafa had never seen him allow with anyone before. Yet his tone contained heat. "Whatever you want to call yourself, you got a lot of explaining to do running out on your mates like you did."

"Running out? I was invalidated out."

"That's not a by-your-leave to scarper from our lives, you bloody bastard. We've all been worried sick about you."

"Not everyone," Augustus said bitterly.

Tim nodded grimly and his tone softened. "Yeah, I heard about that. If she can't have you the way you are she don't deserve you. But what happened? Last time I saw you, you were in hospital half out of your mind on morphine. Never did get a proper talk with you."

"I changed my name and moved to Alexandria. But people kept bothering me so I moved down to Cairo."

Tim took half a step back, his face going cold. "Well, if I'm bothering you …"

Augustus took his hand again. "No. No, you're not. I don't regret leaving, but I should have spoken with you first. I'm sorry I ran out. I just couldn't stand England anymore. I wanted a fresh start. But whatever are you doing here?"

"Gregory came looking for you. He found out you were in Alexandria and he's been here for a few months, but the trail went cold. Then he heard about an antiquities dealer in Cairo, a veteran who wore a mask. He knew it must be you. He cabled me and sent me travel money to come out here because he thought you wouldn't see him."

Augustus sighed. "I would have."

"Yeah, well, the way you ran off how could anyone guess anything about you? He also needed me for some added firepower."

"Firepower?"

Tim shook his head. "Wish I made it in time. I read about his murder in the papers. I guess that's why you're up here, looking into it. You and your Fuzzy Wuzzy."

Moustafa balled his fists.

"Don't call him that, Tim," Mr. Wall said.

Tim grinned, showing bad teeth. He looked Moustafa up and down. "Where did you dig him up? Black as they come. Looks like you dressed a pile of coal in a nightshirt."

Moustafa glared at him. "You're lucky your old comrade stopped this pile of coal from giving you a good thrashing."

"Ha! In your dreams. One hit to the head wasn't enough, I'll give you that. I'd have had you out cold in the next two seconds though, Fuzzy Wuzzy."

"Do not call me that!"

"Tim, stop." Mr. Wall turned Moustafa. "My apologies, Moustafa. My friend isn't as worldly as some of the other Europeans and English you know."

"Worldly, hell!" Tim said. "I spent four bloody years in France and Belgium, didn't I? That's enough travel for a lifetime."

Mr. Wall put a hand on Tim's shoulder. "I'm glad you decided to travel again. It's good to see you."

"You could have seen plenty of me if you hadn't run off."

"I haven't been … well."

Tim bit his lip. "No need to feel ashamed on my account, old pal. Just living through it all is enough to feel proud." He turned to Moustafa and jabbed a thumb in Mr. Wall's direction. "You're looking at a bloody hero, you are. Fought like the best of them. Saved my skin more times than I can count."

"Approximately the same number of times you saved mine. Come, let's sit down."

Moustafa gratefully took the most comfortable armchair, still holding the damp towel to his head.

"How's the old skull?" Tim asked him as he sat on a sofa with Mr. Wall.

"I've had worse," Moustafa said.

Tim laughed. "Spending time with him, I'm not surprised. He got me into all sorts of rucks. A magnet for trouble, he is."

Moustafa tried to imagine these two fighting side by side on the Western Front. The poor Germans.

Tim turned to Mr. Wall. "So how did Gregory meet his end? The papers didn't say much except he was found strangled in his hotel room."

"Not strangled. Suffocated. Someone held his hands while another pressed a pillow to his face. A strong man, by the looks of it. Gregory was wearing a false beard that didn't get dislodged. That shows he wasn't able to move his head at all."

"Gregory was no ninety-pound weakling."

"No, he was not. He had asked the bellboy to come up in half an hour to retrieve a telegram, and had previously asked the concierge how long it would take to reach an address in Cairo."

"That would have been for you. He didn't want to just turn up at your door. Did you find a map in his room?"

"A map? No."

Tim hit the arm of the sofa with a fist. "Damn! They got it."

"A map to what?" Moustafa asked, leaning forward.

Timothy Crawford leaned back, eyes sparkling. "The biggest treasure of the East. Enough to give us each more gold than the Sultan."

"Where?" Mr. Wall asked.

"Right here in Alexandria. Gregory got his hands on a map to the tomb of Alexander the Great."

"Alexander the Great? Impossible!" Moustafa said. "It's been lost for centuries."

Tim nodded. "It has, but Gregory got a line on it. With that map we could have found it, but the bloody Aussies got it now. No good to them, though."

"Wait, Tim. Back up. Tell us from the start."

"All right. I'm getting ahead of meself. You see, I'm a Johnny-come-lately to this whole thing. It all started a year ago when Gregory went to London for the season. He was at his club in Pall Mall when he got to chatting to one of his posh chums. The toff had been an officer in the Egyptian Expeditionary Corps. It was Gregory's birthday, so the man made him a present of a marble slab he'd brought back from Egypt. Had some Greek writing on it. Said Gregory could put it in his garden. Gregory didn't think much of it. He might have been a toff like you, but he acted more like one of the lads."

"You mean he only cared for sport, drinking, and womanizing?"

"I mean he didn't have tomato juice running through his veins. Got a cigarette? I'm out."

Tim slugged him on the arm, which got no more response than a smile. Moustafa was amazed. He'd never seen someone act this way with Mr. Wall before.

"Here you go," Mr. Wall said, handing him a packet of cigarettes.

"Woodbines? Now who's acting like one of the lads? I thought you'd have switched back to the posh brand your parents always sent you."

"They never sent enough, as you know. Woodbines became a habit."

Tim took the packet and held it out to Moustafa.

"Want one, Coalface?"

While Moustafa preferred the sheesha, and certainly did not prefer to be called "Coalface," he recognized an olive branch when he saw one.

As he slid a cigarette out of the packet, he realized that in all their time together, Mr. Wall had never offered him one.

"Thank you," he said. To Tim, not Mr. Wall.

They all lit up. Tim went on.

"So Gregory put it in his garden and didn't think nothing of it," Tim continued. "Then one day another of his posh friends was over for tea. This bloke was more your type. Cambridge educated."

"Cambridge? Well, no one is perfect," Mr. Wall said. Moustafa smiled. His former boss had obviously regained his composure.

"He took one look at the slab and nearly jumped out of his skin. The Greek writing said it was from the tomb of Alexander."

"Impossible!" Moustafa said.

"Why should it be?" Tim said. "So that got Gregory interested. He was never one for the books, but this looked too good to pass up. He asked his gentleman's club friend where he got it from and learned it was sold to him by some Aussie army engineers who had been laying a branch line in Alexandria. They came up with all sorts of stuff."

"Anyone who digs in my country would," Moustafa said.

"I guess you're right. The friend told Gregory the unit and Gregory snooped around the War Office and found out they were still posted in Egypt. So he took the next boat to Alexandria. He had heard you'd moved here and wanted to knock on your door and get you in on the game, since you know more about this tosh than anyone we know. That was four, five months ago. Well, he didn't find you but he tracked down the men who had found the slab and learned they had sold a few other bits and bobs to a couple of antiquities dealers. He managed to buy some back from one of them, an Egyptian. Others had already been sold."

"What were they?" Moustafa asked, his heart beating faster despite his skepticism.

"Another piece of the slab, and a couple of bits of broken statue. Gregory made a sketch of them all. I'll show you those in a minute. More important, he got the engineers to make a map of where they had found it all. Weren't too precise, because it had been the year before, but the map shows enough to give a good idea."

"But the map has been stolen," Mr. Wall said. "Who did that?"

Tim raised his hand. "One step at a time. By God, you used to be the patient one!"

"I was never on the trail of Alexander the Great's tomb before."

"We may not be now," Moustafa cautioned.

Tim went on.

"Gregory went to the other antiquities dealer, some Greek fellow living here in Alexandria. He had some more things, including pieces of the slab. Small bits that didn't have too much writing on them. Gregory slipped up and let spill what was on his part of the slab. That made the Greek shut up. Wouldn't sell him anything, but offered a big price for Gregory's part of the slab. When Gregory realized it was nothing doing, he left. He came back a few days later to try again, but the Greek pressed him, asked him all sorts of questions that showed he had been making enquiries of his own. After that Gregory noticed he was being followed."

"So the Australians learned what they had given up and now want to reclaim it," Moustafa said. "That Australian who came to my bookshop must have been one of them."

"That's right. While asking around among all the antiquities dealers, Gregory heard of an Englishman with a mask living in Cairo by the name of Sir Augustus Wall. He figured out right quick who that really was. He knew he was in over his head, so he decided to go to Cairo and get help from a man he could trust who knew more about this stuff than he did."

"And the Australians followed him," Mr. Wall said in a heavy voice.

"Done him in and got the map. Gregory was going to show it to you. See if you could make out more than he could."

"Why didn't you come with him?" Moustafa asked.

Tim shrugged. "I only got here two days ago. He told me in the wire where he was staying. When I came and found him gone, the manager told me Gregory had reserved a room for me next to his until the end of the month. Left me the whole story in a letter."

Mr. Wall smiled. "That must have been more reading than you've done all year."

"Cheeky bastard. Also left me the key."

"The key to his room?" Moustafa asked.

"No, the key to the map. He worried he might get done, and so he kept the key and the map separate. He had memorized the key. I hope they didn't get that information from him."

Mr. Wall shook his head. "Not Gregory."

"No, you're right. Tough as nails, he was. He took that key to his grave."

Moustafa leaned forward, the pain in his head forgotten. "So are you saying the map is no good without the key, and the key is useless without the map?"

The tough little veteran nodded. "That's right, Fuz—erm, I mean whatever your name is."

"Moustafa."

"Right. The Aussies will see that quick enough, and they'll come on back to Alexandria to look for the other piece of the puzzle. That's why I coshed you. Figured you were with them. The next people who come knocking on this door sure will be."

CHAPTER TWELVE

Faisal woke up in his rooftop shed to the dawn call to prayer, excited and ready to go. After a long, difficult conversation the previous night, Cordelia had made him understand she was buying them tickets to ride on the train to Alexandria for that afternoon.

Faisal had already packed his small canvas bag with a few possessions and collected all the money he had just in case he needed it. He hurried to make some final preparations, which started with eating a huge breakfast. He didn't know when he'd get to eat next. Then he washed himself so he'd look respectable for the train. There would be a lot of Europeans on it. After that he checked his things to make sure he had everything he needed, which wasn't much. Just his penknife, some matches, most of the food from the house, and a blanket.

Once he finished, he figured it was time to get to Cordelia's. He knew he had to be there before the noon call to prayer, and that couldn't be too far off.

He was just about to unlock the front door when he remembered that the Englishman had asked him to guard the house. So he went to an upper window and looked out from behind the wooden screen onto Ibn al-Nafis street.

Everything looked normal. Karim the night watchman was walking home, yawning and no doubt looking forward to his rest. The egg seller stood just below the window with two or three customers. Bisam the water seller walked slowly by, a big keg strapped on his back, calling out "Fresh water! Fresh well water from the villages!"

Across the street, the usual loungers sat at the Sultan El Moyyad Café, drinking tea and talking about nothing in particular. Faisal would never understand how men could sit around at cafés all day. Didn't they get bored? He couldn't sit still for more than five minutes without wanting to get up and move.

So it looked like everything was all right on Ibn al-Nafis street.

Wait. Who was that? An older Egyptian man, with the seamed dark face of a farmer under his cap of camel's wool, stood at the corner opposite the house, watching the passersby. Another man, younger, with a cleaner djellaba and looking like a city dweller, sat alone at the Sultan El Moyyad Café, sipping a tea and talking to no one.

Nothing unusual about either of them, except that Faisal didn't recognize them. You hardly ever saw strangers on this street except wandering vendors, and neither of them looked like that.

Plus both kept looking at the house.

They were subtle about it. Faisal bet no one but him noticed, and it even took him a minute.

Professional thieves or police?

After what happened at Moustafa's shop, Sir Thomas Russell Pasha would probably send a policeman they recognized so there wouldn't be any misunderstanding, and he would only need to send one policeman to watch the house, not two.

So Faisal had to assume they were sent by whoever killed the Englishman's friend. Since the murder happened in Shepheard's Hotel, the murderer was probably a foreigner. Hardly any Turks or Arabs stayed there, and no Egyptians. Since a foreigner would stand out in this neighborhood, the murderer had hired two Egyptians to watch the house.

No way he could walk into the street without them trying to grab him.

Faisal grinned. What those two didn't realize was he had a secret way out, one that even the Englishman hadn't discovered until Faisal showed him. He hurried up to his shed on the roof, grabbed his football (the absolute best thing the Englishman had ever given him), and went to the back wall where it overlooked an alley half-filled with rubble. It was a dead-end, and no one ever went there.

He bounced the football off the blank wall of the opposite building hard enough for it to fly back and hit the back wall of the Englishman's house. From there it zigzagged between the two walls before landing on the ground, bouncing up a few feet before landing again and rolling to a stop against a pile of splintered old boards.

Faisal giggled. He loved doing that.

Taking off his sandals, he tied the straps together and put them around his neck. Then he slung his bag over his shoulder. He climbed over the lip of the wall and searched around with his feet to find the familiar holds.

The house was an old one. The Englishman said several hundred years old or maybe more, built with stones from an ancient ruin. That explained why there had been so many djinn living here before Faisal set charms all around the house. It also meant the stones had lots of cracks between them, cracks Faisal had widened and deepened with a chisel he had stolen back when he had been living here without the Englishman knowing. The handholds and footholds gave him an easy route up and down.

Within a minute he was down in the alley. He shoved the football into his bag and headed out to the street.

Now for the tricky part. The alley curved around the Englishman's house to open up on Ibn al-Nafis street. Both those spies would see him come out. They might already know he lived there and try to follow him. Even worse, they might wait until night and sneak into the alley and discover the route up the wall. Faisal doubted anyone except him could climb it, but he couldn't take that risk. He couldn't let those spies see him.

Faisal walked up to within five feet of the opening of the alley, where neither spy could see him from where they watched. He could just see the far end of the café, where Mohammed, the café's star backgammon player, was playing Youssef, the barber who had a shop next door. From the look on

Youssef's face, Mohammed was winning as usual. The spy sat on the other end of the café, and wouldn't see Faisal until he actually came out of the alley.

Which Faisal wouldn't do until the right moment.

He heard the rumble of an approaching cart. It sounded like the right moment was coming just now.

Sure enough, a donkey cart laden with meal sacks rattled down his side of the street, the driver calling out to the animal and whipping it as it struggled to pull the heavy load.

Just as it passed, Faisal ducked out of the alley and walked alongside, using the cart to shield him from view. The cart was low enough that from the other side of the street the spy wouldn't even see his legs underneath.

He felt very proud of his cleverness until someone called his name.

"Faisal, there you are!"

Abdul stood up from where he had been squatting in the shade of the house next to Faisal's.

Faisal put a finger to his lips.

Abdul had been on the streets for years, and could tell when somebody didn't want to be seen. He fell in beside Faisal.

"What's going on?" Abdul asked in a whisper.

"Never mind. Just go away," Faisal said, hunching low and following the cart.

"Do you have any food?"

Faisal grimaced. The same every morning. They always waited for him. Usually he left the house later. Abdul must have come early.

"No, I don't have any food."

"Do you have any money?" Abdul asked.

The cart driver leaned over, looking curiously at the boys. He gave Abdul, who had no shoes on his filthy feet and only a faded and patched djellaba, a warning glance.

"I'll make sure he doesn't steal anything, sir," Faisal said.

The man nodded and turned to face forward again.

"I'll make sure he doesn't steal anything, sir," Abdul said in a singsong voice. "Aren't you getting all high and mighty!"

"Keep your voice down."

"Do you have any money?" Abdul asked again, louder this time.

"Here," Faisal grumbled, giving him half a piastre.

"I haven't had anything since breakfast yesterday," Abdul whined. "Got any more?"

"Here's a piastre, now leave me alone!"

Abdul laughed and ran off. Faisal let out a breath of relief and continued following the cart, using it to hide him from view.

Faisal walked all the way down the street, passing the other spy on the corner, with no sign that either of them had spotted him. Even the driver of the donkey cart didn't give him a second glance. A nicely dressed boy with a football wouldn't try stealing any of his meal sacks. The old Faisal would never have been able to walk beside the cart like this. The cart driver would have looked at him like he had looked at Abdul.

That made him feel proud and kind of bad at the same time.

On the next block was another café. The plainclothes policeman he had dumped watermelons on sat there, drinking a tea and watching the man on the corner.

Faisal slowed. The policeman noticed him, then looked away, trying to act subtle. Faisal smiled and went over, taking his hand and kissing him on both cheeks like he was a relative.

"Hello, Uncle Mohammed!"

The policeman took the hint. "Oh, it's my favorite nephew. How are you?"

He pinched Faisal's cheek, way too hard. Faisal leaned in a little closer and whispered,

"Good job spotting that farmer on the corner, but I bet you didn't see the other spy in the dark green djellaba and Western style shoes at the Sultan El Moyyad Café."

The look on the policeman's face told Faisal he was right. Faisal grabbed a coin he had left on the table to pay for his tea.

"Thanks, Uncle Mohammad. I was hungry!"

He hurried off before the policeman could do anything.

***

The train station was the loudest, busiest place Faisal had ever seen. A huge crowd of Europeans and Egyptians bustled back and forth under a big arched roof. A giant clock was fixed to one wall next to a big board with writing and numbers on it that Faisal figured showed the times the trains arrived and left.

The building was so big the trains came right into it, separated by wide concrete platforms. A train came in just as Faisal and Cordelia walked inside, chuffing away and sending out billows of smoke and steam.

Faisal's heart raced. It was so loud here. So much going on. He clutched Cordelia's hand. She must be scared by all this noise and all the strange sights. Clutching her hand would make her feel better.

In his other hand he held the small bag with his things. Behind them came two porters with Cordelia's things—a big trunk, three large suitcases, and a round box for her spare hat. One of the suitcases alone could carry everything Faisal owned in the world. What did she need all this stuff for?

She took him first to a little window like they had in the moving picture houses and bought two tickets. Then she led him to one of the platforms where a train waited like a big sleeping metal monster.

They climbed aboard and a conductor led them to a little room in the train with two padded benches facing each other and a window looking out over the platform. The conductor turned to him.

"The second class carriage is in back. Servants go there. Stop holding your mistress's hand. It's disrespectful."

Faisal glared at him. "I am not a servant." He was getting really, really tired of saying that.

The conductor turned to Cordelia and switched to English. He asked a question and got a short answer in reply that didn't sound too polite, and Cordelia always acted polite. The conductor shot him a sour look and left. Faisal stuck out his tongue at him.

Cordelia nudged him. "Stop."

"Sorry."

Faisal stuck his head out the window and watched all the people go by. He spotted Cordelia's two porters putting all her stuff into a railway car with no windows. That was smart. That way no thieves could climb inside as they were going up to Alexandria.

Two foreign women came into their carriage and took the bench opposite them. They looked at Faisal suspiciously and asked Cordelia something in English. She started to reply and they got angry. The conversation went on for a while, both women frowning at Faisal. He did not stick out his tongue. These were European women, and they could get him kicked off the train if they wanted to. Of course Cordelia was European too, but he had better be careful just in case.

A conductor on the platform blew a loud whistle. Faisal could hear doors in the train thumping shut. He poked his head out. Several cars ahead, he could see the tall smokestack of the engine begin to puff like a giant sheesha. His eyes widened as the train began to move. It started slowly, like a boat going down river without any oarsmen to speed it along. Soon it picked up speed, and more speed. The train pulled out of the station and along the track past buildings and streets.

Faisal let out a whoop. They were going so fast! He'd seen plenty of trains, but he never thought he'd get to ride on one.

He pushed his head out more and felt the wind hit him in the face, making his hair fly everywhere. If they kept going this fast, they'd be in Alexandria by lunchtime. The buildings and people zipped by, and up ahead he could see where the big buildings stopped and only the small huts on the edge of town remained. Pretty soon they'd be out of Cairo.

He felt a tug on his shoulder. Faisal brought his head back in.

"Sit down, Faisal," Cordelia said. She looked embarrassed.

Embarrassed about what? Oh, those two frowning European women. They said something in English. The only words he caught were "Egyptian boy," and they weren't said in a nice way. Cordelia said something that sounded like an apology.

Why should those two ladies care if he stuck his head out the window? Probably because he was an "Egyptian boy." He bet an English boy could do that and they'd smile at him and give him candy. Like that fat English boy he had slugged on the steamboat. Those boys got to do whatever they wanted.

It didn't bother him much, because he'd seen all this a million times before. What bothered him was that Cordelia looked embarrassed. About what? Him? He was dressed nice and had washed. And he hadn't belched or anything.

Was Cordelia embarrassed because he was Egyptian? Ridiculous! They were friends.

But maybe, just maybe, she did feel a little bit embarrassed. Europeans hardly ever traveled with Egyptians, and never with Egyptian children unless they were servants. Those two women probably thought he should be in the servants' car with the luggage, and Cordelia had explained that he wasn't a servant. That's why they were frowning and that's why she felt embarrassed.

They always leave in the end, Moustafa had said.

Bah, what did Moustafa know?

He's known way more Europeans than you have.

These thoughts troubled him as the train sped out past the end of town and along the edge of the desert, the green strip of cultivation off to their left, the Nile glimmering in the distance.

But Faisal's young mind couldn't stay troubled for long. There were all the things to see and the excitement of moving so fast and the sandwiches Cordelia had packed in the wicker basket she carried.

The train clattered through the desert and as the sun grew hotter, the women across from them drew the shades. Faisal had to peek through the edge of the shade to see, only opening it a little bit because they complained if he opened it too much. The edge of the farmer's fields never went out of sight, and he saw villages and isolated farmers' huts fly by.

Alongside the track ran a wire set on top of a series of poles. He'd heard this was for the telegraph. Twice on the trip he saw small groups of soldiers fixing the wire. He wondered if the independence people had cut the telegraph line again.

After a couple of hours, the line of cultivation drew closer, and pretty soon it was green as far as he could see. Little rivers ran everywhere, cutting through tall patches of papyrus and other plants. The air grew humid and smelled different. Richer. Birds filled the sky.

He'd never seen a land like this and realized this must be the Delta. Just before it gets to the sea, people said, the Nile spreads out like the top of a lotus flower to make a big green area. Lots of farmers lived here, but there was so much green much of the land didn't even get used. That was different from the little strips of land along the Nile. Every little bit of that got used. He wondered why so many people went hungry in Cairo when there was all this land to farm.

Faisal stared and stared, so entranced by their speed and the constantly changing scenes that he almost forgot to eat the rest of the sandwiches Cordelia had packed for them. After a few hours, they approached the outskirts of a city. He noticed something else too—the air was different. It was cooler and beneath the smell of coal and wood smoke and all the cooking smells a city made, he breathed in something sharp and fresh. He wondered what it could be.

The train passed through some open fields where Bedouin camped in their black camel hair tents and then into a city with lots of European buildings, as many as in the European parts of Cairo.

Then they pulled into a station and there was a great hustle and bustle in getting out. Cordelia paid some porters to help with her mountain of luggage, and together they passed through an echoing hall and through some great arches to a line of waiting carriages.

Cordelia went to one and said something in English. The driver, a thin older man in a white djellaba and brand new tarboosh, replied in English then turned to Faisal.

"We're going, boy. Get your tip and be gone," he said. He didn't say it in a mean way, but it bothered Faisal just the same.

"I'm with her," he said.

"Oh, you're her servant? Strange for a European lady to have a boy servant, but who can understand Europeans?"

"I understand them a little bit sometimes."

"Then you know more than me. Hey! What are you doing? You can't sit back there with her. Sit up here with me."

"Sorry," Faisal grumbled, and sat next to the driver.

"You obviously haven't been properly trained," the driver said, snapping the reins to get the horse to start forward.

The sour mood the driver's words put him in didn't last long, because they started passing through the most amazing city Faisal had ever seen, not that he had seen many. Just Cairo and Luxor.

Huge European-style buildings rose up on each side, with pillars and big arched windows. Everything looked clean and new. A tram rattled by their carriage, and tooting motorcars shot past just like in Cairo.

"This city looks rich," Faisal said.

The carriage driver chuckled. "That's because there are so many Europeans in it, and not only Europeans but also Greeks and Armenians and Jews. There are even Russians."

"We have Greeks in Cairo. What's a Russian?"

"Like a European but more aggressive. They come from a harsh land that's like a desert but with snow. The sun never shines all year around and there are big white bears that eat people. That's why the Russians are so foul-tempered."

"Wow. I wouldn't want to live there."

"Neither would I. Many came here in the past couple of years. A group of Russian barbarians killed their king and all the royal family and stole everybody's money. They say people will be richer that way."

"I guess they're happier here then."

"Yes, but they drink too much. Don't get near a Russian when he drinks."

"Are they worse than Australians?" The Australian soldiers had a bad reputation for drinking and getting into fights.

"Worse than ten Australians. We're almost to the hotel."

They turned a corner, and Faisal's eyes went wide and his breath caught. Before them was a big square, and beyond that a road that ran along a low wall about waist high. Over it he could see water.

And only water. It seemed to stretch as far as he could see. It reminded him of the desert except with water instead of sand. Part of the water was encircled by a wall of big stones and inside floated lots of big ships, bigger than any Faisal had ever seen. Some had masts while others had steam funnels. A couple were made all of metal and had huge guns. The British flag flew from those.

"Is that the sea?"

The carriage driver laughed. "Yes it is. I guess it's quite a sight for you. I grew up here so I'm used to it. You should go swimming. You do know how to swim, don't you?"

"I swim in the Nile."

"Good. When I was your age I used to go to the end of the mole, that's the stone wall that protects the harbor, and swim by that old castle. I suppose boys still go out there. Ask your mistress to let you have a day off. You don't want to miss that. Well, here we are."

They stopped in front of one of the huge European buildings, all made of stone. A Nubian in a red suit rushed out and began taking Cordelia's things. Faisal grabbed her hat box. If he didn't look like he was her servant, they wouldn't let him inside.

The Nubian managed to get all the other bags and boxes, stacking them on his head and walking through a big set of double doors another Nubian held open. Faisal followed behind Cordelia, hoping no one would notice him.

They entered a big front room all of marble. Europeans sat on nice couches talking and smoking. One wall was all mirrors, and when Faisal saw himself in the middle of all those rich Europeans and well-dressed Nubian servants, he felt even more out of place. Even the man who carried the luggage dressed better, and Faisal bet he had never begged for food or slept in an alley.

Cordelia went up to a counter and chatted in English with an Egyptian standing behind it. The Nubian disappeared with the luggage.

Faisal stood there, unsure what to do. Nearby, at the bottom of the staircase, was a Classical statue of a woman. Faisal stared for a second, then blushed and looked away, hoping no one had caught him looking. They put that in a hotel where everyone could see it?

After a minute, another Nubian came and escorted them toward the stairs. Faisal thought they were going to go up, but instead the Nubian opened a metal door like a shutter into a tiny little wooden room with windows on each side. He ushered them in, then got in himself and closed the door behind them.

What are we doing in here?

The Nubian pulled on a lever and Faisal yelped. The room started going up!

"Don't embarrass your mistress," the Nubian said.

"What is this thing?" Faisal gasped, looking out the little window as the ground floor fell away beneath them.

"You've never been in a lift before?"

Faisal didn't answer. His stomach felt funny and he was afraid of opening his mouth in case those sandwiches came out. They passed through the winding staircase like a train going through a tunnel, but up instead of forward. Another floor passed by, then another. Faisal clutched his stomach.

After a moment the little room stopped, the Nubian opened the door, and Faisal rushed out.

"Let your mistress go first! Don't you have any training?"

Cordelia said something to the Nubian, sounding embarrassed again. The Nubian bowed and shot a glare at Faisal behind Cordelia's back.

They walked down a long hallway with more mirrors and lots of doors. Faisal gaped. Each door had paintings of vases and flowers on them, and were lined with gold paint on the edges. Gold on doors! He thought only the Sultan in Constantinople had gold on his doors. Cordelia must have been even richer than the Englishman. Where did all the money come from?

The Nubian opened a door, bowed, and handed Cordelia a key. The luggage was already inside amid ornate furniture and a table with a glass top and legs painted with gold. Maybe they were even solid gold. At the far end, a pair of large open windows showed a view of the sea. The Nubian bowed and left.

Cordelia smiled and got to work unpacking. As she bustled around the room, pulling things out of her steamer trunk and putting them away, Faisal sat in a corner looking around at all the nice furnishings and the view of the sea and suddenly got a funny feeling—distant and sad at the same time.

He'd felt it before when he'd been to nice places like this. He had felt it the worst when he had been on the steamboat going upriver in his own little cabin looking at himself in the mirror. The Englishman had told him to wear a new djellaba so he could pretend to be a servant, but had made him pack his filthy old djellaba so he could use it as a disguise.

He had remembered standing in front of the mirror in his cabin, changing from one djellaba to the other, and wondering which was the right one for him.

Neither were the right one for this place.

He watched as Cordelia put away all her things—so many things—singing a happy song to herself as if staying in hotels with golden doors was the most natural thing in the world. Faisal sighed.

"Sooner or later that Nubian is going to come back and take me to the servant's quarters," Faisal said.

Cordelia stopped what she was doing and said in English, "What?"

"Of course I can't stay here, because you're not my mother or sister, but it would be nice to stay next door and have a view of the sea. But I'm not going to get a view of the sea. I'm going to get a little room in the cellar or in some other building where the window faces a blank wall. If I even get a window, that is."

Cordelia knelt before him, smiled and said in Arabic, "*La takallim arabi.*" "I don't speak Arabic."

"I know you don't. That's the language for people like me, people who don't get to stay in nice big rooms with windows looking at the sea. We live in different places. Moustafa says you all leave sooner or later."

"Moustafa?"

"But you don't need to leave. You're not really here."

Cordelia put a hand on his cheek, looking concerned, and asked him a question in English he didn't understand.

"You're nice. Nicer than most Europeans, that's for sure. But you're not going to get me the room next door."

The Nubian reentered. Cordelia quickly stood.

"Come," he said, gesturing at Faisal. "I'll show you the servants' quarters."

"I told you," Faisal said to Cordelia, and followed the Nubian out of the room.

CHAPTER THIRTEEN

Augustus sat in his dead friend's pension room, thinking about all Timothy Crawford had told him. It seemed fanciful in the extreme that the marble slab Gregory had been trying to reconstruct could really bear the epitaph of Alexander the Great. More likely it was some memorial to him, or from the base of a statue. Likenesses of the great conqueror had been erected all over the ancient city.

Still, even the remotest possibility made his skin prickle.

And then here was Crawford sitting next to him, joking and bragging and laughing at danger like he had in the trenches. It was as if two years hadn't passed.

But two years had passed. They were in Egypt, not France, and he was missing half a face and a fiancée.

"So what have you been up to?" he asked his old friend.

Crawford shrugged. "This and that. Mucking about Rose Hill mostly."

Rose Hill was a village near Oxford, and about as unlike the affluent university town as Scotland was from the Soudan.

"Got work?"

Crawford laughed. Augustus smiled and shook his head. Tim had always been work-shy, in and out of reformatories, and later jails, for a host of infractions. He had risen to the challenge of the war, though. Augustus had hoped it would turn him into a respectable citizen.

On second thought, however, Augustus realized what a daft idea that was. Sitting in cold mud killing your fellow man for four years does nothing to help make someone a boon to society. Quite the contrary.

"It was good of you to come all this way to help Gregory," Augustus said.

"He was a mate, even if he was a toff," Crawford said, punching him in the shoulder. "Hard to put on airs when the air is filled with mustard gas, eh?"

"That was a clever little alarm you set for us," Moustafa said, still holding the wet towel to his head. "How did you manage to set it up without trapping yourself inside?"

"Climbed through the window."

Augustus and Moustafa glanced at each other, went to the window, and leaned out. The nearest window to Crawford's rooms was nearly ten feet away, reachable only along an ornamental ledge barely six inches wide. The street was six stories of clear air down.

"Crikey. Faisal would be impressed," Augustus said.

"Who's Faisal?"

"A constant pain in the neck," Moustafa grumbled.

"I suspect you'll meet him presently," Augustus said. "Now on to more urgent matters. Do you have any idea where these Australians are staying?"

"Not a bloody clue. I'm in the dark as much as you are. I'll show you Gregory's letter, but there's nothing there I haven't told you. I'll show you them sketches and the key too. Come on over to my bunk."

They headed next door, where they found an identical set of rooms, different only in their state of utter disarray. The bed was unmade, empty beer and whiskey bottles lay scattered everywhere, and Crawford had strung up a line of laundry to dry by the window in the sitting room.

"I see you've kept your army discipline."

"Never had any."

"Oh yes, now I remember."

"What's this?" Moustafa asked, pointing to a bag hanging suspended from the light fixture.

"My food," Crawford said.

Moustafa looked at him curiously. "Why did you hang it up?"

"To keep the rats away, why else?"

"You're not in a dugout anymore," Augustus said.

Crawford looked embarrassed. "Well, um, you never know in these Gippo places, eh?"

Augustus put a hand on his shoulder. "It's all right. Show us those papers."

Crawford cleared away enough detritus so they could sit, and Augustus went through all the papers. First the letter, which contained nothing more than Crawford had already told them. Gregory's handwriting, familiar from so many daily memos and after-action reports, tugged at him, as did the mention of his real name. Seeing it written down in black and white made a little tremor go through his body.

All that passed from his mind when he looked at the sketches. Moustafa leaned in.

It was a crude drawing made by Gregory's untrained hand, but it told them enough. It showed the broken upper left corner of a larger marble slab with ancient Greek written on it. Part of the first line was visible, as were the upper parts of the letters of the first part of the second line, allowing him to guess at its content.

A second drawing showed three smaller bits of the slab, each with fragmentary inscriptions. Numbers at the side give the dimensions of the main piece as twenty-five inches by eight inches, with the third side at a steep angle to form a right triangle. The largest of the other three pieces was no more than ten inches, the other two considerably smaller.

Such small, fragmentary inscriptions were brought up by the bucket load on excavations and worksites, and were of little interest to collectors. Augustus was not surprised they hadn't sold until someone had come along who thought they had greater significance.

And the inscription on the main piece made his heart race.

"Here lies the son of Ammon, conqueror of all the …"

"Prepared for the place of reeds …"

Moustafa took in a sharp breath as he read it too.

"God be praised, it really might be it," the Nubian said.

"What does it say?" Crawford asked.

Moustafa looked at him. "Didn't you get ancient Greek in school?"

"All I got in my school was canings."

Augustus cleared his throat. "Only the more, um, affluent schools teach Latin and Greek."

"He means the snooty brats get all sorts of useless learning while the rest of us get prepared for the workhouse," Crawford told Moustafa, then cocked his head. "You telling me you can read this chicken scratch?"

Moustafa drew himself up. "Yes, I can read ancient Greek. I can read Latin and hieroglyphs as well."

"Are you joking?"

"He's not," Augustus told him.

"So what does that damn thing say?"

"It identifies the entombed as the son of Ammon," Augustus replied.

"I thought it was supposed to be Alexander the Great."

"When Alexander conquered Egypt, he journeyed to Siwa Oasis, where the oracle of Ammon declared him son of the god and thus the rightful pharaoh."

"I wonder how much that cost in donations," Crawford snorted.

"He was hardly short of resources," Augustus replied. "Let's look at the rest of these fragments."

The other three fragments bore smaller parts of the inscription. One bore the words "loyal general," another "with Isis and Anubis," and the last simply said "forty."

"That doesn't tell us much," Crawford grunted when they translated them for him.

"The loyal general would be Ptolemy Soter," Moustafa said. "He was Alexander's right-hand man and claimed Egypt for himself after his commander's death. Isis and Anubis were Egyptian gods. Since Alexander claimed godhood for himself, he would have been associated with them. As for the significance of the number forty, I have no idea yet."

Crawford chuckled and nudged Augustus. "Looks like a porter and speaks like a bleeding professor."

"So what do historians know about the burial place of Alexander?" Moustafa asked Augustus, ignoring Crawford's latest slight. "All I know of it is that he was buried near the palace in a glass or crystal sarcophagus."

"We do know a bit more, but I suppose it wasn't taught in Koranic schools in the Soudan," Augustus said.

"I never went to school, Mr. Wall."

"Oh dear! My apologies. I keep forgetting you're an autodidact. Well, never mind. University would probably ruin you. It does for most minds."

"He never went to school?" Crawford asked.

"I was born in a very small village in the Soudan," Moustafa told him.

"You've come far," Augustus said, "and you are correct that Ptolemy placed his commander's tomb somewhere near the palace, although we don't know precisely where. Odd, considering that it was a bit of a pilgrimage site in the ancient world. People would come and pay their respects. His most famous visitor was Octavian, who after the battle of Actium had the tomb opened so he could place a gold wreath on Alexander's head. He botched the job, however, and broke off the fellow's nose."

Moustafa let out a belly laugh. "That's one of the things I love about history, such details. You know it is true because no one would dare make up a story like that about an emperor of Rome!"

"Indeed. Other emperors visited it when they came to Egypt. The last story we have is of Caracalla. He visited in the year 215 and rifled through Alexander's things, such as his ring and tunic, before leaving them on the coffin."

"On the coffin?" Crawford asked. "Why not take them, or at least put them back?"

"Strange, isn't it? We have this from John of Antioch, who doesn't explain why this was done. Probably simple curiosity. He wanted to touch Alexander's things, then didn't feel right taking them or putting them back. Perhaps he was afraid Alexander would stand up and smite him."

"He sounds like a Roman Faisal," Moustafa grumbled.

"Come now," Augustus said. "He might have been one of the Rome's more brutal emperors, but give the man a little more credit."

"And there are no stories after that?" Crawford asked.

"None whatsoever of the interior of the tomb. St. John Chrysostom taunted the pagans in the fourth century by saying no one knew where the tomb of their hero was anymore. There are some later records from the Middle Ages of a chapel venerated by the Alexandrians that stood atop the tomb of Alexander. There's no evidence they were correct in their belief, and none of the accounts give an exact site. The actual tomb appears to have vanished."

"If it had been looted, there would surely be some record of that," Moustafa said quietly, finally taking the damp cloth away from the noticeable bump on his head. "The treasure inside would have been immense."

"The murderers must think the same thing," Augustus said.

"And the bastards have already shown they're willing to kill for it," Crawford said.

"But could they really have found new evidence for a tomb people have been trying to find for more than a thousand years?" Moustafa said incredulously.

"I'd like to think so, but you're right. It's highly unlikely. The real issue is that they think they have, and that's why poor Gregory got murdered."

Moustafa fell silent for a while, then whispered. "But what if they have found new evidence?"

Augustus chuckled. "Then we'll take it from them and you'll get to be the most famous archaeologist of your generation."

"You too, Mr. Wall."

"Good lord, no! Journalists and curiosity seekers pounding on my door every hour of every day? No, thank you."

"I'll take the fame," Crawford brightened. "I'll charge newspapers for interviews at ten bob a time. Get lots of ladies too, I imagine."

"The kind of ladies you like don't read," Augustus quipped.

"Oh, getting clever, are you? Well, clever lad, figure out this then."

Crawford jabbed his finger at the key to the missing map. It had a list of numbers with captions beside them.

"1. Branch line.

2. Tool shed.

3. Mound of rubble.

4. Column bases.

5. Bedouin encampment.

6. Small ruined mosque."

Augustus considered for a moment. "The branch line confirms the original story of the Australian engineers finding it during railway work. It's difficult to determine the significance of these other entries without the map. They do seem sufficiently important that the map would be of little use without the key."

"The column bases hint at an ancient site," Moustafa said. "The mound of rubble might too."

"But what about all these engineering works?" Crawford asked. "They could have wrecked the entire tomb."

"I doubt it," Moustafa replied. "It was probably cut deep within the bedrock. There is a set of Greco-Roman catacombs not far from here that go down more than a hundred feet into the rock."

"Guess you're right, professor. And there would have been a big fuss if they had found the treasure. Hard to keep something like that silent. Rough boys, the Aussies. I met some once. Good for a pint and a fight at any time of the day."

"The letter mentioned the unit was the 3rd ANZAC Engineering Regiment," Augustus said. "We should track them down."

"Already done that, old pal. They got barracks near the central railway station, and I know the drinking houses and brothels they like to go to."

"I suspect you've checked them out quite thoroughly," Augustus said with a smile.

"Got to do me research, just like the two of you."

"We'll take a look tonight. But what we really need is the engineers' maps, to find out where all the branch lines go. Perhaps we don't need Gregory's map if the key gives us sufficient clues to match it with one of their maps."

"But that means breaking into regimental HQ. That's a sight more bother than nicking the rum ration."

"Indeed it is," Augustus said, sitting back.

For the moment, it seemed like they were stuck.

"So where you staying?" Crawford asked.

"The Windsor Palace."

"Well la di da. You should bunk here. If them Aussies come sniffing about, I'd like some backup."

"All right, but we can't simply sit around here waiting for something to happen."

"Always the eager one. No worries, old pal. We'll take the war to them. And I've already set up a plan to do just that."

CHAPTER FOURTEEN

On the walk over to the Windsor Palace Hotel, a luxurious institution overlooking the Corniche and the harbor, Mr. Wall went into a tobacconist's for some cigarettes. Crawford took the opportunity to pull Moustafa aside.

"You been with him a while, right?" Crawford asked in a low voice, watching the doorway to the tobacconist's.

"I worked in his antiquities shop for a year. We've been on more than one murder investigation together."

"Right, so you know him pretty well then. Tell me, how is he? How is he really?"

This look of sincere concern on this loutish man's face took him aback. Crawford really was more than just an old war comrade. Moustafa took a deep breath, and decided to tell him the whole truth.

"When he meets danger, especially if there's any gunplay, he is liable to think he's back in the trenches. It's a strong hallucination although he has never mistaken friend for foe. He is also highly antisocial, practically a recluse who rejects any and all invitations from the English community in Cairo. He is the only Englishman of any standing who is not a member of the Gezirah Sporting Club or Turf Club. He is also all too eager to get into danger. He feels a rivalry with Cairo's chief of police and tries to solve cases before the police do."

Crawford shook his head. "Always did want to prove he's smarter than anyone else. So he's pretty far gone, then?"

"Only when he's in danger," Moustafa said, suddenly feeling defensive for his former employer. Who was this brute to judge?

"And he goes looking for it?"

Moustafa nodded.

Crawford's eyes got a faraway look. "Yeah, that's happened to a lot of the lads. You spend months and years stuck in some mucky hole cursing your luck and pining for home, and when you finally get there all you can think of is the trenches. Hard to put it behind you. It's a horrible life, I tell you, but it's sharp. Really sharp. Every minute you're more alive than you could ever be at home. You could die at any moment, and that makes those moments like diamonds. Been back in my hometown two years now and I can't stop thinking about the front. It's barmy to miss it, but I do."

"Are many sick like him?"

"Not quite like him, no. Some take to the bottle." Crawford laughed sheepishly. "Or get themselves into trouble with the law. Others just mope about. Then there are the mad ones, I mean the truly mad ones that get locked up and you never see them no more. We lost a good mate that way."

Mr. Wall stepped out of the tobacconist's and tossed a couple of packs of cigarettes to Crawford.

"I'm sure you're short of funds as usual," Mr. Wall said.

"Thanks. Yeah. Gregory sent me money for the trip and paid for the room, but thought he'd be around to give me more once I got here. I never seem to have enough nick."

"It's remarkable what gainful employment will do to remedy that situation," Mr. Wall said.

They entered the Windsor Palace, passing through a spacious lounge the size of a ballroom, complete with dainty paintings of bucolic European scenes on a ceiling held up by gilded Corinthian columns, and into the marbled front hall. The clientele here was a mixture of nationalities, the vast majority, of course, being European.

"Blimey," Crawford whispered. He turned to Moustafa. "They let you in here?"

"Why shouldn't they?" Moustafa snapped. "I am staying in the room next to Mr. Wall."

And when the porter took me up to that room he gave me a look like I was Faisal in his street clothes.

They walked to the lift. Crawford shook his head and said, "Let's take the stairs."

"Why?" Moustafa asked.

"We're taking the stairs," Crawford grumbled, gesturing at the lift. "I hate those things. Bloody death traps, they are."

"It's only a …" A warning look from Mr. Wall made Moustafa's words trail off.

"So here's my plan," Crawford said as they walked up the stairs. "I was going to do it without you but now that you're here it's even better. Take a look at this."

He produced a newspaper cutting from his pocket.

"A memorial service for the late Peter Saunders will be held at the Anglican chapel, 41 Essex Street, at 8pm. All are welcome."

The date was for that night.

"You're planning an ambush in a house of worship?" Moustafa asked.

"Why not? The bastards won't be on their guard. We'll have the service and see who turns up. Since the papers published his real name and not the one he was going by, only the murderers will show and not anyone he might have gotten to know here." He nudged Mr. Wall. "Remember when we were billeted in that wrecked cathedral and the Bosche made a night raid on us? You were slamming away at them with a Lee Enfield from behind a statue of Jesus himself."

"Poor chap got a few extra stigmata, if I remember correctly," Mr. Wall said, a smile coming to his lips.

God help him, he really does miss it.

They made it to the correct floor and went to Mr. Wall's room, a spacious suite overlooking the harbor.

"Nice. I should bunk here." Crawford said.

"You'll need a weapon," Mr. Wall said, moving to the closet.

"You blokes have more than those two pistols?"

"Much more," Moustafa grumbled.

Mr. Wall hauled out his weapon bag and put it on the bed with a thump. He itemized the contents as he pulled them out one by one.

"Two Lee-Enfield rifles, with bayonets and a hundred rounds of ammunition for each."

Crawford took one of the rifles in his hands and studied it with admiration. "Look at that. I haven't had one of these in me hands since November of '18."

"A German MP18 …," Mr. Wall continued, pulling out his next item.

"A bloody Storm Battalion submachine gun? How the hell you ever get that?"

"Connections, my friend, connections. Three Mills bombs and three flash grenades of my own making …"

"Jesus, Mary, and Joseph. It's a bloody arsenal!"

"And a final surprise." Mr. Wall twisted the head of his cane and drew the sword from its shaft.

"What do you think, Tim? We ready for battle?" he asked, flourishing the blade.

Mr. Wall let out a hysterical laugh that made Moustafa and Crawford exchange worried glances.

***

The church Crawford had chosen was not one of the main ones close to the center of the European quarter, but a smaller one near the edge of the Egyptian district, a modest little neo-Gothic stone building that reminded Moustafa of prints he had seen of England. It would have looked more at home in some green field than it did in an Egyptian port.

But from what he had heard, the English imported England wherever they went. They certainly had in Egypt and the Soudan.

Night had fallen, and a cool breeze blew in from the sea. This district was mostly given over to offices and had grown quiet. A café across the street offered them shelter. A few office workers, mostly middle-class Egyptians in local imitations of Western clothing, sat talking over their tea. Much of the conversation was about the protests. After a few initial stares at Mr. Wall's mask, everyone went back to their conversations. Moustafa studied the café goers closely, and felt relieved not to spot any hostile expressions. He and Mr. Wall sat near the back, obscured from view from the street but still able to look through a window at the entrance to the church.

"Your friend picked the location well," Moustafa said.

"He always did have a keen eye for terrain." Mr. Wall chuckled. "Funny to think of him in that chapel, pretending to pray."

"He is … quite unlike you, Mr. Wall."

"Delicately put, Moustafa. What you mean to say is he is a foulmouthed, uncouth, uneducated, drunken lout. Guilty on all charges. He's also the best friend I ever had."

The best friend he ever had? While Moustafa had heard many men speak of the bond that war can build between people, could Timothy Crawford really be the best friend he ever had?

Moustafa wondered if Mr. Wall's madness had started before, or after, his terrible wound.

"It's a pity we didn't have a third pistol. I feel naked without my automatic," Mr. Wall grumbled.

"It's better for your friend to have it, since he's positioned inside," Moustafa said.

"Yes, I suppose so, and I can't hide that Webley unless I take on loose native clothing such as yours. It's such a bother."

Moustafa shook his head. He sounded like a young child who had forgotten a favorite toy.

"Well, at least I have my sword cane and the flash bombs," Mr. Wall said.

"Yes, Mr. Wall. At least you have those," Moustafa reassured him.

"Look at that," Mr. Wall whispered.

A pair of white men in inexpensive suits, their skin deeply tanned from long residence in Africa, approached the entrance to the chapel. They looked to be in their twenties. They glanced around briefly before going inside.

"That might be our friends," Mr. Wall said. The only other people they had seen enter in the last fifteen minutes was a middle-aged couple and a trio of elderly women. "But where's their watchman?"

"I don't know. Perhaps he's in here," Moustafa replied, checking out the other tables. Everyone seemed occupied with their own affairs. That meant nothing, though.

Mr. Wall left some coins on the table. "Let's go."

"Wait. I'll stay here for a minute and see if anyone follows you in."

"Good idea."

Moustafa studied him for a moment. "Are you sure you'll be all right?"

"Crawford and I have faced no shortage of danger together."

"I have no doubt, it's just that …"

"You mean I might go stark raving mad in the middle of an Anglican chapel? Entirely possible. But I have you along as nursemaid. See you in a minute."

Mr. Wall rose and left. Moustafa watched him go, thinking on his words.

Nursemaid. Maybe that's the true reason he wants me along on all these mad adventures. Not just for my strength and my languages, but to take care of him.

I'm his nursemaid. And so is Faisal.

Mr. Wall entered the church. A moment after he did so, an Egyptian strolled by on that side of the street, a young, tough looking fellow wearing a plain gray djellaba and carrying the small box of a shoe shiner.

Moustafa studied him. While most shoe shiners were boys, men were not unknown in their ranks, but something about this fellow seemed off.

Firstly, he walked with too much confidence, not the hunched humility of a poor man who served others for a living.

Secondly, he didn't come into the café, the obvious place to gain custom. Instead he squatted by the entrance to the church, keeping his box close in front of him.

If gambling wasn't a sin, I'd bet that box contained something other than shoe polish.

Moustafa waited another minute. No one else entered and the shoe shine fellow didn't move from his post. Taking a deep breath, Moustafa rose and moved out of the café. As he did so, he glanced at a mirror positioned by the door.

And caught a glimpse of an Egyptian in a cheap Western suit and tarboosh looking at him over his newspaper.

It was too late to do anything but continue on his way. Turning around would have made it obvious Moustafa suspected something, so he went through the door and cut to the left to get out of sight of the café's windows. He leaned against the wall. Next to him was a printer's shop, now closed.

He took the time to light a cigarette. Moustafa didn't actually like cigarettes. A sheesha in the evening was his pleasure, but working with Mr. Wall had taught him the value of having a prop as an excuse to linger.

Sure enough, the man in the tarboosh walked out, newspaper tucked under his arm. He stopped as he saw Moustafa glaring at him.

"Don't move." Moustafa said.

The man looked Moustafa up and down, taking in the glowering face and the impressive muscles born from a childhood of farming and an adulthood of archaeological excavation.

"I-I don't have much money on me."

"You know that's not what I'm after." Moustafa tore the newspaper from his grasp, thinking it hid a gun. But the man's hands were empty. He quickly patted him down as the man sputtered a panicked protest.

He had nothing on him.

"Who sent you?" Moustafa demanded, looming over him.

"W-what are you talking about?"

A passing Egyptian couple stared at them. Moustafa began to feel unsure of himself.

And then a movement out of the corner of his eye alerted him to the real danger.

The shoe shiner put his hand inside his box.

Moustafa sprang away from the man he had been questioning, hoping to get the poor fellow out of the line of fire.

He darted to the left, the man staring at him in astonishment.

Moustafa put his hand on the pistol in his pocket and saw the shoe shiner wasn't even looking at him. He had pulled out a cigarette.

Working with that madman has made me think like him, and act mad in public too!

He glanced at the man he had been questioning, and saw him scoop up his newspaper and hurry down the street, the tassel on his tarboosh wagging from side to side like the tail of a dog. Moustafa crossed the street, his gaze darting to the left and right. He saw no more suspicious characters, but felt sure this shoe shine man was more than he seemed. The cigarette meant nothing.

I better be right. I can't accuse two men in as many minutes. Someone will call the police.

The shoe shiner hunched low to shield his cigarette from the sea breeze blowing down the avenue. He struck a match to light it, tossed the match to the side, and hunched down a little lower.

Almost low enough for Moustafa to miss him putting his hand in the box again.

This time it came out with a snub-nosed revolver.

Moustafa whipped his gun out of his pocket to fire.

Or at least tried to. The Webley was a big gun with a six-inch barrel, and that barrel, or at least the top sight on it, got caught on the fabric of his djellaba.

The shoe shiner leveled his revolver. Desperate, Moustafa fired through his own pocket.

The bullet cracked off the stone wall of the church just above the shoe shiner's head. Although it missed, it made him flinch and his shot missed Moustafa by several inches, panging off the metal shutters of the closed print shop.

Moustafa didn't dare struggle to extricate his revolver. He didn't have time. Instead he fired another unaimed shot.

This one hit the wooden box, causing the shoe shiner to flinch and yelp. Moustafa got a brief glimpse of blood on the man's shin as he fired again.

This shot came closer, and once again ricocheted off the shutters.

Moustafa fired a third time. The shoe shiner slammed into the wall behind him, a dark red stain on the front of his djellaba.

Cursing, Moustafa finally yanked his gun out of his pocket and leveled it, but he had no need. The shoe shiner slumped against the wall, unmoving.

It was only then that Moustafa noticed everyone up and down the street screaming and running away.

So much for subtlety.

He bolted for the entrance to the church.

Then three things happened at the exact same time—he felt a burning sensation on his side, he heard the shrill sound of a police whistle, and he heard the sound of a shot inside.

As Moustafa kept running for the door, he looked down at the side.

He had thought he might have been grazed, but no, his djellaba was on fire! The powder burns from his own pistol must have set fire to the cloth.

Slapping the flames with his free hand, he managed to put them out as he barged through the front door, bowling over the elderly couple who had entered a few minutes before, and who were now fleeing the sound of further shots somewhere further inside the building.

"Excuse me!" Moustafa shouted, leaving a trail of smoke as he ran into the church.

He found himself in the nave. Candles and a few weak electric lights allowed him to see a modest Anglican church with a Gothic-style arch. Rows of pews took up much of the space. He spotted a couple of people crouched behind them, obviously hiding from the shots. Moustafa had entered at one end of the nave. At the other end stood the altar. Between him and the altar were two side chapels.

Another shot. Two figures burst out of the side chapel, running fast. One turned and fired behind him.

Moustafa crouched behind a pew. He saw they weren't Mr. Wall and Crawford, but at the same time he didn't recognize the man who had drawn a gun outside his shop. He hesitated, not wanting to fire at someone innocent, and hoping they would assume he was just another frightened churchgoer.

The two men ran in his direction, headed for the exit. Moustafa lowered his gun out of sight behind the back of the pew.

Crawford and a man in a hooded djellaba burst out of the side chapel. It took a moment for Moustafa to recognize the shoes and pants of Mr. Wall poking beneath the hem of the djellaba. Crawford fired at the fleeing men, his bullets cracking against the pews.

Now knowing his quarry, Moustafa raised up and aimed. The men were almost to the exit. Getting a bead on the one who was slightly ahead, he began to squeeze the trigger.

Just then, a panicked parishioner rushed out from his hiding place and ran for the door, getting in the line of fire. Moustafa growled in frustration and pulled up his gun.

The two gunmen disappeared out the door.

"After them!" Mr. Wall shouted.

Together they rushed to the door, only to have to leap back as a bullet thumped into the thick wood. They paused. Moustafa crouched low and peeked around the doorway, leading with his gun.

The two Australians were already halfway down the street.

A police whistle shrilled in the distance.

"Damn it!" Crawford shouted. "The law's coming."

"That's what happens when you have gunfights in churches," Moustafa grumbled.

"Next time we'll have to fight in a mosque then," Crawford said.

Moustafa shot him a look. The police whistle shrilled again, closer.

"We had best get going," Mr. Wall said. "I hope no one saw my distinctive feature."

"I don't think so," Moustafa said.

They walked out of the church past the man Moustafa had killed.

"Good job, Shaka Zulu," Crawford said, looking at the dead body.

"Maybe next time we'll get the whole lot."

The police whistle shrilled again. They hurried in the opposite direction, ducked down a side street lined with hotels and apartments, and slowed to a stroll, hoping no police would come this way. Mr. Wall pulled off the djellaba and put it in a bag Crawford had slung over his shoulder. Crawford pulled out an English workman's cap and put it on his head, as well as a light jacket. It wasn't much of a disguise, but hopefully enough to fool panicked witnesses.

Their luck held and they saw no police. They took a zigzag route back to the hotel.

"We pulled it off," Crawford said with a grin.

"No, we failed," Moustafa growled, clutching his djellaba so the giant hole in the side didn't cause a scandal.

"Got one," Crawford said. "We'll get the rest soon enough."

"It will be twice as difficult next time," Moustafa said, "because now they know we're after them."

CHAPTER FIFTEEN

Faisal had been right. The hotel man led him down to the cellar, where a series of little rooms opened onto a common room with a few cheap divans.

"Here you go," the Nubian said, opening the door to a room no bigger than his shack on the roof. Other than a bed and an electric light, it was entirely empty. There wasn't much room for anything else anyway. "There's a sink and toilet down the hall."

"I don't even get a window?" Faisal whined.

The Nubian raised his eyebrows. "Oh, His Majesty wishes a window! Would Your Highness prefer a sea view? Settle in and go see if your mistress needs anything."

With that, the hotel employee walked off. Faisal stuck his tongue out at him.

After bouncing his football off the walls and ceiling of his little room for a minute to make himself feel better, he headed back to Cordelia's room. It was a long climb up all those stairs, but he didn't dare take that lift thing. He had no idea how to use it and he probably wasn't allowed anyway.

Cordelia let him in and had him sit. Then she pointed to the telephone and said something. He understood the words "telephone," "hotels," and "Augustus."

So she was going to call him, or maybe call around the hotels to see where he was staying.

Faisal sat where he was told and watched as she picked up the phone, talking with someone. After a minute she hung up, then used the phone again.

He felt amazed at how easy it was for her. If he called around to all the hotels in Alexandria asking after a rich Englishman, they'd tell him to get off the phone, or say it was none of his business who stayed at their hotel. For Europeans, everything seemed easy.

After a few minutes, Cordelia put down the phone and smiled at him.

"Yes?" he asked.

"Yes."

Cordelia put on her hat, a big white thing that looked like a giant saucer with flowers on it, then put on a pair of white gloves. Then she picked up a parasol. Why did she need that if she already had that huge hat? Then she picked up the bag she kept all her medicines and bandages in.

"Are they hurt?" Faisal asked, forgetting to ask in English. He didn't know how to say that anyway.

Cordelia said something in a reassuring voice, then gave a little shrug. Faisal thought he understood. They weren't hurt yet, but they probably would be sooner or later. He was glad she came along. She might have another life to save before they found the murderer.

That made him shiver a bit.

They went down the lift again, making Faisal even more nervous, and crossed the front room of the hotel where Faisal felt like everyone stared at him. He walked a couple of steps behind Cordelia, feeling uncomfortable being with her but not wanting to look like he was alone.

He felt better once they got out onto the big square. He saw more Egyptians here. There was a stone fountain in the center gushing water high into the air. Tidy flowerbeds surrounded the fountain, gravel paths running between them.

They walked along one of the paths, Cordelia admiring the flowers and Faisal admiring the view of the bay. Who wants to look at flowers where there's a sea and big ships to look at? Faisal wished Mina was here. It would be nice to have someone to talk to about all the things he was seeing. She'd probably be more interested in the flowers too. Girls were like that.

A European man in a tan suit and hat walked toward them, looking at Cordelia. Faisal studied him. He didn't look like the man at the bookstore, but the way he stared at Cordelia made Faisal suspicious. Had they been found out already?

Faisal noticed he carried a walking stick with a big brass knob where you held it. He wondered if it had a sword hidden inside.

The man stopped, tipped his hat to Cordelia, and said, "Good afternoon."

"Good afternoon," Cordelia said, continuing to walk.

The man fell in beside her. Faisal was still a couple of steps back and the man didn't notice him at all.

The European started chatting to Cordelia in English and she replied. Soon they had struck up a conversation. He paused by some flowers, picked a red one and handed it to Cordelia, then picked a big purple one that he stuck in his buttonhole.

These Europeans can do anything. If I picked a flower a policeman would beat me.

They continued, the Englishman following her across the square and then crossing the seaside road, acting all important by holding up traffic so they could cross, like he was a policeman or something.

Faisal's suspicions grew. What did the fellow want?

They got onto the walkway along the Corniche, a broad paved area with a low wall separating them from the water. It was set a bit above the water, and Faisal could look down on it. A line of big stones ran along the Corniche down there, and several Egyptian men sat fishing just like on the Nile.

Now he could get a closer look at all the ships. There were small wooden boats that looked different from the feluccas and dahabiehs that sailed along the Nile. Egyptians were on these too, fishing further out in the harbor. There were also a couple of bigger ships, all steel and big funnels, and those two warships from which the British flag flew.

They were huge, with guns bigger than houses. He bet they could blow up the entire city. No wonder the British ruled over everything.

Faisal forced himself to look away from all the interesting things out in the water. He needed to find out what this man wanted.

He still walked alongside Cordelia, chattering away like an old friend. Cordelia didn't chatter back. Instead she looked straight ahead and barely said anything at all. The Corniche was busy with people, both Egyptians and Europeans. A few food stalls had been set up too, and Cordelia kept walking around groups of people or stalls, putting them between her and the man, but he kept right alongside her, asking her questions and that she gave short answers to, looking away from him while he stared at her, not noticing the amazing ships at all.

Cordelia began looking a bit annoyed. She was still smiling, but that smile had gotten stiff, like she had to tighten her muscles to keep it on her face. Faisal had seen her do that before, usually when Faisal did something to embarrass her in public.

She stopped and said something to the man that ended with "goodbye," but when she started walking again, he walked right alongside her. His voice changed, getting softer, almost whispering. Cordelia blushed.

Faisal got impatient. He hated being ignored. Thinking through what he needed to say in English, he quickened his steps to get between them. The man blinked and looked at Faisal, obviously noticing him for the first time.

"We go Englishman hotel?" Faisal asked Cordelia.

He did not expect the response he got.

Cordelia brought a hand to her mouth, turned bright red, and suddenly burst out laughing.

The man clouted him on the head, harder even than Moustafa when he was really mad.

Faisal ended up sprawled on the pavement.

Cordelia's laughter cut off, sharp. She shouted at the rude European, shaking her parasol at him while he sputtered something that sounded like he was defending himself. People started to gather.

Faisal picked himself up, rubbing his head. That really hurt!

An older European couple stopped, a pot-bellied man and a woman on his arm who had an even bigger hat than Cordelia's. They frowned at the rude European and said something to him in English. More people stopped to stare, both Europeans and Egyptians. The man said something that sounded like an apology, but Cordelia didn't look like she was impressed. She continued to shout at him. He backed off.

Faisal fumed. Did no one care that he just got knocked flat?

He spotted a little cart a few steps away. A boy a few years older than him had a metal grill filled with coals and was roasting corn. These carts were common along the banks of the Nile where people took evening strolls. Faisal hurried over like he often did when he saw one of the corn sellers. This time, it wasn't because he was hungry.

He plucked one of the corn cobs off the grill and, before it could burn his fingers, hurled it at the rude European.

Smack! Right in the face.

Everyone looked stunned for a second, the man especially. He had a big red mark on his face the shape of a corn cob. Then he let out a bellow, raised his walking stick in the air, and rushed for Faisal.

Ha! No one could catch him in a crowd. Faisal darted between the people, zigzagged around food stalls, jumped up on the little wall between the pavement and the water, gave the man a crude gesture, and jumped back into the crowd.

The rude European continued after him, losing ground.

Then Faisal realized he had made a mistake. He was running in the direction Cordelia had been going, which must be the direction of the Englishman's hotel.

His Englishman. Not this rude Englishman. He must be English if he spoke English. Faisal hoped they weren't staying at the same place.

He needed to get rid of this dummy, so Faisal slowed down, letting him catch up a bit, then darted into traffic, passing around a horse carriage and cutting in front of a motorcar.

The rude Englishman hesitated. Faisal made another crude gesture at him. A carriage driver shouted at him to get out of the road. Faisal ignored him.

Sure enough, that rude Englishman followed him into traffic. Sadly, no one ran him over. Faisal led him on a chase to the sidewalk on the far side of the street, then back the way they came.

By the time they got back to the square with the fountain, the rude Englishman lagged way behind, huffing and puffing and wiping sweat from his brow. Why did so many Europeans come here when they always complained about the heat?

Faisal lost him easily enough and circled back to find Cordelia not far from where he had left her. The older European couple was still with her. They looked at Faisal uncertainly, as if worried he'd throw a corn cob at them too. Cordelia said a few words to them and they went away.

"Hey!" someone shouted in Arabic.

Faisal turned to see the older boy with the corn grill.

"Sorry about stealing from you," Faisal said.

The boy laughed. "The look on his face was worth it! And that Englishwoman paid me for it. Five piastres! I couldn't believe it. Is that how much roast corn costs in Europe? I need to move there."

"Europeans don't know the prices of things," Faisal replied.

"They sure don't. Feel free to throw my corn at Europeans anytime."

"Um, all right."

Cordelia and Faisal walked along the Corniche for a minute. Faisal kept looking up at her. She had a funny expression on her face, both annoyed and a bit smiling at the same time.

"Mad Faisal?" he asked.

Cordelia smiled down at him, a better smile this time. "No."

"Mad Englishman?"

"Yes." Then she said some more in English he didn't understand. It sure sounded mad, though.

Faisal didn't know the word for corn, so he pantomimed throwing the corn cob and the man staggering back, clutching his face.

He thought Cordelia would laugh. Instead she stopped, bent down, and said, "Thank you, Sir Faisal."

Then she kissed him on the cheek.

Augh! What did she do that for?

They continued along the Corniche. Faisal wiped his cheek when she wasn't looking. That was gross, but kind of nice at the same time. Or maybe it was more nice than gross. He wasn't sure.

Cordelia stopped and pointed at a big stone building seven floors high. The bottom floor had arches with windows in them. The upper floors all had big windows too, and balconies so people could stand out and look over the harbor. A big British flag flew over the entrance, fluttering in the breeze and bright in the sun.

"Sir Augustus," Cordelia said.

Faisal laughed. The Englishman pretended he didn't like Europeans and he stayed at a hotel full of them, with a room looking out on British warships!

On second thought, that wasn't so funny. Tucked away in the old part of Cairo with only Egyptians for neighbors, it was easy for him to forget about Europe, but if he stayed here for a while with his own kind, he might start missing Europe.

Alexandria was where all the Europeans came and left. He could easily hop on a boat or a train and go back to Europe if he started feeling homesick.

Faisal couldn't let that happen.

Then he noticed something that made him worry even more.

Standing by the entrance to the hotel, smoking a cigarette, was the man who had shot at him.

Faisal ducked behind Cordelia just as a policeman stopped traffic to let people cross the street.

"What?" Cordelia asked him, realizing something was wrong.

"Man. Cigarette." Faisal ran his finger across his throat.

Cordelia looked across the street but didn't seem to see who he was talking about. Still, she seemed to get the message. She looked back at him, indecisive.

"Man ... " Cordelia waved a finger around Faisal's face. "Faisal?"

The crowd began to pass by them to cross the street. Was she asking if the killer would recognize him? Faisal nodded.

Cordelia thought for a moment, looking around, then her face lit up with an idea.

She opened up her parasol and handed it to him.

Faisal laughed. What a silly idea! But a good one too. Cordelia crossed the street, Faisal tagging along beside like he was a servant trying to shade his mistress with the parasol, but instead he used it to cover his own face.

They made it across the street and through the front door of the hotel with only a few people laughing at him.

Let them laugh. It was better than getting shot at.

Glancing uncertainly over his shoulder, Faisal could see through the glass door that the man still stood there, watching the street.

Faisal trembled. Someone would get shot before long. He just knew it.

CHAPTER SIXTEEN

Augustus sat with Timothy Crawford and Moustafa in his suite at the Windsor, busy planning their next move when they heard a knock at the door.

All three of them sprang into action. Tim got behind the door with the compact automatic, Moustafa moved behind the bureau with his revolver. Augustus, not having time to dig out his cache of weapons, satisfied himself by drawing his sword cane.

"Who is it?" he called through the door, while standing to one side in case his question got a bullet for a reply.

"It's Cordelia."

Augustus muttered an oath he hadn't spoken since his days in the trenches, making Moustafa gape, and opened the door.

Cordelia and Faisal walked in.

"What the devil are you two doing here?" Augustus demanded.

"Helping you solve the murder," Cordelia said in a smug voice. "Would you mind ever so much putting that sword away?"

"You'll do nothing of the sort," Augustus snapped, drowning out something Faisal tried to say. "You're getting on the next train back to Cairo."

Cordelia gave him a haughty expression. "And who are you to order me about?"

"I'll ring your brother."

I'd rather ring your neck.

"You certainly will not. You snuck up here just like I did."

"That won't stop me," Augustus said, once again drowning out Faisal, who was jumping up and down now.

"Well, if you're going to be uncivil, then we won't tell you about the man watching the hotel."

Augustus blinked. "The what?"

"The man watching the hotel. I believe that's what Faisal is trying to tell you. Either that or he needs the restroom."

Augustus turned to Faisal and switched to Arabic.

"What's this about a man watching the hotel?"

"That's what I was trying to tell you! He's the same man who was at Moustafa's shop."

Moustafa strode forward while Tim stood in the background, utterly confused.

"Are you sure?" the Nubian asked.

"Of course I'm sure. Hey! You're hurt."

Cordelia noticed the burned hole in Moustafa's djellaba at the same time and moved to the Nubian's side.

"Let me take a look at that. I brought my medical bag."

"It's nothing, madam," Moustafa said, bunching up the djellaba so his skin didn't show through.

"You look like you got a burn. I have some ointment for that. Now take off that djellaba and let me help you."

Moustafa looked scandalized. "Certainly not!"

Cordelia clucked. "I'm a nurse. You can't show me anything I haven't seen before."

Tim Crawford stepped forward. "Well, luvvie, I got a bit of a pain you might be able to help me with."

"Her brother is Cairo's chief of police," Augustus told him.

"Oh."

Tim retreated.

"And who is this?" Cordelia asked, frowning.

"An old war friend. A bit rough around the edges but he can be trusted. Tim, would you guard the lift and stairwell while I clear up this riot they've foisted on us?"

"Right." Tim watched as Cordelia took a bashful Moustafa into the bathroom. Then he turned to Augustus with a grin. "Sorry to sweet talk your bird, there, pal."

"She's not my bird, or any other member of the animal kingdom."

"Riiight." Tim looked down at Faisal. "So who's this, then?"

"This is Faisal."

"A nipper? You adopt him or something?"

"More like he adopted me."

"Well, he looks like he'll burst if he doesn't spill what he's got to say. I'm off."

"You have the automatic?"

"Of course."

"Try not to kill anyone on your way to the lift."

"I'll do me best."

Tim left. Augustus turned to Faisal, hands on hips. Faisal suddenly didn't look so sure of himself.

"Zehra sent me a cable informing me of your escape. How did you manage it?"

"I hid inside a crate with one of Suleiman's fake mummies inside."

Augustus felt tempted to inform him that Suleiman made his fake mummies with real human bones, then decided against it. He didn't want to give the boy nightmares.

"Didn't I tell you specifically not to follow me up here?"

"You can't solve murders without me."

"I happened to have solved one up here before."

Faisal stared. "How did you come up here without me knowing?"

"It was before I moved to Cairo. I lived here for a time. A mistake. I also made a mistake thinking you'd be obedient. I give you a roof over your head, plenty of food, and pocket money, and you don't listen to a word I say!"

Augustus tried to sound angrier than he was. Faisal grinned, not fooled. "What you're really mad about is that I brought Cordelia with me."

"That certainly doesn't help matters."

"She's useful. She's helping Moustafa right now. And she helped me get up here and find you."

"Yes, I'll have to have a word with her about that."

Faisal plopped down on the loveseat, looking around. "Is there any food?"

"Not for disobedient little boys there isn't."

"That's all right. We can get something later. So what have you found out so far? And how did Moustafa get hurt?"

"None of your business what we've found out. I can't have you on this case."

"But I found the spy for you!"

"Yes, we'll deal with him in a minute."

"Oh! I nearly forgot. Some Englishman was bothering Cordelia. He might be a spy too. I threw a corn cob at him to make him go away."

"You could have been shot."

"No. He was stupid."

"You shouldn't go around throwing things at people."

"I had to. What about that spy at the door? Did that other Englishman go down to kill him?"

"His name is Tim Crawford. I didn't ask him to do so but it's entirely possible he did anyway."

"How did Moustafa get hurt? Did I miss a gunfight?"

"You did miss a gunfight." The boy looked relieved. "Moustafa got his pistol tangled in his pocket and he had to fire with it still inside. The powder burned his djellaba and his skin."

Faisal put his hand over his mouth to hide his smile. He glanced at the bathroom.

"You better stop laughing before he comes back out here," Augustus said.

"All right Englishman, but you have to admit it's funny."

Ignoring that, Augustus asked, "Do you think that man followed you here?"

"No, I would have noticed him on the train or as we walked over here. We're staying at a big building just like this. It's got a lift and gold doors and everything!"

"Please try to stay on topic. So are you quite sure he's waiting out front?"

"Yes."

"Go out to the balcony and peek down. See if he's still there."

"If he looks up he'll see me. He might know I'm with you and that will tell him what room you're in."

"He can always ask that. The front desk was quite accommodating with Cordelia's enquiry," Augustus grumbled.

"Yes, but he doesn't want you to know he's out there. He probably knows you'll ask if anyone has been asking after you."

"Hmm. You have a point."

Faisal brightened. "See, you can't solve these mysteries without me! You have to keep me around, even if someone gets murdered in England."

"What's this about murders in England?"

Faisal looked everywhere but at him. "Well, um, I suppose people get murdered in England too. If someone gets murdered there you'll need my help. Are there djinn in England?"

"Stop talking nonsense. Here, I have a way of keeping you out of sight."

Augustus went to the closet and fetched his munitions bag. From it he retrieved a small trench periscope. It was a compact model that could be collapsed like a telescope to a size that could easily fit in a large pocket.

"What's that?" Faisal asked, bouncing off the loveseat and walking over.

"It's a periscope. See how it opens? Now look through here. It allows you to see around corners."

"What? Wow! This is great. Why haven't you shown me this before?"

Faisal turned this way and that, bending and twisting so he could look all around. He tried to walk while looking through the eyepiece and stumbled against the coffee table.

"Do your best not to kill yourself. Now what I want you to do is to lie on the balcony and poke the end of the periscope over the edge. Then you can look down and see him. Make sure you only put the very end over the edge. We're high up enough there's little chance of him noticing, even if he's looking up."

"Do I get to keep it?"

"That depends on if you behave yourself and actually do as you're told for once."

"I always do what I'm told," Faisal said, skipping over to the glass door to the balcony.

"You have a rather loose interpretation of reality."

Augustus eased open the glass door just enough so the boy could worm through on his belly. Grinning, Faisal crawled through and peeked over with the periscope. He turned it for a moment, getting used to the strange way of seeing, before finally spotting his quarry.

"He's still there."

"Is he looking up?"

"No, he's looking around the street."

Augustus opened the door further, got on his belly and crawled out onto the balcony.

Out into No Man's Land, crawling on his belly through a gap cut in the wire.

NO.

"You all right, Englishman?"

Faisal was giving him a worried look.

"Quite all right. Just feeling a bit foolish in this ridiculous position."

"Were you going away in your head?"

"No. Show me where he is."

"You don't have to be embarrassed by it."

"Let's focus on what's important, eh?" Augustus snapped.

Augustus took the periscope and with Faisal's direction spotted the man watching the door several floors below. Looking at him from above,

Augustus could only see his slouch hat and a cheap but decent suit. The man turned to look to the right and left regularly, keeping watch on the entire street.

"Why isn't he watching from the Corniche?" Augustus mused. "He'd get a better view and would be less conspicuous."

"Maybe he wants to meet you," Faisal suggested.

Cordelia and Moustafa emerged from the bathroom.

"Are you boys having fun?" Cordelia asked.

"No," Augustus replied, crawling back into the room. Faisal followed.

"Are you all right?" Augustus asked the Nubian.

"Much better, Mr. Wall, thanks to Miss Russell."

"The burn isn't too bad," the nurse said. "More painful than dangerous. I put some salve and a bandage on it."

"And sewed up his djellaba, I see."

Indeed, the gaping hole had been repaired, although so much material had burned away that one side of his garment had a bunched-up look to it. The poor fellow would have to go shopping as soon as possible.

"Where's Tim?" Moustafa asked, looking around.

"Guarding the lift and stairs."

Moustafa glanced at Faisal, who sat on the loveseat next to Cordelia's hat and parasol. "What are you giggling about?"

Faisal put on an innocent face. "Nothing."

Moustafa checked his revolver, now transferred to the other pocket. "I'll go join Tim."

"Try not to set yourself on fire," Augustus said. Faisal giggled again.

"I'll do my best, Mr. Wall."

As soon as Moustafa closed the door behind him, Augustus rounded on Cordelia.

"It's not decent for you to be in my suite."

"I am well aware of the bonds of decency, Augustus, but it is indecent to force a woman out into the street when there's danger lurking."

"There wouldn't be any danger lurking if you had stayed in Cairo. Faisal said a man accosted you on the street."

"Not one of the murderers. Simply a pest."

"Yes, Alexandria seems full of them."

"I will ignore that remark seeing as you need my help," she went on calmly. Augustus didn't like her tone. It was like she was patiently explaining a simple matter to a thick child.

"We most certainly do not need your help," Augustus replied.

"You might want to ask Moustafa for his opinion."

"Your medical services are much appreciated. Now kindly go back to Cairo where you belong."

Cordelia gave him such a strong look he almost took a step back.

"I *belong* wherever I am."

"Why do you insist on running about and putting yourself into danger?"

Cordelia's mood immediately lightened. She gave him a coy smile. "Come now, don't you know? Can't you see? For the same reasons you do."

"It wasn't your friend who got murdered," Augustus grumbled. The cheek of this woman!

At least they were speaking in English. Faisal watched, all eyes and ears, but thankfully did not comprehend.

Cordelia's smile turned sympathetic. "No. This case is different for you. But the other cases weren't personal and you chased down the murderers all the same. You did it because you wanted the excitement, the action. You wanted to be at the center of things. I don't know what your life was like before the war, Augustus, but I suspect it was much like mine. Comfortable. Pleasant. And you didn't give a thought to how excruciatingly dull it was until you got thrust into world-shattering events and a very different mode of living."

"I scarcely think squatting knee-deep in mud and getting shot at counts as living."

Cordelia's eyes got a faraway look. "Or being elbow deep in blood as the artillery pounded all too close to the hospital. Or cringing as German planes buzzed over the building, strafing the ambulances and dropping bombs despite the giant red crosses we had painted everywhere. It was horrible. I felt frightened and sickened every minute I was there and only duty to country and those poor suffering men kept me at my post, and yet when my prayers were answered and the Armistice was signed and we all got home, I found myself wishing I was back."

Augustus bowed his head. Yes, it had been much like that for him. He thought himself mad for thinking so. He had thought perhaps he was trying to relive events and have them turn out differently. But again and again he had met men who had not suffered as much as he had who felt the same.

And now he had met a woman who felt the same.

Cordelia went on, gazing out the window.

"So I returned to Abingdon and found myself at a loose end. I volunteered at the Radcliffe Infirmary and while I found some satisfaction in my work it wasn't truly fulfilling. I realized that even though I now had an occupation, I was still living much the same dull, predictable life I had been before the war. I thought travel would stimulate me. Aunt Pearl, who has spent much of her life traveling, offered to take me to Egypt. That helped for a time, but soon I found myself in the same dreary routine of dinners, walks, and tea dances that I had been in before."

"We are excellent at recreating England wherever we go. That's why I live in the native quarter."

Cordelia glanced around the room as if in accusation and said, "That was not an option for me. I began to despair, until I had the good fortune to be abducted by French anarchists."

"I have apologized a hundred times for that and I do so again."

Cordelia laughed. "I was not being sarcastic, Augustus. It was terrifying, of course, and yet it was the most alive I had felt since November of 1918. And I got to meet such interesting people—you and Moustafa, and this delightful little boy. Don't play with that."

Cordelia plucked her hat out of Faisal's hands. He had put one hand in the cap portion and had been flipping the brim to make it spin like a top.

Putting it on her head, she said, "You are correct that it is indecent for me to be in your suite unchaperoned. Although Faisal has proved quite capable in protecting me from unwanted advances, prying eyes would not think so. I care about my reputation, so I will retreat to the rooftop restaurant

I saw advertised on a sign in the lobby. I will wait there until you need me."

"You might be waiting for some time," Augustus said without heat.

Cordelia lifted up her bag with a significant motion, plucked her parasol from Faisal, who had been aiming it like a rifle, and departed.

Augustus let out a sigh of relief.

"Should I go with her?" Faisal asked.

"No. She'll only get herself in more trouble and you're best out of it."

Faisal leapt off the loveseat. "If she gets in trouble I need to be there to help her. What if that spy who stopped her in the street comes back?"

"He wasn't a spy. He simply wanted to, um, show her the sights."

"Like a tour guide?"

"Something like that."

"Maybe I should go with her just in case."

Augustus stopped him before he went out the door. "Wait. I have a job for you right here. It's time to stop all this sneaking about. Do you remember how to use the telephone?"

Faisal brightened. "Sure!"

"Good boy. Now you stay here with the periscope and keep an eye on our Australian friend. I'm going down to the lobby and I'll ring you." Augustus reached into his pocket and picked out several small coins.

"Thanks, Englishman. I was almost out of money."

"They're not for spending. They're for throwing."

"Throwing? Oh! You want me to distract the Australian so you can sneak out of the hotel?"

"Almost. We'll come up behind him and stick him up, as the Americans in those gangster movies you like always say. Now I'm going to go down to the lobby. Tim, Moustafa, and I will stay out of sight of the front door. I'll ring you to make sure he's still out there and then you'll start throwing coins to get him to look up. Make sure you're not seen."

"I'm good at that."

"Not good enough. I shouldn't be seeing you here in Alexandria."

"But I'm useful!" Faisal whined.

"Yes, and also stubborn. Here, take the coins."

Faisal looked at them. "Wouldn't it be better if I go down to the street and distract him?"

"Risk your life to pocket a few piastres? No. I've put you in enough danger as it is. I can't risk you getting hurt again."

Faisal paled. "I … I won't get hurt."

"You won't get hurt because you'll stay up here and do as you're told for once."

Faisal hesitated for a moment, then said. "All right, Englishman, but if I see you in trouble I'll come down."

"Very well," Augustus said, heading out the room. As he got into the corridor he said quietly to himself, "If this fellow is too quick for us, my boy, it will all be over before you have a chance to make it to the street."

CHAPTER SEVENTEEN

Moustafa waited in the lobby, just out of sight of the glass doors. From his vantage point he could see Tim sitting in an armchair pretending to read a newspaper and hidden from view of the doors by a column. Mr. Wall stood at the concierge's desk at the back of the lobby.

Mr. Wall put down the phone and nodded. Moustafa walked toward the door, passing Tim. He did not look at him, and sensed he did not need to. If that crude little man had survived four years in the trenches, he knew how to handle a situation like this.

As Moustafa got to the glass doors, he saw the man in the slouch hat jerk his head in the opposite direction, as did the liveried doorman standing nearby. Faisal had done his job.

Moustafa opened the door just as another coin pinged off the sidewalk. The Australian looked up. Moustafa resisted the urge to do the same. The Little Infidel would have ducked back out of sight anyway.

The Australian didn't even notice Moustafa until he grabbed his right hand and shook it.

"How nice to see you again, my Australian friend!"

The man's eyes widened. His left hand went for his pocket.

Just then Tim moved in behind him.

"Good to see you, mate!" he said for the doorman's benefit, then continued in a whisper. "Make a move and I'll plug you. Act nice and walk in with us."

The man stiffened, then took on a relaxed air.

"Good to see you too," he said, his voice barely wavering.

This man is used to danger and shows no fear when a gun is pointed at him. Why is it I'm always meeting people like this?

The oblivious doorman bowed and opened the door for them, and the three of them entered the lobby—Moustafa first, then their prisoner, followed by Tim.

"No need for rough stuff," the Australian said in a low voice as they walked through the lobby. "I'm on your side."

"Were you on my side when you were firing your gun outside my bookshop?" Moustafa growled.

"No. Things have changed since then."

Crawford snorted. "Bloody right things have changed, you Aussie bastard. We got you now."

They got in the lift, standing still and quiet as the operator pulled the lever to bring them to the proper floor. Tim shuddered as the doors closed, his eyes widening and casting looks all about him as if he were trapped in a cage. Moustafa stared at him a moment until Crawford noticed, gave him a scowl, and tried to compose himself. Moustafa turned back to the Australian, focusing on him instead.

Why is he afraid of a simple thing like a lift? This man doesn't appear to fear anything else in the world.

When the doors opened, Tim practically leapt out. The Australian followed with Moustafa right behind him. Once the lift moved back down and they walked a bit down the hallway, where they saw no one about, Moustafa patted the Australian down.

"Where's your gun?" Moustafa asked.

"They took it," the Australian said.

"Why did you put your hand in your pocket then?"

"A bluff."

"Who took your gun? Why?"

"My mates. Or who pretended to be my mates. I want to talk with the man in the mask."

"Tell me what's going on," Moustafa growled.

"Take me to your boss and you'll hear."

Moustafa was about to reply when Tim nudged him. A servant walked down the hallway, his slippers making no sound as he passed across the thick carpeting.

"Very well," Moustafa said. "He wanted to speak with you anyway."

They took him to Mr. Wall's room, where they found him waiting. Faisal sat on the loveseat, going pale when he saw the man who had almost killed him.

The side of Mr. Wall's face visible behind his mask turned up in a wry smile.

"Well, well, well, we might have a solution to this riddle at last."

"He didn't have a weapon on him," Crawford said, closing the door behind him. "Said his mates took it."

"How odd." Mr. Wall sounded intrigued.

The Australian glanced at Faisal. "Is he the one I almost hit?"

"Shouldn't you remember the face of a child you almost killed?" Mr. Wall asked, picking up his sword cane and grasping the pommel. He looked about to draw it.

"All the Gippos look the same to me. I was shooting at the copper, not the kid."

"I'll be sure to inform him of that, but I doubt he'll forgive you. I certainly don't."

"Neither do I," Moustafa said, pushing the prisoner into an armchair. "Tell us what's going on."

The Australian made a confident smile and reached into his pocket for a packet of cigarettes.

"Start talking or I'll throw you out the bloody window," Crawford said, drawing close to him.

"Not if I do it first," Moustafa added, hemming their prisoner in on the other side.

The Australian seemed unphased by this remark. He lit his cigarette, crossed his legs, and said, "You're looking for the treasure just like the rest of us."

"And what treasure would that be?" Mr. Wall asked.

"Don't act cute. You know. The tomb of Alexander the Great."

Moustafa felt a tingle go through his body. Until this man said it, he hadn't quite believed.

Now he knew it was true. But could they really have a clue to the location of archaeology's most important lost tomb?

"So why are you here?" Moustafa asked. "You didn't bring a weapon and it seemed like you wanted to attract attention."

"I did. I want to join your side."

"Join us? After you nearly killed an officer of the law outside my shop?"

The Australian grinned. "Fair play, you're angry, but I think you'll change your tune when I lead you to the treasure."

"You don't know where it is," Moustafa scoffed.

"Not yet," he conceded. "But the lads are close, so close they all got to arguing about shares and who deserved how much. Day before yesterday I argued a bit more than what's good for me, and they threw me out on my ear, taking my gun while they were at it."

"Did they kick anyone else out?" Moustafa asked.

"Two others. The rest of the lads got us boat tickets to send us off back home. That was our parting gift, like that would be enough. They made us get on the boat and watched to see we stayed on it. I bribed a couple of natives to put me in an empty steamer trunk and carry me off, right under their noses!"

"It's a good thing you didn't shoot that boy over there," Mr. Wall said, lighting a cigarette. "You two have much in common. So have all of you been mustered out?"

"I have. Some of the others. Some are still here on guard duty thanks to the natives all drumming up trouble over British rule."

Wanting to rule your own country doesn't count as drumming up trouble, Moustafa thought. He kept that to himself as the man continued.

THE CASE OF THE ASPHYXIATED ALEXANDRIAN

"We're getting close, and I can lead you to the dig site. We've been good at hiding it, so you won't find it without me."

"You mean we won't find it without the map you stole from my friend, after you murdered him," Mr. Wall said.

"I didn't kill him."

"But you were part of the gang who did. You're lucky I don't let this human hand grenade of an ex-Tommy kill you with his bare hands. I've seen him do it. An unlovely sight, even when performed on Germans. I'm tempted to do you in myself. I've watched his technique."

The Australian raised his hand. "Easy there, mate. I wasn't the one who done him."

"Perhaps not. While you are certainly fit, the man who killed Gregory had immense physical strength. You could have been the man who held his arms, though."

The Australian shook his head. "It wasn't me, I swear."

"Who was it, then?" Moustafa asked.

The Australian jutted out his chin at him. "I'll tell you if we make a deal."

Moustafa let out a bitter laugh. "As if you're trustworthy!"

"I didn't have to come here."

"You only want money."

"Of course I do. But I'll help your English pal get his revenge, and you'll help me find the tomb, and we'll all be richer in the bargain."

Moustafa blinked. It was the first time a foreigner had referred to his former boss as his friend. While they were certainly not friends, it was nice to have someone assume he was something other than a servant.

Mr. Wall stepped forward, fiddling with his sword cane, which he had still not drawn.

"You can't find the treasure, can you? You have the map but not the key."

The man's jaw dropped. "How did you ... oh, the key was hidden, was it? My mates only got half the puzzle."

"The key was memorized. The perfect hiding place," Mr. Wall said, telling only half the truth.

"Where is the map?" Moustafa demanded.

"With them. I was never allowed to see it. I was just a private, you see, and it's the officers that run the show. Same as in the army. And they stiffed us, same as in the army."

Moustafa frowned. "Do your friends have names? Do you?"

The Australian looked him up and down. "They're not my friends, and I'll tell you their names if we make a deal. But here are my conditions. I get an equal share of the treasure, and you hide me from them. I give you instructions to where they are and what they're doing, but I don't want them knowing I'm still here, you see? They're a nasty lot. And once we find the treasure and split it evenly, you let me get out of Egypt with no trouble."

Moustafa and Mr. Wall looked at each other. Moustafa stayed silent. It was Mr. Wall's friend who got murdered, so it was his decision.

"Very well," Mr. Wall said at last. "We have an agreement. But if I find you are the killer, or helped the killers directly in any way, your life is mine."

The man in the slouch hat did not seem overly worried about this. "You'll get your men."

"So what are their names?"

"There's seven Aussies. They've hired five Gippos. I don't know the names of the Gippos. They gave names, but they lied, I'm sure of it."

"So what are the names of your associates?" Moustafa asked, growing impatient.

The man in the slouch hat gave him a gap-toothed grin. "Lieutenant, Captain, Master Sergeant, Corporal One, Corporal Two, Private One, and Private Two."

Moustafa grabbed him by the lapels and shook him.

"Don't play games with us. Give us their names!"

The man's grin only widened. "Those are the only names I know. We didn't go by real names. I was Private Three."

Moustafa's hand balled into a fist. "Tell me your real name before I knock your teeth out."

Private Three glanced at Mr. Wall. "You're seeing the new Egypt here, mate. You toffs mucked up your colonies like you mucked up the war."

"Answer his question," Mr. Wall said.

"Private Jack Turner. Formerly 3rd ANZAC Engineering Regiment. Got mustered out late last year, along with most of the rest of the gang. The Lieutenant pulled some strings and got us work permits to stay here so we could search for the tomb. Said we were working on a water pump at a private estate."

"This lieutenant, if he got you the work permit you must know his name."

Jack Turner shook his head. "The name on the permit is of a rich Alexandrian family. They got an estate west of town. That's where we sleep while we're searching for the tomb, and it's on their land we're supposed to be building the water pump."

"You're going to show us this place," Moustafa said.

"All right. We can take the tram most of the way, then walk. But don't get so quick with your guns like you did outside. It's a family living there."

"You're one to talk," Moustafa said, pointing to Faisal, who had grown bored and was playing with Mr. Wall's trench periscope.

"I told you I wasn't aiming for him. He got in the way."

"Let's go," Mr. Wall said. "We'll take a look at the place from a distance and then try to get in at night. Are there dogs?"

"No dogs. You know how the Gippos don't like dogs."

"All the better. Let's go."

Moustafa raised a hand. "Wait, Mr. Wall." He turned to Jack. "You said most of you have been mustered out. Who among you hasn't?"

"The Master Sergeant. When the 3rd ANZAC got sent home, the 4th ANZAC Engineering Regiment took over our work. Bloody useless. The Master Sergeant had some specialist knowledge about building railway bridges and volunteered to be seconded to the 4th."

"In order to keep an eye on what they were doing, and what might turn up."

"That's right."

Moustafa's brow furrowed. "Wait. If he's still in the army you must have seen him in uniform. You'd know his name because it's sewn on his shirt."

The man paused for a second. "He always changes into civvies before meeting us."

Moustafa locked eyes with him. He sensed this fellow was lying, perhaps about many things, but also sensed that the only way to wring the truth out of him would be torture, and that was something Moustafa could only threaten to do.

Mr. Wall put on his hat and twirled his sword cane.

"Come," he said. "The day is wasting. Let's take a look at this country estate for treasure hunters."

CHAPTER EIGHTEEN

Faisal really needed to learn more English. He had to sit, bored out of his mind, as they talked with the man who almost shot him. Faisal knew better than to interrupt, because the Englishman and Moustafa never explained anything to him until they felt like it.

When they finally did explain everything, he felt better. If they had to check out a house in the daytime, it was only because they would want him to break in at night. He was still useful.

They walked out of the hotel room. More talking in English, and this time no explanation. Why couldn't they all talk in Arabic?

And then he had to ride the lift down. Even worse than getting into that strange moving room was being crowded in there with that gunman. Tim was smart and took the stairs.

The Englishman must have seen Faisal shrinking away because he said,

"Oh, Faisal, our new friend told me to apologize on his behalf for nearly shooting you. He was aiming for the policeman."

"Is he sorry he nearly shot me or sorry you caught him?"

The Englishman smiled. "Cheeky boy. He wanted us to catch him, like I told you. I think he really is sorry he put you in danger."

Was the Englishman sorry for putting him in danger all the time? Maybe that's why Faisal got so many moving picture shows and big meals.

"I don't trust him," Faisal said.

"For once I agree with the Little Infidel," Moustafa grumbled.

"I don't trust him either," the Englishman said, "but I trust his greed. Besides, he's our only solid lead."

Once they got on the street, the Englishman turned to him.

"Moustafa and I are going with this chap to check on something. I want you to stay here with Tim."

"Don't you need our help?"

"Not at the moment. Tim is a bit too hotheaded for this sort of work, and we don't need your particular skills in the daytime."

"You can't be sure."

"I want to keep you out of danger." When Faisal opened his mouth to object, the Englishman added, "Don't worry, I'll fetch you when I need your help."

"What about Cordelia?"

The Englishman tried to hide a smile but didn't do a very good job. "We'll leave her in the upstairs restaurant for a few years."

Faisal grinned. "You're so mean to her. I don't think she likes you anymore."

"God, I hope not. Will you stay with Tim? We should only be a couple of hours."

Faisal shrugged. "All right, Englishman."

"Good boy," the Englishman said, making Faisal smile.

He turned to Tim and switched to English. After they talked, the Englishman and Moustafa left with the man in the slouch hat.

Faisal and Tim stared at each other uncertainly for a moment. What was he supposed to do with someone he couldn't even speak to? Well, he couldn't really speak to Cordelia either, but he'd known her for a while. Tim was a stranger.

Tim looked around and said something in English, pointing to a place across the street. Faisal shrugged and followed him.

It was one of those big European cafés, with columns and chandeliers and waiters in stiff white shirts. European waiters! He'd only seen European waiters in moving pictures.

Faisal stopped at the door. He couldn't go in there. Sure, he saw a few Egyptians sitting inside along with all the Europeans, but rich Egyptians with Western suits and gold watches. This was no place for him.

"Come on!" Tim said, dragging him across the threshold.

They found a table and sat. A waiter came and stopped right by Faisal's chair, looking down his long, straight nose at him. Faisal wilted. They were going to get kicked out for sure.

Well, *he* was going to get kicked out.

Tim said something in English. The waiter looked down his nose at him too.

That was surprising. Waiters weren't supposed to do that to Europeans. Maybe European waiters were allowed.

Tim repeated what he said, loudly and slowly, pointing at himself and Faisal. The waiter walked away so stiffly it looked like Karim the watchman had put his stick somewhere bad. The thought of it made Faisal giggle.

Tim grinned and said something, punching Faisal in the arm.

Ow! Faisal tried to show it didn't hurt. While Tim acted friendly, he didn't have to be so rough.

The waiter returned with two big cakes. There was chocolate and cream and all sorts of other things Faisal didn't recognize. He set them down with a thump and walked away.

"Thank you," Faisal said. He just managed to remember to say it before he took the first forkful. That was hard to remember with a big cake in front of you.

"You're welcome, little Gippo," Tim said.

The waiter walked by, not bothering to even look at them. Faisal didn't care. He had cake.

Tim leaned over and pointed to himself. "English."

"Yes," Faisal nodded. "English."

Tim pointed at the waiter. "French."

"Oh, French." That explained it. The Englishman had talked about the French. They didn't like the English. He said the French had never forgiven the English for saving them from the Germans.

That seemed pretty ungrateful.

"Frog," Tim said, whatever that meant. "Ribbit."

Faisal stared. "Frogribbit?"

Was that even a word?

"Ribbit," Tim said, saying it low in his throat like he was belching.

Faisal could do better than that. "Rrrrribbit!"

Tim seemed impressed. They ate more cake and kept saying ribbit, especially when the waiter walked by. The waiter didn't look too happy about it but he could see Tim was tough.

Faisal could tell him a thing or two. If Tim's play punches hurt so much, imagine what his real punches felt like.

At last the cake was done and they leaned back in their chairs, their bellies full. Tim let out a belch. The rich European couple at the next table frowned at him. He blew them a kiss.

Faisal giggled again. Tim was as crazy as his own Englishman. Were all Englishmen crazy?

Tim gestured to Faisal and made a belching sound. Faisal stared. Tim repeated the gesture, thinking Faisal didn't understand.

But he did. Did an adult really want him to belch in a café?

Faisal looked to the left and the right. That European couple was still frowning, and the frogribbit waiter stood close by. Faisal got the giggles.

"Go on," Tim said, laughing.

Faisal let rip the biggest, throatiest belch he had ever made. Everyone turned and stared. Faisal and Tim cackled with laughter.

Faisal drummed his feet on the floor, laughing his head off. While everyone looked grumpy, the frogribbit waiter especially, no one said anything. No one wanted to get Tim angry. Faisal was safe as long as he was with him. Nothing could touch him. He let out a second belch and laughed some more.

Faisal pointed to the cake. "How say in English?"

It was an important word.

"Cake."

"Cake tomorrow?"

"Yerdamnrite, little Gippo!"

Faisal blinked. Was that a yes?

"Yes," Tim said slowly and clearly. "Cake tomorrow."

Faisal grinned a chocolatey grin. Tim leaned back, belched, and lit a cigarette.

Once Tim finished his cigarette, he pulled out some coins and rapped one against the marble table until the frogribbit waiter came, all snooty and looking down at them. Faisal belched. Tim gave him a wink, said something to the waiter that sounded rude, and paid.

They left, everyone looking glad to see them go, and walked along the Corniche for a while. Tim seemed happy. He kept talking about the Englishman, calling him "Sir Augustus" and laughing. He must have known that Sir Augustus was a false name the Englishman lived under so everyone in Europe left him alone. Tim also mentioned another name, and from the way he said it and the words "France" and "Germans," Faisal knew this was someone from the war.

Tim fascinated Faisal. He was so different than the Englishman, all loud and pushy, but he was kind of the same too. Every now and then he'd grow quiet and look out over the water, and his face would change. Just for a second, he'd look like the Englishman did so often. Sad and angry at the same time.

And like the Englishman, he would remember himself and put his face back to normal, laughing to cover himself.

One time he didn't. A soldier came along, limping badly and using a cane. He had a patch on one eye and kept one hand in his pocket. A lot of wounded soldiers did that when they had lost fingers. Faisal had seen that plenty of times in Cairo.

Faisal looked at Tim, and just as he thought Tim had that dark look the Englishman got sometimes. As the soldier hobbled past them, Tim whispered, "Poor bugger."

What did that mean? Faisal thought he might know.

"Poor buddar," Faisal said.

"Poor bugger," Tim corrected, managing a smile.

"Sir Augustus poor bugger?"

Tim nodded, his face going dark again. "Yes."

"Tim good friend Sir Augustus."

"Damn right."

"Damrite?"

"Yes."

"Faisal good friend Sir Augustus."

Tim cracked a grin. "Damn right!" he punched Faisal on the shoulder.

Ow! He knew that had been meant to be playful, but it hurt! He sure was strong. Maybe even stronger than Moustafa. When Tim looked out over the harbor again, Faisal rubbed his arm. He didn't want Tim to think he was weak.

He thought through the English words to ask Tim the main question on his mind.

"Tomorrow Tim go England?"

"Tomorrow?" Tim laughed, and said something Faisal didn't understand.

No, tomorrow wasn't the right word. That meant *bokra* and they wouldn't have solved this murder by *bokra*. How did you say *baed ghad*?

Faisal waved his hand. "No. Tomorrow tomorrow."

"Later," Tim said loudly and clearly.

"Later," Faisal repeated.

Tim grabbed his shoulder and shook it, saying something encouraging. At least it sounded encouraging. He was smiling, anyway. When Moustafa shook him like that he was always shouting. Tim sure had a strange way of showing he liked someone.

"Um, Tim go England later?"

"Yes."

Faisal paused, summoning up his courage. "Sir Augustus go England later?"

Tim looked thoughtful, shrugged his shoulders, and said something Faisal didn't understand.

But it made him tremble and get a sick feeling inside.

"No?" Faisal asked.

Tim repeated what he had said, clearly and slowly, as if Faisal would magically understand the words if he did that.

"Yes?"

Tim repeated the same thing again.

So not a no and not a yes. That meant maybe.

That meant Tim would try to get the Englishman to go back to England with him, but wasn't sure if he could manage to.

But he would try, and he was the Englishman's old war friend, maybe his best friend in the whole world. He could probably convince him. Maybe he would even find mysteries for the Englishman to solve back home. Tim probably met lots of people who got murdered. He seemed like that kind of person.

The Englishman was going to leave!

Tim took him more places and they did more things that day, but it was all a blur.

CHAPTER NINETEEN

The house stood on several feddans of land just outside the western fringes of Alexandria. Being at the mouth of the Nile Delta, the land here was moist and green, most of it given over to the cultivation of grain. A breeze blew in from the Mediterranean that somewhat offset the heat of the sun.

The house was a large, rambling whitewashed structure of two stories, with balconies looking out over the sea and surrounding land. Its flat roof was enclosed with a low wall in the Egyptian style, allowing the women of the family could enjoy the sun without being seen. The bottom floor was obscured by an ugly concrete wall topped with broken glass that glinted in the sun. While it marred the view of the house, it added a good deal of security.

The house stood alone, surrounded by open fields except to the west where a date palm grove offered some shelter for an approach. Several other farmhouses stood within sight.

"This is going to be a tough nut to crack," Augustus said. They sat in a hired carriage two-wheeled with the top up, that and the leather sides hiding them from view. Augustus peeked out, the shade against the harsh brightness of the Mediterranean sun hiding him further.

"The master of the house has a lot to hide," Jack Turner told them.

"Tell me about him." Augustus glanced at the driver, sitting up front with his whip, wearing a gray djellaba and a dirty yellow turban. While Augustus had already determined the man spoke almost no English, he still felt nervous talking to his companions with him sitting so close.

"He's a big landowner named Mahmoud Naguib. Has his fingers in a lot of pies. I know he smuggles, and I think he does a lot of other things besides."

Augustus noted the side gate and the lorry tracks going to and from it.

"He gets shipments by lorry?"

"That's right."

"When do they come?" Moustafa asked.

"All times of the day and night, mostly night. I never saw a pattern to them. You thinking of hopping on the back of one and getting in there?"

Augustus and Moustafa exchanged glances. That was exactly what Augustus was thinking. It looked like Moustafa thought the same.

"How well guarded is the place?" Augustus asked.

"There's always a watchman sitting in the garden. When the trucks come in some of the other servants come out to help unload it. Not a good way to get in."

"We could wait until late at night and pop over that wall," Augustus said.

Jack nodded. "If you do it late enough, you might catch the watchman asleep. You'll have to be quiet, though."

Faisal is as quiet as a church mouse. He could get in. If I explained to him exactly what we're looking for, he might be able to find it.

What am I thinking? If they catch him, who knows what they'll do? They've already shown themselves to be ruthless.

"A pity we can't just go in guns blazing," Augustus said. "But we can't endanger Mr. Naguib's family."

"You don't mind endangering that little mite you got dogging your footsteps," Jack said.

"I didn't want him up here. He followed me!" Augustus snapped.

"He followed you to this black fellow's bookshop too, eh?"

"Quiet," Moustafa grumbled.

"I already said I was sorry about nearly hitting him. I was trying to plug that copper. I'd never put a nipper in danger, not even a Gippo."

"Quiet, or I'll pull out your entrails and give them to my daughters to skip rope with," Moustafa said.

"You sure learned some English," Jack said with a chuckle. He turned to Augustus. "You teach him that?"

Augustus ignored him. They were now passing out of view of the country home. Augustus tried to focus on the terrain, the ditch by the road and patches of high vegetation that would hide an approach, and the other houses they had to avoid, but he couldn't concentrate. That lout's words had stung deep. His actions had nearly gotten the boy killed down in Luxor. Now Faisal had dogged his footsteps all the way to Alexandria. He couldn't put him in danger again.

But with the boy popping up everywhere, how could he help it?

That problem went around and around in his mind for another mile until Moustafa leaned forward and told the driver to turn around and head back to town on the same road.

They made another pass by the Naguib home, but Augustus barely looked at it. Too risky.

"There's another way," he said in a low voice.

"What's that?" Moustafa asked.

"Break into regimental HQ. They'll have the maps there. We can match it to the key."

"Are you bleedin' stupid?" Jack asked.

"I would be if I went myself, but I know someone who can slip in and out of there like a ghost."

"Won't it be dangerous?" Moustafa said, his look showing Augustus he knew who he meant.

"For us, yes. The worst that would happen to him is that he'd be arrested, and if that happens I can cash in my chips with Sir Thomas and get him out."

Jack stared at them. "Anyone going in there would be shot on sight. Wait, you're talking about that kid, aren't you? Bloody hell, you're salty. Yeah,

I guess they wouldn't plug a little chap like him. But is he up for it?"

"He broke into the Citadel once," Augustus told him.

The Australian's jaw dropped.

"You shouldn't have told him that, Mr. Wall."

"No one will believe him."

"If I told myself, I wouldn't believe it neither," Jack said.

They returned to Alexandria in silence, with Augustus thinking about how to handle a break-in of that magnitude. When Faisal broke into the Citadel, he had a disguise and a man on the inside helping him. They didn't have that now.

"What did you tell Miss Russell?" Moustafa asked as they entered town and drew up along the Corniche, which led to their hotel.

"Nothing. For all I know she's still on the rooftop café."

Moustafa looked away and muttered something the way he always did when Augustus did something he didn't approve of.

They were almost to the hotel when Moustafa got his attention and pointed. Tim and Faisal stood at the low wall, looking out at the bay.

"Driver, you can stop here," Augustus said.

He paid and they hopped out. Faisal spotted them and waved.

"Sorry for leaving you on babysitting duty," Augustus told his old friend as he strolled up.

Crawford cracked a smile. "Babysitting? Hell, he's a good little nipper. Not a pest like these shoeshine boys and beggars that swarm about like fleas."

"Really? I thought he was the greatest pest of them all."

"Him?" Crawford gave the boy a punch on the arm. Faisal winced and smiled at the same time. "He's been loads of fun. We terrorized the Frogs in some patisserie, then walked along the Corniche and got lunch. He's got a hell of an appetite. Worse than us when we got leave and finally faced a table set with something more than bully beef. So what did you find out?"

"No show at the country residence, I'm afraid. There's a family living there."

Crawford shook his head. "That's too bad. Can't launch a night raid like we did with the Hun. Oh, your girl showed up."

Augustus took in a sharp breath. "Jocelyn?"

"Who?"

"Never mind. You mean Miss Russell."

"Yeah, she hunted us down on the Corniche and asked where you were. I played stupid."

"Not a challenging role."

"Steady. I got plenty of brains."

Augustus smiled. "Yes, you are impressively muscled between the ears."

Tim barked out a laugh.

"You always were a snooty bastard." Tim turned to Faisal, pointing at Augustus and saying slowly and clearly. "Snooty bastard!"

Faisal got a quizzical look on his face. "Snotty bustard?"

Moustafa smacked Faisal upside the head. "Show some respect!"

Crawford shook a fist in his face. "Oi, Shaka Zulu! Anyone smacks my little Gippo friend again and I'll start doing some smacking of me own, you got me?"

Moustafa glowered at him. "My name is Moustafa Ghani El Souwaim."

"Your name can be King Henry the Bloody Eighth and it don't make a damn bit of difference."

"Gentlemen, we have a mystery to solve," Augustus said. He couldn't afford a falling out between these two, even though it would be fascinating to see who would win in a physical conflict, the fiery little rock of an Englishman or the mountain of Nubian muscle.

Moustafa and Crawford glared at each other for a moment, neither wanting to back down.

Faisal jumped up and down between them like he did when he had something urgent to relate, or at least something he thought was urgent.

"Cordelia says you should come to her hotel when you got back."

Augustus blinked in surprise. "How did she relate that to you?"

"We talk just fine. We talk about all sorts of things."

"Mostly to do with you eating something, I imagine. Is she cross with me?"

"Of course she's cross with you. She's cross with me too, because she wanted to take me back with her but I stayed with Tim because you told me to. Is he going back to England after we solve the murder?"

"I expect so."

"Oh." Faisal looked worried.

Moustafa cut in. "While you deal with that, I'll go with Jack Turner and take a look at Regimental HQ."

Mr. Wall gave him a smile. "Retreating in the face of overwhelming force, eh? Smart man."

Tim cut in. "Speaking of overwhelming force, your gal made me promise to ring her up when you came back. She was pretty angry with you. I'll try to cool her down and get her to stay away."

"I seriously doubt you'll manage."

"Probably not. Still, I never break a promise to a lady."

"Have you ever met one before?"

Tim turned to Faisal. "Snooty bastard, like I said. All right 'Sir Augustus', I'll go try to keep your lady from wringing your stupid neck. See you at the hotel."

He headed off.

"That man is infuriating," Moustafa grumbled.

"You'll get used to him."

"I don't want to get used to him. Let's go, Jack," Moustafa said.

Once Moustafa had left with the Australian, Augustus and Faisal headed for the Metropole.

"So are we going to break into that country house?" Faisal asked.

"No, it's well guarded and there's a family living there. We can't risk having them caught in the crossfire. We're going to have to find another way."

"Bluddy ell."

Augustus turned to him. "What did you say?"

"Bluddy ell. It's what Englishmen say when something bad happens."

"Not proper Englishmen. Don't say that again."

"Tim says it all the time. He also says bleedin eedjit, blimmy, steekin frog, dam, sh—"

"Stop!"

Faisal looked up at him curiously. "Why?"

"Don't learn any more English from Crawford. He's more foul-mouthed than Moustafa in a bad mood."

Faisal perked up. "All those are bad words?"

"Now what am I supposed to say, Faisal? If I tell you they're not bad words, you'll keep using them. If I tell you they are bad words, you'll teach them to all your lice-ridden friends."

"Not all my friends have lice!"

"I'm very glad to hear it."

"No, really. Mina doesn't have lice."

"Who?"

Faisal rolled his eyes. "Mina. The daughter of Waleed, the *fuul* stand owner. You sent him to a doctor, remember? Why don't you ever remember these things?"

"Perhaps because I'm too busy solving murders."

"I'm busy solving murders too, and I remember."

At the Metropole they had the front desk call up to Cordelia's room. Augustus fidgeted as the Egyptian behind the desk talked in a low voice with her a minute, then hung up.

"She says she will be right down, sir. You can wait in the sitting room. This is her servant, yes?"

"Um, yes."

"I'll send him to the servant's quarters."

"No, he needs to stay with us for … further instructions."

The man bowed. "Very well, sir."

They headed for the lounge.

"What's a frogribbit?" Faisal asked.

"A what?"

"A frogribbit. It's what Tim called the French waiter in the patisserie."

Augustus groaned. "Don't make a hard day any harder."

He sat in one of the armchairs. Faisal sat in the one next to it. A frown from one of the other guests made Augustus motion to Faisal.

"Those are for guests only."

Faisal got up and stood next to him. "I am a guest."

"No, you're a pest."

Faisal paused for a moment. Augustus could practically hear the wheels turn in his head.

"When is Tim leaving for England?"

"That's up to him."

"But soon. Right after we solve the murder?"

"I expect so."

Faisal looked at the floor. "I won't be a pest anymore, Englishman."

Augustus lit a cigarette. "I seriously doubt that."

Cordelia swooped into the lounge, her white sundress billowing behind her. A young man stepped up to say something, motioning to a free chair next to the one he had just vacated, but she stormed past him so quickly she nearly set the poor chap spinning.

"How dare you leave me behind?" she said without preamble.

"You cannot be left behind when you weren't supposed to come along in the first place," Augustus replied.

Cordelia ignored that, like she had ignored every other sensible thing he had ever said to her. Instead she sat in the chair next to his and leaned in close to him, eliciting a jealous glance from the young man across the room, who had retreated to his own chair.

"Mr. Crawford told me everything," she said, her eyes sparking with delight.

Augustus tensed. "Everything?"

"I asked where you were and he explained at length why I should go back to Cairo post haste."

"Oh no."

"Did you find a way to break into that country estate?"

"What a question from the sister of a police officer!"

"Well, did you?"

"There's a family there and we cannot risk any gunplay."

"What about the regimental HQ?"

"Good Lord, he told you about that too? I knew Crawford lacked subtlety, but this!"

"He enumerated what you were doing as a way to dissuade me from trying to intrude. He said 'this is no job for a lady'. He's quite mistaken."

"You're not a lady?"

Cordelia reddened. "Insulting me won't dissuade me either. Now listen. You cannot break into regimental HQ yourselves, and it's too risky for Faisal to do alone. He doesn't know what he's looking for and if they catch him they'll beat him black and blue. I have another way."

"There is no other way."

Cordelia raised her chin and looked down her nose at him. It didn't have much of an effect, the nose being pert and little. The eyes were much more imposing.

"I can go on an official visit."

Augustus had to admit he had not been expecting that. "I beg your pardon?"

"I have in my possession a letter of introduction from my brother. This will get me and my servant Faisal," she gestured to the boy, who had been listening with uncomprehending enthusiasm, "in for a tour of the facilities. I'll ask to see the map room, and when I find the map you are looking for, I'll give a signal to Faisal and he'll steal it."

"Why in the world would they let a woman into a military base?"

Cordelia stood a little straighter. "Because I am the sister of Cairo's chief of police, and I will lead them to believe that I am on a tour of inspection on his behalf. Thomas often sends his friends to be his eyes and ears when he is too busy to do so himself. Everyone knows that. Would it be so surprising if he sent his sister?"

"Somewhat, yes. And they won't think it odd that they were not informed ahead of time?"

"Thomas is famous for his snap inspections."

Augustus paused. That was true. Sir Thomas had a habit of showing up anywhere he liked, and at any time, to make sure his officers and informants were on the job.

Still, this plan seemed risky.

"His authority is limited to Cairo," Augustus said.

"As the head of Egypt's main police precinct, his authority extends all across Egypt. In the past year he's solved crimes from Aswan to the Sinai."

"And if you're caught?"

"Faisal is a child and it will be a simple enough matter to free him. Thomas will listen to me, and to you."

"True enough. I was wondering more about your fate."

"My brother kicks me out of Egypt and I go to India to rejoin Aunt Pearl."

"A fate worse than death."

"Don't be cruel. She's a dear old woman, and I'm willing to risk ejection from the Protectorate to help you find the murderer, and …" her eyes lit up, "… what he was looking for."

Augustus sat back, at a loss for the moment. He tried to think of a better plan and couldn't. Cordelia and Faisal both looked at him, waiting for him to speak.

How else to get into the engineering regiment's map room? He could think of no other way. Cordelia was correct, Faisal would be useless on his own, but perfect if accompanying Cordelia in the guise of a servant. Augustus could probably get in himself, but as a man would be watched more closely, and a muscular native like Moustafa wouldn't be allowed in as his servant, not with the present disturbances.

Good Lord, she has me. She's found a way to wheedle into one of my cases and there's no other way forward.

But if Sir Thomas hears about this, Cordelia won't be the only one ejected from the Protectorate …

CHAPTER TWENTY

Regimental HQ for the 4th ANZAC Engineering Regiment was a series of low prefabricated buildings surrounded by barbed wire in a western district of Alexandria mostly given over to small villas and a scattering of humbler dwellings in between.

Like in the outskirts of many Egyptian cities, Bedouin had pitched their tents on unused land between the more permanent homes. Children played in the grassy fields of the Nile Delta, while women drew water from one of the many small channels the Nile broke into in this region before flowing to the sea. Old men sat smoking at the entrances to their tents or in a small outdoor café of mudbrick a little way down the street.

Moustafa noted that the engineering regiment, like the Bedouin, had taken over some wasteland between two large villas. He hoped the soldiers' residence here would be as impermanent as the Bedouin's.

Moustafa and Jack walked along a broad street in front of the base, where a series of shops had opened up, no doubt to take advantage of the soldiers' ready money. Jack had to wave away offers of fake antiquities, indecent picture postcards, canned goods, and bottles of beer. A small open-air bar sat in the shade of a cluster of palms. A few off-duty soldiers sat drinking and laughing.

"So this is it," Jack said once they had cleared a space between the hawkers. "Barbed wire all around, and as you can see the guard towers on the two corners have a clear view in all directions. That boy you want to send in won't have a chance."

"Don't be so sure. Do these shopkeepers ever get in?"

"Are you joking?"

"During the war some did."

Jack grinned. "Mostly ladies, if you want to call them that. They don't let any natives in anymore, not after all the riots in the past year."

"No, I suppose not."

So how are we going to break in? Mr. Wall might be able to bluster his way in, but he'd never get to the map room.

No doubt he'll come up with some insane plan, something involving danger to himself and everyone around him. Why do I keep getting pulled into these affairs?

"Let's make a circuit of the base," Moustafa said. "I want to see it from all angles."

"All right. Oh, bloody hell!" Jack ducked behind a palm tree. "That's the Master Sergeant. Don't let him see me."

Moustafa moved to stand beside the palm, adding to the man's cover. He scanned the crowd and found the officer Jack had mentioned, recognizable from the chevrons on his sleeve.

He was a hefty, florid-faced man with a handlebar moustache. He wore a Webley revolver just like Moustafa's in a holster on his belt. Tucked under one arm was a bulky satchel that looked heavy.

"We should follow him and see where he goes," Moustafa said.

"I can't. If he spots me, he'll recognize me for sure."

Moustafa looked at him. While he had insisted Mr. Wall buy him a new hat and coat to disguise himself a little, he was still a distinctive looking individual. Anyone who knew him would recognize him from a long way off.

"This is too good of an opportunity to pass up," Moustafa objected, unsure how to proceed.

"Follow him. He doesn't know you. I'm the only one in the gang who ever laid eyes on you. I'll make myself scarce and join you at the hotel later."

Moustafa glowered at him. He didn't dare let this fellow out of his sight.

"Come on," Jack urged. "He's getting away."

Indeed, the Master Sergeant was walking down the main street toward a tram stop, nothing more than a small concrete floor covered by a wooden awning to shield waiting passengers from the strong sun. If he got on that tram, they'd lose him.

Moustafa turned back to Jack. "Do you have your passport and army papers?"

"Of course. We have to carry them at all times."

"Give them to me."

Jack's eyes went wide. "What?"

"Give them to me. That way I know you'll come back. If you don't, you'll be stranded here and sooner or later you'll get picked up by the authorities."

Jack gave the Master Sergeant a worried look, grumbled, and handed the papers over.

"I get those back the minute we meet again," the Australian told him.

Moustafa nodded. "You will."

The approaching rattle of the tram cut Moustafa off from saying more. He hurried to the stop, where the Master Sergeant now stood. The tram could be seen just down the street. Moustafa walked at a rapid pace. Once he glanced over his shoulder, only to find Jack Turner had disappeared.

Moustafa made it to the tram stop just in time, and managed to join the small crowd of people getting on.

Being native, he had to get into the second-class car in the back, while the Master Sergeant rode in the first-class car up front.

Moustafa growled in frustration. The tram car was so full he couldn't even see the man through the window!

The tram rattled along. Moustafa tried to push to the front of the car so he could see through the windows at the end, which afforded a view of the car ahead. He usually avoided that spot, as it made the acid boil in his stomach to see foreigners get the better car. At least there were only two carriages on this branch line. If there had been a car between them, there'd have been no hope of spotting the man he followed.

After a minute, and several protestations from other riders, he made it.

Only to find that the first-class car was full enough that he still couldn't see the Master Sergeant.

The tram rolled to a stop. Moustafa poked his head out, scanning the Europeans leaving the other carriage. A couple of Armenians in cheap business suits got off his carriage, grumbling at him for getting in the way. He ignored them.

The bell clanged without the Master Sergeant making an appearance, and he pulled his head in before the doors closed.

They rattled along for another couple of blocks, Moustafa growing increasingly impatient, before coming to another stop. He put his head out again, causing a student trying to get on to say, "excuse me." Moustafa didn't budge, eyes fixed on the Europeans getting off and on.

"Are you riding this tram or not?" the second-class conductor barked.

The bell rang again. Still no sign of the Master Sergeant.

The conductor came up to him. "Well, are you?"

Moustafa pulled his head in. "Sorry. I'm … with someone in the first-class car and I'm waiting for him to get off."

"Oh, you're a manservant, are you? Well, you should have asked your master what stop he was getting off on."

Moustafa resisted the urge to toss him under the wheels of the tram, or up on the roof where he'd get electrocuted. Instead Moustafa forced himself to smile and turned away.

At last! The crowd had thinned out enough in the other carriage for him to spot the Master Sergeant sitting near the front. While there were two other soldiers up there, he was the only one of such massive size, equal to Moustafa's own hulking frame.

Mr. Wall said the man who suffocated his friend had great physical strength.

Moustafa felt a chill go through him despite the close air.

Look at that man. Just a few days ago, if I'm right, he murdered someone with his bare hands, and now he sits in the tram like a regular citizen.

Despite the many cases he had solved with Mr. Wall, he had never gotten used to the sort of people he met because of them. He didn't want to get used to them.

Bringing them to justice, however, that gave him a true sense of satisfaction.

And I'm the only one who cares about justice. Well, on this particular case so does Mr. Wall, but this is the sole exception. He just wants to be clever and have a chance for some gunplay. Faisal just wants to be useful so Mr. Wall gives him things.

No, that isn't fair. As thieving and greedy as the gutter rat is, what Faisal really wants is a home. The lice must have dug through his skull to feed on his brain if he thinks that madman can provide him one.

And Cordelia? What did she want?

He had no idea.

The tram continued into central Alexandria. As it slowed for another stop, he saw the Master Sergeant stand. Moustafa edged to the door.

The tram pulled up, the doors opened, and both of them got out. The Master Sergeant didn't look back as he walked down the street with a determined gait, holding the heavy satchel under one arm.

Moustafa wondered what it contained. Despite the man's great size, he shifted it onto his other shoulder, and gripped it from the bottom with his hand to relieve some of the weight from the shoulder strap.

Moustafa trailed him down a quiet side street flanked by European-style buildings of plainer decoration than those along the Corniche. They looked like apartments for clerks and modest shopkeepers. Indeed, the few people he saw passing appeared to be just that. In the ground floors were various small businesses with signs in Greek or Armenian.

He grimaced as he saw a couple of the signs had been defaced with paint. There were some in the independence movement who thought the Greeks, Armenians, and Jews should be kicked out of the country. Ridiculous. Those families had been here for generations. Centuries, even. And they had become some of the most prosperous people in the country. It was simple jealousy. In meetings in his bookshop after hours, where only trusted friends were invited, Moustafa had forcefully told anyone who would listen that all Egyptians, no matter what their background, would be needed to build the new nation.

His thoughts snapped back to the task at hand as he saw the Master Sergeant pass through a low doorway. The sign above it read in Greek, "Giorgos Alexopolous: Translator and Notary Public."

Moustafa slowed his steps and passed by the dirty window. Inside he saw a cramped office with a filing cabinet, a large bookshelf, and a counter with stacks of forms. The Master Sergeant's back was turned to him. He stood before a desk overflowing with papers behind which sat a hunched old Greek with a fringe of messy white hair. A pair of spectacles sat on his nose. The Greek did not look out the window.

Moustafa passed by, not daring to hesitate in front of the window and draw attention to himself.

Once he got out of sight of the window, he turned, putting his hand in the pocket where he kept the revolver. Taking a deep breath, he passed by the window a second time, hoping he would remain undetected.

He caught a glimpse of the Master Sergeant pulling a portion of a marble slab out of his satchel. Moustafa's heart flipped in his chest.

Another fragment of the dedication?

The man behind the counter obviously thought it was significant. He rose to his feet, eyes going wide.

That was all Moustafa saw before he passed out of view.

Stopping a few steps beyond the window, he glanced up and down the street. No one seemed to have noticed him. If he passed the little shop a third time, that might change.

But he had to. God had smiled upon him and dropped a vital clue right in his path.

Summoning his courage, he turned and passed the window a third time.

And stopped.

The Master Sergeant and the Greek man had disappeared from view.

Peering inside, he saw a doorway behind the desk leading out of sight.

He could see the rest of the front office and they weren't there.

What to do? The officer was dangerous, and Moustafa didn't know what role this Greek played. Translator for the tablets? Antiquities smuggler? There was no shortage of organized crime in Alexandria, and the Greeks played a big role in it.

He wished Mr. Wall was here, or even Tim or that mangy Australian. Handling this alone would be tricky.

But he had no choice. There was no time to fetch them.

Giving a furtive look over his shoulder to make sure no one was looking, he opened the shop door …

… and winced as a little bell above the door rang. Moustafa quickly locked the door behind him.

The Master Sergeant rushed out of the back room, his face flushed. When he saw Moustafa he stopped short.

"What the bloody hell are you doing here?" the Australian demanded.

They stood only a few feet apart, the Master Sergeant just to the side of the counter.

Moustafa put on a deferential air. "Sorry, sir. I just came to the good Mr. Alexopolous to have a letter—"

"He's busy. Be off with you!"

Moustafa could see beads of sweat on the man's brow. His hands were red too, as if from exertion.

"But sir—"

"You heard what I said. Come back later."

The Master Sergeant looked about to say more, but then he paused, his eyes straying down the pocket where Moustafa still had his hand.

The pocket where the revolver was hidden.

Whether the officer could see it or not, Moustafa was never certain. At the very least he guessed it was there, for the next moment he went for the pistol in the holster by his side.

Moustafa knew he would have no time to pull out his cumbersome Webley revolver out of the pocket of his djellaba before the soldier managed to draw his own, so he did the only thing he could do—he rushed the man, crossing the few feet between them in a split second and slamming into him while grasping the wrist of the hand that was just drawing the pistol.

The Master Sergeant hit the shelves on the back wall, snapping one of them and covering both men in a cascade of papers as they fell together to the floor.

Moustafa fell on top and managed to place his knee on the Master Sergeant's gun arm. Leaning on it with all his weight and pressing down on the wrist with one hand, he used the other hand to punch the Australian in the face.

Any ordinary man would have fallen unconscious from the first punch, but Moustafa soon learned this was no ordinary man.

The Master Sergeant shot a punch right up into Moustafa's jaw.

The Nubian swayed, momentarily stunned, took another punch, then heaved his weight to give the Australian a hammering blow to the face.

The Master Sergeant let out a grunt and protected his face with his free hand. Moustafa rained more blows on him, but couldn't get a strong hit behind the man's defenses.

That gave the Australian the chance to build up the strength to twist his body, pushing Moustafa half off him.

Moustafa grabbed the gun arm with both hands, suddenly fearful the Master Sergeant would yank it free.

A punch in Moustafa's ribs almost allowed him to. The Australian pushed him again, and they ended up side by side on the floor, each trying to knee one another as Moustafa kept a firm grip on his opponent's gun hand.

The Master Sergeant gave Moustafa an especially good one and reached with his free hand for the gun. Moustafa batted the weapon away just as he was changing it from one hand to the other.

The gun skittered across the floor and under a far shelf.

With a frustrated roar, the Master Sergeant heaved Moustafa off him. The Nubian rolled to the side, knocking over a lamp, and sprang to his feet. The Australian got on his feet too, just out of reach.

Both glanced at the front window of the store, checking if their fight had been noticed from the street outside. No one stood staring at the window.

The Master Sergeant let out a little laugh, smiling at Moustafa.

He edged around Moustafa to get between him and the front window. Moustafa stepped back a few paces, followed by his opponent, until they had stepped out of view of the street and into the back room.

Moustafa didn't dare try to draw his pistol during this lull in the fighting. The Master Sergeant would be on him before he got his hand in his pocket. His embarrassing experience in front of the church had taught him that he could not get his gun out quickly enough.

A glance around the back room showed him what he expected to find—the old Greek lying strangled on the floor.

It was a small office, with shelves filled with folders and papers. On a battered wooden desk lay the stone slab, with a piece of paper next to it.

The slab was of the finest marble, and bore a couple of lines of ancient Greek. The piece of paper had identical lines on it, obviously copied out by the poor man now lying dead on the floor.

He took this all in within a second, for a second was all the Master Sergeant allowed him before hurling himself at Moustafa a second time.

Strong hands grasped Moustafa around the neck, instantly cutting off his breath. He struck at the man's arms, but they were like a vice around him. Desperate, Moustafa tried to extract the gun from his pocket, but the Master Sergeant saw the move and slammed him against the wall, pinning him and keeping the pistol pressed against the wall and Moustafa's body.

Moustafa struck him again and again. The Master Sergeant grunted at each blow, but his grip did not weaken. He simply stood there, choking the life out of him, eyes glaring into Moustafa's as the Nubian's blows began to weaken.

In a final desperate gamble, Moustafa clamped his hands around the man's throat. Those crazed eyes bugged a little.

Years of spadework on archaeological digs had given Moustafa's hands great strength, but the Master Sergeant was strong too, and Moustafa already felt himself slipping. He focused his entire energy into pressing in on the man's throat. Through dimming vision he saw the Master Sergeant's face go red.

Moustafa's lungs burned, his head pulsed, and still he kept his grip.

Soon his vision dimmed to almost nothing. He didn't even feel the man's stranglehold on him, couldn't even feel his own hold on the Master Sergeant. He had only his will, a will to keep on choking the man, a will to keep on living.

And soon even that passed, and Moustafa knew nothing more.

CHAPTER TWENTY-ONE

Faisal stood behind Cordelia, holding the parasol over her head as she talked to an officer at the gate to the army base. His heart beat so fast and hard he felt sure the stern-eyed sentries would hear it. While he had broken into plenty of places, he had always snuck in or wore a disguise. Walking into a place in the day time when everyone could see you was too risky.

The Englishman had tried to reassure him, saying that the letter she was showing to the officer came from her brother, the chief of police, and would get them in easily.

Sure, but then what?

Once they got in, Cordelia would go on a tour and ask to see the map room. Through the Englishman, she had told him she would signal to him by patting him twice on the shoulder when she found the right map.

If he needed a distraction, he was supposed to ask her, "Are you cool enough, madam?" and she would draw their attention away.

Then he was supposed to steal the map.

Riiiiight. Steal it as the map people stood there showing off their maps? When the officer showing Cordelia around talked to her? Then Faisal had to walk around for the rest of the tour hiding the map?

Sure, why didn't they ask him to weave a flying carpet while he was at it?

He wished he wasn't so good at swiping things, because now everyone thought he could work miracles.

As usual, the adults kept talking and talking. Faisal held the parasol over Cordelia's head as the officer read the letter and blah blahed to the Englishwoman. They still hadn't been let through the gate. Men with rifles stood to either side, bayonets flashing in the sunlight and hurting his eyes. They all had stern faces. Up in the tower by the gate, a man sat behind a machine gun that could probably kill a thousand people before you took a single breath.

Faisal remembered the base he had visited in Bahariya. The soldiers had been friendly there. One had even given him chocolate and let him climb into an armored car.

These soldiers were different. They acted suspicious, giving Faisal mean looks. Maybe it was because of all the independence demonstrations, or maybe the Australians were meaner than the English. He didn't know. The Australians had a pretty bad reputation. They drank a lot and smashed up shops and didn't like Egyptians at all. Faisal stuck close behind Cordelia.

At last, the officer let them in. He walked right beside Cordelia, chatting away. Cordelia was all smiles and walked close to the officer as if she liked him. Faisal didn't think she did, though.

They entered a broad parade ground with two tall flagpoles in the center. One flew the British flag. The other flew another flag that had the British flag in one corner, while the rest was blue with some stars on it. Maybe that was the special flag for map people or something. On three sides of the parade ground stood long, low buildings. Faisal trotted behind Cordelia and the officer, still holding the parasol.

When they got to the first building, the officer turned to Faisal and said something that kind of sounded like Arabic but not close enough for Faisal to understand what he meant.

Faisal stared at him.

The officer frowned and repeated himself.

He's probably telling me to wait here. Maybe if I pretend I don't know what he's saying he'll let me come along.

The officer pointed to Faisal, then pointed to a thin strip of shade by the building.

I can't pretend I don't understand now.

Of course they wouldn't let me inside! Why didn't we think of that?

It turned out that Cordelia had. She said something to the officer and handed Faisal her handbag, plus a fan. Faisal closed the parasol, resisting the urge to pretend it was a gun and shoot the officer, and opened the fan.

They entered the building together, Faisal carrying the bag in one hand, the parasol tucked under his arm, and using the other hand to fan Cordelia.

Great. How was he supposed to steal the map with both hands full?

They came to a room with a few overstuffed armchairs and little tables. Several officers who had been talking and smoking rose and bowed to Cordelia. The officer showed her a chair and she sat while Faisal stood next to her, fanning.

The officer sat in a chair opposite and they began to blah blah again. Some of the officers joined them. Cordelia chattered away merrily and the officers all smiled, saying what sounded like nice things and staring at her. Nobody paid any attention to Faisal.

After a couple of minutes, a soldier brought out a tray of tea and crumbets. Faisal's stomach growled. He told it to shut up. Those soldiers wouldn't offer him a snack, not if he stood there fanning Cordelia for a thousand years.

The soldiers and Cordelia talked and talked and talked. Faisal had never realized he could be terrified and bored at the same time. Faisal's stomach kept growling but Cordelia ignored him. He knew she was playing a part and trying to get the soldiers to relax around her, lower their guard, but it was still annoying. She had slipped back into her English world, with tea and crum bets served in nice cups and dishes, and polite officers who pretended the Egyptian boy wasn't there.

The Englishman pretended to be different from these people. He avoided other English people most of the time because they reminded him of Europe and the war. Faisal could tell he missed his own kind, though. He had breakfasts with Sir Thomas Russell Pasha and sometimes went to talks at one of those big European meeting halls.

And now one of his old war friends had come. That would make him think of England more.

Would the Englishman slip back into the English world just like Cordelia?

One of the officers snapped his fingers at Faisal, jerking him out of his thoughts. The officer frowned at him. Faisal stared, wondering what he had done wrong, and then realized he had forgotten to keep fanning Cordelia. He started fanning again. The rest of the Australians kept talking as if they hadn't noticed. Maybe they hadn't.

At last Cordelia and the officers stood. The officers all bowed and there was some more blah blahing before finally the officer who had met them at the gate ushered them out of the room.

From there he took them to a large room with long tables. From a window in one wall Faisal could see a big kitchen. Rich cooking smells came out of it, making Faisal's stomach grumble again. Would he have to stand by Cordelia fanning her while they ate lunch?

Luckily, he didn't have to endure that torture. They soon left the room and passed through several others. It was all boring. Faisal was surprised the officer believed Cordelia's tale about her brother wanting to inspect the base. Why would Sir Thomas Russell Pasha care about some boring rooms in Alexandria?

"The English love inspections," the Englishman had explained to him. "It's their way of pretending everything is under control when it isn't."

They left the building, crossed the parade ground, and entered another building with a big wire on top of it. It looked like one of those wires that went to homes that had electricity, except the wire only hung between two tall poles. That didn't make any sense.

When they entered, Faisal suddenly remembered. Inside was a wireless set. He had seen one in Bahariya, run by an officer from some place in Europe called New Zealand. You could talk on it and people would hear you miles and miles away, in other countries even. His servant boy, Ahmed, had explained how it worked but Faisal didn't understand it.

An operator hunched in front of the wireless set, tapping away at a little metal bar that made beeping noises. Faisal remembered this too. The beeps were some sort of code that made letters. It was very complicated and you were supposed to be quiet when the beeping was going on. Even the officer shut up for a minute.

The operator stopped hitting the metal bar, and the wireless set started to make a crackly sound. Suddenly some beeping came through. The man at the wireless set started writing down words.

Faisal's skin prickled. While he'd seen this before, it still gave him the jitters. Too close to magic. He knew it wasn't, that it was only another clever thing the Europeans had thought up, but if something was clever enough, wasn't it a sort of magic?

They left the wireless room and went on to look at some less interesting stuff.

Then something Cordelia said made him perk up. She said "maps," which was English for *khareeta*. The Englishman had made him learn that word, making him say it at least a thousand times as if Faisal was stupid or something.

But he wasn't stupid. They needed him to solve all these murders, after all.

Cordelia wasn't stupid either. She acted like maps were the most exciting thing in the world and that the officer was the nicest man ever to show them to her. She moved closer to him and chattered away, looking him in the eyes and smiling. The officer looked very pleased with himself.

While Faisal knew it was all pretend, he didn't like seeing Cordelia act indecently. European women went around alone all the time, and talked with any man they liked, but even they didn't act like this with men who weren't their husbands.

Cordelia was a decent woman and should act like it, just like his mother was a decent woman who died giving birth to him.

You know what they say about her in the neighborhood. Even the girls who sit in the windows with the red candles say the same.

Faisal shook himself. No, they were all lying. And what they say about the window girls isn't true either.

"Faisal."

Cordelia's voice snapped him out of his thoughts. She and the officer had walked toward one of the buildings and Faisal, lost in his thoughts, hadn't noticed. She stood several paces away, the officer a couple of paces further on. He didn't look like he wanted Faisal to come at all.

Cordelia gave Faisal a wink.

Faisal had to bite his lips to keep from laughing. Of course it had all been an act to fool that stupid Australian officer. Cordelia was a decent woman just like his mother!

The officer led them to another building across from the radio building. They entered a large, airy room with big windows that let in a lot of light. In the center was a funny slanted table. A soldier stood in front of it drawing lines on a half-finished map. A bunch more maps hung on the wall, while at another table two more soldiers were looking at a map and talking about it.

On the far wall stood a bunch of shelves with stacks and stacks of maps piled on them. Faisal almost groaned in despair. There must be hundreds! How would they find the right one? How could Cordelia get them to show her the right one?

Maybe she would hint at it somehow. She was blah blahing to the soldiers now, all of whom had turned to speak with her while the officer who had been showing them around stood close to her like she belonged to him. Faisal fanned her to give himself a reason for being there.

He didn't need to. None of the Australians paid him any attention.

After some more boring conversation, the man who had been drawing the map showed her the half-drawn map. This wasn't what they wanted, but Cordelia acted all interested anyway. She was good at that. Faisal felt like going to sleep.

He would have if he hadn't been so scared. There were three soldiers in the room, and Faisal had to fan Cordelia with one hand, hold the parasol and handbag with the other, and somehow grow a third hand to steal the map, all without anyone seeing?

The officers brought out a big stack of maps and started showing them to Cordelia. Faisal peeked around her to see the maps too. They all looked the same, with little squiggles and lines drawn on them. How did people read these and know where things were?

He leaned in closer, trying to make sense of all those lines.

A glance from one of the soldiers made him duck back and keep fanning Cordelia. He didn't want to draw attention to himself.

The foreigners kept blah blahing, but Faisal paid attention now, because they kept saying the word "train". He knew that one. It meant *'atr*. The place they were looking for was near a train line.

Cordelia acted very interested, and they started spending more time on each map. Faisal fanned her more eagerly.

Then he nearly dropped the fan from excitement. Cordelia, without looking at him and without pausing as she talked to the officers, patted him twice on the shoulder.

That was the signal. He stared at the map he was supposed to steal, trying to memorize it.

How to do that? All these maps looked the same!

Cordelia helped. When it came time to put that map on the pile of maps they had already looked at so they could look at another one, she put it at a bit of an angle, so a corner stuck out from the pile. The soldiers were so busy looking at her they didn't notice.

Faisal waited for his chance, allowing them to go through another couple of maps.

How to do this? All three soldiers still stood around with Cordelia, making a half circle in front of the table.

Then he saw a lit cigarette sitting in an ashtray next to a couple of half-drawn maps, and got an idea.

He could make a bigger distraction than Cordelia ever could.

But first he needed the soldiers' attention drawn elsewhere, just for a second or two.

"Are you cool enough, madam?" he asked.

The signal for her to make a distraction.

"Yes. Thank you, Faisal."

She went back to blah blahing with her new soldier friends. After a moment, she took her handbag from him and pulled out a handkerchief. She fumbled it, kind of obviously on purpose, and out of her purse tumbled her handkerchief, a pen, and a little box. The little box opened as it fell to the tile floor. A little white poofy thing fell out in a burst of white powder.

The men all hurried to grab the things for her, two even knocking their heads together with a loud *clonk*. That made even more of a distraction.

Faisal stepped out of the way of the soldiers who were so eager to help the lady they had forgotten she had a servant to do those things, reached over and put the cigarette on the half-finished map.

The soldiers all came up at once, two of them rubbing their heads. They had all gotten a prize. One had the handkerchief, and returned it with a bow to Cordelia. He got a thank you. The second one, rubbing his head, presented her with the pen, bowing as he did so. He got a thank you as well. The third stopped rubbing his head long enough to try and reassemble the box with the poofy thing and only managed to get white powder all over his uniform. After a moment he gave up, bowed, and got a thank you from Cordelia.

They all looked very proud of themselves for picking up things off the floor, and were so busy bowing and blah blahing they didn't notice the thin curl of smoke coming up from one of the unfinished maps.

Cordelia gestured toward the map they had been studying and said something. They all went back to looking at it. Faisal turned, fanned the cigarette for a second to get a little tongue of flame to shoot up from the paper, and went back to fanning Cordelia.

Just as he suspected, Cordelia's distraction hadn't been enough to get the officers away from the stack of maps. His own distraction would take care of that soon enough. Foreigners should really leave that sort of job up to the professionals.

Faisal tried to ignore the spreading flame behind him and leaned in to study the maps. The same officer gave him another look like he wasn't welcome, but this time Faisal ignored him. He wanted to be seen doing something other than setting fire to maps.

One of the officers sniffed and looked around curiously. At first he didn't look in the right place, the silly Australian, but then his eyes went wide and he hollered.

All three officers rushed to the burning map, nearly knocking over Faisal and Cordelia.

Faisal stepped over to the pile of maps, slipped the right one out of the pile, rolled it up around the handle of the parasol, and dropped it inside.

He stepped back next to Cordelia as the officers shouted and slapped the burning map with their hands, burning their fingers as well as the map. They knocked over an ink bottle that made a big black mess over another map, which got two of the soldiers arguing. One looked like he was about to punch the other before the officer separated them, shouting at them until they noticed the flames weren't out yet. Then they all went back to smacking at the map.

Cordelia nudged Faisal and gave him a wink. He put on his best innocent face.

After what seemed like ages, and not before knocking over more things and nearly having another fight, did the three Australians finally put out the fire. By then the map was almost burned up. The table had a big black scorch mark on it and smoke hung in the air.

The officer came over and talked to Cordelia. It sounded like he was apologizing. Then he turned and shouted at the two other soldiers, who came to attention. He shouted again and they marched out of the room.

After some more apologizing, the officer took them out of the map room and toward the front gate. The two soldiers from the map room were marching back and forth across the hot, sunny square at double time. They looked like they'd be marching for a while.

As they got to the front gate, the officer scowled at Faisal.

Uh-oh. Did he suspect something?

The officer pointed at the parasol, said something in English, and pointed at Cordelia.

Oh, right, he was supposed to be shading her.

But the map was curled up inside!

Faisal put his hand inside the parasol and curled the map as tightly as possible around the central rod. Then he made the sleeve of his djellaba as loose as he could, put the parasol upright, and tried to slip the map into his sleeve.

It didn't fit.

Oh, he knew what he was doing wrong. He needed to make the map looser so it could go around his hand and slide right into his sleeve.

He tried that, but couldn't get it to fit right. Some part of the edge of the map kept getting caught on his sleeve.

Faisal struggled with the map. It was still hidden inside the upright parasol so it looked to the others like he couldn't get the parasol open.

The officer grumbled the way foreigners do when they think an Egyptian is being lazy or stupid.

There, almost. If he could just get the map tucked in …

The officer shouted something and snatched the parasol from his grasp. Faisal let out a yelp of fear, thinking the map would tumble down at his feet.

Instead it slid right down the sleeve of his djellaba. When the officer grabbed the parasol, he had nudged the map just the right way for it to fit.

Faisal kept his arm up, like he was reaching for the parasol. The officer opened it and handed it to him.

"Thank you," Faisal said in English.

The officer only grumbled. Faisal held his breath to keep from giggling. The idiot thought Faisal was thanking him for helping him with the parasol.

Cordelia walked out of the front gate of the army base, past the guards and the big machine gun, and out onto the street.

Faisal walked right behind her, his arm held high, the map rustling inside his sleeve, keeping his other arm across his face so those men with the machine gun wouldn't see him smiling.

CHAPTER TWENTY-TWO

Augustus pored over the map, trying to align the details he saw with the key Gregory Marshall had written.

It was frustratingly slow going. Cordelia, who had safely been sent back up to the rooftop terrace, had stolen a map of the western rail lines that was of too large a scale. That left Augustus with an extensive area to cover.

"Is that helpful?" Faisal asked, eating an enormous éclair he had earned as a reward and getting chocolate and cream everywhere.

"Yes, very helpful."

Or it will be once I find the right spot. This key is just so damned vague!

He looked at the key again.

"1. Branch line.

2. Tool shed.

3. Mound of rubble.

4. Column bases.

5. Bedouin encampment.

6. Small ruined mosque."

The map was exact enough to show tool sheds, unfortunately the engineers had put up one every mile or so. A few spots were marked as mounds of rubble or ruins, but they were all quite large, and it was hard to know if the mound on Gregory's map had been large enough to have made it onto the engineering map. The Bedouin encampments weren't on the map at all, being impermanent structures, and he didn't see any markings for a small ruined mosque.

Augustus drummed his fingers on the table in frustration.

"Want some of this chocolate thing?" the boy asked.

"No, thank you," Augustus replied, continuing to trace the line of the railway with his finger. He found a spot marked "ruined house". That was the second he'd come across. Could one of these houses have been mistaken for a mosque?

"It's good," Faisal said. "We got it at a place called a patisserie. Cordelia got it for me. I wanted to sit down but she said no."

"French patisseries generally don't let Egyptian boys onto the premises," Augustus said, muttering a curse as he came across a third ruined house.

"I got to sit down with Tim."

"Rules don't apply to him."

"Why not?"

"Simply look at him and you can figure that out for yourself."

"Where is he?"

"On watch downstairs. Didn't you see him when you came in?"

"No."

"Good. He hasn't lost his touch."

"He's a crazy man. Nice, though."

"A diamond in the rough."

"A what?"

"Nothing. I'm working, Faisal."

"Is he your best friend?"

"He is indeed. The best I ever had."

Faisal was blessedly silent for a moment. That, naturally, did not last.

"Did you miss him?"

"Yes I did," Augustus admitted. "It wasn't until he showed up here that I really understood how much."

Now the little pest had made him lose his place! Was this the third ruined house he had come across or the second? He better go back to the start and follow the branch line again.

Well, one of the branch lines. He hadn't started on the second one yet.

"Do you miss England too?"

"Not at all. I do believe I mentioned I'm working."

Hints rarely worked with Faisal. Too bad Moustafa wasn't here to smack him.

Another pause. Augustus knew it wouldn't last.

"But Tim lives in England. So that means you must miss England a little bit."

Augustus groaned. "What are you driving at, Faisal?"

The boy had finished his éclair and was busy wiping his fingers around his mouth and chin and licking off the residue.

"Um, nothing."

"Then why are you talking?" This boy was so irritating sometimes it actually hurt.

"It's just … um …" Suddenly Faisal looked like he had an idea. He leapt off his seat. Augustus noticed chocolate stains on the armrest. "I know! You could get Tim to live here. Then you wouldn't have to miss England."

"I don't miss England. And I seriously doubt Tim wants to live in Egypt. I'd end up having to spring him from jail and Sir Thomas would scold me over breakfast."

"That's right! You can't move back to England because then you wouldn't be able to have breakfast at the big hotel anymore."

"Move back to England? Whatever are you talking about?"

Faisal went pale. Before Augustus could ask him what was the matter, there came a furious knocking on the door.

"Mr. Wall, it's me!"

That was Moustafa's voice.

Augustus opened the door and the Nubian rushed in, the new djellaba Augustus had bought for him disheveled and torn. Part of his face was swollen and he carried a large satchel across his shoulder.

"What happened? Where have you been?" Augustus asked.

Moustafa poured out a tale about tracking down the Master Sergeant and getting into the fight of his life. He was so excited he didn't make much sense, and before Augustus and Faisal could make out what exactly had happened, Moustafa swept the papers and map off the table and set the satchel down with a loud thud.

"Moustafa!" Augustus cried. "This is quite unlike you."

"This is a case quite unlike the others!" he said triumphantly, unlacing the satchel.

He pulled out a heavy slab of marble inscribed with a line and a half of ancient Greek.

The sight of one word made Augustus suck in his breath.

For a moment he couldn't speak.

Finally, clearing his throat, he said, "My ancient Greek isn't as good as yours, my good fellow. Does that say … what I think it says?"

"Yes. Hegemon. '… and Hegemon, laid here.'"

"And this next line," Augustus whispered. "'… by Ptolemeis, his …' and the line breaks off. I bet this fits in with the fragment that says 'loyal general.'"

"Yes! Ptolemeis his loyal general! And Hegemon confirms it."

"What does Hegemon mean?" Faisal asked.

"It means supreme leader," Augustus replied. "A title Alexander took on after the death of his father Philip of Macedon."

Faisal poked his head between the two men and peered at the slab of marble. "So it really is his gravestone?"

Augustus and Moustafa didn't reply, too amazed to think it really was possible.

"Well, is it?" the boy asked again.

Augustus shivered.

"Yes. Yes, I do believe it is," he replied in a quiet tone.

"Wow! A gravestone of a king should sell for a lot in your shop."

"Oh, I don't think I'll be selling this."

He ran an appreciative hand across the smooth marble and shivered again.

Then he shook himself, breaking the spell, and looked at Moustafa.

They still had a murder to solve.

"So the Master Sergeant was bringing the portions of the slab to this Greek fellow to translate," Augustus said. "That's good on two accounts. It means they don't have a translator among their own number, and they don't know what this vital piece of evidence means."

"That's right, Mr. Wall."

Augustus studied the Nubian for a second. The fellow had been so excited and so full of news when he had come in that at first Augustus had failed to notice just how badly bruised he was.

"He nearly took you," Augustus said. "That's quite an accomplishment."

"I was unconscious for some time," Moustafa said. "He was a man of incredible strength."

Augustus drew in air through his clenched teeth. "The man who smothered Gregory."

Moustafa nodded. "I doubt they have two men that strong."

Augustus felt a flare of anger against his former employee for taking the chance of revenge away from him. He tamped that emotion down as unworthy.

We still have some more justice to deal out, Gregory.

Augustus extended a hand. "You have done me a great service, Moustafa, and I thank you."

Moustafa took his hand. "You are welcome, Mr. Wall."

"Did anyone see the fight?" Faisal asked.

"I don't think so," Moustafa said.

"But there are two dead bodies in that shop," Faisal said. "And one is a soldier. Did anyone see you go in or out?"

"That's possible," Moustafa said, worry growing on his face. "At least they won't be discovered for some time. As I left, I took the key from behind the desk and locked up. Then I threw the key away."

"No one raised the alarm, and no one followed you," Augustus said. "You will be safe for the moment."

"It won't be long before they are found," Moustafa said grimly. "The proprietor's family will no doubt have a key, and will go into the shop looking for him sooner or later. They might have discovered the bodies already. There will be an investigation. Someone is bound to have seen a Nubian enter. And the police will add that report to the one of a Nubian involved in the gunfight at the church."

"That's a problem," Augustus admitted. "And add to that your disheveled and injured state when you came into the hotel, and it won't be long before the police come knocking. I had some dealings with the local police when I lived here. They aren't an entirely useless lot. We need to hide you."

"But we're so close!"

Augustus smiled. The hunt was more important to Moustafa than his personal safety. God, he missed having this man at the shop!

"We need to hide you all the same," Augustus said. "I know! We'll switch you over to Tim's lodgings. You can get there without the front desk man seeing, and since it's under a foreigner's name no one will suspect you are there. Go clean yourself up. I'll call for a carriage and we'll hustle you into it and whisk you away. In fact, perhaps we all should move over there just to be on the safe side."

"Very well, Mr. Wall. But we need to figure out this map."

"We will be safer doing that from a more secure place."

Augustus suddenly remembered something lost amid the excitement of the slab and vengeance for Gregory. "Wait. Where is that Jack Turner fellow?"

Moustafa stared at him. "He hasn't come back?"

"No. Did he give you the slip?"

"He was afraid of being recognized if I followed the Master Sergeant so I let him go."

"You what?"

"I took his papers. Here they are."

"Hmm. He wouldn't have scarpered without those. What could have happened to him?"

"Perhaps he met someone else he recognized," Moustafa said.

"Oh dear. You're right. The only people who might recognize him are his old associates. That wouldn't be too healthy for him."

Faisal's eyes widened. "Then we need to get out of here! He'll tell on us to save himself."

"You have great insight into the psychology of deceitfulness," Augustus said. "Yes, we'll leave now. Moustafa, grab your things. Just the essentials. I'll pack here. Faisal, go upstairs and fetch Cordelia. Tell her she should go back to her own hotel. Can you do that?"

"Sure, but then what?" the boy asked. Moustafa was already heading out the door.

"We'll fetch you when we need you."

"But I don't even know where you're staying!"

"It doesn't matter. We'll fetch you. You've been a great help." The boy looked at him uncertainly. "Go. It's important that you hurry. Cordelia might be in as much danger as we are."

Augustus doubted that was true, but getting the two of them out of the hotel seemed the safest plan.

Plus it offered a way to shake them both.

After ejecting Faisal, Augustus called the front desk to arrange for a motor cab, and within five minutes they were downstairs and climbing in. As he expected, Tim appeared out of nowhere and joined them.

They had the cab drop them off a block away from Tim and Gregory's lodgings and finished the journey on foot.

"Isn't this putting ourselves in danger of meeting those Australian blokes?" Tim asked as the entered the building.

"Yes, but it's getting us out of danger from the police," Augustus said, giving a brief account of Moustafa's adventures.

Tim looked over the Nubian appreciatively. "Killed him with your bare hands, did you? Good work. I thought you'd had a ruck. I noticed some bruises I didn't give you."

Before Moustafa could snap out a reply, the lift door opened. Augustus tensed to see a middle class Egyptian in a suit and tarboosh waiting on the other side.

They passed him without a word. The Egyptian glanced at them curiously.

We do make an odd trio, don't we? And seeing one of our number duck away and fearfully take the stairs doesn't exactly help us look inconspicuous. I hope you don't think on it too much, my good chap.

They met Tim on his floor, went to his room, and locked the door.

As Tim cleared away the mess, Augustus and Moustafa laid out the map and key.

"So the problem I've been having is that they stole a map of too large a scale," Augustus explained.

Tim laughed. "You never were happy, were you? Here a woman and a kid bluff their way into a military base and His Highness doesn't like the map they bring back!"

"I'm not unappreciative of their services, but I cannot escape the fact that the map may prove inadequate."

"Bloody ungrateful, you are," Tim muttered. "Let's have a look."

They stared at the map and the key for several minutes.

"I see what you mean," Tim grumbled.

They stared for several more minutes.

"Oi, how about this spot?" Tim pointed to a spot on the second branch line, the one Augustus hadn't fully examined.

There was, indeed, a tool shed there, and a rough patch labeled "ruins." A point a little further away bore the label "old saint's tomb."

"Possibly," Augustus mused, "but the key doesn't mention a saint's tomb. It mentions a mosque."

Tim shrugged. "Same thing."

"They are not," Moustafa objected.

"Sure they are. You go pray at both, don't you? I've seen it. There's a tomb not far from here. Gippo ladies wailing there day and night."

Augustus and Moustafa exchanged glances.

"You might be right!" the Nubian exclaimed. "Perhaps the engineers mistook the ruined tomb as a ruined mosque. If the local villagers still go there to pray, and it's in a ruined state, the engineers might have assumed it was a mosque where the minaret had fallen down."

"We should go," Augustus said.

"In the daylight?" Moustafa asked.

"We will be able to see better. I think our friends are digging at night. If it's right on the branch line, they cannot risk being seen by men in their regiment."

"But this spot is close to this village marked here. Wouldn't they attract attention from the villagers?"

"Not if they paid them off," Tim said. "Jack said they'd taken on some local help. I'll bet a month's wages those Gippos came from that village."

"Let's go," Augustus said.

We might have found it, he thought as they hurried out the door. *Let's just hope they haven't posted a sentry.*

Actually, I do hope that. It will give me a chance to avenge Gregory.

I haven't forgotten you, old comrade. Not even with a prize before me as big as this. I'll be killing every one of them before this is all said and done.

CHAPTER TWENTY-THREE

As excited as Moustafa felt about the prospect of finding the spot where the famed Alexander may rest, he tried to keep his head. They had not found the tomb. In fact, they had not even found the general area of the tomb. Tim Crawford's guess was a good one, worthy of following up, but it was still only a guess.

And even when they got there, they would still have much searching to do.

They alighted from the motor cab at a cluster of villas two miles from the spot where they needed to go. They had told the driver they were visiting one of the rich Alexandrians who lived there, and said they wanted to walk the rest of the way to enjoy the weather, which was pleasant and cool thanks to the breeze off the Mediterranean. It was always cooler here than in Cairo, making it a favorite spot for those Cairenes who could afford to get away in the summer.

Thanks to the reward they had earned on the last case, Moustafa was now one of those people.

Crossing paths with this madman had not been an entirely negative experience.

And now he was searching for an archaeological site that he never in his wildest dreams ever thought he'd see.

All three men scanned the area, hoping to spot any ruins. Moustafa was disappointed to see none, and yet this didn't surprise him. This area had been cultivated and built on for some time, and now a brand new set of railway tracks, as yet unused, cut through it. The branch line had been laid to connect the various small communities outside the city boundaries, such as the scattering of villas through which they now walked. The line was also to allow the rich farmland outside the city easier access to the city market. According to the map the Little Infidel had stolen, the line had another ninety miles to go, and when finished would bring a whole new farming region within a day's delivery of Egypt's second city.

That could only be of benefit to Alexandria and Egypt as a whole, and yet the Egyptian people were trying to push out the British. Moustafa hoped that when that happened, the Egyptians themselves would take up the job of building up the new nation's infrastructure.

It was already late afternoon and the wealthy of the neighborhood were out for their daily rides. A few Egyptian men on horseback trotted through the fields, talking happily. A carriage passed, bearing a couple of veiled women out for a visit. A few servants passed on some job or other. No one paid much attention to the Nubian and two Europeans walking through. This wealthy suburb seemed untouched by the independence struggle.

Soon they put the villas behind them and walked along a dirt path that paralleled the branch line. Fellahin worked the fields, stopping to stare at the foreigners as they passed.

"Now that we're off the main road, we're attracting attention," Moustafa said.

"I don't see how we can avoid it," Mr. Wall replied.

Moustafa scanned the area. They were getting close now.

"There," he said after a minute.

He did not dare point, for they were in sight of a small village of mudbrick huts. A couple of little girls, drawing water from a rivulet flowing past the village, stopped and stared with their mouths hanging open. Moustafa could just see the dark form of a woman in one of the doorways, watching them. In the fields next to the village a couple of men hacked at the soft earth with hoes. While they did not stop to watch the passing strangers, Moustafa felt sure they saw. In Egypt, people always saw.

"Where?" Tim said. "Oh, you mean that rise over there?"

"Yes," Moustafa said.

The branch line ran just to the north of the road they were on, and a few hundred yards to the north of that rose a low mound of earth, about a hundred meters above the floodplain and looking to be about a mile in length. From his vantage point he could not see how wide it was, although from what he recalled from the map it was about a half a mile wide, one of the scattered outcroppings of bedrock that formed islands in the delta. Alexandria stood on just such an island.

"Makes sense," Tim said. "Wouldn't want to bury your king someplace the floods could get him."

"Are you turning into an archaeologist?" Mr. Wall asked with obvious amusement.

"I mucked about with enough dead bodies in the war to make me a professor."

They left the road, passing on a narrow raised path between two fields. About a hundred yards to their left a group of half a dozen fellahin working on fixing a water pump stopped their work and turned in their direction.

"Go back to Europe, foreigners!" one shouted.

"Egypt for Egyptians!" another shouted, brandishing a wrench.

Tim narrowed his eyes at them. "I can't understand Gippo, but that didn't sound too friendly."

"It wasn't," Moustafa said. "Let's go."

The farmers continued to shout. Tim put a hand in his pocket.

"If they approach, let me handle it," Moustafa said.

"Don't worry, Shaka Zulu. If all they do is wave tools in the air I won't start shooting," Tim said. "But if I see a gun, it's open season."

Moustafa wondered what he'd do if it came to that. He could not let this Englishman gun down a group of fellahin for simply wanting a nation. On the other hand, if a mob formed, he'd be one of its victims too.

Luckily the men did nothing but shout, and Moustafa and his

companions hurried on through the fields to the mound.

As they approached, they could see the outcropping better. It was covered with tall grass swaying in the wind, colored by sprays of purple and red wildflowers. Here and there a palm tree was silhouetted against the sky, but these were few and small, for the ground was too rocky. Moustafa could see the bedrock poking through the vegetation in several places. At the near end of the eminence stood a crumbled stone building about ten feet square with a domed roof.

"The shrine," Moustafa said, his heart beating faster. This might really be the spot!

"But where's the Bedouin encampment?" Mr. Wall asked.

"I don't know. Maybe they left."

I hope so, or this is the wrong place.

As they climbed onto the tracks, raised above the surrounding fields on a bed of packed gravel, they caught sight of the remains of a small wooden structure nearby, now nothing but a heap of ash and a few blackened boards.

"I suspect that's our tool shed," Mr. Wall said. "Egypt for the Egyptians. Hurrah! A great blow for independence."

Moustafa bridled at his tone. He did not like to hear the movement mocked, least of all by some Englishman.

But he had to admit Mr. Wall's sarcasm was deserved. The movement was destroying as much as it was building. Burning toolsheds, cutting telegraph wires, and breaking the windows of Greek shops was no way to start a nation.

"Those Gippos are still watching us," Tim said, looking over his shoulder.

"They're called Egyptians," Moustafa said.

"Whatever they're bloody called, they're still watching us. We're being so obvious I feel like I'm waving a red flag in the middle of No Man's Land. What the hell are we wandering about in broad daylight for?"

"It's the only way we can spot possible places for the tomb," Mr. Wall explained as they walked down the other side of the railway embankment. "The men digging for it aren't trained archaeologists like we are and might have missed something."

"What if they're up there now?" Tim asked. "Then what do we do? Shaka Zulu and I only have pistols, and you only got that little pig sticker."

"They'll only be digging at night. It's too conspicuous otherwise," Mr. Wall said.

As if to demonstrate Mr. Wall's point, off in the distance they heard the sound of a train. A steam engine approached, pulling a flatbed stacked with railroad ties and a tender heaped with gravel. It chugged past and headed for the end of the line, soon dwindling out of sight.

"You want to kick us out and we're still building your country," Tim grumbled. "I pay tax, I do, and it all goes to bleedin' foreigners."

Moustafa glowered, but said nothing.

"Come now, Tim," Mr. Wall said. "You have to work to pay tax."

"Well if I did work, my tax would all go to bleedin' foreigners."

Moustafa ignored the little man as they ascended the side of the slope. It felt hotter now that they were shielded from the sea breeze. The Englishmen's breath grew labored. Moustafa kept looking around. As annoying as that runt of a foreigner was, he had a point. They were terribly exposed, and news of their visit would be sure to reach the ears of the Australians. They must have spies and allies in the area. It would be the only way they could do any work in peace. While a passing train would ignore any lights atop the ridge, the locals would come to investigate.

They'll come investigate us when we dig up here too.

As they made it to the top of the ridge, a strong breeze hit their faces and tugged on their clothing. To the north, Moustafa could see the distant blue line of the Mediterranean past a stretch of green fields and marshland. Looking to the east, past the cracked and crumbling saint's tomb standing on the end of the eminence, his eye followed the line of track back to the cluster of villas and beyond, where a smudge of smoke on the horizon marked the city.

Nervously he turned to the south, the way they had come, and saw two villages in the broad fields, the one by the tracks they had passed, and a larger one a little further to the south. Irregularities in the mound kept him from seeing to the west.

Moustafa examined the top of the mound, and took a deep breath. Yes, this had been an ancient spot. It was obvious to anyone with the least bit of training.

The small plateau ran about a mile to the east and west and a little less than half a mile wide from north to south, running roughly parallel with the railway line. Moustafa guessed that at one time the top had been flattened, but now the windswept grass undulated over a rough surface, and here and there were larger knolls out of which stuck stones, some of them showing straight edges from having been worked. Moustafa bet the stone blocks used in the saint's tomb had been looted from this site.

"Where's the mound of rubble and the column bases?" Mr. Wall wondered aloud.

"Let's go forward a bit so the Gippos downhill can't see us," Tim suggested.

They walked until they got to the center of the little plateau, noticing more worked stone as they did. It was eerily silent here except for the constant rustle of the wind through the grass.

"I've seen enough mounds of rubble to make a Belgian village," Tim grumbled.

"They weren't always rubble, you know," Mr. Wall said, smiling as he looked around. He was obviously enjoying himself.

"All the ones I saw were."

They began to move west along the center of the plateau. Moustafa's sharp eye spotted a couple of fragments of statues—the fingerless palm of a hand, a portion of a leg, and what looked like the dome of a head half covered in grass and dirt.

"What I wouldn't give for a dig permit at this place," Moustafa whispered.

"I hereby grant you one," Mr. Wall said. "Usable only at night while heavily armed and only after we find a likely spot."

"Won't the Aussies and Gippos be digging at night?" Tim asked.

"The term is Egyptian, you half-sized excrescence from a baboon's bottom!" Moustafa growled.

Tim grinned and made a mock bow. "My apologies, Shaka Zulu. Won't the Aussies and *Egyptians* we're planning on getting into a gunfight with going to be digging at night? *Egyptians*, mind you. Got to be respectful to the blokes before blowing their fuzzy heads off."

"Why you—"

"Look," Mr. Wall said, pointing with his cane. What Moustafa saw made him temporarily forget to strangle Tim.

A mound of stone, several feet taller than the rest, stood before them. It was a jumble of stone and column drums, as well as smaller bits of rubble in between, and only partially covered by clumps of grass. As Moustafa approached and studied it more, he could see bits of an architrave jutting through.

"This was once a temple," he whispered.

"How can you tell?" Tim said. "Looks like a quarry after a two-day barrage of heavy artillery."

"I believe you are correct," Mr. Wall said, presumably to Moustafa.

Moustafa's heart skipped a beat as he pointed. "Look!"

A little to the south of the mound was a scattering of five column bases, ripped from their foundations and lying every which way amid the grass.

"Two items from the key so close together? We must be close," Mr. Wall said.

As they approached the area, Moustafa and Mr. Wall spread out, scanning every unevenness in the ground, every fragment of statuary or masonry, every potsherd. Moustafa took a deep breath of sea air and smiled. He missed being on excavations, and missed this initial phase of surveying the ground. Even just a slow walk across an archaeological site could tell you so much.

His trained eyes studied the terrain. Yes, this flat, open bit marked a submerged road. Here and there flagstones poked up through the thin topsoil. And there was a row of buildings to the south, the landward side. None terribly large, perhaps the family tombs of lesser nobles. Yes! Here was a fragment of a funerary stela showing a woman lighting a fire at an altar. And a large amount of potsherds crunched under his feet, broken and deliberately left behind after visiting families had eaten meals with the departed.

But the tomb, where was the tomb they sought?

It soon became obvious the Australians didn't know either. They found evidence of half a dozen different test excavations scattered around the promontory.

Excavations? Bah! Simple holes in the ground done with no concept of modern archaeological method or care of preservation. In one test pit they had cut right through a mosaic floor. In another they had dug into an obviously subsidiary building, giving up after finding and scattering various small pottery figurines around the area. In another case they had dug horizontally into the large mound, not realizing this was the heap from a collapsed temple, and if the tomb was close by it would be under the structure, not in its ruins.

That realization prompted Moustafa to poke around the mound further, but he saw no evidence of an entrance to any subterranean chamber and no inscriptions that would give them any clue.

He glanced over at Mr. Wall, who didn't seem to be having any better luck. Tim, not knowing how to help, lay nearly out of sight at the top of the mound, keeping watch over the surrounding countryside.

For an hour they searched all along the top of the ridge, finding nothing, or at least not what they hoped for. It was a prime archaeological site, well worthy of further investigation, and yet paled in comparison to what they sought.

"We're never going to find it this way," Mr. Wall called over as he poked about the foundations of one of the larger buildings. "We need a full crew and several field seasons."

"Once we take care of the murderers, perhaps you should request permission from the authorities," Moustafa suggested.

Because they would never say yes to me.

Mr. Wall looked over at him and smiled. "And I wonder who I would get to run the excavation."

THE CASE OF THE ASPHYXIATED ALEXANDRIAN

Moustafa's heart did somersaults in his chest.

"Do not joke with me, Mr. Wall," Moustafa said cautiously.

"I am not joking. Come. We have to plan for tonight. I'll fetch Tim from his perch and we'll go back to the city."

"All right, Mr. Wall."

Moustafa walked along the ruined avenue one last time, the sea breeze fading away as he got within the lee of the mound. His gaze roved over the rough area of grass and shrub where every few feet a worked stone protruded out of the soil. In front of the mound ran a low bump that must be the foundation of a wall, and a parallel bump about ten feet to the side marked the other wall. In the middle was a shallow swale where the grass waved in the sea breeze.

Waved in the sea breeze? But this was the one place on the ridge where the breeze didn't touch.

And only the grass in the center of the swale waved. The grass around the edge remained still.

Curious, Moustafa moved to the edge of the swale, got down on his hands and knees, and crawled forward.

He could feel the breeze now, cold and damp and coming not from the sea, but coming out from the ground itself.

Moustafa crawled forward another couple of feet, felt the ground beneath him shift a little, and quickly scampered back.

In the instant he had retreated, he had seen a narrow, dark fissure at the lowest point of the ground.

The breeze had come up from there, up from an underground chamber funneling the sea breeze from some other open portion of the hill.

"Moustafa, I am beginning to think you are a genius."

Mr. Wall's voice made him look up. His former boss stood several paces up the slope of the mound, with Tim standing next to him. Mr. Wall could see the waving grass where no breeze should be, could see Moustafa lying on the ground, and had divined its meaning.

"I think it might be a vertical shaft entrance to catacombs like those of Kom el Shoqafa," Moustafa said.

"It could very well be, but don't those date to much later?" Mr. Wall said, the excitement in his voice at odds with his words of caution.

"They could have been built up around the tomb, or near to it. The breeze coming up out of that hole is such that there must be a great space below."

"Let's check the seaward slope and see if we can find another entrance."

They spread out and descended the far slope, the salty breeze much stronger here. For half an hour they found nothing. Finally, Tim let out a cry and motioned them over.

"How about this?" he said, pointing to a tumble of large masonry. It took a moment for Moustafa to notice one of the dark gaps between the stones did not end after a few inches. Moustafa stuck his face up against it.

He could see nothing, but he smelled the cool air of the interior, and felt an open space beyond. Letting out a whistle, he heard it echo into the far distance.

He trembled a little as he stood back.

"May God be praised," he whispered.

"Fine, don't thank me at all," Tim said.

"Pity we didn't think to bring torches," Mr. Wall said, peering into the hole. Then he stood back and studied the stone surrounding it. "The blocks here are too large to move without a serious labor force. I think our best plan is to try the entrance above. We'll have to buy ropes."

Despite his excitement, Moustafa forced himself to think scientifically. "One thing makes me wonder. All the reports said Alexander was buried within the city itself."

"That's true, but only the earliest accounts," Mr. Wall said. "Perhaps the tomb in the city was a mere cenotaph, with the body placed elsewhere."

"Or this might be the cenotaph," Moustafa said, although he didn't want to entertain the thought.

"We will find out shortly enough. We'll come back tonight and start to dig."

Tim Crawford turned to him. "Are you stupid? Every Gippo within three miles has seen us up here. Those Aussies will know about it before dinner and be waiting for us."

Mr. Wall's face turned hard. "You want to get the men who killed Gregory or not?"

"You know I do, but walking into an ambush?"

"An ambush laid by people in the engineering corps and a few tough but inexperienced fellahin. We're trench raiders."

Tim paused a moment, then said quietly, "Sure, we're trench raiders. The best of the lot. And we survived the war by not putting our heads in the noose. You don't waltz into an ambush when the enemy has better terrain and superior numbers."

"We can't attack the Australians where they're staying and we don't know what other places they frequent. We're not even sure if we'll see our informant again. Can you think of a better idea?"

Tim looked at Moustafa as if to get support. Moustafa looked away. What could he say? Tim was right, it was a foolish step. But Mr. Wall was also right. This was the only way to confront the murderers directly.

"You good with a gun?" Tim asked him.

"I've been an associate of Mr. Wall for a year now."

Tim snorted. "Then you're good with a gun. Let's do it."

Moustafa passed a hand over his face, suddenly regretting the day he was born. He knew something terrible would happen tonight. He didn't need Nur's dreams to tell him that.

CHAPTER TWENTY-FOUR

Faisal was nervous, which felt better and worse than being bored. He had been bored for a couple of hours when Cordelia went to her room and he got sent back down to his little box in the basement. He had nothing to do there except kick his football around, making it bounce off the walls and ceiling and door every which way. That was fun because the harder you kicked, the harder it was to predict where it would come at you.

But then one of the hotel staff came and shouted at him for making so much noise. So he had to stop and then had nothing to do until the little bell above his door rang, signaling that Cordelia wanted her "servant" to come help her with something.

"Something" turned out to be going for a walk.

They strolled onto the square in front of the hotel. Instead of crossing the street to walk along the Corniche to look at the sea and pass all those tempting food stands, they walked along the landward side of the street.

"Where we go?" Faisal asked in English.

Cordelia answered with something he didn't understand.

"Where we go?" Faisal asked in slower English.

"Don't worry, Sir Faisal."

Faisal took a step to the side. Last time she called him that, she kissed him. Yuck.

Faisal looked around. Maybe she was worried that the European who had been chatting to her would come back. The Englishman had explained to him that he hadn't been a spy for the murderers, but Faisal wasn't so sure.

They walked along the main street facing the port for a little while, Faisal having to shoo away beggars and Egyptians offering boat rides and tours.

"My mistress is on very important business," he told them.

She did seem to think so. Cordelia walked with that confident, determined look she got sometimes, especially when the Englishman told her she couldn't do something.

Cordelia turned right, inland, and followed a street lined with nice European shops. All of them had big windows full of things Faisal could never afford—suits and shoes and giant ladies' hats.

There were other things too, like walking sticks and gramophones and gold boxes to hold cigarettes.

He had stared at shops like that all his life, looking at the things on display as if they weren't real, like they were images in clouds instead of actual objects he could ever own. It must be strange to be able to go into those shops and buy whatever you wanted.

"One minute," Cordelia told him, and entered a shop.

Faisal kicked a stone across the street and did as he was told. He'd never get to go in those shops. He stood there, bored, as Europeans entered and left. After a minute, he took a peek through the window.

Cordelia was trying on a hat! Didn't she have enough hats? He thought they'd come up here to help with the mystery, and Cordelia was standing here trying on a hat.

Well, the Englishman did leave her behind.

He had left Faisal behind too. The Englishman didn't want either of them along.

Grumbling, Faisal paced back and forth. Tim was probably talking about England right now, telling the Englishman all about how he should come back home and be with his old war friends. He'd convince him. Faisal was sure of it.

And there was nothing Faisal could do to stop him.

Faisal slumped, despairing. This might be the very last day the Englishman was in Egypt, and Faisal was wasting it watching Cordelia try on hats!

No. The Englishman wouldn't leave until he had found the people who killed his friend. So he'd be around for a few more days. Would Faisal even get to see him?

Probably not. He'd be stuck with Cordelia the whole time.

Then Faisal saw someone across the street who made him forget about what might happen in a few days and worry about what might happen in the next few seconds.

That foreigner who had followed Cordelia was walking down the sidewalk on the other side of the street.

The moment after Faisal spotted him, he spotted Faisal.

He stopped, glowered, and rapped his cane on the pavement like the Englishman did when he was really, really mad.

Except the Englishman never hit him. This man would.

The European strode across the street.

Faisal looked both ways, unsure what to do. There were both Europeans and Egyptians on the street just like last time, and last time no one helped him except Cordelia.

But he had to protect Cordelia, not the other way around.

Halfway across the street, the foreigner raised his cane like he was going to smack Faisal with it.

"That's him!" Faisal shouted, pointing. Several people turned to look. The man stopped, uncertain. "That's the foreigner who insulted the protest movement. He called Sa'ad Zaghloul a son of a dog and said all the independence heroes should be lined up and shot. I heard him! And he beat a corn seller on the Corniche!"

"Typical!" an Egyptian man pulling a cart grumbled. "All foreigners should be kicked out."

A burly Egyptian in a Western-style suit put a hand on Faisal's shoulder. "Are you sure he said all this?"

"Sure I'm sure," Faisal said, then realized he might be caught in a lie. "He said it in English, but my mistress told me what he said and I saw him beat the corn seller with my own eyes."

The man still stood in the middle of the street, looking around at the angry faces, all Egyptian, looking back at him. Faisal noticed that some foreigners were staring curiously, while others moved away. Perhaps they spoke Arabic.

"And this is the man?" the frowning Egyptian in the business suit asked, jabbing a finger in his direction. That seemed to startle the foreigner. He took a step back.

"Yes, he said horrible things about Egyptians. Dirty things. My mistress blushed when she heard them, and said no European would dare say such things about another European."

"They never do," a Nubian porter growled, coming up beside him. "They're as thick as thieves."

"They think they own us!" another Egyptian shouted.

Faisal nodded to the small but growing crowd around him. The European had lowered his cane and retreated back to the other side of the road. "He said the British shouldn't have stopped the slavers in the Soudan. They should have sold Egyptians down there instead."

"Bah! Why bother? They keep us as slaves right here."

The European started walking away with a hurried step.

"He's getting away!" the porter cried.

"He can't insult our nation and get away with it. I'm tired of their kind."

The Nubian switched to English. "Hey, you!" The European looked fearfully over his shoulder. "Yes, you. Come here. We want to talk to you. You have some explaining to do."

The European quickened his pace. Several of the men crossed the street.

Then several things happened at once. The European broke into a run, and the group of half a dozen Egyptians and Nubians ran after him. From further down the street, two Egyptians rushed to intercept them, one blowing a whistle.

Plainclothes police! What were they doing here on a boring street of shops?

"Stand back! Disperse!" one of the policemen said.

The two of them got between the European and the group chasing him. A couple of Egyptians ran off as soon as they realized they faced policemen. The rest stopped and started shouting.

"Countrymen! You work for our oppressors?"

"Let us through! He insulted all Egyptians!"

While the plainclothes policemen were able to stop the men Faisal had talked to, they didn't notice the European, halfway down the street now, get tripped by an Egyptian shopkeeper. He stumbled and fell to his knees.

Suddenly several Egyptians appeared out of nowhere to rush him.

The European swung his cane to clear the space around him, then tried to rise.

That was a mistake, because he had to stop swinging his cane for a moment.

The Egyptians closed in, knocking off his hat, wrenching the cane from his grip, and tearing his suit.

Screams and shouts everywhere. All the Europeans started to flee, a couple of them getting slaps from the Egyptians. One European man pulled out a pistol, pointing it around him uncertainly, then bolted.

The plainclothes policeman blew his whistle again as his partner tried to keep back the first crowd. When the Egyptians and Nubian simply ran around him, the two officers turned and hurried back to help the European, who was now getting slapped by several people at once.

Faisal watched all this with a mixture of glee and a growing sense of alarm. He'd seen riots and big fights before, and he knew there always came a point where everything got out of control, where shouting and trying to calm people down no longer worked, where a few insults and slaps turned into real violence.

He shrank into the doorway of the women's shop and noticed the door was closed and locked, the blinds drawn. Cordelia and the other ladies must be hiding inside. That was good. He had to stay put and make sure the crowd only went after bad Europeans. He wished the Englishman was here. He could take care of all this much better.

More shouts and slaps and running feet. Seeing they were outnumbered by the crowd, one of the officers pulled out a revolver and fired in the air, poking a hole in a British flag hanging from one of the buildings.

The crowd scattered, one of the men attacking the European getting in a final kick.

For a moment Faisal thought that would be the end to it, but the crowd reformed at the end of the street, joined by more Egyptians who came to see what was going on. The shouts rose to a roar. The two policemen, both with pistols drawn, stood in the street near the doorway Faisal was hiding in. They looked uncertain what to do. The European, his clothes all torn and his face red from slapping, followed the last of the Europeans down the other end of the street.

No, not the last. One European woman about halfway down the street hid in a doorway. She looked rich, with a nice white dress and big hat like Cordelia. What was she still doing here?

"Fellow Egyptians!" the porter shouted at the two policemen. "Why do you draw guns on your countrymen and protect the invaders?"

"Disperse!" One policeman said as the other blew on his whistle again.

A cobblestone flew out of the crowd, bouncing off the doorway where Faisal hid, making him yelp. The two officers held their ground.

Another cobblestone flew through the air, and another. The last one nearly hit the man with the whistle, who had to jump back a couple of feet to avoid it.

A roar came from the crowd, the sound of a hungry predator confident of getting its prey.

The mass of Egyptians and Nubians, still growing, began to advance. Faisal shrank further into the protection of the doorway. He was right between the two sides. When they met, he'd be in big danger!

Faisal looked sadly at the door. If this was an Egyptian shop, like a normal Egyptian shop for normal Egyptians, he could pound on the door and they'd let him inside.

But if they hadn't let him in when things were normal, they sure wouldn't when there was a riot in the street.

Several more cobblestones flew at the policeman, who had to do a little dance all around the street to keep from getting hit. That encouraged the crowd, which advanced more quickly.

One of the policemen fired just over the heads of the crowd.

That stopped them. They jeered and threw more stones. Once again the police had to back away, and once again the crowd advanced.

A flurry of stones sailed into the street. The two policemen finally broke and ran. The crowd swarmed past Faisal's doorway. That poor foreign woman would be killed for sure!

In the next moment, the crowd stopped, then rushed back the way it had come. What was going on?

Faisal dared a peek, and saw a line of mounted police, led by a shouting, red-faced English officer, trotting down the street in a solid line, waving their long truncheons at the crowd.

None of the rioters stayed long enough to get hit. They sprinted down the street to the intersection and ran off in both directions. The mounted police followed. Faisal squeezed himself into the doorway and tried to make himself invisible.

Then suddenly he was being thrown into the street. The world spun and he landed hard on the cobblestones. The two plainclothes policemen stood at the doorway, along with the European lady.

"Open up in the name of the law!" one of the officers demanded in Arabic, pounding on the door.

Faisal picked himself up and backed away. The horsemen had reached the end of the street and stopped, content to let the rioters run away. He could still hear shouts from beyond the line, but nothing got thrown at the mounted police and Faisal knew it was all over.

At least for today. There might be another riot tomorrow. How did these things start, anyway? People were getting crazy.

Someone peeked nervously from behind the blinds. One of the officers flashed a badge, and the door opened.

To Faisal's surprise, the police didn't enter. The woman did. Curious, Faisal got closer, but not too close. He didn't want one of the policemen to throw him on the street again.

Between the two policemen he could see the European woman speaking angrily with Cordelia. With both of them talking in English and talking at the same time, Faisal couldn't understand any of it. After a moment, the woman gestured at Cordelia, said something that sounded like an order, and the two of them walked out the door.

"Faisal!" Cordelia cried, and hurried over to him. She asked something in English and looked him over.

"How are you I am fine," Faisal replied.

One of the plainclothes policemen stepped up, spoke with Cordelia for a moment, then turned to Faisal.

"Cordelia Russell is under protective police custody. We're taking her back to her hotel."

"Is she under arrest?"

"No. But she must do as she's told." The officer pointed at the other woman. "This is Lady Dorothea Russell, Sir Thomas Russell Pasha's wife. She came up here specifically to fetch her since her husband couldn't get away given the situation in Cairo."

The policeman didn't seem to think Faisal deserved any more explanation, because he turned and the whole group of them started walking down the street, Lady Dorothea keeping a hand on Cordelia's arm. Cordelia looked over her shoulder at him, worried.

Faisal tagged along behind.

"I'm supposed to guard her," he said.

The policeman snorted. "You? I have orders to keep her away from everyone she came up here with. You and your friends are a bad influence."

"Bad influence? She wanted to come up."

The policeman turned. Faisal stopped.

"Get lost," the officer said.

"What's going to happen to her?"

"She'll be sent back to Cairo to see her brother. He'll decide what to do. Most likely she'll be packed off to England."

With that, the officer turned and rejoined the others. Faisal stayed put, unsure what to do. Cordelia gave him a final look over her shoulder before they rounded the corner and disappeared.

They always leave in the end. That's what Moustafa always said.

And the Englishman will leave too.

Faisal hurried to Tim's apartment building, hoping they'd be there. He'd found out where Tim lived easily enough. He knew the Englishman had called the front desk to hire a motor cab, so he had gone down there himself and asked for the address since his "mistress" wanted to join them. The Egyptian at the front desk had given him the address without a second thought.

Pretending to work for the English gave you some of the advantages the English had. Not all of them, just some.

Faisal worried they might be at the Englishman's hotel. He didn't dare go in there alone. The apartment building had regular Egyptians living in it, so Faisal could blend in.

He ran all the way there, passing knots of angry men talking about the fight.

"We should demonstrate in front of the police station!" one shouted.

"We should burn the hotels!" another shouted.

That worried Faisal, but not too much. When people shouted and waved their arms around, they were usually just letting off their anger, not making it grow.

He hoped.

Huffing up the flights of stairs, he got to Tim's door and pounded on it.

To his relief, Tim opened up. He hadn't taken the Englishman away yet.

"Hello, Little Gippo."

"Hello."

Faisal entered to find the Englishman, Moustafa, and Tim arranging all sorts of equipment on the floor. They had shovels and pickaxes, as well as some electric torches. On the sofa was a long coil of rope and a big burlap bag that clanked as Moustafa picked it up as if it contained a lot of metal objects.

"How the devil did you find us?" the Englishman asked.

"Um, I guessed."

"Nonsense," Moustafa grumbled. "How did you find us?"

"It doesn't matter. He'll just make up some story," the Englishman said, not looking up from his work.

"What's all that stuff?" Faisal asked.

"Tools for a little excavation we're planning," the Englishman said. He sounded happy.

"Where?"

"Outside the city. We want to get to it before those Australians do."

"You're going to dig up some djinn?"

"Yes, so it's best if you stay away."

Silly Englishman. He didn't believe in djinn, so why would he say that except to scare him?

He was trying to leave him behind. Faisal wasn't about to be left behind again.

"Where's Cordelia?" the Englishman asked.

Should he tell? Maybe not. "At her hotel."

"Good. You go back there and protect her," the Englishman told him.

"I'll make sure Cordelia is safe," Faisal replied.

He turned away to look out the window and hide his smile. He knew Cordelia would be safe, so he didn't have to watch over her. Saying he'd make sure he was safe wasn't a lie. If he said he'd stay at the hotel with her, that would be a lie. He was getting pretty good at telling the truth and still doing whatever he wanted.

And what he wanted was to see the treasure they were going to dig up, and solve whatever problems the Englishman would get himself into.

He got the feeling he didn't have much time left with him, so he had to make the most of it.

CHAPTER TWENTY-FIVE

Augustus and Tim lay in the damp mud of a farmer's field, watching the dark bulk of the ridge silhouetted against a starry sky. They could hear a few distant voices from the nearest village, visible only as a ragged line of softly lit windows. Somewhere a woman sang a simple, rhythmic song that had probably accompanied work for hundreds if not thousands of years.

Moustafa had disappeared into the shadows to their left to watch the road. They hadn't heard a sound from him for ten minutes.

"Amazing how quiet that Nubian can be," Tim whispered.

"He's a good man in a fight. You'll see."

Augustus gripped the MP18 submachine gun. Both other men had rifles. Augustus had shared the Mills bombs and homemade flash grenades between himself and Tim. They had been waiting in the field for an hour, and other than a couple of villagers strolling down the road intent on a nighttime visit with a friend, they had seen no one.

"We should get up there soon." Tim whispered. "I don't think they got there before us, and since they didn't, we should take the high ground first."

"It will be difficult to defend with just the three of us. Too large," Augustus whispered back.

"Yeah, but at least we can pick our ground, and we're out of the city so the kid and that lady won't get in the line of fire."

"In our last case, Cordelia followed us," Augustus said, scanning the dark fields. "A gun battle is no place for a woman, although there's no use telling her that."

Tim's grin was visible even in the dim light. "Do you fancy her?"

"Good Lord, no."

"Why not? She's not half bad. And the way she bosses you around she acts like she's your girl. Careful, mate, or she'll slap a ring on your finger and make that bossing official."

"She was interested once. I cured her of that affliction."

"A diehard romantic, I see. Mind if I make a play?"

"She's the younger sister of Cairo's chief of police. Don't you remember?"

"Oh, right. Maybe not, then. Who's this Jocelyn I heard your Nubian pal mention? Oi! Look at that face light up. She's the real stuff, eh?"

"Don't be crude, Tim."

Tim elbowed him. "She's a nice one, I'll bet. Where is she?"

"Palestine. I wired her. I hope she can make it. She was a great help on the last case."

"Last case? You talk about these murders like they come as regular as the morning post."

"Sometimes it feels that way."

Tim edged closer to him and his voice took on a conspiratorial air. "So what's she like, eh? This Jocelyn girl."

"She's hardly a girl. She's a widow and a mother."

"Oh, experienced then. Lucky you."

Augustus frowned. "Tim ..."

Tim raised his hands in a placating gesture. "Uh-oh. She's special. All right, I'll say no more. Looking forward to meeting her. Must be interesting if she fell for you."

"What's that supposed to mean?"

"Don't get like that. I mean she must be some bookish toff like you."

"She does read more than the sports pages, that's true."

"Hey, I read lots more than that."

"When?"

"When we was in the trenches. I had to read all those maps and action reports."

"And the Quartermaster's manifest in order to see where the rum ration was stored."

"You see? I'm a well-read man."

Moustafa's voice came out of the shadows. "You two talk too much."

"You're sneaky, Shaka Zulu. Didn't hear you come up," Tim said.

"You would have if you had been listening instead of talking," Moustafa grumbled, crawling into view. "You act like you're going to a party instead of a gunfight."

"We'll be getting to that soon enough," Tim said. "No need to rush it."

"I've seen no one," Moustafa said.

"Tim suggested we get up on the mound. I think that's best," Augustus told him.

"All right."

They rose and, crouching low, moved across the fields, pausing at the raised edge of each in order to survey their surroundings.

The three of them were weighed down not only by their weapons, but also by two long coils of rope, harnesses, a mallet, a hammer and chisel, a crowbar, a dozen metal stakes, and other tools. Augustus hoped they would get a chance for a little nighttime archaeology.

The extra gear didn't slow them down at all. Back in the war, the officers sent them over the top with a ridiculous amount of impedimenta, so the two veterans felt advancing through soft earth with thirty kilos of gear hanging from them to be the most natural thing in the world. Moustafa was so strong he didn't notice the weight either.

They met no one as they drew nearer the mound. Artillery rumbled in the distance. Augustus tried to maintain focus. They found a deep shadow between a cluster of three palm trees and a farmer's tool shed.

"You two wait here," Tim said, "and I'll scout the way up."

Tim disappeared into the night. Augustus kept a watchful eye, looking slightly away from the slope in order to improve his night vision, a trick he had learned in the trenches. For some reason you could see less at night if you looked directly at the object of interest. Nevertheless, he didn't see his old friend or anyone else.

He didn't hear anything either. When it came to night work, no one was better than Timothy Crawford, and only Augustus and a couple of other men, now gone west, were his equal.

Augustus had done a lot of night work in the war. Thankfully, Crawford hadn't been along for his last mission.

He shared a shell crater with a few others between the forward and support line, having spent most of the predawn hours stringing telephone wire for the signals men. The Germans had a knack for hitting the wire with their artillery, or simple luck borne from pummeling their lines on a regular basis.

The work had gone on for longer than planned, as was generally the case, and sunrise found them stuck in an exposed position. So they had settled in a deep shell crater to have their breakfast and wait until late afternoon, when the sun would shine in the Germans' eyes and they could make it back safely.

The officers wouldn't complain too much about this brief vacation. It happened all too often, and at least the crew had strung all the telephone wire, the last line frantically laid as the sun began to pale the eastern horizon and everything started to become visible.

Now the four of them lay against the sloped side of a muddy shell hole a good ten feet deep, the bottom a pool of stinking water. They couldn't light their cigarettes or pipes—the Germans might spot the trails of smoke—so they contented themselves by eating their cold rations, the only food they'd get until nightfall.

"A whole day without work," Private Wright said, shoving his steel helmet over his eyes and crossing his hands over his chest. "I think I'll take a nap."

"Not a bad idea," Sergeant Young replied. "I'll keep first watch."

Sleep tugged him down, but duty forced him to say, "No, I will. I'm the senior officer."

"Lucky you," Private Wright said. "Since you're so senior, you can take watch until nightfall."

The others chuckled.

He smiled. It had taken a long time to accustom himself to this sort of joking from the lower classes. Now he knew it was a sign of acceptance.

Private Wright made a show of settling into the mud and making snoring noises. Not too loudly, of course. While the German line was two hundred yards away, all the men had taken up the habit of being as quiet as possible when not in the trenches.

Sergeant Young used his bayonet to cut an apple in half. He leaned over and handed him half, giving his superior officer a jaunty salute as he did so. That produced another smile. Salutes had been dispensed with years ago.

Corporal Haroldson decided to take a kip as well, while Private Smith gnawed on a hunk of bread that looked a bit past its prime.

He leaned back and munched on his apple. Despite his weariness and the stench that rose up from the cordite and an unburied body that he couldn't see but most certainly could smell, he felt oddly content. He'd found comradeship in the army, and a confidence he had lacked in his easy academic life before the war. Five years ago, if asked whether he could crawl all night through mud and barbed wire, diving into shell holes or pressing himself flat against the mud when a flare went up, all the while stringing telephone wire in a complex system between various frontline and communication trenches, and he could not have even imagined the kind of man that could perform such a feat.

Now he was that kind of man. As hateful as this war was, and as many good friends as it had taken from him, it had changed him at least partially for the better.

A brief whistle followed by a sharp bang to their right made everyone inch down a little further into the shell hole.

"Morning hate's coming a bit early," Private Wright grumbled without opening his eyes.

"They could at least let us sleep, the bastards," Corporal Haroldson said.

Another whistle and bang came from the same direction. German field artillery, called "whizz bangs" by the men for their distinctive sound, had decided to send some shells over.

It did not concern him or his men overly much. This was a common occurrence, and because the heavy artillery hadn't joined in, it did not herald an attack. If the Bosch had wanted to come over the top, their big guns would have started up a couple of hours ago to pummel the British lines.

The thud of a trench mortar came from the German position. There was a long, low whine and a crump as the shell impacted.

Sergeant Young grinned at him. "Bet you a shilling we're going to have to lay that bloody telephone wire again."

"I'm not taking that bet because I'm afraid you're right," he replied.

Another trench mortar fired, then a third. The men wormed their way down until they were half in the pool of filthy water at the bottom of the crater. He felt the cold water soak through his clothes and boots. It didn't matter. He'd been wet and cold so much in the past three years he barely noticed anymore.

He pulled out a half-empty packet of biscuits, crumbled from spending too long in his pack and a bit chewy from the perpetual damp.

"Looks like there are enough crumbs to make half a biscuit for each of us," he said. "Here you go, chaps."

Private Wright, who was lying closest to him, flipped his hat off his eyes and reached for one.

"Ta."

Another thump from a German trench mortar. A long whistle, growing closer. And closer. He and everyone else curled up, a sickening feeling in each man's gut when they could tell, with their expert ears, that it would land right on top of them.

Then a blinding impact, and nothing more.

A nudge to the shoulder brought him out of it.

"All you all right, Mr. Wall?"

"Yes, why wouldn't I be?" he grumbled.

Moustafa stared at him, trying to study his half-face in the gloom. Why did everyone have to be so irritating just because he indulged in a few memories?

"Psst," Tim's whisper came from somewhere to their front right. "Seen anyone?"

"No. You got back quickly," Augustus said.

Tim crawled into view. "Been gone half an hour."

Oh dear, I've been out of it that long?

"I took out a sentry," Tim reported in a voice so low as to almost be inaudible. "A Gippo crouched behind a bush right at the top."

"How do you know he was a sentry?" Moustafa asked, accusation roughening his voice.

"Because he had a shotgun and was watching the land all around. Snuck up on him and gave him a second mouth with me knife. He won't be sounding any alarms unless it's with a trumpet at the pearly gates."

"Did you see anyone else?" Augustus asked.

"No. I would have taken care of them too. I didn't have time to search the whole area, though. Thought it best for us to go up together now that this side of the mound is clear."

Augustus crawled forward. Moustafa and Tim spread out to either side and together they quietly picked their way up the slope.

The sound of artillery returned. Augustus shrugged it away.

At the top, they came to the bush Tim had mentioned. An Egyptian in a black djellaba lay behind it, dead. Augustus did not see the shotgun. Tim would have unloaded and hidden it in order to deny it to the enemy.

Together they made a slow, careful circuit of the entire promontory and found no one. A second, quicker patrol down the middle yielded the same result.

"They're not here," Augustus said.

"You sound disappointed," Tim said.

"Bloody right I am. I'm going to kill every one of those murderers."

"Relax, mate. We'll get our chance. That Gippo was on guard looking out over the road to town. That's where they figured we'd come from, and I bet that's where they'll come from."

"That villa is to the northeast of here," Augustus said. "Their most likely route is to take a small, north-south path the map indicated to get onto this main road, before cutting west to make it here."

"I know, pal. I can read a bloody map. I'm going to keep that dead Gippo company and see if our Aussie friends show up."

"While you do that, let's go look at the entrance I found," Moustafa said to Augustus. The excitement in the Nubian's voice crackled like lightning.

THE CASE OF THE ASPHYXIATED ALEXANDRIAN

Tim snuck off into the shadows and Augustus and Moustafa went to the strange depression at the foot of the ruined temple.

Moustafa got on his hands and knees, crawling around until he found the spot by feel. They didn't dare shine a light.

He got to work with a short-handled spade and cleared off the topsoil in a matter of minutes, Augustus clenching his teeth each time the metal scraped stone. This work was too noisy, and it would soon get much noisier. The villages stood far enough away that the fellahin wouldn't hear, but anyone coming up the slope would. He hoped Tim had picked the right side of the mound to watch.

Once Moustafa had cleared the topsoil, the hard work began. The night was moonless, but there was enough starlight for them to see he had uncovered several worked blocks that had tumbled down on top of each other, the spaces between them filled with smaller fragments. Augustus guessed this had once been a vault that had collapsed with the weight of time.

Together they felt around for the smaller loose stones. Some they could pull out by hand. Others they needed to pry out with a crowbar. As they worked, they could feel the larger blocks begin to loosen.

After working for several minutes in silence, Moustafa spoke.

"It's going to be tricky getting the center stones out without causing the whole thing to collapse."

"We might not be able to manage. At least let's keep us from collapsing along with it, eh?"

They fastened a rope around one of the smaller blocks near the edge and as Moustafa pulled on it, Augustus stood as far away from the edge as he could and pried with the crowbar.

After some huffing and puffing in this awkward position, it finally came free, thudding onto its side on top of another stone and sending a cascade of smaller stones down into the depths. After far too long, they heard them smash against a hard surface.

"I hope there wasn't a mosaic down there," Moustafa said.

"If there was, there isn't anymore."

Moustafa looped another rope around the stone they had moved and together they hauled it off the other stones. Its extra weight might cause the whole thing to collapse, sending up a din that even the distant villages would hear.

Augustus probed the declivity with the end of the crowbar, testing its strength. A couple of stones shifted a little, sending dirt and pebbles into the depths, but nothing larger fell.

"Well, I wouldn't dance a jig on it, but it will hold for a time," Augustus said.

"Let's see what we have," Moustafa said.

Augustus smiled. The Nubian sounded as a excited as a child on Christmas morning.

They lay down and crawled as close to the edge as they dared, their heads over the black hole they had made. Moustafa pulled out a torch, stuck his hand into the hole to shield the light as much as possible from view, and switched it on.

Beneath them yawned a circular opening like a well, hewn from bedrock. It measured about twenty feet in diameter, and had a stone staircase and railing spiraling down its sides. The first couple of turns of the stairs were filled with rubble, making it impassable.

Moustafa inched forward, sticking his arm further into the hole.

"Careful," Augustus said.

The light of the torch could not penetrate to the bottom.

"You find anything?"

Tim's whisper startled them so much, Augustus and Moustafa nearly toppled over the edge.

"Bloody hell, you could have warned us," Augustus whispered as they crawled back out of danger.

Tim chuckled. "The warning would have startled you just as much. You should have seen the two of you, squawking like a pair of old hens."

"I thought you were on watch," Moustafa said.

"I was, but you two were making so much damn noise I thought I'd make a circuit of the ridge to make sure the Gippo farmers hadn't sent up a hue and cry."

"Any sign of them?" Augustus asked.

"No."

"Good. Take a look at this," Augustus said, taking the torch from Moustafa and handing it to him.

Tim wormed his way far too close to the edge and peered down. After a moment he crawled back. Even in the dim light Augustus could see his old friend shudder.

"Looks like you found a pharaoh's tomb," he said, trying and failing to keep the tension out of his voice.

An old memory came back to Augustus, who put a hand on Tim's shoulder.

"It's all right. It will be me or Moustafa going down, not you. Let's clear a bigger hole so one of us can get down there."

Tim paused, then shook his head. "You see them rocks piled every which way? You pull any more out and the whole thing will cave in. They'll be sure to hear us then."

"He's right, Mr. Wall. Tim should go down. He's the smallest and he can fit in the hole we've already made."

"No, we can make it bigger," Augustus insisted.

"No we can't, old pal. I'll go."

Augustus looked at him, trying to read his expression in the darkness. "Are you certain?"

Tim paused, then let out a curse. "Yes. It needs doing."

"What's the matter?" Moustafa asked.

"Nothing," Augustus said. "Let's get the harness tied to the rope and then secure the other end around that column drum over there."

As they worked, Augustus whispered to Tim, "You don't have to do this."

"I'll do it, mate. No worries. I'll do it for Gregory. Poor bugger. Pity we couldn't have a proper memorial service for him," Tim said.

Augustus gave him a wry smile. "Since when did you go to church?"

"Since half my friends got killed."

"You might want to reassess the brawling and womanizing then," Augustus replied, glad to get the conversation on a lighter tone.

"Didn't Moses have a pack of wives when he was a hundred years old? I'm just getting started early."

"You have as loose an interpretation of your religion as Faisal has of his."

"So why is he with you, anyway? Doesn't he got a mum and dad somewhere?"

"His mother is dead. He never mentions his father. I think he was a drinker."

"Why do you say that?"

"He gets snippy anytime I want to enjoy a whiskey in the evening."

"Isn't it a sin for the muzzies?"

"It is," Moustafa grumbled, "not that it stops some of us."

"Mother dead and a lousy father," Tim grumbled, testing the line to make sure it was secure.

Augustus remembered that Tim had been in a similar situation. While Augustus had spent his leave visiting family and a fiancé, Tim had done in England what he did in the rear areas on the front—get in fights and scour the area for available women.

"He was living on the street when I first met him," Augustus said. "Filthy and covered in lice."

"Probably smelled as bad as you did back in the war."

"You weren't exactly a rose garden yourself. He turned out to be quite the little spy. He helped me crack a case, and has proved most helpful on several more."

"And in return you let him live with you."

"Actually he decided that himself. There's an unused shed on my roof. He noticed I never go up there, so he cleared out the back and put in a bed."

Tim laughed. "Clever little bugger! And it took you ages to discover him, eh?"

"I never did. After a few months he showed me and insisted he stay."

Augustus decided not to mention leaving him at an orphanage. Tim had been in and out of juvenile homes as a lad and probably wouldn't approve of his trying to institutionalize the boy. It seemed no one but Moustafa thought it had been a good idea.

Tim chuckled and shook his head. "Clever little brat, if he fooled you all that time."

"Indeed."

"So how old is he?"

"I'm not sure. I doubt he knows himself. Funny thing with these street boys, they seem both older and younger than their age. At times he's like a child, all enthusiasm and jumping about and coming up with ridiculous ideas, and at other times he's as serious as a Presbyterian minister. He's seen too much for one of his years."

That's partially my fault, Augustus chided himself. *At least he's out of danger.*

And on that point, as usual, Augustus was wrong.

CHAPTER TWENTY-SIX

Moustafa let out a cry, dove behind an exposed masonry block, and pulled up Faisal by the hair. The boy let out a yelp.

"How did you pull a boy out of a rock like he was a jack-in-the-box?" Tim asked, astonished.

"I don't know what a jack-in-the-box is, but this boy has a bad habit of showing up where he doesn't belong." He turned to Faisal, gave him a good shake, and asked, "How did you follow us, anyway?"

Faisal shrugged. "Held onto the back of the motorcar, as usual."

"We checked," Mr. Wall said.

"Not good enough," Faisal replied.

"How did he sneak by me?" Tim asked.

"He can sneak past anyone," Moustafa said. He gave the boy another shake. "Now sneak back to Alexandria where you belong."

"Easy there, Shaka Zulu. You shake him again and I'll start shaking you."

Moustafa glowered at him. Mr. Wall stepped between them.

"Actually, now that he's here, we might put him to use."

Moustafa had a bad feeling he knew what the madman would say next. He was quickly proven correct.

"We can send him down the hole," Mr. Wall said. "He's lighter, and will be easier to lower down."

He said this in English, which kept the boy from running off in panic.

"Send him down that hole? You gone barmy?" Tim asked.

He did a long time ago, Moustafa thought.

"It's safe," Mr. Wall said.

"Says you," Tim scoffed.

"He's small and agile. He'd be better at it than you. It's only an exploratory look. The main priority is to find Gregory's murderers."

Tim shifted from one foot to the other. Even in the poor light Moustafa could tell he was uncertain, perhaps struggling with something. He did not seem anxious to go down there.

Good God, does he believe in djinn too? I've never asked an Englishman about their superstitions. Perhaps he's as afraid as the Little Infidel.

"What are they talking about?" Faisal asked.

"About who's going down that hole," Moustafa replied.

"I am," Faisal groaned.

"Now don't start talking a lot of nonsense about djinn!"

"I think you're the ones afraid of djinn. That's why you always send me into the tombs."

"Well, you shouldn't have followed us!"

"You need me."

Tim cut in. "Look, it isn't right sending a nipper down there all alone. But you're right that he's smaller and might be able to squeeze in places I can't. And if our friends decide to join the party he's safer down there than up here. Tell you what. We'll both go down. And if there's trouble up here you haul me up so I can help with the fighting. I'll leave him down there so he won't get hurt."

"Are you quite certain?" Mr. Wall sounded doubtful.

"Yeah, you bloody bastard." Tim forced a laugh and punched him in the shoulder. "Hey, we might even find the old stiff. Then we can go to England with his royal corpse and sell a peek at a bob a time."

Mr. Wall laughed. "Yes, Tim. We'll go to England and do that."

"What are they saying?" Faisal whispered to Moustafa in Arabic. He looked nervous.

"Just joking around."

"But aren't they saying they're going to—"

"It's nothing, Little Infidel. Just focus on what you need to do."

Mr. Wall turned to him. "Moustafa, why don't you get Tim tied in. I need to speak with Faisal alone for a moment."

"All right."

Moustafa had already tied one end of the rope around the drum of a fallen column. Now he secured the harness to the other end. It was a simple loop to put the body through, with two smaller loops to secure the legs.

Tim seemed familiar with the device and got himself in. Moustafa could hear him breathing heavily, and as he helped the veteran cinch up the rope, could feel the sweat and heat radiating from him.

"Are you all right?" Moustafa asked.

"Don't mind about me, just keep an eye out for the Aussies. Bloody hell, how does he get me to do these things?"

"I often ask myself the same question," Moustafa grumbled.

"Wait. Don't you work for him?"

"No. Well, he pays me when I'm with him on these ridiculous adventures, but …"

Tim let out a strained laugh. "But that's not why you run around savage nations searching for murderers and dead kings, eh? You're as mad as he is, and I'm twice as mad as the two of you put together. I crossed a damn sea to volunteer for this job."

"You had better give me the bombs. You don't want them going off down there."

"The man has a point," Tim said, handing them over. "You take care with this line, eh? I took a look at those stairs and there's no way we're getting up them. Just a heap of rubble at the top and this damn hole is too far to reach from it."

"We'll be here. Just take a brief look around and we'll pull you up. Oh, and if you can, look for that other entrance on the seaward side."

"I remember it. It's all caved in but I'll see how bad it is. Once we take care of Gregory's murderers we can come back with more time and better gear. What's taking them so long?"

Tim and Moustafa looked over to where they could see the dim outlines of Mr. Wall and Faisal. Moustafa grunted.

"He's afraid of djinn. Mr. Wall is probably trying to convince him for the hundredth time they don't exist."

"All worried about the boogeyman, is he? Like he doesn't have better things to worry about running around with you lot. Don't worry, I'll make him keep his chin up."

"Take care if you find any tunnels. They might be unstable after all this time. Many of the tombs in my country are dangerous to go in."

"I'll try not to shoot any mummies."

"Try not to bump into any columns or speak too loudly either," Moustafa warned.

Tim let out a little gasp. "Is it that bad?"

"It could be. Just be careful."

Tim looked down at the hole and took half a step back. Moustafa wanted to ask him what was the matter, but something in the veteran's attitude told him not to.

The man was plainly terrified. But why? He must have been through far worse in the trenches.

He looked more afraid of going down that hole than getting in a gunfight.

CHAPTER TWENTY-SEVEN

Faisal couldn't understand everything Tim and the Englishman had said to each other. He didn't need to. He knew enough English to figure it out. Tim had said "we," and "go," and "England." Then the Englishman laughed and said yes.

He really was leaving with Tim.

The Englishman would use him for one last adventure and then sail back to England and forget all about him, just as Moustafa said all foreigners do.

The Englishman made a motion with his head for Faisal to follow him and walked a few steps away. Faisal did as he was told, trying to think of something he could say. But the words didn't come out.

"Why the long face?" the Englishman asked, peering at him through the gloom. "Are you nervous about going down there? Remember what I said about djinn. They don't exist. And in that hole we might find a fabulous treasure. You could end up living in a palace just like the one the Hanzades have."

While you live in a palace in England, Faisal thought.

Still he didn't say anything. The Englishman put his hands on Faisal's shoulders.

"Faisal, I need you to be strong. Not for me, but for Tim. I have to tell you something about Crawford he wouldn't want me to reveal. You see, he's afraid of enclosed spaces. Being shut in without much room to move really frightens him."

Faisal had a hard time imagining Tim being afraid of anything.

"Didn't he live in the trenches with you?" Faisal managed to ask.

"Well, yes. That was all right because it was open at the top. But one time during an artillery barrage the trench caved in and he got buried. He nearly suffocated before we dug him out. After that he was always afraid of being underground. He could only stand entering the dugout because it was more dangerous to stay outside. Even so, he always insisted on being right next to the doorway. When we were on leave in Paris he wouldn't even use the Metro. Insisted on taking the bus everywhere."

"So why did he agree to go down this hole?" Faisal asked, wondering what a metro was.

"Because being brave means sometimes doing things we don't want to do, like you are about to do. So I want you to take care of him. He'll put on a brave face, but he's going to be very nervous. If you act brave, then he'll keep his chin up in order not to look bad in front of you."

Faisal wondered if this story of Tim being afraid of underground places was really true. Was the Englishman trying to get him to go down the hole with this story?

"Don't worry, Englishman. I'll take care of him."

But who's going to take care of me?

The Englishman tousled his hair. "Good boy."

"And after we find what you want, you'll come back to Cairo, right?"

"Of course. Where else would I go?"

"Um, nowhere. But you'll come back to Cairo, right?"

"Yes, I'll come back to Cairo." He could tell the Englishman was getting impatient. It didn't take much.

"Promise?"

"Yes, I promise!"

Faisal stared at him. Had the Englishman just lied to him?

No, maybe Faisal had misunderstood what he and Tim had been

saying to each other.

No, he hadn't misunderstood. He was good in English. He could tell what they had said.

Couldn't he?

More confused than ever, Faisal sighed and said, "All right. Lower me and Tim down the hole."

They went back to find Crawford already tied to the rope, which was wrapped around a big stone to add friction and make it easier for Moustafa and the Englishman to lower them down without getting so tired they'd drop them. At least Faisal hoped so. He'd seen builders back in Cairo do this but he never thought he'd be the one on the end of the rope.

Crawford motioned Faisal over. Heart beating fast, Faisal held the rope while Crawford gripped him with one arm while holding an electric torch with the other. The soldier's arm felt like a band of iron around him. Faisal could hear Crawford breathing fast, and even in the darkness he could see his face shining with sweat.

He really is scared. I hope he doesn't drop me.

Crawford sat down at the edge of the hole, his legs swinging in the air. Faisal sat in his lap like a little child, his heart beating fast. Beneath their feet he could see only darkness.

Crawford said several words Faisal wasn't supposed to repeat and leaned out over the hole, the rope going taut.

Faisal gripped the rope harder. His breath caught as Crawford kicked off from the edge, keeping his leg out to push off the from the side of the hole as the rope jerked, then steadily lowered them into the darkness.

Crawford clicked on the electric torch and shone it around.

Faisal wished he hadn't. Now he could see how deep this hole was. The Englishman and Moustafa were lowering them down the center of a big spiral staircase cut into the stone. The top part of the staircase was filled with rubble, and he noticed with a clenching heart that there was no way to climb over that rubble and reach the edge of the hole. Further down, Faisal could see the worn, dusty steps winding downwards, down and down toward … something.

He still couldn't see the bottom, even when Crawford shone the light down there.

"How are you today?" Faisal asked in English.

Crawford whispered several more bad words.

"No problem," Faisal whispered, trying to sound encouraging. He should feel mad at Tim for taking the Englishman away, but the soldier was so scared Faisal felt sorry for him.

"Big bloody problem," Tim whispered.

He was right, of course. Since he had one arm gripping Faisal so hard he could barely breathe, Faisal could let go with one hand and pat him on the shoulder.

"No problem."

"Crazy little Gippo."

Crawford said this in the way that adults tell children everything is all right when it isn't.

It grew cool, a damp draft wafting up from somewhere below. The creak of the rope as it held their weight echoed softly in the dark space, sending chills down Faisal's spine. Something was going to hear that for sure.

Faisal kept looking around. That one light wasn't enough to banish all the shadows, and he felt like every one of them was ready to leap out at them. And Crawford wasn't shining the light up near the hole at all. There could be a djinni with a scimitar up there ready to cut the rope. Then they would fall into the darkness, into the waiting arms of a whole horde of djinn.

He gasped as he saw a doorway by the side of the staircase open up into a large chamber. Crawford shone his light into it. It was a big room with stone benches on three sides. They didn't get to see more, because Moustafa and the Englishman continued to lower them down.

Faisal glanced nervously above them as they continued their descent. That room was dangerous, he just knew it. He hadn't gotten a chance to check out every corner for djinn, which meant there were some hiding in there for sure.

Maybe they'd be scared of Crawford. He sure hoped so. Faisal wanted to clutch the talisman around his neck, made especially for him by a wise woman back in Cairo, but he needed to hold onto the rope and pat Crawford's shoulder to make him feel better. He could feel Crawford's heart beating fast and hard in his chest like some big motor. Faisal patted harder. He had to make sure Crawford didn't faint or run away or something because then he'd be down here all alone.

Crawford shone his torch below them and said something in English. The floor came into view, a smooth mass of gray stone with a few stones scattered around that had probably fallen from above. The staircase reached to the floor of a round room. Two passageways opened on either side.

Their feet touched stone. The rope slackened a bit as Moustafa and the Englishman continued to play it out. Crawford looked up, put two fingers in his mouth, and let out a sharp whistle.

Faisal winced. He was going to call every djinni in the place!

They listened. The Englishman did not answer. Even though he was far above them, he should have been able to hear. Faisal supposed he didn't want to attract any attention. What did he have to worry about? He wasn't in an underground city of djinn and dead people!

Dead people? He didn't smell any dead people. It didn't stink the way the Englishman's shop did when he got a shipment of mummies, or like that fake mummy Faisal had to share a box with. There really wasn't any smell down here at all except damp.

But this was a place of the dead for sure. So if he wasn't smelling them, that could only mean one thing.

They weren't dead.

Faisal kept close to Crawford as the veteran got out of the harness and unslung his rifle. The snap of the safety coming off sounded like a gunshot in the darkness. Now that Faisal had a hand free to hold his talisman, he held it with all his might.

Crawford looked around, clutching his rifle as hard as Faisal clutched his talisman.

He handed Faisal the torch, which didn't make him feel much better. Sure, if you shone the light in one shadow you could keep the djinn away, but what about all the other shadows?

Faisal shone the light down one of the passageways and saw that after a few feet it was mostly filled with rubble. The ceiling looked rough, with deep cracks in it that ran onto the top part of the wall.

Oh great, not only are there mummies and djinn and who-knows-what down here, but the ceiling is falling down too.

Faisal turned and shone the light down the other passageway …

… and gasped.

A djinni stood right there looking at him.

It was the weirdest one he had ever seen, with a jackal's head and a body like two snakes, but wearing armor on its chest like the Romans had. The Englishman had shown him pictures of Roman soldiers. He hadn't told him the Romans had djinn.

Faisal ducked behind Crawford, who chuckled and gestured at the djinni with his gun.

"No problem, little Gippo," he said, followed by some things Faisal didn't understand. They sounded reassuring, anyway.

Faisal peeked around Crawford and discovered the djinni had turned to stone. Had Faisal's talisman done that, or had the djinni been scared of Crawford? If even other Europeans were scared of him, maybe djinn were too.

But djinn were tricky. They always tried to fool you into thinking you were safe. You never knew what they'd do next.

He'd have to be careful.

Slowly Crawford approached the passageway. He may not have been scared of the djinni, but he kept his rifle ready just in case. The djinni stood like a statue in the center of the passage, which continued beyond it into the darkness.

Tim stopped at the entrance to the passage, cursed for a while, then looked at Faisal. He must have realized he looked scared because he put on a brave face, croaked something that sounded like "no problem," and walked into the passage.

As they entered, they could see the sides of the doorway had carvings of two coiled cobras with circles on their heads. The Englishman had told him those circles were suns, and that the ancient Egyptians worshipped the sun. That made them pagan sorcerers and extra dangerous.

Faisal tried to get right in the middle of the entrance so he would be as far away from both cobras as possible, but the entrance was so narrow he could reach out and touch them if he had dared.

That meant, of course, that they could reach out and touch him.

Or bite him with their poisonous fangs.

Or wrap themselves around him and squeeze the life out of him.

Or cast some sort of serpent spell on him.

He ended up not entering the doorway at all, instead standing just out of reach in front of it, staring at both of the cobras and waiting for them to make the first move. He let out a little sob of fear. He hadn't meant to. Only babies did that and he didn't want Crawford thinking he was a baby, but he couldn't help it.

Crawford passed through the entryway and Faisal hissed through clenched teeth, convinced those snakes and that other djinn in the armor would attack him from three sides.

The veteran turned around.

"Oi, little Gippo," he whispered, motioning for Faisal to follow.

Faisal shook his head.

Crawford let out a chuckle and asked something. Faisal pointed to the djinn and shook his head again.

Crawford said something more and then slapped one of the serpents right in the face!

Faisal yelped and jumped back.

"No problem, little Gippo," Crawford said, and smacked it again.

"Big problem, Crawford!"

"Big problem?" Crawford jerked a thumb in the direction of the jackal-headed Roman djinni. "No problem!"

He turned and kicked the djinni between the legs. Faisal cringed and covered his eyes. Now that thing was going to come to life for sure.

But it didn't. When Faisal dared to peek, he saw the djinni was still a statue. Crawford said something to Faisal as he kicked the djinni again, and then did something even worse.

He turned his back on Faisal, facing the statue, set down his rifle, and started fiddling with his trousers.

He's not going to …

The sound of liquid splashing against the statue confirmed Faisal's worst fears.

Crawford was peeing on the djinni!

That was disgusting and stinky and really scary and kind of funny all at the same time.

It was also amazing. The djinni just stood there and did nothing.

Crawford did up his pants, laughed, and grabbed his rifle.

"Come on, little Gippo."

Faisal blinked, trying to figure out what just happened.

He could think of a few possibilities.

One: his talisman had kept the three djinn from coming alive.

Two: The djinn were too scared of Crawford to come alive even when they got slapped and peed on.

Three: The djinn were waiting until just the right moment to come to life and eat them. Probably slowly, in revenge for getting slapped and peed on.

Four: They really were just dead stone statues like the Englishman always said.

Since number four was obviously wrong, Faisal gave himself a one-in-three chance of getting eaten when he passed by.

Then another idea came to his head. Maybe Crawford knew they were going to come to life, and made them angry on purpose so they'd attack him and not Faisal.

What a hero Crawford was! Maybe he could even defeat the djinn, or at least give Faisal time to run away.

That almost (almost) made Faisal forgive him for planning to take the Englishman away.

Faisal carefully passed between the two snakes, still clutching his charm and trying to shine the torch on both cobras at the same time, which was impossible, then made a big step over the stinky puddle Crawford had left. Then he hurried a few more steps to get the three djinn well behind him, just in case.

After a few feet he stopped, having found something new to be afraid of.

He stood at one end of a long passageway just a little narrower than his outstretched arms. On the walls, in three rows from top to bottom, were stone slabs with writing on them. Some had pictures too. Faces, mostly.

Stone faces of men and women staring out at him.

The ceiling was low, the air stuffy and dusty. Slowly Faisal walked forward.

"Little Gippo," Crawford whispered. His voice came out hoarse.

Faisal stopped and Crawford got ahead of him. Even in the dim light of the torch Faisal could see his knuckles were white as he gripped his rifle, and sweat poured down his face now.

The Englishman had told the truth. Crawford really was afraid of underground places. Not French waiters or Australian gunmen or even djinn. Just underground places.

He had been scared going down the shaft, but that must not have been too bad because the shaft was pretty big and he could still see the way out. Now that he was in this cramped little tunnel deep below the ground, even Crawford couldn't handle it anymore.

"Don't worry, Crawford," Faisal whispered. "This won't fall down like your trench."

Of course Crawford couldn't understand him, but maybe he'd feel better with someone talking to him. Faisal pointed at the funny letters on the stone slabs.

"English?"

Crawford shook his head.

Faisal took another look at them. The letters looked familiar. For a moment he stared and scratched his head, then he had it!

They looked just like the signs in the Greek shops.

"Greek!" he said, pointing to the letters.

Crawford said something, shrugging his shoulders. Maybe they didn't have Greeks in England.

They continued forward, Crawford saying "bluddy ell" every few steps, and came to an intersection. Another passageway lined with marble slabs went off out of sight to the left and right.

They stood for a second, unsure which way to take. Crawford pointed to the right. Just at the edge of the light, Faisal noticed one of the slabs had fallen to the floor, uncovering a sort of stone shelf in the wall.

As they crept toward it, Faisal's curiosity grew. Could this be the treasure everyone wanted to find so much?

They came to the broken slab, a portion of a face staring up at them from the floor. Faisal shone the torch into the stone shelf the fallen slab had revealed.

And shrank back in terror.

A skeleton lay on the shelf. Shreds of clothing still clung to the dusty bones, and clumps of hair to the grinning skull.

On shaky feet, Faisal backed up until he bumped into the opposite wall. That made him jerk and pull away, because he finally understood.

He looked one direction and then the other, and all he saw were slabs like the one that had fallen. And he saw another intersection, no doubt with another hallway lined with stone slabs.

Hundreds of slabs. Hundreds of skeletons.

They were in a city of the dead.

A hand rested on his shoulder. Faisal leapt in the air.

He spun around, expecting to see a skull leering at him.

Faisal almost fainted with relief. It was only Crawford. Of course he wasn't afraid of the dead. He hadn't been afraid of the German army, after all, so why be afraid of an army of skeletons?

Crawford's confident face suddenly transformed. His eyes darted back the way they had come, suddenly alert. He motioned toward the torch and said something.

A faint sound echoed down the tunnel, like big stomping feet.

The djinn! They were finally transforming from statues into living beings!

The banging continued, growing faster. It sounded like a whole bunch of djinn all running together.

Faisal clutched Tim, praying the djinn wouldn't find them. They didn't seem to be getting closer. He looked around. The dead people weren't coming out of their graves either.

Maybe, just maybe, they would get out of this.

Then Tim did something that made Faisal howl with terror. He pulled himself away from Faisal's grip, grabbed his wrist, and hurried out of the city of the dead, pulling Faisal with him.

"Don't run toward them!" Faisal wailed. "They'll find us."

Tim ignored him. The footsteps continued, sounding irregular, not like footsteps at all. Faisal imagined djinn with three legs, or five, waddling around the maze trying to find the Egyptian boy and English soldier who had dared enter their realm.

Faisal yelped as they approached the Roman snake djinni and his two cobra friends. To his surprise, he saw they still hadn't moved, and yet he could hear the footsteps.

What was going on?

They dashed out into the central chamber, and Faisal's superstitious mind did a flip flop from summoning up ghosts to facing an even worse reality.

Those weren't footsteps, they were gunshots.

Gunshots coming from up on the surface.

Faisal and Crawford stared up at the hole far, far above them, and saw flashes of light every time a gun went off.

After a moment, the gunshots died away.

The rope that still hung from the hole shook a little, like it was doing a little dance. Faisal stared at it, confused.

Then a sliding, whooshing sound from above made him look up again.

The end of the rope came rushing down at them, the rope crumpling up. Crawford yanked him back as the rope slapped onto the ground and lay in a heap like a dead snake.

Faisal and Crawford stared at it for a moment.

"Bluddy ell," Faisal said.

CHAPTER TWENTY-EIGHT

They came on them in a rush. The only warning was a rustle of movement from the landward side of the ridge. Augustus and Moustafa were standing by the hole, the rope slack against its lip. When the movement started, both men leapt in opposite directions.

A bullet passed directly between them.

Augustus was too experienced to remain surprised for long. He grabbed the German submachine gun from where it lay on the ground, rolled to the right as another bullet sought him out, and snapped off the safety.

A trio of flashes in rapid succession from his left told him they were going for Moustafa as well.

Augustus gave a short burst at where he had seen the muzzle flares, and rolled away as his own firing revealed his position.

The answering fire came so close he felt dirt and stone kicked up by the bullets thump against his jacket.

Augustus rolled more, only to get stopped short by the column drum they had tied the rope around.

A bullet cracked off the marble. Augustus leapt to his feet and sprayed a long, blind burst at the shifting shadows. He saw no evidence he had hit anything. The moonless night made aiming difficult for both sides.

At least the burst acted as suppressing fire. He bolted to the right, stumbling in the dark as he tried to put as much distance between him and the enemy as possible. The ancient blocks that tripped him up turned into barbed wire, and the shouts in English and Arabic turned into German. The smell of mud and rotting bodies replaced that of sea air.

He found himself in No Man's Land, alone with a captured enemy machine gun. How had he ended up here? No time to think about that. He was on a mission, that was all he knew. Something about Gregory Marshall. Gregory was lost and he needed to find him.

He stopped, ducked down, tried to make himself as flat against the earth as possible.

Strangely dry for No Man's Land. It should be mud. And why was the night so balmy?

He checked his equipment and found other things that were strange. He was not wearing a helmet or a uniform. It was too dark to see properly, but he appeared to be wearing a summer suit.

What the devil was going on?

He wasn't entirely unprepared, however. In his pockets he found two Mills bombs and a third bomb he couldn't recognize by feel. Homemade? Perhaps one of Corporal Black's inventions. That man was a genius for creating death and destruction from a jam tin and a few simple chemicals.

But what was the mission?

Gregory. I'm supposed to find Gregory.

That's right, isn't it? Something to do with Gregory, anyway.

The big boor must have gotten himself in trouble again.

Well, he'd get him out of it. Gregory had saved his skin on more than one occasion. Like with Timothy Crawford, it had become a bit of a competition to see who could save who more often.

Down to business. The starlight gave only a faint view of the area, and at the moment he could see no one. All was silent. The Germans had gone to ground. Behind him rose a large mound, unusual for No Man's Land. The sides looked rocky and steep.

Was there an observation post on top? Perhaps he and Gregory had already taken it out, because the Germans had come at him from the other direction.

He froze as the soft, unmistakable sound of rustling clothes came to him from his front left, audible even to his ringing ears. So the Germans hadn't shifted position much after their exchange of fire. Fools for not taking advantage of the darkness and confusion to move as he did.

Perhaps they were new recruits. The quality of the German soldiers had declined over the years as their best men got used up.

Keeping close to the ground, he wormed his way forward, getting behind what felt like a large block of worked stone. That mound behind him must be the ruins of a sizeable building. A factory or church, perhaps.

More movement. It sounded like at least two men directly to his front. They had shifted since he had last heard them. Another sound, much softer, came from further to his right.

He kept as still as the stone behind which he hid, waiting for the Germans to move again.

A few seconds later they did. The rustle of clothing, the click of metal on stone, the crackle of grit ground under a knee. Amateurs. Pure amateurs. Perhaps he had already done away with the *Sturmtruppen*. He held one of their guns, after all.

The sounds moved closer. The sound to his right did not repeat. Judging from the last location, those to his front were the chaps he had just exchanged fire with. He had no idea about the fellow to the right.

A shadow shifted about twenty yards ahead of him. Bracing his submachine gun, he let out a short burst. In the flare he saw a body jerk and flail. A longer burst took out the man's companion. He had a brief glimpse of a third before the man to his right got into the fight, sending a shot that cracked off the stone block he was using as cover.

Shifting his fire, he gave a long burst in the direction, stopped firing, rose and bolted to the left several paces before throwing himself on the dirt.

Groans from the men he had hit. He felt pretty sure he hadn't hit the more disciplined man to the right.

Searching through the pockets of the summer suit he inexplicably wore, he found another magazine for the MP18. There was no way to silently remove and replace a magazine, so he waited until the German groaned again to mask the sound.

Not well enough. He got the old magazine out, but as he clicked the new one into place, fire came from both locations.

Fine by him. Since they fired more or less blind, the bullets didn't come close, but he returned fire at the muzzle flare of the further man, the one who looked like he had some sense.

Silence again. Had he hit him?

Several shots rang out in the distance. Another firefight was going on back the way he had come.

No time to worry about that now. Using the gunfire as cover for his movements, he crawled in a half-circle around to the location where he had last seen the small group he had fired at.

One was still groaning, and he heard another man whispering. What amateurs! If the Kaiser was feeding men like this into the line, the war would be over by Christmas.

They didn't even see him coming. As he got behind their position, he could see three dark forms. One lay motionless, arms outstretched. Another writhed in pain as the third bent over him, whispering reassuring words, a rifle in his hand.

A quick burst took care of them both.

The snap of a rifle to his left told him the chap he had fired on previously was still in the game.

Not for long. A long burst, cutting low through the dark, lit up the area and showed a man pirouette and fall.

Time to find out what that other firefight was all about. Maybe Gregory was over there.

He began to crawl in that direction. The firing died away as the opposing sides went to ground.

They had sounded a good distance away. He had a faint memory of another soldier standing beside him when the fight started, but could not for the life of him remember who that was.

And there was still the mystery of his unusual apparel.

All senses alert, he continued to crawl through No Man's Land. He could see he was on quite a sizeable ridge. A few lights shone in the distance below. It looked like a village and a scattering of houses, lit by oil lamps. Why did they give away their position, and why wasn't this commanding position held by an entire regiment of Germans or English? The place should be bristling with artillery and bunkers. None of it made any sense.

He stopped short. A black hole yawned before him. From below he could feel a cool draft.

An enemy dugout!

Well, there was only one way to deal with that.

He pulled a Mills bomb out of his pocket. All he had to do was drop this down there and the shrapnel would kill anyone inside.

"Don't do that," a familiar voice whispered beside him.

He turned, blinked. "Gregory, there you are."

His comrade-in-arms lay beside him, his familiar face smiling at him from under the brim of his steel helmet. He wore a mud-smeared uniform and carried a Lee-Enfield rifle.

Gregory looked strange, though. Far too visible in this poor light, as if he gave off his own slight radiance.

"I've found the enemy bunker, Gregory. Let me blast it and we can get out of here."

"Silly boy, you're not in the war."

"Don't be daft. Now that I've found you, let's get the job done and get back to our own lines."

"Snap out of it, old man. You have a friend and a child down there."

"What?"

"That's not a German dugout, you silly bugger. You're in Egypt."

"Egypt? This is France."

Gregory's usually positive features grew grim.

"You can't keep coming back."

A chill ran through him. Something tugged at his gut. "I never left."

"You only think that. You only stay here because you can't face being done with it. It was hard for me as well, I don't mind telling you. I'd be on the cricket grounds ready to bowl, a batter standing before the wicket ready for me, a sunny sky overhead, and clean, decent people in the stands, and I'd freeze. Simply freeze. It didn't seem possible I had come from the mud and the blood and ended up in a place where I didn't have to be afraid of every sound, where I didn't have to wonder if I'd live to have my next drink. It didn't seem fair, considering all the lads we left behind. It didn't seem right. But I had to accept it. So I'd take a deep breath, thank my luck and promise myself never to forget, and get back to the business of living."

"Easier for you," he mumbled. "It was always easier for you."

"You always were a bit too serious, a bit too grim. This didn't help."

Gregory reached out a phosphorescent finger and touched him on the cheek.

Cheek? No. On the mask!

"Oh, Lord," Augustus sobbed. "You had cricket and friends and a face. It was easier for you to live in the present. What do I have?"

"You have the people down in that hole, you bloody idiot. And the people back in Cairo. Now watch it, I hear movement over there. You may not be in the war anymore, but you are in a fight."

Augustus snapped his head up, staring into the gloom. He heard rustling to his front.

He made a motion to Gregory, but of course he was gone.

Augustus winced, trembled, struck his forehead with his fist.

More movement.

He edged to a better position behind a stone, and realized it was the column drum that they had secured the rope to. The dark rope showed up clearly against the white surface.

Clearly enough for him to see that one of the bastards had cut it.

Augustus felt his skin prickle. Tim and Faisal were trapped down there, both entombed with their own fears.

More rustling in front of his position. It sounded like a group of them.

That got confirmed a moment later when several shots came at him at the same time.

Thanks to the darkness, none of those shots hit. It still felt like a miracle.

Without thinking, Augustus yanked out the pin and lobbed the grenade at the Egyptians and Australians.

It detonated, sending up screams from the men. In the brief flash Augustus could see there were several of them. He tossed the second Mills bomb to finish them off.

A rumble from below told him he had made a terrible mistake.

The ground shifted, and the covering over the catacomb entrance caved in. Augustus had to scamper away from it as the edges caved in too.

Then another flash and detonation ripped through the night.

It came from the direction where Moustafa had disappeared, and it didn't sound like a Mills bomb, it sounded like a charge of dynamite.

More rumbles came from below. It felt like the entire ridge was shifting.

Augustus had a horrible vision of ancient tunnels, their walls and ceilings weakened over the course of two thousand years, collapsing onto Tim and Faisal and sealing them in a living tomb.

CHAPTER TWENTY-NINE

Moustafa picked himself up from where the dynamite had blown him. He was shaken, battered, but still in one piece. When the first shot came, Moustafa had run off into the shadows for cover. His rifle, and Mr. Wall, got left behind.

The gunfight that had ensued proved that his former employer was doing what he did best.

Armed with only the pistol from his pocket, Moustafa felt very exposed. At least the night was dark.

Sounds of approaching movement, however, told him the Australians and his own countrymen were still hunting him. They couldn't see him, and he feared they'd try and seek him out with another charge of dynamite.

The last one had shaken the entire ridge. He prayed nothing caved in below his feet.

Moustafa cut to the left, making a big circle around where he had last seen the Australians and Egyptians. He had to get back to the hole and find out what had happened to Tim and Faisal.

More firing along the ridge. It sounded further away now, as if Mr. Wall was retreating.

Nothing made that man retreat except far greater odds, and usually not even then.

How many of those thieves were up here?

By a miracle Moustafa made it back to the entrance without being spotted, stopping a good ten yards away.

Even with the poor light, he didn't have to get any closer to see it.

What was once a small hole barely big enough for a man was now a gaping chasm.

The entire entrance had caved in, taking some of the surrounding soil and stone with it.

Moustafa shuddered. Tim and Faisal were trapped down there, perhaps even dead already, and there was no way for him to get to them.

Wait, there was a way. The entrance on the seaward side!

Moustafa knew he had to find the other entrance and get it open immediately. They didn't have enough rope to lower another line, and with the rope cut, Moustafa could only imagine Tim's panic. The boy wouldn't be any help either. He'd think he was trapped with an army of djinn and would do nothing but stand there blubbering and soiling his djellaba.

But how to find the entrance in the dark in the middle of a gunfight?

The ridge had gone silent again, both sides creeping in the dark searching for someone to kill. Moustafa now understood they had been tricked. Spies in the villages had told the Australians about their visit earlier in the day, and instead of setting up an ambush, the thieves had waited until they came up here. They knew Mr. Wall was an antiquities dealer, and probably knew Moustafa's archaeological experience as well. So they would know that letting them have the run of the ridge might uncover the entrance. Only then did they spring the trap.

Moustafa groped in the dark for a minute before finding the crowbar where he had left it, thankfully well away from the edge of the pit. Now he could hopefully pry open the entrance.

Just as he grabbed the crowbar, a movement to his right made him turn. Something rushed at him, and he darted to the side, falling to the ground as a rifle butt missed his head by inches.

Moustafa made a hasty swing at the man's legs with the crowbar, missed, and had to roll again as the rifle butt came down a second time.

Desperately rolling away, he felt the earth crumble beneath him and he had to scramble toward his attacker to keep from falling over the edge. Even so, as he tried to get to his feet, a portion of earth came off beneath it and he fell flat on his face.

Some shots fired by Mr. Wall or one of the thieves made the man with the rifle hesitate. In the split second it took for the man to realize the shots weren't coming for him, Moustafa grabbed one of his legs and yanked him off his feet.

The man landed on his back with a thud and a grunt.

Moustafa was on him in an instant. The thief, who Moustafa could now see was an Egyptian, tried to raise his rifle. Moustafa grabbed it, and for a moment they struggled. Moustafa put his weight on top of him and crushed the rifle down on his throat. The Egyptian struggled and gasped, legs kicked and Moustafa began to crush his throat with the barrel of the rifle.

A shot from the dark left a streaking pain across Moustafa's back. It was barely a graze, but the surprise and sudden pain made him jerk and release his hold.

The Egyptian beneath him didn't waste any time. He brought a knee up against Moustafa's side, hitting him painfully just below the ribs, and pushed him off.

Moustafa rose to a crouch and swung a meaty fist hard into the side of the man's head.

His opponent fell next to the hole. There was a hurried, desperate scramble, a slipping along the crumbly edge, and he vanished into the depths.

Moustafa edged away, then froze as he heard the hammer cock on a pistol.

"You speak English?" a whisper came from the dark shape in front of him.

Moustafa's back burned from the graze, and he knew that even in his poor light, there was no way the man would miss.

A burst of machine gun fire drowned out his response.

"Yes," Moustafa repeated once it was over.

"What's the hole? What have you found?" The man's voice sounded excited, almost shrill. Moustafa could tell gold lust had brought the Australian to this point, and that he'd kill Moustafa in a heartbeat if he didn't get what he wanted.

Thinking fast, Moustafa said, "A labyrinth. Just as was written in the famous *Ancient Studies* of Leo Africanus. It is as complex as it is extensive, and probably runs the length and breadth of this ridge."

The man paused. Moustafa bit his lip. Africanus never wrote a book called *Ancient Studies*, and no writer had ever claimed Alexander was buried in the middle of a labyrinth.

He was banking on the hope that this Australian engineer had never read much about Alexander the Great or had even heard of Leo Africanus. Anyone who was well-read in history and archaeology would see right through Moustafa's lie.

"How do you get through?"

Another burst of fire. Mr. Wall and this bandit's companions were in a different part of the ridge, too far away for either side to help the two men facing each other by the chasm leading to perhaps the greatest treasure ever buried.

"Our companions down below are working on that right now," Moustafa said. "Once they've mapped a bit of it, I was to go down and translate the hieroglyphs to find clues as to how to get to the tomb."

"Yes, you're that Nubian who can read ancient Egyptian."

So they had heard of him. Moustafa rose to his feet.

"Watch it!" the man warned, taking a step back.

Moustafa put his hands in the air.

"Don't shoot." Moustafa tried to give his voice a panicked edge. "I-I'll help you get through the maze. I have no loyalty to Mr. Wall. He only pays me. If you know about us, then you know I quit his service months ago. I hate working for the English, and I hate his friend even more. Just spare my life, and the life of the Egyptian boy who's down there. I'll give you what you want."

The man paused. Another burst of fire came from along the ridge. Moustafa felt sweat trickle down his back, stinging as it ran across the graze from the bullet.

"All right," he said at last. "You bought your life."

"And the boy?"

"What do I care about the boy? Sure. I'm not going to kill a kid."

Moustafa let out the breath he had been holding. He felt bad making up a bluff that wouldn't save all his friends, but the story of hating the English was the only one he could come up with, and was the most believable. These Australians were still in Egypt more than a year after the war to suppress the independence protests, after all.

Another burst of fire. A stray bullet whined past them. Both men crouched. As Moustafa did so, his foot shifted and bumped into something that gave off a metallic clank as it hit a stone.

Moustafa glanced down, moving only his eyes.

It was the crowbar, its black iron making it all but invisible in the darkness.

"We got to move away," the Australian said. "Walk to your left. I'll be just behind you. You try to run, I'll plug you."

Moustafa let out a little gasp as if in pain and bent down, reaching his arm around to clutch his back. He hoped the Australian could see the move.

"Get up," his captor demanded.

"You hit me with that shot. The bullet streaked right across my back. The pain is getting worse."

"That's the shock is wearing off. Too bad for you. Get to your feet."

"Aaah," Moustafa gasped again, falling to one knee and putting his hand out to support himself.

And grasp the crowbar.

"Enough shamming. You won't buy time that way, Gippo."

"Give me a minute."

"You won't have it," the Australian said, taking a couple of steps forward and training the gun on him. "You don't get up this instant I'll—"

Moustafa swung the crowbar with all his might. The man screamed as Moustafa felt and heard his hand break. Moustafa rose and gave him a clout on the head that dropped him.

As he bent down beside the Australian's body to retrieve the gun, a loud boom and a thud rocked the ridge. A flash in the direction of the firefight showed the engineers were throwing dynamite at Mr. Wall. The responding blast of a Mills bomb told him Mr. Wall was still in the fight.

The ridge shook again, as if a giant bell had been hit with a hammer. More rumbling came from below.

He had to get Tim and Faisal out of there!

He paused. What about Mr. Wall?

That mad Englishman wasn't helpless, while the other two were. And it was two lives for one.

And—Moustafa could barely admit this to himself—one of those lives was Egyptian, and in the end that counted for more.

Moustafa ran around the mound and down the seaward slope, desperate to find the other entrance. If he could pry it open with the crowbar, call out to those trapped inside, maybe, just maybe, they could find their way out. He would not have the Little Infidel's death on his conscience. The boy did not want to die, and Mr. Wall, deep down, did.

That, and not their nationalities, was the true difference.

Moustafa told himself that as he scrambled down the slope and forced himself to believe it.

He stopped, looking around the darkened slope. With the reflected starlight off the sea, and the lights of fisherman's cabins dotted along the distant shore, this side of the ridge was slightly brighter than the rest, but he still couldn't see the tumble of half-buried masonry that had once been the entrance.

He'd have to risk turning on his electric torch. He reached into his pocket, only to find it gone, lost in the struggles on the top of the ridge.

Now what?

Another blast rocked the ridge, and a low moan came from further down the slope and to his right. For a moment he froze in superstitious terror, then berated himself for still having a little bit of the villager left in him. That had been the air getting forced out of the entrance.

Moustafa hurried in that direction until he could feel the draft coming out of the little gap they had dug earlier in the day.

He felt around for gaps between the blocks, then froze. Had he heard a noise coming from further down slope?

Peering into the night, ears straining, he didn't hear or see anything for half a minute until those maniacs on the ridge set off another bomb. Unable to shoot each other in the dark, they were now intent on blowing each other up.

Hadn't they had enough of that in Europe for the past four years?

The way they kept setting off explosives, he needed to get the entrance open *now*. He'd just have to pray there was no one in the fields below, except perhaps some curious farmer wondering what was happening.

Moustafa set the crowbar between two blocks and heaved. The crowbar slipped out, making him stumble. He set it in again, more firmly this time.

Muscles straining, face breaking out in sweat, Moustafa hauled on the stone. It didn't move. He braced his legs and tried again, back lacing with pain from the graze he took from that bullet.

With a dry scrape, the stone shifted. Moustafa reset the crowbar and heaved at it again.

The stone toppled out with a thud, followed by the patter of smaller stones and earth.

Moustafa groped around, feeling the hole he had made. It was a start, but he did not think Tim could fit through it. He felt the edges of the surrounding stones and noticed one was a bit displaced. Probing with the end of the crowbar, he found some purchase and pressed down on the length of iron. The stone slid halfway out.

He felt around, unable to find a good spot to put the crowbar. Gripping the edge with his hand, he pulled on one end until it stuck out of the hole enough to lean on. It fell onto the first stone with a loud crack.

The hole was big enough now even for Moustafa, although he couldn't go in since he had no light. He peered inside, sensing more than seeing a passageway. The firing up on the ridge continued.

A loud series of thuds inside made him jerk back, a draft wafting in his face, a plume of dust making him blink. That sounded like a cave in, but there hadn't been an explosion. The whole structure had been weakened enough that it was falling of its own accord.

They had to get out of there right away, but didn't even know there was another exit now.

Disregarding the danger to himself, Moustafa cupped his hands and shouted,

"Tim! Faisal! The entrance on the seaward side of the ridge is open! Follow the sound of my voice! The entrance on the seaward side is open! Tim! Faisal!"

The bright yellow beam of an electric torch flicked on, catching him in its spotlight. The words choked in Moustafa's throat.

"Don't move," came an order in Arabic.

The snick of a bolt being pulled back added emphasis to the words.

Another rumble came from inside the ridge. Another cave in.

CHAPTER THIRTY

Faisal yelped as Tim grabbed his wrist and yanked him down the passage. There was a burst of gunfire from up above. Faisal couldn't tell if that was aimed at them but he guessed Tim didn't want to wait around and find out.

Once they got out of the line of fire, they stood there for a minute, breathing hard. If the Englishman or Moustafa were down here, they'd want to switch off the electric torch so they could hide, but there was no way Faisal would suggest that. Stuck in the dark with all those djinn?

Tim didn't suggest it either. It would probably make him even more afraid of being underground. He kept swearing and looking around, sweat running down his face.

A loud boom from above, followed by another, and right after that the sound of rocks and dirt falling.

The whole passageway shook, dust and fragments of rock trickling down on them. Suddenly Tim wailed like a little kid and curled up on the floor, arms over his head. His gun and torch clattered to the floor.

Faisal grabbed the torch before it could roll away.

"Tim? Tim!" Faisal shook his shoulder.

Tim looked up at him, and the soldier looked so terrified and ashamed Faisal felt sorrier for him than anyone he could ever remember.

Maybe that's why he came to take the Englishman back home. He needs him more than I do.

The passageway echoed with the sounds of more falling masonry. Tim trembled on the ground. He had been nervous before, but with all the shaking and bits of roof falling in, he couldn't control himself anymore.

That got Faisal scared too.

Scared of the cracks in the roof and the dust that trickled down, yes, but also scared of something even worse.

Because soon the djinn would soon realize nobody was protecting him anymore.

"Tim, we have to see if we can still get out," Faisal said. He knew the soldier wouldn't understand him, but if he talked in a calm voice, maybe he'd feel better.

But Faisal couldn't keep his voice calm.

Faisal shone the light down the way they had come. Dust hung in the air and he could barely see. It was almost like a sandstorm, and djinn lived in sandstorms.

He shone the light the other way. The Roman snake djinn and the two cobras stood in their places, waiting their chance. Beyond lay the tunnels of the dead. All those bodies, with carved faces looking out of the graves …

Faisal shuddered.

"Get up! Please get up!" Faisal said, shaking Tim again. "Don't leave me yet!"

Tim raised his head and looked at him. He licked his lips, stared at the ceiling for a moment, then cringed and looked away.

"This isn't fair!" Faisal shouted. "*You're* supposed to protect *me*!"

Faisal kicked him. Not hard, just to show how mad he was.

Tim looked at him again, surprised.

"Get up!" Faisal kicked him again.

Anger flickered across Tim's face, which looked like a demon's with the light shining on it from a weird angle.

Uh-oh. Faisal took a step back.

Tim rose. Faisal took another step back.

"No problem, Little Gippo," Tim said. His voice came out husky.

"Come, Tim," Faisal said, gesturing toward the entrance passage.

Tim nodded, looked around, nodded again. "R-right."

He picked up his rifle.

Faisal tugged on his shirt. "Come. Tim go England."

"Right. Bloody England." Then Tim said something Faisal didn't understand. It sounded like he didn't believe he'd see England or any other place ever again.

Faisal felt the same.

"Tim go England," Faisal repeated as they walked down the hall, the torch dim in the haze. "Englishman go England."

"Right."

Faisal's heart sank. There it was. Tim had admitted it. He was going to take the Englishman away and Faisal would be out on the street again.

That wouldn't matter if the djinn ate him, or the ceiling came down.

Faisal peeked at the ceiling while trying to keep Tim from noticing he was doing so. He didn't want Tim panicking again.

And he sure would if he saw the ceiling. Big cracks ran along the stone, and every couple of steps they stumbled over chunks that had fallen.

The ceiling and floor grew worse as they continued. They stumbled more, barely able to see as the torch shone against dust that made their eyes water and lungs cough.

The dust thinned, and they came to the central chamber with the spiral staircase.

What was left of it. A large heap of rubble filled the circular room. High above, the hole they had come through looked much bigger. Faisal felt hope rise in him; maybe now they could go up the ancient stairs and get out.

He shone the torch up to the top of the stairs, and his heart sank. The stairs near the top had crumbled and fallen onto the stairs below. There was no way to get up there now.

Tim groaned, covered his face, and looked like he was about to sink to the floor again.

"No!" Faisal shouted at him. It didn't matter if the djinn heard him.

They were coming sooner or later. "No, Tim. Look."

Tim managed to look up, quaking as he saw there was no way out. Faisal punched him in the chest.

"No. Look Faisal."

Tim looked at him, terror in his eyes.

Faisal touched his own chest. "Egyptian boy." Then he jabbed Tim's chest. "English soldier."

Tim looked confused. How to make him understand?

"You …" what was the word for strong? Faisal made a muscle and slapped his arm. "Me boy. You fight. Go to England." Tim stared at him. Why don't they learn Arabic when they come here?

They always leave, Moustafa had told him so many times. *They only show interest in you while they're here and then they forget all about you.*

Anger rose up in Faisal. This man came to take his friend, and now he was acting like a baby when both their lives depended on him.

Frustrated, Faisal slugged him as hard as he could in the face. "Fight, soldier!"

That anger flashed in Tim's eyes again, and this time it didn't go away.

And this time Faisal didn't back off.

"Yes?" Faisal asked.

The anger faded, but the fear didn't return.

At least not so much.

Tim put a hand on Faisal's shoulder.

"Yes, Little Gippo. Sorry."

"No problem. What we do?"

Tim looked down the passage they hadn't tried, and found it even more full of rubble than before. Tim couldn't fit through there. He turned to the one they had just escaped, took a deep breath, and started walking into it.

Faisal, gripping the torch, followed.

They passed the three stone djinn and entered the maze of the dead. All those faces stared at them. In a couple of spots the stone slabs covering the graves had sheared off, revealing the skeletons within. Faisal tried not to show his fear. It might set off Tim again.

They walked down one of the narrow passages, stone faces staring at them from either side. Tim's heavy breathing sounded loud in the enclosed space. He gripped his rifle tight, his shirt damp with sweat. Faisal came right behind him, lighting their way with the torch.

They came to a corner, turned, and had to climb over a heap of stones from where the ceiling had caved in. Tim let out a little groan.

"No problem, Tim. You and friend go England."

"Bloody right," Tim whispered.

Living on the street is better than dying. Just get me out of here.

They found themselves in another corridor the same as the last. At the far end they could see another turn. Faisal wondered if that would lead to a third corridor of dead people.

It did, bringing up the terrible thought—what if this entire hill was full of dead people? What if they got lost forever and ever in a maze of skeletons?

Then there was the electric torch to think about. Faisal had played with them enough to know they only lasted a couple of hours. He tried to figure out how long he had been down here and found he couldn't say for sure. And had Tim and the others used it before he showed up?

Sooner or later that torch would flicker and die, and they'd be trapped in the dark with all those bodies. The djinn wouldn't be afraid of Tim at all then.

Faisal pushed him. *"Yalla!"*

He had forgotten how to say "hurry up" in English. He should have remembered. The Englishman was always saying it to him, along with "don't" and "no" and "stop that".

The Englishman was always telling him not to do things. He acted like Faisal was a big burden and a pest. Sure, he fed him and gave him a place to stay, but he always acted like Faisal was nothing but a bother.

That was another English word he knew. "A bother."

Maybe he had been. Maybe that's why the Englishman wanted to go back to England.

Just as they were about to get to the end of the corridor and to another turn, a boom shook the whole place. Tim and Faisal screamed. A slab sheared off right next to them. They leapt back an instant before it shattered on the floor where they had been standing.

Tim let out a string of bad words and picked his way over the broken pieces of slab. Faisal followed, trying not to look at the body inside.

When they turned the next corner they didn't find another narrow passage of dead people. Instead they found something very different.

A larger hallway of white marble, cracked now from the explosions. One way it ran into darkness. In the other direction it opened up. They went that way and found themselves in a giant chamber, its floor littered with rubble. The domed roof had deep cracks and looked ready to fall. In front of them stood an arched doorway sealed by a heavy iron door. An altar stood in front. To either side of the doorway were Classical statues. Greek writing in big letters was carved over the door.

Tim whispered something Faisal didn't understand. It sounded like he was so impressed he had forgotten to be scared of being underground.

Faisal was so impressed he had forgotten to be scared of djinn.

A spark of hope lit up inside him. Maybe that door led outside! All the Egyptian temples he had seen had grand entrances. Maybe the Greeks did the same. If they could get that door open, they'd be free!

Another boom rocked the chamber, throwing Faisal off his feet. Small stones from the ceiling pelted him. A loud crash jabbed his ears. He coughed and blinked his eyes as the air filled with dust.

After a minute he got on his hands and knees, ears ringing, wiped his eyes, and gasped.

Tim lay flat on the floor, blood matting his hair. A stone the size of Faisal's fist lay next to him. He did not move. Beyond, between the two statues, the door had fallen off its old rusty hinges and slammed onto the floor.

The way out!

Faisal got to his feet. He shone the torch up at the ceiling and saw the cracks had spread. One big chunk of stone looked like it was barely held up by the rock surrounding it.

They had to get out of here.

They?

Faisal took a look at Tim. He could see him breathing, but he was unconscious. Faisal wasn't sure he was strong enough to drag him out.

And then a terrible thought rose up in him.

If he dragged Tim out, assuming he could, Tim would wake up and take the Englishman back to England. Faisal would be on the street again. Everything he had fought so hard to get in the past year and a half would be gone. He'd be the street boy nobody cared about. No house. No bed. No food. He'd probably even lose his friends because he wouldn't be able to feed them anymore.

He'd have nothing.

But if he escaped now, he could tell the Englishman that Tim had been hit by a rock from the ceiling. That wouldn't even be lying.

Well, yes it would.

A new sound echoed through the corridors from the way they had come. A chill ran down Faisal's spine. It sounded like a voice!

What was it saying? He couldn't make out the words. It was too distant, too drowned out by the crackling of the weakening stones in the roof, by the constant trickle of dust and grit from above.

But he could recognize part of it.

"Faisal ... Tim ..."

The djinn were calling for their names! They had seen Tim get knocked out and now they were brave enough to come after them.

Slowly Faisal backed away from the opening to the corridor and moved toward the dark doorway revealed by the iron door now lying on the floor.

"Faisal ... Tim ..."

I'm not leaving Tim, Faisal told himself. *I'm only going to check if this is really the way out. I'm not leaving Tim.*

Liar.

"Faisal ... Tim ..."

Faisal turned and bolted for the doorway. The iron door clanged under his sandals as he ran over it.

He stopped short just beyond the threshold.

Beyond was a circular, domed chamber about ten paces across. It was all of the whitest marble, with Greek words running all around it in what looked like pure gold. In the center was a large glass coffin. Inside lay a man in strange purple clothing. A purple robe was draped over part of the glass coffin, and a ring and a wreath of gold leaves lay next to it.

But Faisal barely noticed these things. He couldn't keep his eyes off the man.

He looked almost alive. Sure, his face and hands were all thin and dried up, and his nose had broken off, but he was better preserved than any mummy he had ever seen. Faisal could tell what he looked like in life.

He looked Greek, with black hair and olive skin almost like an Egyptian, but with European features. He didn't look very old, perhaps in his thirties. Maybe he had died in battle. He had a sword in a sheath by his side. But Faisal didn't see any marks on him. The Greek looked too noble to hurt, as if in battle everyone would be too afraid to try and strike him. He looked like how Faisal always imagined a king might look.

With such a grand tomb, he must have been a king.

For some reason, Faisal didn't feel afraid of him. He looked too noble to be a djinn, too dignified to come alive and eat him. Faisal wondered what kind of king he had been, and decided that he had probably been good to his friends and terrible to his enemies.

"Sorry," Faisal said. "I didn't mean to break into your tomb."

The king didn't reply. Faisal sensed he could hear him, though. With all the magic in this place he must have been able to. The Englishman had said the ancient kings built grand tombs so they could live forever.

A faint call from behind him made him turn toward the open doorway. Those djinn voices again. They hadn't arrived yet. All he could see was Tim lying unconscious on the floor.

For the moment he wasn't afraid of the djinn. They wouldn't dare enter a place like this.

He turned back to the king.

"I don't know what to do," Faisal whispered.

The king lay silent in his crystal sarcophagus.

"I don't want to leave him but if I take him out I'll end up on the street. I'll probably die there. Most street boys do. Tarek died of a fever last winter. Waaiz got killed when an abandoned building he lived in fell down. And Ramy disappeared. Just vanished. People say some men sold him to a Yemini slaver. I don't want to die or disappear."

The king did not respond.

A crash outside made Faisal jump. Another part of the ceiling had fallen somewhere. He needed to find the way out and he needed to do it now.

Dragging Tim will only slow you down. You both might end up dying, and what's the good of that?

He moved closer to the king in his glass tomb.

"If I leave him, the Englishman will be really sad. And it would be kind of like killing him. But if I take him, I'll die on the street. It would be kind of like killing myself, and that's a sin."

Faisal took a step closer.

"Tell me what to do."

Faisal reached out to touch the glass tomb. As he did, his hand brushed the wreath of gold leaves and one snapped off. His thief's reflexes caught it before he even knew what he was doing.

Blinking at the gold leaf in his hand, he suddenly knew the king's answer.

He had to do the right thing, even though he'd end up on the street. The gold leaf was a gift. He could sell it and get some money, maybe even set up a little market stall. It would be a chance. He'd lose everything he had, but he'd get a little chance.

Faisal turned to the dried up, noble face of the ancient Greek and opened his mouth to speak.

Just then another explosion rocked the chamber. An ominous cracking above and a series of echoing thuds from outside told him the entire place was going to come down.

"Thanks! Bye!" Faisal said, stuffing the gold leaf in his pocket and bolting from the tomb.

He ran out into the larger chamber, ducking to the left as a big stone slammed to the ground and pelted him with fragments.

Faisal got to Tim, turned him over and tried to drag him with one arm while holding the torch with the other. He found he wasn't strong enough to do that.

He paused. Maybe he could drag Tim with two hands, but then how would he hold the torch? Another thud echoed down the hallway. The entire maze of tunnels was falling down bit by bit.

Tim's rifle lay nearby. Moustafa grabbed it, figured out how to unhook the strap from the gun, tossed the weapon aside, and looped the strap around his neck. Then he wound the strap around the torch and tied it off. It hung down to his belly and didn't give very much light except at his feet, but it was sure better than nothing.

"All right, Tim, let's go, and please wake up whenever you feel like it."

Just as he grabbed Tim under both arms and began to pull back out of the big chamber, another block of stone fell, crashing down in front of the king's tomb and toppling one of the Classical statues. That set off the rest of the dome and it all came down in a roar.

Crying out in terror, Faisal pulled at Tim as hard as he could, backing into the passageway. The floor trembled, the passage filled with dust, and he couldn't see where he was going. The torch was a dim glow below him, barely illuminating Tim. Faisal kept bumping against the walls and moved more by feel than sight.

Coughing from the dust, Faisal dragged Tim down the one passageway they hadn't tried. He kept glancing over his shoulder not only to see where he was going, but to see if any djinn were coming at him. For the first time ever, he was more scared of something else at the moment—the roof caving in. Every few seconds, the passageway would resound with another thud as a heavy stone somewhere in the maze sheared off the ceiling and crashed on the floor.

They came to a larger room, and Faisal gasped as he saw he had backed through a doorway flanked by a pair of djinn. Both had human bodies and animal heads. They were pretending to be stone.

Or maybe they really were stone. One was missing half its head and the other had a big crack down the middle.

Maybe this cave-in is killing the djinn, or at least making them run away. I better run away too, or I'm the one who's going to get killed.

Faisal's arms and back ached. Tim was heavy, and dragging over heaps of rubble and around corners was almost more than Faisal could bear. He knew he'd make much better time if he left Tim, but he couldn't. That king would never leave a friend. You could just look at him and tell.

You might die.

Then he would die. He wasn't going to leave someone behind when there was a chance to save him. The Englishman would never do that, and neither would Moustafa. He didn't get to act different just because he'd spent most of his life on the streets.

Faisal stumbled and fell. Getting up, he dragged Tim across the rest of the room and through a portal on the other side. A hallway ran for a little bit and then branched in two directions. Faisal took a guess and turned right.

A terrible shaking of the passageway almost threw Faisal from his feet. The thuds of falling masonry thundered again and again, coming so quickly they turned into a sustained roar. Faisal grunted as a piece of ceiling the size of his fist struck his shoulder.

Dragging Tim turned into agony. His ears filled with roaring, his watering eyes half blind from dust, every muscle screaming in pain. Faisal couldn't even be sure where he was going anymore. He kept dragging the soldier, knowing these were the last moments he had on earth.

I did get some fun, near the end.

And at least I didn't leave Tim behind.

Through the rumble in his ears he heard voices. The djinn making their way out of the maze? Maybe. Or maybe they had decided to eat him as a snack on their way out. It didn't matter. He wasn't getting out of here anyway.

The haze of dust grew brighter, and the babbling voices took on words.

"This way!"

"Over here!"

Faisal looked over his shoulder, coughing and blinking. The haze glowed with a diffuse yellowish light.

"You're almost there!"

An ear-splitting roar drowned out what they said next. With a final desperate effort, Faisal picked up speed, Tim bouncing over the heaps of rubble until Faisal's back struck the edge of a cut stone block. He coughed, then breathed fresher air.

He looked over his shoulder. There was a hole in the wall, and Egyptians on the other side with torches.

It could be the bad Egyptians they had been hunting, but at this point he didn't care. Groaning with effort, Faisal dragged Tim up the heap of rubble, banging his head against the ceiling, and hauled him outside.

They both collapsed on the grass. Faisal gulped fresh air.

With a final, thundering crash, the entrance to the maze collapsed. The men with the torches backed off.

Faisal got on his hands and knees and checked Tim. The soldier groaned and Faisal let out a breath of relief.

The Egyptian men came up to him. Now that he was outside, he could see they wore police uniforms.

"Are you all right, Little Infidel?"

Faisal looked to his left. Moustafa stood a little way off, handcuffed.

"Yes. Tim is hurt but I think it's not too bad."

"You're all right?" one of the policemen asked. What a dummy. Didn't he hear what Faisal just said?

"I'm all right. No thanks to you. Why didn't you help?"

The man's eyes were wide. "And risk getting buried?"

Faisal stood. He was so angry he forgot to be tired.

"Idiot!" Faisal kicked him in the shin.

"Ow!"

The policeman made a grab for him. Faisal darted away and ran down the slope for the dark fields.

"Get him!" one of the policemen said.

"Run, Faisal!" Moustafa shouted.

"Stop!" a policeman ordered.

"Don't shoot!" one of the policemen said. "He's just a child."

I am not a child!

But if you want to think that and not shoot me, go ahead.

Faisal ran as fast as he could down the slope and into the fields beyond, just in case they changed their minds.

The sound of running footsteps behind him. At least two of the police officers were chasing him. Electric torches probed the night.

The field was planted with vegetables and was completely open. If they shone the torches anywhere near him, they'd spot him for sure.

Up ahead Faisal spotted a field of half-grown grain, its waist-high stalks waving in the salty breeze. Faisal made for it.

The bobbing, searching lights settled on him.

"Stop!" one of the policemen shouted.

Since you won't shoot me, why should I?

Faisal dove into the field, crawling amid the stalks of grain.

"Where did he go?" one policeman asked the other. Faisal kept crawling, moving to the right. The lights searched over the grain. Faisal froze and the lights passed him over. He was as invisible as a djinn.

The sound of swishing grain told him the policemen had entered the field. Faisal crawled away from them, moving fast when the lights shone elsewhere and stopping when they came close. He didn't want them to see the grain moving as he passed through like a felucca leaving a wake on the river.

A distant shout from the ridge.

"All right!" one of the policemen said. He heard them move away.

Faisal counted to a hundred and dared a peek over the top of the grain. Two lights bobbed across the field of vegetables and rejoined the many lights by the entrance. There were lights on top of the ridge too, and they came down to join the lights at the entrance. Faisal could see many English and Egyptian policemen, as well as his friends.

Or former friends.

Because once they got out of jail, they would be sent back to England.

He could see a crowd of foreigners and Egyptians, many of them wounded, under guard of one group of police. A little to the side stood Moustafa and Tim and the Englishman. Tim looked worn out, and the Englishman had his arm around him, talking with him. Even if Faisal had never seen them before he would have been able to tell they were best friends.

Standing now, not really caring if the police spotted him, Faisal watched as the two best friends talked in English, probably about going home. The police had stopped looking for Faisal, and his former friends didn't look for him either.

The English policeman in charge shouted an order and the group of officers led their prisoners away.

Faisal watched them go until the lights of their torches dwindled and winked out in the distance.

CHAPTER THIRTY-ONE

In all the adventures he had been on with Timothy Crawford, Augustus had fully expected to one day see the inside of a jail cell.

He had never dreamed, however, that it would be his fault.

He and Tim shared a cell in the dank, thoroughly unpleasant cellar of the Alexandria central police station. Moustafa was stuck in a cell on the opposite side of the hallway, with a drunk and rowdy Bedouin he had already pummeled into submission.

At least the cell was reserved for Egyptians. In His Majesty's glorious prison system, Europeans and Africans were kept strictly apart.

The way Moustafa paced around the tiny cell, cursing as only he knew how, Augustus would not want any foreigner stuck in there with him, saying the wrong thing.

Augustus did not pace, but he did curse and he did worry. Once the police ascertained their identity, he might find himself forcibly placed on the first boat out.

Where could he go? Start all over again in some new place? Palestine? India?

Of course he could always go back to England, but his false name would hold no water there, and he'd have to face far too many awkward questions and half-hidden sympathetic looks from people from his old life.

No. Not England. Where then? And what of his life here?

And Faisal! He couldn't let the boy end up back on the streets, and he couldn't very well take him along. It wouldn't be fair to take someone that young away from everything he knew to some foreign land that spoke a foreign language. Taking him to England would be ten times worse. He knew how Faisal would be treated there.

So he'd ask one last favor of his long-suffering friends. They'd make sure the boy was all right.

The sound of snoring took him out of his thoughts. Tim lay on the other cot, a bandage around his head and fast asleep. Augustus smiled. Being incarcerated was a regular occurrence for that chap, nothing to make a fuss about.

"In how many countries have you visited jails, old friend?" Augustus murmured. "England, France, Belgium, and now Egypt. That makes four. Perhaps others I don't know of? Are you trying to collect the whole set?"

There was the rattle of a heavy key in a lock, and the barred door to the hallway clanged open. Two native officers, led by a hulking British sergeant, tromped down the hall, their hobnailed boots clanging down on the stone floor.

A good effect, Augustus mused. *I always wondered why prison guards wore hobnailed boots and now I know. I guess I could have asked Tim and known earlier.*

His old war chum rubbed his eyes, yawned, stretched, and let out a loud belch just as the three policemen stopped in front of their cell.

The sergeant studied Tim with distaste for a moment, then signaled for them to come forward.

"Put your hands through the bars!" the sergeant barked.

"You're not going to say please?" Tim mocked him.

"Tim, please," Augustus said.

Tim chuckled. "You always were a wet blanket. We're nicked. Might as well have a bit of fun with it."

Augustus groaned and put his hands through the bars so one of the native policemen could clap a pair of handcuffs on him. Then he did the same with Tim.

"Back up!" the sergeant ordered.

They backed up.

One of the policemen unlocked the door.

"Out!"

"You don't need to shout. We're not deaf, you know," Tim grumbled.

"OUT!"

"We'll be deaf before this is all over," Augustus said.

Tim grinned and nudged him with his elbow.

They were beyond hope now. His social standing and connections would keep him from prison, so his main worry was to ensure that Tim and Moustafa also got out, and that Faisal would be cared for after his departure.

I'll have to think up some better way to guard him so he doesn't sneak onto the boat as I'm sent into exile.

They handcuffed Moustafa and brought him out of the cell, not even sparing a glance at the pummeled Bedouin who lay groaning on his cot. From what Sir Thomas had told him, beatings were as commonplace as rats in Egyptian jails.

Without another word, they were marched up a narrow stone staircase under a low, dripping ceiling to a back room of the police station where the temporary holding cell for lesser criminals was located. Passing by the large barred area with its collection of drunks and brawlers, they came to the front office, where a long desk was staffed by a couple of officers. Another officer hauled in a shifty looking Armenian who loudly proclaimed that he would never pickpocket anyone in his life and how dare the police sully his reputation.

The sergeant and two native police steered them through this room and through a side door marked "Chief of Police."

What Augustus saw in there nearly made him faint.

A man in a civilian suit who he took to be the chief of police sat behind a large oak desk, and in front of it sat Cordelia and Lady Dorothea Russell.

Cordelia looked worried. Lady Dorothea looked furious.

Augustus stared at Sir Thomas's wife, wondering how she could have gotten up here so quickly. She wore a women's hunting costume with a long khaki dress and matching jacket, the pockets bearing impressions of having been stuffed with shotgun shells.

"Have you been hunting, Lady Dorothea?" Augustus asked.

Lady Dorothea stood, shot an angry glance at Cordelia, who visibly wilted, and turned to Augustus and his companions.

"Thomas sent me to the desert with a hunting party to get out of danger from the protests, and then just as quickly summoned me back when we found Cordelia had gone missing. Once we discovered you and Moustafa had also disappeared, it didn't take much investigative ability to determine where the three of you had gone."

"Four. Have you seen—"

Lady Dorothea did not let him finish his question.

"I should have known you wouldn't listen to my husband and come up here on your own."

Augustus cleared his throat and, carefully considering his words, said, "Sir Thomas told me he is short staffed and couldn't put enough men on Gregory's case. And considering he was my friend I—"

She stamped her foot. "Going behind my husband's back and ignoring his express orders is bad enough, but involving his sister is quite unacceptable! Are you not a gentleman?"

Cordelia finally found the courage to speak.

"I came up here on my own, Dorothea. He tried to leave me behind and I came anyway."

"Well, I never! Don't you think you've created enough scandal moving into a flat on your own? Taking on work when you are a woman of independent means? Don't you ever consider your brother's position? His reputation? You're to return to Cairo with me at once."

Cordelia stood. "I will not!"

"You will," the chief of police said. For a moment, Augustus had forgotten he was there. "My officers will escort you to the station, where you can take the five o'clock train."

The man pressed a buzzer and the sergeant who had released them from the cells entered.

"Come," Lady Dorothea said in a tone that brooked no argument.

"We need to find Faisal," Cordelia objected, although she did stand and move to the door. "He's gone missing."

"Who?"

"I'll find him," Augustus said. "Or more likely, he will find me."

"Enough delay," Lady Dorothea snapped. "You're coming back to Cairo and you are going to behave."

"You're not my mother!" Cordelia objected as they walked out of the room.

"Thanks to God I am not! When you first came to Cairo I thought we'd find a husband for you. And now you're not even looking. Instead you're running off with men who are not your relations and chasing criminals."

"What I do is my affair."

The sergeant, with a pained expression on his face, closed the door, cutting off any further sounds of the argument other than two muffled feminine voices shouting at each other until they thankfully faded into the distance.

The chief of police let out a sigh, pulled a cigarette out of a silver box on his desk, and lit it.

"Give your sergeant danger pay," Augustus advised.

"I am already over budget on danger pay this month thanks to you. Sit."

Augustus sat, as did Tim and Moustafa. For once, Tim did not offer one of his cheeky comments.

"I've spoken with Sir Thomas on the telephone, and he had me get in touch with Sir Hugh Davison, my predecessor."

At the name, Augustus perked up.

"Yes?"

"Sir Hugh vouched for you. He said you gave a great deal of assistance in solving the case of the khedive's jewels."

By which he means to say I solved the case with virtually no help from the authorities.

Augustus bowed his head in what he hoped was a fair simulation of humility.

"I am only too glad to be of service to the crown."

The new chief of police did not look impressed, judging by the glare he shot Augustus.

"He also said, and now that the ladies are gone I can share this, that you were a right pain in the arse."

Tim broke out in laughter. Augustus frowned at him, his frown deepening when he saw Moustafa put his hand in front of his face, trying and failing to hide his own laughter.

"I see nothing humorous about any of this!" the police chief said, cutting off the laughter sharp. Or at least most of it. "You have interfered with police business and engaged in a small-scale battle not only in the nearby countryside, but also in an Anglican church! Then there is the little matter of a Master Sergeant and a Greek shopkeeper found dead in a place of business, and a large Nubian seen leaving the scene. I don't suppose that would be you, Mr. Ghani El Souwaim?"

Before Moustafa thought of an answer that would neither incriminate nor perjure himself, the police chief went on.

"Don't say anything. It's too early in the morning for lies and I'm sure I'll get my fill of them in the course of my usual work day. At least I didn't get any lies from the prisoners you captured. They started singing the minute they saw the inside of a prison cell. It got a bit confusing with everyone pointing fingers at everyone else, but enough of a picture emerged to see you are telling the truth. After a fashion."

Augustus cleared his throat. "Yes. I am aware that I have gone past the bonds of the law, but I did so to stop even greater crimes. If you must mete out punishment, please do so on me and not my companions. I was the one who planned and organized this mission to Alexandria."

The chief of police waved an impatient hand. "I'm not punishing any of you, at least not yet. Sir Thomas vouched for you, as did Sir Hugh, and that coupled with the confessions we wrung from those thugs is enough."

"Speaking of the thugs, did you find out who besides the Master

Sergeant killed my friend?"

"They all say it was someone they called Private One. You killed him last night."

Augustus took in a sharp breath, and let it out slowly. "I most certainly hope so."

"Even if you didn't, it won't make any difference. These men will in all likelihood hang. Oh, we also brought in another Australian, an ANZAC corporal named Jack Turner."

"He broke with the gang and was of some help in us finding them," Moustafa said for the first time.

"And he's been singing like a canary ever since we brought him in. We found his papers in your hotel room."

"I hope you return them to him," Augustus said. "He wants to go home."

"After a year or two at His Majesty's pleasure, he probably will," the chief of police said, then waved his hand as if shooing away a crowd of tour guides at the pyramids. "You are all free to go, but you are confined to your hotels until we finish our investigations. It shouldn't take long. And your weapons will be confiscated until this matter is cleared up."

"Very well. Oh, may I have my cane back? An old war injury to the leg—"

The chief of police frowned. "You mean your sword cane? No, you may not have it back. Now get out of my office. Sergeant!"

An officer entered. "Yes, sir?"

"Remove these handcuffs and send these fools on their way."

"Yes, sir." The sergeant looked disappointed.

"The chief of police seems like a pleasant chap," Augustus said as they stepped into the predawn air. The sergeant had escorted them to the front door of the station and stood there, silhouetted by the light from inside. To Augustus he looked like Charon by the shores of the River Styx.

"He didn't hang us, I'll give him that," Tim said.

They walked down the street, utterly exhausted.

"It's too bad we can't find a motor cab at this hour," Moustafa said.

"We'll go back to the hotel, catch a couple of hours of sleep, then be up at dawn to find one," Augustus said. "We need to retrace our steps and locate Faisal."

"Here I am," Faisal said, popping out of a darkened doorway.

The three of them stopped and stared at him in shock.

Augustus got over his surprise first. Living with the boy, he had learned not to stay surprised at anything he did for terribly long.

"How did you know what I was saying? I was speaking in English."

"My name is the same in any language, you silly Englishman. So what were you saying about me?"

"We were about to go in search of you. How did you get back here so quickly? Surely you didn't hang on the back of a police car."

"Of course not! I walked most of the way, then tucked myself in the back of a farmer's wagon who was coming to market. I sure am tired, though."

Faisal walked past him and up to Timothy Crawford.

"Sorry, Tim," the boy said, looking glum.

"Sorry? What you got to be sorry for?" Tim said, slapping him on the shoulder. "You saved me life, you did."

Faisal did not look cheered up by Tim's demeanor. He gestured down the street. "Sorry. I … go."

"You went for help and didn't find anything? That what you mean? Well, you came back and did it all yourself. No need to say sorry, Little Gippo."

"What's the matter, Faisal?" Augustus asked in Arabic.

"Nothing," the boy said without looking at him. "Are you mad at me for not finding the treasure?"

"No, I'm happy you saved my friend. He and Moustafa told me all about it. I'd give you the Victoria's Cross if you were eligible."

"I don't know what that is."

"A medal. You did very well, Faisal. What did you see underground? Tim told me about some statues that sounded like they dated to the Greco-Roman period, and some tombs in niches on the walls. But he was hazy after that. The stone that struck his head seems to have blotted out some of the memories of your explorations."

Faisal shrugged, looking at the ground. "Nothing much. Just some djinn Tim scared into statues, and some little tombs on the walls with faces on them. We didn't find any treasure."

"Did you see any writing? Or any grand tomb?"

Faisal slowly shook his head.

Augustus cursed his luck. The entrance had been too small to send down himself or Moustafa. Instead they had to rely on a superstitious boy and a near-illiterate. It was almost as bad as not sending anyone at all.

"Mr. Wall, from what little they've said, it sounds like the catacombs of Kom el Shoqafa. Scholars have theorized that many such catacombs were dug in the Greco-Roman period," Moustafa said. "Alexander wasn't buried there. It was simply a much later burial place."

"But the inscription!" Augustus objected.

"We fooled ourselves. It was so fragmentary we saw what we wanted to see. Most likely it came from a statue of Alexander in the ruins of that temple. That's all. If they had come across the tomb we sought, the boy would have grand tales of treasure and a man in a crystal sarcophagus."

Faisal slumped, looking at the ground. Augustus put a hand on his shoulder.

"It doesn't matter, Faisal. We avenged my friend and we're safe. It's a pity about the catacombs, but justice has been done. That's the main thing."

"So we're all done here," Faisal said.

"Yes. Let's go." They began to walk again.

Augustus didn't understand why the boy trudged along the street all downcast.

The poor boy must be more exhausted than any of us.

"We have a few things to clear up with the police, but yes, our work here is done."

Faisal looked at the ground, kicking a discarded husk of corn ahead of him. "So Tim is going back to England soon."

"Yes, I suppose so. Why the long face? Will you miss him?"

"No. I mean, yes. But ..." the boy's voice became all but inaudible. "I guess you're going too."

Augustus stopped. Faisal stopped too, not quite able to look at him.

"What are you talking about?" Augustus asked.

"Can you at least buy me a train ticket so I can get back to Cairo?"

"You think I'm going back to England? Are you mad? Why would I want to return to that dreadful place?"

Faisal looked up at him, confused. "But it's your country."

"Wretched weather, dreadful food, polite society? I'd rather go back to the trenches. At least I have the better option of staying here."

Faisal brightened. "Really? You hate England so much?"

"You cannot begin to comprehend my loathing for that place. And in addition," Augustus cleared his throat. "I have certain, um, obligations here. Responsibilities, you might say. An old friend reminded me of them. Well, not exactly. It's, um, hard to explain."

"Responsibilities? You mean like your shop?"

"That's the least of them," Augustus grunted.

"Solving murders?"

"That does seem to have become a regular duty of mine, yes."

"Having breakfast with Sir Thomas Russell Pasha?"

"Don't be ridiculous. You know perfectly well I'm talking about you!"

Faisal jumped up and spun in the air.

"Great! Now let's go find a food stall. There must be one open someplace."

Augustus looked at his watch. "It's four in the morning."

"So? The workers will be getting up and the farmers will start coming in from the villages soon. I bet there are some food stands already open."

Augustus shook his head and they strolled down the street.

"We barely escaped with our lives and have the police breathing down our necks, and all you can think of is finding something to eat."

"Why not? I'm hungry, and that's your responsibility."

CHAPTER THIRTY-TWO

Three days later ...

Alexandria's port shone in the sunlight of early morning. There was a bustle on the dockside as porters, stevedores, passengers, and well-wishers all jostled to get to their ships. Several steamers were docked at a row of piers, and moored out in the vast semicircle of the port were dozens of ships of all descriptions—rusty old freighters, imposing steel battleships flying the Union Jack, even one of the new oil tankers that slaked the world's increasing thirst for gasoline.

Moustafa looked with longing at those ships, and the blue sea beyond stretching to the horizon. He had traveled far in life, all the way up the Nile from a little village in the Soudan to a professional job in Cairo.

And now he wanted to travel more. There was so much out there to see, so much the world could teach him.

But not today. Today it was Timothy Crawford who was traveling. While Mr. Wall had tried to get him to stay, Tim didn't feel comfortable in Egypt, certainly not with the police now having his name on a list.

"There she is," Tim said, pointing to a freighter moored at the next pier.

While his head was still swathed in bandages, he had regained his usual energy and was even giving Faisal a piggyback ride. Mr. Wall strolled alongside, Tim's suitcase in one hand and his sword cane in the other. All matters with the police had finally been cleared up, thanks in no small part to Sir Thomas Russell Pasha.

The only loss was Mr. Wall's German machine gun. He had to pretend it was the gang's weapon in order to avoid trouble, and had complained bitterly about its loss.

"That's the ship on the next pier?" Moustafa asked.

"That's right. In a few days I'll be back in Blighty. Food I can eat, water I can drink, and all the rain I could ever want. You should visit some time."

"I would very much like to."

"'I would very much like to,'" Tim mimicked. Grinning at Mr. Wall. "Bloody hell. Looks like a bootblack and talks like a professor. He'd make a hell of a show at the British Museum, wouldn't he?"

"I plan to do that at the Egyptian Museum," Moustafa said.

"You will, too. Any of those scrawny professors give you any fuss, just lay into them. One hit from those fists of yours and you'll be playing football with their heads."

"A tempting prospect," Moustafa said and laughed.

The steamer's whistle let out a blast.

Faisal, still clutching onto the veteran's back, pointed at the ship. "Tim, look!"

"That's right, Little Gippo. That's me ship and that whistle tells me I need to double time onto it. Off you get."

Tim shucked off the boy like he was dropping a backpack after a long march. Faisal laughed and landed on his feet. The crowd swirled around them as passengers pressed forward to queue up in front of an official standing at the head of the gangway.

"Home sweet home in just five days," Tim said.

He turned to Moustafa and took his hand. "You're all right, Shaka Zulu. We could have used a few of you on the Western Front."

Moustafa smiled. "From the way you fight, I can see you did just fine on your own."

Tim jabbed a finger in Mr. Wall's direction. "Me and him were the terror of the trenches, I tell you." Tim turned to Faisal, grabbed him by the middle, turned him upside down, and shook him. "And you, you little Gippo. You take care of my pal, you hear? He's a snooty bastard but he'll stick with you through thick and thin."

"Yes, yes," Faisal said, laughing.

"You don't even know what you're saying yes to, you little sneakabout. Don't matter. I know you'll take care of him."

Tim set him upright and tousled his hair so roughly Faisal almost fell over.

Slowly Crawford turned to Augustus.

"All right, old pal. I'd try to get you to come with me to England but I know you won't. You got a new life here and it looks like a good one. Just try not to get into too much trouble, eh?"

"I'll be careful."

Tim laughed. "Like hell you will. If you ever need any help, if anyone gives you any trouble, just wire me and I'll come sailing over, and God help whoever crossed you."

They clasped hands.

"Damn good to see you again, no matter what name you're calling yourself," Tim said.

"You too."

Tim balled his free hand into a fist and jabbed at Mr. Wall's ribs, stopping half an inch before hitting him. Almost at the same time, Mr. Wall swung for Tim's head, stopping just shy of his ear.

Tim laughed. "Still just a second too slow. Well, I'm off! Hey, look at that bit of fluff heading to the ship. She looks like she's on her own. Won't be for long!"

Tim shoved through the crowd to get right behind a young woman struggling with her bags, made a deep bow, said something, and took them from her. They headed for the gangway together.

Moustafa, Mr. Wall, and Faisal watched for a moment and then turned away. They walked back up the pier, occasionally stopping to look back at the ship, Crawford now lost in the press of passengers. As they left the pier, they turned right, moving with the jostling crowd along the port to get to the gate where a string of carriages and motor cabs would be waiting. As they did, they passed another pier where a passenger ship was docked, its steam funnels quiet. In front of the pier was a one-story customs house, a long line of disembarking passengers waiting their turn to get through the officials. A low fence and several policemen kept them from the main part of the harbor.

Mr. Wall stopped short and stared. Moustafa followed his gaze.

There, near the front of the line, stood Jocelyn Montjoy. She had only one large steamer trunk and a small bag, and wore a loose khaki shirt and trousers, and her usual military boots and pith helmet shading a lean, brown face. From a distance, she looked like a small, beardless man. To Mr. Wall she was anything but.

"Jocelyn!" Mr. Wall shouted, rushing up to the fence and waving. A policeman turned and raised a cautionary hand. Mr. Wall ignored him, jumping and waving and acting more like Faisal than the dour antiquarian Moustafa knew so well.

The woman turned and her face lit up as she spotted him.

"Augustus!"

She left her spot in line and rushed up to the fence. The policeman said something, but Moustafa couldn't catch it because Faisal was tugging on his sleeve.

"Look, Moustafa, it's Jocelyn! The Englishman was sad with Tim leaving but now he'll be happy again."

"Yes, I suppose he will." Moustafa thought about the woman waiting for him at home, a respectable woman who knew how to dress with modesty. He had only been gone a few days and still he missed her. It would be good to get back.

"Eeew!" Faisal turned away as Mr. Wall and Jocelyn kissed. Moustafa turned away from the scandalous sight too. Even most Europeans didn't do that in public.

A madwoman for a madman.

"Have they stopped yet?" Faisal asked, still turned away.

"I don't know. I'm not looking either."

Faisal tugged on Moustafa's sleeve again. "Let's leave them alone. I saw a patisserie near here. Have you ever been to a patisserie? I have some money. I'll treat you."

Moustafa frowned. "I'm not going to use stolen money to eat cake!"

"It's not stolen. Tim gave it to me because it's no use in England."

"They probably won't let you in," Moustafa said.

"They let me in when I was with Tim. And why shouldn't we be allowed in? I'm clean and I have money. You're the one who's always talking about how we should be free to do what we want in our own country."

"That's true, Little Infidel. You're quite right," Moustafa said thoughtfully.

They started walking toward the entrance. Faisal chattering away about all the different varieties of cakes in the last patisserie Tim took him into.

"All right, Little Infidel. You win. We'll go in. After the independence marches of the last couple of days I don't think they'd dare try and stop us. I've never been much for sweets but after this case I think I've earned it," Moustafa said.

Faisal jumped up and spun in the air. "Me too! It's too bad Jocelyn didn't come soon enough to help us with the murder."

Moustafa let out a deep sigh.

"I have no doubt there will be another one soon."

Faisal looked up at him. "You think so?"

"Oh, yes. Let's get some of that cake. We're going to need it."

CHAPTER THIRTY-THREE

The carriage carrying the Englishman, Jocelyn, and Faisal pulled up in front of the big castle at the end of the mole protecting Alexandria's harbor. It had a broad arched gate and towers overlooking the water. A soldier stood on guard at the gate, and several cannons poked over the tops of the walls.

The castle stood at the end of the barrier between the sea and the harbor, but Faisal could see a second barrier curving away from it in the other direction. At the end, he could just make out some boys diving and swimming in the water. So far away, they looked like tiny brown sticks.

"Go have your swim, Faisal," the Englishman said. "You're earned it. We'll be at the castle."

"You sure you can get in?"

"The chief of police gave me a letter of introduction to the commandant. Since this castle is of historical interest, they will allow us to study it."

"Um, all right."

"You sure you don't want to come in?" the Englishman asked. "You might like it."

Jocelyn nudged him. "I think he'll like swimming more."

"That's for sure!" Faisal said. He could tell the Englishman wanted to be alone with Jocelyn and he only invited him to be nice. It was great having the Englishman in such a good mood.

"You know how to find the hotel?" he asked Faisal.

"Yes."

After Cordelia had left, he had been kicked out of the servants' quarters of the Metropole. Now he was at the Windsor with the Englishman. In the servants' quarters. The Englishman had made a big fuss about that, but the hotel wouldn't budge.

It didn't matter. The room was warm and safe. Much better than the streets. The gold leaf the king gave him was well hidden under the mattress. Faisal hadn't decided what to do with it yet. It didn't feel right keeping it since he didn't need it for food. Maybe he could spend it on someone who didn't have a home.

What did feel right was leaving the king to rest in peace. Faisal tried not to lie to the Englishman, at least not too much, but he had decided not to mention finding the king in the glass sarcophagus. The Englishman and Moustafa would have dug away the whole ridge to get to the tomb. That wouldn't be right, not after all the king did for him.

"Now remember," the Englishman said," it's called the Windsor. You can just make it out on the Corniche right over there."

"Yes, yes, the big white one. I know."

Jocelyn laughed. "Stop mothering him, Augustus. He's big enough to get home by himself."

"He always does," the Englishman said.

Faisal waved goodbye and passed the castle, kicking his football along in front of him. Three boys walking the same direction came up to him. Two wore nice djellabas like him; the other was a Greek boy in short pants and a shirt.

"Nice football. Where did you get it?" one of the Egyptian boys said.

"He gave it to me," Faisal said, pointing back at the Englishman.

"Wow. Do you work for him?" the Greek boy asked.

"No. He adopted me. My mother was a good woman who died giving birth to me. My father was in the Egyptian Expeditionary Force with that Englishman. They fought together and won lots of medals, but then a

German cannon killed my father and hurt the Englishman. That's why he wears that mask. As my father lay dying he asked the Englishman to take care of me, so I live with him now."

Faisal liked that story. He was going to tell it from now on.

"You going swimming?" they asked.

"Sure."

"I'm Mohammed," the first boy said. "This is Ibrahim and Alexander."

Faisal laughed.

"What's so funny?" the Greek boy asked.

"Nothing. It's a good name. The Englishman says he was the greatest king ever. I'm Faisal."

They climbed over the giant stones of the mole, getting splashed by the spray as the waves broke on its seaward edge. Faisal couldn't kick his ball and had to carry it.

"Maybe we can play some football after we swim," Alexander suggested.

"Sure. I know lots of tricks."

It took a long time to get to the end of the line of big stones. The castle got smaller and smaller behind them. Faisal could no longer see the Englishman and Jocelyn. Maybe they were two of the little heads he could see poking over the top of the wall. He waved but nobody waved back.

Some boys played in the water to the side of the barrier, their dirty djellabas spread out on the rocks and getting splashed by the waves.

"Let's swim!" Faisal said.

"Not here," Mohammed said, making a face. "We don't swim with them."

"It's better at the end," Ibrahim explained. "It's deeper and you can dive really far. You can't dive here because there are stones right under the water."

"Oh," Faisal said, pretending to understand. If it was better at the end, why were those boys swimming here? Maybe they were a rival group and there had been a fight or something.

They hopped and clambered over the big stones. Faisal felt great. The sun was bright but not hot. The wind blowing in from the sea kept it cooler, tousling Faisal's hair like the Englishman did when he was really happy. Out to sea floated the blue fishing boats and a couple of big British warships, and beyond that—nothing. It was amazing to see water stretch all the way to the horizon.

Even better, he had helped solve another mystery and the Englishman was going to stay in Egypt. Jocelyn arriving made that doubly sure. It looked like everything was going to be great from now on.

They finally made it to the end of the mole, the castle far behind them. A dozen Egyptian and Greek boys swam in the water or dove off a big stone at the very end of the barrier. All the nearby rocks were covered in djellabas or shirts and short pants, turning the end of the mole into a dozen different colors like the glass windows in the houses of the rich.

"Don't dive off the side," Alexander told him. "Look, see how when the waves pull back you can see the rocks underneath the water? Dive there and you'll break your leg."

"Or your head!" Mohammed said. "Same on the other side. Just dive off the end. It's really deep there."

"All right."

The boys kicked off their sandals and started taking off their clothes. Faisal looked back the way they had come.

"What if a girl comes along?"

"No girls ever come out here, and if a tourist comes, we throw rocks at them until they go away."

Faisal laughed. "That's what we do on the Nile!"

He pulled his djellaba over his head and draped it over one of the rocks.

The boys all stared at him.

"What?"

One of them pointed at the scar on his chest.

"What's that? It looks like a bullet wound."

"It is a bullet wound."

The boys gasped.

"How did you get shot?"

Faisal swelled with pride.

"Oh, that happened in the war," he said like it was nothing special.

"You weren't in the war, you're too young!" Mohammed said.

"Oh, I wasn't a soldier, but I was with the Egyptian Expeditionary Force. My father loved me so much he couldn't stand to be away from me, so he brought me along. We went on all the marches together and everything. I helped the soldiers by keeping watch around camp and loading their guns. Things like that."

"Really?" The boys didn't sound convinced, but the scar made them think twice.

"Sure. That's how I got shot. A German sniper saw me keeping watch at the edge of camp one night and shot me."

"Wow!"

"It was strange, but it didn't hurt all that much," Faisal shivered a little as he remembered what really happened. "I just felt all weak and sort of floated away. My father was so sad. The Englishman too. They cried and cried thinking that I was going to die, but an English nurse saved me. Her name is Cordelia."

"Tell us more stories about the war!"

"Yeah!"

"What were the Turks like?"

"And the battles?"

"Later," Faisal said. "I came here to swim, so let's swim!"

He hopped across the last rocks and leapt off the end one, right where he had seen another boy do the same.

Faisal felt a thrill as he sailed through the air and splashed in the water in the midst of a whole crowd of swimming boys.

He came up spitting and coughing.

"Ugh! The water tastes all salty."

All the boys laughed. "That's because it's seawater! Haven't you ever been to the sea before?"

"No, just the Nile."

"Well, don't drink it, silly."

He sure wouldn't. It tasted terrible.

And now he had another problem. The waves pushed him away from the barrier, and he had to swim hard to keep close to it. The water tugged at his feet too, first one way and then another.

"It's weird to swim in this stuff. It won't stay still!"

"You'll get used to it."

The boys were still laughing at him. Faisal needed to impress them again.

"Hey!" he called to one of the boys who had just climbed onto the barrier, skin glistening from the water. "Throw my football down. It floats."

"You can't play football in the water," the boy said.

"I invented my own game for when I'm swimming with my friends in the Nile. I call it water football. We use our hands instead of our feet."

The boy tossed the ball in and Faisal grabbed it, having to struggle even more against the waves now that he could only use his legs. He quickly organized the boys into two teams and told them spots on the water that counted as goals. Pretty soon they were all tossing the ball back and forth, trying to pass it to people on their own team, or wrestling with players on the opposite team. The ball went every which way and nobody made a goal, but everybody had fun and got their heads dunked underwater a lot.

"You should live up here, Faisal." Alexander said. "You're great!"

"Yeah, then we could play water football every day," Mohammed said.

"And you can tell us all your stories about the war," Ibrahim added.

"That would be fun." Faisal thought of Mina and all his other friends in Cairo. "Well, maybe I could come up here a lot. It's not too far on the train."

"I've been on the train!" one of the other boys said.

Why not come up on the train? Maybe he could bring Hamza and Mehmed and all the other street boys. If he asked really, really nicely, the Englishman might pay for it. They'd love it, and he could have two groups of friends instead of just one.

And these were boys with homes. They wouldn't always ask him for money and food. That would be nice.

They continued to play, laughing and splashing around, until a shout from one of the boys sunning himself on the barrier stopped their game.

"Get out of here!"

At first Faisal thought a girl or a tourist had come to the end of the barrier, but when he looked all he saw were four more boys.

In a moment all the boys in the water started shouting.

"Get out!"

"Go away!"

"Go further down where the others are."

"But we can't dive there!" one of the boys whined.

"So what? We don't want you dirtying up our spot."

Faisal swam closer to the barrier. He could see the boys didn't have sandals, and that their djellabas and hair were filthy. They were street boys.

"Why can't they swim here?" he asked, although he thought he knew why.

"They're street boys, what do you think?" Mohammed said.

"So?"

"So they're dirty!" Alexander said, sticking out his tongue at them.

"They won't be dirty once they dive in the water," Faisal said.

"They're dirty on the inside too," one of the other boys said. "They eat trash and sleep in alleyways. You want to swim with someone like that?"

"Come on," one of the street boys said. "We won't bother you."

"You're already bothering us!"

The boys started getting out of the water, a good dozen of them, cursing and shaking their fists. The four street boys backed off.

"That's right, go to your spot!"

"Yeah, know your place!"

Faisal treaded water, a sick feeling growing inside him. The street boys trudged away. One looked over his shoulder. He looked hurt, but not surprised.

"That took care of them!" Ibrahim said. "Let's get back to our game."

He dove into the water. Several more followed him while others stayed on the rocks making crude gestures at the street boys.

Faisal swam over to Mohammed, who had the ball at the moment.

"Give me the ball," Faisal said.

"But it's my turn," he objected.

"Just give it to me."

The boy tossed it to him. Faisal swam to the edge of the barrier and climbed up.

"You going to dive?"

"Pass the ball to me while you dive!"

"No, pass it to me!"

"Try to make a goal from the air. Then we'll all try and see who gets the high score!"

Faisal picked up his djellaba, draped it over his shoulder and, with the football tucked under his arm, started walking away.

"Hey, Faisal, where are you going?" Ibrahim asked.

"Leaving so soon?"

"Yeah, where are you going?"

Faisal shot them an angry look over his shoulder but did not slow down.

"To swim with them."

HISTORICAL NOTE

While the main characters and story in this novel are fictional, the historical background is as accurate as I could make it. Also, some of the minor characters are real.

The anecdotes and attitudes of Sir Thomas Russell Pasha come from his autobiography, *Egyptian Service 1902-1946*, an excellent glimpse into the mind and times of this important historical figure.

Another real figure is that of Heinrich Schäfer. I am glad to say he finally did finish his *Principles of Egyptian Art* which, while a weighty academic tome, is still one of the most thorough introductions to the art of ancient Egypt almost a hundred years after it was written.

These and many other books on Egypt in the old days I read during various research trips to the Bodleian Library, Oxford, one of the world's great repositories of knowledge, and on frequent visits to that sanctuary for Cairene bibliophiles, the American University in Cairo bookshop.

I also relied on William Edward Lane's classic study, *Manners and Customs of the Modern Egyptians* and the 1929 edition of the *Baedeker's Guide to Egypt and the Sudan*. A more modern guide to the country is the *Blue Guide to Egypt*, now sadly out of print. The 1993 edition has an extensive section on Cairo and proved an invaluable companion on my many rambles through the medieval districts where much of the Cairo action takes place.

For descriptions of Alexandria, a major source was E.M. Forster's *Alexandria: A History and A Guide*, written during the First World War while Forster served in the city with the Red Cross. Lawrence Durrell's *Alexandria Quartet*, while set a couple of decades later, also helped with atmosphere and scenery. I also drew on *Alexandria: City of Memory* by Michael Haag.

The catacombs that Tim and Faisal explore were inspired by the catacombs of Kom el Shoqafa, built during the 2nd to 4th centuries AD. These atmospheric tombs and tunnels are one of the most impressive sites in the city and well worth a visit, assuming you aren't claustrophobic and don't believe in djinn. I wrote about the catacombs of Kom el Shoqafa in an issue of my newsletter, which, by the way, is a great way to keep up with what I'm writing and where I'm traveling.

The Windsor, where Augustus stayed, and the Metropole, where Cordelia had a room and Faisal was consigned to the basement, are still in existence. I visited both while staying in the slightly later Cecil Hotel. I had the pleasure of staying there for several nights with a room looking out over the Mediterranean. Several of the Alexandrian passages were written while trying not to be distracted by such a view.

More details of Alexandria's hotels came from Andrew Humphreys's detailed and beautifully illustrated book, *Grand Hotels of Egypt in the Golden Age of Travel*. Another good book about the British in Egypt is Anthony Sattin's *Lifting the Veil: British Society in Egypt 1768-1956*.

This book was written during two long visits to Cairo, Alexandria, and the Western Desert. I would be remiss not to thank my many Egyptian, Sudanese, and expatriate European friends who helped me with their local knowledge and encouragement. A very special thanks goes to the Middle Eastern historian Alan Rush, who provided a home and extensive library in downtown Cairo.

About the Author

Sean McLachlan worked for ten years as an archaeologist in Israel, Cyprus, Bulgaria, and the United States before becoming a full-time writer. He is the author of numerous fiction and nonfiction books, which are listed on the following pages. When he's not writing, he enjoys hiking, reading, traveling, and, most of all, teaching his son about the world. He divides his time between Madrid, Oxford, and Cairo.

To find out more about Sean's work and travels, visit him at his Amazon page or his blog, and feel free to friend him on Goodreads, Twitter, and Facebook.

You might also enjoy his newsletter, *Sean's Travels and Tales*, which comes out every one or two months. Each issue features a short story, a travel article, a coupon for a free or discounted book, and updates on future projects. You can subscribe using the link below. Your email will not be shared with anyone else.

Amazon: http://www.amazon.com/Sean-McLachlan/e/B001H6MUQI
Goodreads: http://www.goodreads.com/author/show/623273.Sean_McLachlan
Blog: http://midlistwriter.blogspot.com
Twitter: https://twitter.com/@writersean
Facebook: https://www.facebook.com/writersean
Newsletter: http://eepurl.com/bJfiDn

Fiction by Sean McLachlan

Tangier Bank Heist: An Interzone Mystery

Right after the war, Tangier was the craziest town in North Africa. Everything was for sale and the price was cheap. The perverts came for the flesh. The addicts came for the drugs. A whole army of hustlers and grifters came for the loose laws and free flow of cash and contraband.

So why was I here? Because it was the only place that would have me. Besides, it was a great place to be a detective. You got cases like in no other place I'd ever been, and I'd been all over. Cases you couldn't believe ever happened. Like when I had to track down the guy who stole the bank.

No, he didn't rob the bank, he stole it.

Here's how it happened . . .

Available in electronic edition!

Three Passports to Trouble (Interzone Mystery Book 2)

Back in the days when Tangier was an International Zone, the city was full of refugees. People fleeing Stalin. People fleeing Franco. People fleeing the Nuremburg Trials. Tangier offered a safe haven from the chaos of Europe.

The International Council had to keep a delicate balance, tolerating everything from anti-capitalist agitators to Germans with murky pasts. It was the only way to keep the peace, and it worked.

Until an anarchist was found dead with a fascist dagger in his chest.

And I got stuck with the case just when I had to smuggle a couple of Party operatives out of town.

Available in electronic edition!

Flight to Fez (Interzone Mystery Book Three)

Only in Tangier could a literary event turn into a murder scene.

I'm "Shorty" MacAllister, private detective. I've investigated all sorts of crazy cases in this lawless town, tracking down con men and Nazi fugitives, anarchists and bank robbers, all the while running my own secret angle.

But I never thought that when I went to hear my friend Jane Bowles read her latest story I'd end with a murdered man in my lap, and an old war buddy getting pinned with the crime.

After that, things got a whole lot more complicated.

Available in electronic edition!

Trench Raiders (Trench Raiders Book One)

September 1914: The British Expeditionary Force has the Germans on the run, or so they think.

After a month of bitter fighting, the British are battered, exhausted, and down to half their strength, yet they've helped save Paris and are pushing towards Berlin. Then the retreating Germans decide to make a stand. Holding a steep slope beside the River Aisne, the entrenched Germans mow down the advancing British with machine gun fire. Soon the British dig in too, and it looks like the war might grind down into deadly stalemate.

Searching through No-Man's Land in the darkness, Private Timothy Crawford of the Oxfordshire and Buckinghamshire Light Infantry finds a chink in the German armor. But can this lowly private, who spends as much time in the battalion guardhouse as he does on the parade ground, convince his commanding officer to risk everything for a chance to break through?

Available in electronic edition!

Digging In (Trench Raiders Book Two)

October 1914: The British line is about to break.

After two months of hard fighting, the British Expeditionary Force is short of men, ammunition, and ideas. With their line stretched to the breaking point, aerial reconnaissance spots German reinforcements massing for the big push. As their trenches are hammered by a German artillery battery, the men of the Oxfordshire and Buckinghamshire Light Infantry come up with a desperate plan—a daring raid behind enemy lines to destroy the enemy guns and give the British a chance to stop the German army from breaking through.

Available in electronic edition!

No Man's Land (Trench Raiders Book Three)

No Man's Land—a hellscape of shell craters and dead bodies. Soldiers have fought over it, charged across it, and bled on it for a year of grueling war, but neither side has dominated it.

Until now.

An elite German raiding party is passing through No Man's Land every night, attacking the British trenches at will. The Oxfordshire and Buckinghamshire Light Infantry need to reassert control over their front lines.

So the exhausted men of Company E decide to set a trap, a nighttime ambush in the middle of No Man's Land, where any mistake can be fatal. But the few surviving veterans are leading recruits who have only been in the trenches for two weeks. Mistakes are inevitable.

Available in electronic edition!

Christmas Truce

Christmas 1914

In the cold, muddy trenches of the Western Front, there is a strange silence. As the members of a crack English trench raiding team enjoy their first day of peace in months, they call out holiday greetings to the men on the German line. Soon both sides are fraternizing in No Man's Land.

But when the English recognize some enemy raiders who only a few days before launched a deadly attack on their position, can they keep the peace through the Christmas truce?

Available in electronic edition!

Warpath into Sonora

Arizona 1846

Nantan, a young Apache warrior, is building a name for himself by leading raids against Mexican ranches to impress his war chief, and the chief's lovely daughter. But there is one thing he and all other Apaches fear—a ruthless band of Mexican scalp hunters who slaughter entire villages.

Nantan and his friends have sworn to fight back, but they are inexperienced, and led by a war chief driven mad with a thirst for revenge. Can they track their tribe's worst enemy

into unknown territory and defeat them?
Available in electronic edition!

A Fine Likeness (House Divided Book One)

A Confederate guerrilla and a Union captain discover there's something more dangerous in the woods than each other.

Jimmy Rawlins is a teenage bushwhacker who leads his friends on ambushes of Union patrols. They join infamous guerrilla leader Bloody Bill Anderson on a raid through Missouri, but Jimmy questions his commitment to the cause when he discovers this madman plans to sacrifice a Union prisoner in a hellish ritual to raise the Confederate dead.

Richard Addison is an aging captain of a lackluster Union militia. Depressed over his son's death in battle, a glimpse of Jimmy changes his life. Jimmy and his son look so much alike that Addison becomes obsessed with saving him from Bloody Bill. Captain Addison must wreck his reputation to win this war within a war, while Jimmy must decide whether to betray the Confederacy to stop the evil arising in the woods of Missouri.

Available in print and electronic editions!

The River of Desperation (House Divided Book Two)

In the waning days of the Civil War, a secret conflict still rages…

Lieutenant Allen Addison of the *USS Essex* is looking forward to the South's defeat so he can build the life he's always wanted. Love and a promising business await him in St. Louis, but he is swept up in a primeval war between the forces of Order and Chaos, a struggle he doesn't understand and can barely believe in. Soon he is fighting to keep a grip on his sanity as he tries to save St. Louis from destruction.

The long-awaited sequel to *A Fine Likeness* continues the story of two opposing forces that threaten to tear the world apart.

Available in electronic edition!

The Case of the Purloined Pyramid (The Masked Man of Cairo Book One)

An ancient mystery. A modern murder.

Sir Augustus Wall, a horribly mutilated veteran of the Great War, has left Europe behind to open an antiquities shop in Cairo. But Europe's troubles follow him as a priceless

inscription is stolen and those who know its secrets start turning up dead. Teaming up with Egyptology expert Moustafa Ghani, and Faisal, an irritating street urchin he just can't shake, Sir Wall must unravel an ancient secret and face his own dark past.
Available in electronic and print editions!

The Case of the Shifting Sarcophagus (The Masked Man of Cairo Book Two)

An Old Kingdom coffin. A body from yesterday.

Sir Augustus Wall had seen a lot of death. From the fields of Flanders to the alleys of Cairo, he'd solved several murders and sent many men to their grave. But he's never had a body delivered to his antiquities shop encased in a 5,000 year-old coffin.

Soon he finds himself fighting a vicious street gang bent on causing national mayhem while his assistant, Moustafa Ghani, faces his own enemies in the form of colonial powers determined to ruin him. Throughout all this runs the street urchin Faisal. Ignored as usual, dismissed as usual, he has the most important fight of all.

Available in electronic and print editions!

The Case of the Golden Greeks (The Masked Man of Cairo Book Three)

They thought the case was solved.

When an eminent Egyptologist is murdered giving a lecture in front of a packed hall, Cairo's chief of police quickly rounds up those responsible.

Or at least some of them.

Sir Augustus Wall, antiquities dealer and amateur sleuth, knows there's more to the crime than it seems. With little to go on but an exotic murder weapon, a map of a desert oasis, and some gilded Greek mummies, he sets out across the Sahara with his assistant Moustafa Ghani and the street urchin Faisal, who is the only person to have seen the killer's face. They soon find themselves in the midst of international intrigue on Egypt's remote border with Libya.

Can they discover what mystery lies beneath Bahariya Oasis?

Available in electronic and print editions!

The Case of the Karnak Killer (The Masked Man of Cairo Book Four)

A scandal in America. A murder in Cairo.

Sir Augustus Wall, antiquities dealer and amateur sleuth, is hired to track down a blackmailer who threatens the reputation of an American millionaire. When blackmail turns to murder, he must travel up the Nile by steamboat to find the killer.

Joining him are Faisal, a street urchin who makes himself equally useful and troublesome; Heinrich Schäfer, a leading Egyptologist; and Jocelyn Montjoy, an adventurous woman who has captured his heart.

But complications set in before the hunt even begins. Unwelcome fellow passengers threaten to derail the investigation, and Augustus has fallen out with his right-hand man, Moustafa Ghani. Can a new team of investigators help him solve his most challenging case yet?

Available in electronic and print editions!

Radio Hope (Toxic World Book One)

In a world shattered by war, pollution, and disease...

A gunslinging mother longs to find a safe refuge for her son.

A frustrated revolutionary delivers water to villagers living on a toxic waste dump.

The assistant mayor of humanity's last city hopes he will never have to take command.

One thing gives them the promise of a better future—Radio Hope, a mysterious station that broadcasts vital information about surviving in a blighted world. But when a mad prophet and his army of fanatics march out of the wildlands on a crusade to purify the land with blood and fire, all three will find their lives intertwining, and changing forever.

Available in print and electronic editions!

Refugees from the Righteous Horde (Toxic World Book Two)

When you only have one shot, you better aim true.

In a ravaged world, civilization's last outpost is reeling after fighting off the fanatical warriors of the Righteous Horde. Sheriff Annette Cruz becomes New City's long arm of vengeance as she sets off across the wildlands to take out the cult's leader. All she has is a sniper's rifle with one bullet and a former cultist with his own agenda. Meanwhile, one of the cult's escaped slaves makes a discovery that could tear New City apart...

Refugees from the Righteous Horde continues the Toxic World series started in Radio Hope, an ongoing narrative of humanity's struggle to rebuild the world it ruined.

Available in electronic edition!

We Had Flags (Toxic World Book Three)

A law doesn't work if everyone breaks it.

For forty years, New City has been a bastion of order in a fallen world. One crucial law has maintained the peace: it is illegal to place responsibility for the collapse of civilization on any one group. Anyone found guilty of Blaming is branded and stripped of citizenship. But when some unwelcome visitors arrive from across the sea, old wounds break open, and no one is safe from Blame.

Available in electronic edition!

Emergency Transmission (Toxic World Book Four)

Trust is the only thing that can save the world.

The problem is, everyone has their own agenda.

When an offshore platform starts emitting toxic fumes that threaten to destroy the last outposts of civilization, the residents of New City have to team up with a foreign freighter to fix it. But a lingering mistrust remains, and neither side has the resources to stop the leak.

That is, until help comes from the least reliable source.

Can old enemies finally set aside their differences for the greater good?

Available in electronic edition!

Tales from the Toxic World

A scavenger with a wondrous artifact from the Old Times sets out to avenge his past ...

The sheriff of a post-apocalyptic shantytown investigates a baffling murder ...

Two fishermen in a toxic sea make a startling discovery ...

A peddler has to compromise his faith to help others and not end up dead ...

Here are nine stories from a grim future that's all too possible. The world has been destroyed by war, pollution, and environmental degradation. Now only a few lonely outposts struggle to keep the light of civilization lit amid vast toxic wasteland filled with human predators.

This collection is a long-awaited addition to the popular Toxic World post-apocalyptic science fiction series. It's sure to please fans and newcomers to the series alike.

Available in electronic edition!

The Scavenger (A Toxic World Novelette)

In a world shattered by war, pollution, and disease, a lone scavenger discovers a priceless relic from the Old Times.

The problem is, it's stuck in the middle of the worst wasteland he knows—a contaminated city inhabited by insane chem addicts and vengeful villagers. Only his wits, his gun, and an unlikely ally can get him out alive.

Set in the Toxic World series introduced in the novel *Radio Hope*, this 10,000-word story explores more of the dangers and personalities that make up a post-apocalyptic world that's all too possible.

Available in electronic edition!

The Last Hotel Room

He came to Tangier to die, but life isn't done with him yet.

Tom Miller has lost his job, his wife, and his dreams. Broke and alone, he ends up in a flophouse in Morocco, ready to end it all. But soon he finds himself tangled in a web of danger and duty as he's pulled into scamming tourists for a crooked cop while trying to help a Syrian refugee boy survive life on the streets. Can a lifelong loser do something good for a change?

A portion of my royalties will go to a charity for Syrian refugees.

Available in electronic and print editions!

The Night the Nazis Came to Dinner and Other Dark Tales

A spectral dinner party goes horribly wrong…

An immortal warrior hopes a final battle will set him free…

A big-game hunter preys on endangered species to supply an illicit restaurant…

A new technology soothes First World guilt…

Here are four dark tales that straddle the boundary between reality and speculation. You better hope they don't come true.

Available in electronic edition!

The Quintessence of Absence

Can a drug-addicted sorcerer sober up long enough to save a kidnapped girl and his own duchy?

In an alternate eighteenth-century Germany where magic is real and paganism never died, Lothar is in the bonds of nepenthe, a powerful drug that gives him ecstatic visions. It has also taken his job, his friends, and his self-respect. Now his old employer has rehired Lothar to find the man's daughter, who is in the grip of her own addiction to nepenthe.

As Lothar digs deeper into the girl's disappearance, he uncovers a plot that threatens the entire Duchy of Anhalt, and finds that the only way to stop it is to face his own weakness.

Available in electronic edition!

Writing Books by Sean McLachlan

Writing Secrets of the World's Most Prolific Authors
What does it take to write 100 books? What about 500? Or 1,000?
That may sound like an impossibly high number, but it isn't. Some of the world's most successful authors wrote hundreds of books over the course of highly lucrative careers. Isaac Asimov wrote more than 300 books. Enid Blyton wrote more than 800. Legendary Western writer Lauren Bosworth Paine wrote close to 1,000.
Some wrote even more.
This book examines the techniques and daily habits of more than a dozen of these remarkable writers to show how anyone with the right mindset can massively increase their word count without sacrificing quality. Learn the secrets of working on several projects simultaneously, of reducing the time needed for each book, and how to build the work ethic you need to become more prolific than you ever thought possible.
Available in electronic and print editions!

History Books by Sean McLachlan

Wild West History
Apache Warrior vs. US Cavalryman: 1846-86 (Osprey: 2016)
Tombstone—Wyatt Earp, the O.K. Corral, and the Vendetta Ride (Osprey: 2013)
The Last Ride of the James-Younger Gang (Osprey: 2012)

Civil War History
Ride Around Missouri: Shelby's Great Raid 1863 (Osprey: 2011)
American Civil War Guerrilla Tactics (Osprey: 2009)

Missouri History
Outlaw Tales of Missouri (Globe Pequot: 2009)
Missouri: An Illustrated History (Hippocrene: 2008)
It Happened in Missouri (Globe Pequot: 2007)

Medieval History
Medieval Handgonnes: The First Black Powder Infantry Weapons (Osprey: 2010)
Byzantium: An Illustrated History (Hippocrene: 2004)

African History
Armies of the Adowa Campaign 1896: The Italian Disaster in Ethiopia (Osprey: 2011)

Purchase copies of any of these titles here:
http://www.amazon.com/Sean-McLachlan/e/B001H6MUQI

Printed in Great Britain
by Amazon